Eminent Eclipse

J.B. CHADWICKS

J&B Press

First published by J&B Press
An imprint of J&B Publishing Company

EMINENT ECLIPSE

First Edition
Printed in the United States of America

For information address:
J&B Publishing Company
P.O. Box 10526
Alexandria, VA 22310

ISBN 978-0-9998046-0-5 (paperback)
ISBN 978-0-9998046-1-2 (e-book)

PREFACE

Although this book incorporates references to real events, it is a work of fiction based on the imagination of the author. Any resemblance or similarity to actual persons, groups, companies, names, or organizations is purely coincidental. The ideas presented in this book are inspired by information that is publicly available. This novel is intended for the reader's enjoyment.

ACKNOWLEDGEMENTS

I want to give a special thanks and acknowledgment to my parents, friends, and family—especially my wife—who have all supported and encouraged me along this journey for over a decade. Because of their support, this book was made possible.

To all of those who dream, dream big. Persevere, for the journey may be long and arduous, but the experience, learning, and satisfaction in the accomplishment will be worth it.

INTRODUCTION

The world is ever-changing and incessantly plagued by civil, political, social, and economic unrest as the major nations of the world vie for superiority. As advances in science, medicine, telecommunications, and technology proliferate, new threats arise to challenge not only the national security of the United States of America but the security and stability of other countries as well. If you read the newspaper, watch the news, or search the Internet, every week there is a new story about the threat of cyberattacks. The threat has existed in the shadows for years; only now is the threat being brought to light. This novel is inspired by real-world events. There are many more examples, but this list below offers a glimpse into the threat of cyber warfare and cyber espionage:

- September 22, 2017: Securities and Exchange Commission's computer systems hacked . . . the breach may have allowed access to nonpublic information that was used for illegal profit-making and gains on the U.S. stock exchanges.
- July 7, 2017: U.S. government suspects Russians are behind recent cyberattacks on power plants, including nuclear facilities.
- June 13, 2017: U.S. cyber experts warn that Russian malware could be modified and used to attack and disrupt U.S. electrical systems . . . malware attack in Ukraine in December 2015 shuts down power in Kiev . . . similar software could be used against the United States.

- May 15, 2017: Experts warn that cyberattacks could increase in frequency and intensity . . . unprecedented ransomware attack affects hundreds of thousands of victims in approximately 150 countries . . . victims include individuals, hospitals, universities, businesses and government agencies . . . future attacks will only get worse.
- March 8, 2017: Hacking tools the CIA uses are made public . . . electronics, smartphones and other devices connected to the Internet are vulnerable . . . U.S. company trade secrets at risk.
- October 7, 2016: The NSA arrests contractors accused of stealing classified information . . . the arrest highlights the issue of insider threats.
- August 30, 2016: The FBI investigates possible foreign hacking of U.S. elections systems and websites.
- August 18, 2016: NSA hacking tools are exposed . . . files were released containing codes and information.
- July 25, 2016: Washington, D.C., power outages leave museums in the dark.
- September 1, 2015: The United States to levy sanctions against China for cybercrimes.
- December 23, 2015: Iranian hackers claim responsibility for cyberattack against U.S. dam . . . hackers access the dam's control systems . . . this is only the beginning.
- June 2, 2015: Congress passes USA Freedom Act to rein in NSA surveillance powers.
- January 5, 2015: North Korea repudiates the United States for sanctions against the country over cyberattacks targeted at U.S. companies.
- November 13, 2014: Banks are fined billions for rigging stock market.

- November 13, 2014: U.S. officials report that China hacked into U.S. weather systems.
- May 23, 2014: U.S. intelligence officials offer insight into China's hacker army . . . Beijing recruits and trains thousands of young men to serve as hackers.
- April 10, 2014: Reports the NSA used the Heartbleed bug to gather critical information on individuals through vulnerabilities on the Internet . . . tens of millions of computer servers exposed.
- February 21, 2013: The United States targets insider threats . . . White House intervenes as the number of thefts of trade secrets and cyberattacks rises.
- February 4, 2013: Power goes out during the Super Bowl in New Orleans.
- August 3, 2012: U.S. Senate fails to approve cyber security legislation . . . bill would have established security standards to prevent large-scale cyberattacks on the nations' critical infrastructure including water supplies and the electrical grid . . . the United States is more at risk than ever, but Congress fails to act.
- July 16, 2012: The Washington, D.C., Metro investigates computer outages . . . software shutdowns cause all metro lines to close twice in a week.
- June 20, 2012: Reports claim the United States and Israel used the Flame virus to slow Iran's nuclear program . . . the United States denies involvement.
- August 26, 2010: The Pentagon reports it was attacked by a "malicious code."
- July 9, 2009: Cyberattack traced to North Korea . . . the hacking effort that began July 4 crippled many U.S. websites.

- August 14, 2008: The continued surge in electricity demand strains the U.S. power infrastructure . . . five years after record Northeast blackout, the U.S. electrical infrastructure remains inadequate.
- August 14, 2003: More than 50 million residents lost electricity as power line problems in the Midwest caused the worst blackout in U.S. history.

1

It was a cold, rainy, November Saturday night in Manhattan. A faint light flickered in the alley above the back door of a Chinese carryout restaurant. A U.S. intelligence official, nearly unconscious, huddled behind a dumpster. The blood flowed from his side, and he felt a burning sensation from a recent gunshot wound radiating through his body. He had barely escaped. Things had gone wrong. Armed men sprinted through the alley, shouting in Russian and English. The intelligence official shuddered with chills as his senses were bombarded by the sounds and sights of the damp, dreary night.

He hoped they wouldn't find him and feared what would happen if they did. They wanted the information he possessed. Thoughts raced through his clouded mind. *What happened? Who are these men who are chasing me?* Grasping his wound and fighting the cold darkness, he continued to hide near the dumpster behind a pile of rain-soaked cardboard boxes and trash bags. His blood flowed into the puddles.

2

In the drab fluorescent light of his cubicle, Matt O'Shea worked tirelessly at his computer. His space was as confined as a honeycomb where worker bees were grinding away each day. Matt and his colleagues kept a bottle of pain pills near the coffee maker to aid with the long days and nights of staring at computer screens. The past several months had been grueling as they completed major updates to their software and control systems to meet deadlines. The local Washington, D.C., power company, Lucigen, was installing new computer systems and software to support plans for updating its physical power infrastructure across the region. Matt found himself working more and sleeping less.

As a computer programmer turned hacktivist, Matt had been recruited by the National Security Agency (NSA) to take an undercover position for the U.S. government. His job at Lucigen was his cover. Matt didn't know why, given his computer skills and background, he had been stuck working on computer network systems for an energy company. It made no sense, but it was good pay, and he was glad to have a job, even if the work hours lately had been inhumane.

Matt was a computer science major from MIT. The faculty and staff had encountered many talented students over the years, but none quite like Matt. His abilities were unparalleled, and MIT had recruited the seventeen-year-old with an offer of a full academic scholarship. His professors advised him that his potential would be infinite if he kept on track. Matt was in the second semester of his senior year and looking forward to graduation. He'd been working on an advanced algorithm for his dissertation for nearly a year. He was so proud of it. He considered it a masterpiece—the best work he'd ever done. It would revolutionize cyber security and monitoring on a global scale. Early in the semester he thought it'd be a good idea to put it on open source to get input from other programmers. It would give him plenty of time to make modifications before the end of the school year when his dissertation was due. Oddly enough, he received no responses—nothing. What was even stranger was the vague call he received months later from the dean of the Computer Science Department asking Matt to come immediately to his office to discuss an urgent matter.

When Matt entered the dean's office, he was met by the university president, his computer science professor, several armed FBI agents, and two businessmen in dark suits. Matt was instructed to sit on the sofa while the men in the suits sat across from him. For nearly two hours they interrogated Matt, asking him a wide range of questions, many of which focused on the computer program he'd written. Matt later learned that hacktivist groups and foreign governments had usurped his code from open source. They'd been using it to hack into financial and utility companies to skim funds to support their activities. It wasn't until one of the groups grew bold and tried manipulating commodities and stock prices on the New York Stock Exchange that they had been discovered. The federal authorities ultimately traced the code's origins back to Matt. In his naiveté, Matt had no idea that his program had been stolen and modified for illegal activities. He was merely trying to gather input from fellow programmers to improve his code. He'd never once considered something like that could happen and, in his mind, it was an honest mistake.

The dean informed Matt that, due to the gravity of the situation, he would not be allowed to graduate unless he agreed to certain conditions. Matt had less than a month before graduation, and he'd finished all of his course requirements except his dissertation, which he thought would be his crowning achievement. The dean said Matt had to agree to turn over all of his research files and computer equipment to the authorities. The FBI required Matt to sign a gag order that restricted him from speaking to anyone about the incident. If he complied he would be allowed to graduate, they would not press charges, and Matt would avoid prison, but his activities would be under surveillance for the foreseeable future.

He didn't know what to do. He would lose months of hard work. Devastated, Matt was escorted like a criminal into a police car and back to his apartment. The FBI agents rummaged through his drawers and closets, picking the place apart from top to bottom. They confiscated all of his computer equipment and electronics, anything that could be connected to the Internet. Matt watched in disbelief and anger.

It wasn't long before other MIT students caught wind of the FBI's presence on campus and the agents' visit to Matt's apartment. Some students had seen Matt escorted from campus by the federal authorities, and others had seen the agents at his apartment. Rumors and social media stories about Matt—all of them false—spread like wildfire over the Internet. Due to the gag order, Matt wasn't able to speak up to defend himself, so he simply had to take it. He would graduate, but not with honors, and the flurry of social media activity ruined all that he'd worked for over the years. Disgraced and with his name and reputation tarnished, he withdrew from the world and hid in the confines of his ransacked apartment in Boston. He knew he'd never get a job doing anything computer related. A bleak and hopeless future awaited, and the injustice of it infuriated him.

What happened with Matt's code was never publicized because the fear of alerting investors and the public to the stock market and financial system manipulation could have led to an economic crash. The U.S. economy was already fragile, so government authorities kept it all quiet. Aside from financial markets, the hackers also had been manipulating utility bills of residents across the country. The hackers would discreetly change the reading of a gas or electric bill so that it would raise a resident's monthly bill by a few cents or a few dollars, which customers would unassumingly pay. The hackers would then enter the utility company's accounting systems to reconcile the actual readings with the monthly payments. The system would show that the customer overpaid that month. But rather than applying the overpayment to the next month's bill, the computer was directed to send it online back to the utility customer's bank account, though that didn't happen. Instead, the overpayment was routed to an offshore account held by the hackers. The dollar values of the discrepancies in each transaction went unnoticed for months because they were so small, and utility bills generally vary each month.

Months after that fiasco, once things had settled down, Matt quietly relocated to Washington, D.C., where he kept a low profile working part time in retail and service jobs where he could blend in, and people wouldn't ask many questions. But he did still dabble in the occasional small-scale programming job. He knew the authorities monitored his activities, but he took his chances to make some extra money. Matt also found ways to get involved in the hacktivist communities without being detected by using aliases, public computers, and Wi-Fi networks. He found ways to fight back against the system, the people, and the authorities who had unjustly tarnished him and his future. Matt made it his mission to find who had stolen and modified his code. They had wrecked his life, and he vowed to track them down and make them pay the only way he knew how—by hacking and destroying their systems.

After being out of school for over two years, he was reacclimating to everyday life when he got a strange visit at his apartment one evening from two men dressed in black suits who were accompanied by a well-dressed bald man in his late fifties or early sixties. The gentleman stood silently to the side and observed while the two government officials extensively questioned Matt. Initially, Matt was afraid they'd found out what he'd been doing online and were there to arrest him, but that wasn't the case. Matt didn't talk much. He just listened as he sat on his couch, all the while keeping an eye on the older man standing at the other side of his living room. Matt had no idea of the importance that man played in the U.S. cyber world or U.S. government intelligence community.

Given his experience and expertise with computers and codes, not to mention the unwanted notoriety gained while at MIT, Matt was recruited by the NSA to work as a mole and monitor the industrial control software systems and information technology activities while working for Lucigen. Matt was initially put off as to why they didn't want to use his computer engineering expertise for covert government operations and why the NSA wanted him working as a network systems contractor. In exchange for his service, the NSA gave him a hefty salary, a clean record, and a new identity as a cover for his job. Given the cost of living in D.C., Matt was tired of working part-time jobs in restaurants and retail where he scraped by on minimum wage and tips. Matt considered himself fortunate to be given a second chance, especially after his MIT debacle and the recent death of his only brother from a car accident only a few months prior. This opportunity gave him the sense of hope that he had been lacking the last two years.

■ ■ ■

It was nearly five o'clock on Friday. Matt was shutting down his computer when John, his cubicle-mate asked, "Anything planned for the weekend?"

"Nope, same old stuff. I'll probably just hang out around the apartment."

"You know you should get out more. Hey, I know this cute girl who works in the Marketing Department. I can introduce you. I think she'd be just your type. She seems friendly."

"I'm not interested in dating right now."

"Who said anything about dating?" John paused a moment. "At any rate, you'd better get out of here before the boss comes by and asks you to work this weekend. The company is doing another round of software updates."

"I know, I know," Matt replied hastily. "Why is it these computers are always so slow when you have a need for speed?" It had been a long week, and he was ready to go home. Matt fumed with frustration at his computer. Rocking in his chair, he glanced restlessly over his shoulder to see if his boss was coming, but he was nowhere in sight. Matt's anxiety began to fade, though he knew that if he didn't leave soon, he'd get stuck working all weekend.

Matt stood up quickly to scope out the scene. The "bossman" as they called him, had no real name, or at least they didn't call him by it. He was the quintessential, stereotypical bad boss. Forget words like empowerment, valuing your employees, trust, respect, and all that jargon the management consultants blab about. To the bossman, you were nothing more than an object, a tool to be used. Your job was to produce results or else. Matt was a contract worker at Lucigen and, like most such workers in the D.C. metro area, he was expendable. But Matt had a more meaningful purpose, especially in his undercover NSA role with their Tailored Access Operations (TAO) unit. Neither his boss nor his colleagues—including John—knew his *real* job.

At times, working long hours in the confined cubicle felt like prison. Given the nature of the contract work, he had to clock in and out. For security purposes, all the doors in the information technology and computer network sections of the building had passcode entry. Matt needed the money and wanted an opportunity for a fresh start. Otherwise, he wouldn't have taken the deal with the NSA. He owed a loan shark a lot of money after he lost a high-stakes poker match, and he had medical and legal bills from his brother's car accident, so his financial situation had become dire. Part of the arrangement with the NSA was that his debts would be paid if he helped with some "special covert cyber projects." He didn't know what that meant at the time, but given his financial predicament, he couldn't refuse.

■ ■ ■

It was after 5 p.m., and Matt was edgy. His computer wouldn't shut down, and he knew that his boss could walk into his cubicle at any moment. Matt's bag was packed, and he was ready to go. Swearing under his breath, he leaned over his desk and waited for the screen to go blank. Then John began his dry cough, the office signal indicating that the bossman was making his end-of-day rounds. *Should I leave without turning my computer off? Should I step away for even a minute and then come back?* Matt's mind raced. Finally, he turned to leave, but it was too late. The wrecking-ball-shaped wretch of a man blocked his way. There was no escape. Knowing what would come next, Matt's stomach reeled as he clenched his fists against the arm of his chair. Matt gritted his teeth as the words came out of the bossman's mouth.

"Matt, I need you to work this weekend, Saturday and Sunday. We're behind on our system updates."

3

On the train ride home that night, Matt contemplated what the morning would bring. The more he thought about it, the more he wished he'd taken John up on the offer to meet the girl from the Marketing Department. Maybe he could call John later and arrange something for Saturday night. Matt glanced at all the different people on the train. They looked like zombies off in their own worlds. No one looked happy. *For crying out loud people, it's Friday; you all should be excited!* Then he wondered if they were a reflection of himself. Perhaps he had become a zombie just like all the others living out their measly existences.

Despite all of the walking dead around him, there was an angel in his midst, an attractive young Asian woman sitting across from him on the train. She was smiling warmly at him, her face flawlessly silky. Surprisingly, he didn't recall seeing her board, but she sat adjacent so that they nearly faced each other from opposite sides of the train. Her long black hair and light brown eyes glistened under the florescent light. She was slender and athletic which made her miniskirt, knee-high leather boots and tailored gray blouse fit her physique flawlessly. Her lightly tanned skin and warm, glossy, blush lips made her exotic and inviting.

Matt found himself glowing on the inside. He smiled gleefully back at her, the temptation hard to resist. Despite her apparent shyness, she radiated a fiery liveliness that he couldn't decipher. *What was it about her?* Matt was skittish, so he looked away, unable to hold her gaze. But she noticed him and sheepishly grinned as she modestly recrossed her legs.

Matt couldn't help but admire her beauty. Feeling himself coming alive, it had been months since a woman had shown him any interest, certainly nothing like this. Matt wasn't sure if she was flirting with him or if he was simply imagining it. Either way, he felt compelled to talk to her. He searched for the courage but found none.

The metro train halted at the next stop. The young Asian woman casually prepared to exit the train as she stood by the door, her back to him. Matt could feel his insides burning. She turned and glanced at him as she exited, smiling warmly with friendly eyes. Matt smiled back, wanting so much for his feet to move, but they wouldn't. The voice of the train operator announcing the closing doors echoed in his ears, his last chance before she would be gone forever. Matt took a deep breath and began to stand, but it was too late. The doors closed, and she strutted down the platform, turning back momentarily with one last cheerful grin and a subtle, flirtatious wave.

"Shit. I blew that one," Matt mumbled under his breath.

4

It was Friday night, November 9, hours after his team had left early for the Veterans Day weekend, but NSA Deputy Director Michael Stevens was still busy at work. Michael sat quietly at his desk typing. Looking forward to the long weekend, he took a moment to peer out his window that overlooked the courtyard. He never tired of watching the quiet, fall sunset. The seventy- to eighty-hour weeks for the last six months had been grueling, and he needed a break.

Michael was attractive, in his late forties, with chiseled facial features, a charming smile, blue eyes, and blond hair that he wore in a high and tight haircut. Standing six-four and weighing two hundred and twenty eight pounds, he carried a commanding presence. His oak-like build served him well when he had played quarterback for the U.S. Naval Academy. While on active duty, the navy paid for him to attend grad school at MIT where he earned an advanced degree in computer engineering and cyber security. It was also through his MIT network that he had learned about Matt O'Shea and recommended that the NSA hire him. The NSA had been keeping an eye on Matt ever since he'd left Boston and moved to D.C.

Michael spent much of his navy career in Asia—China, Japan, and South Korea—with a couple of tours in D.C. at the Pentagon. Many of his assignments were as a principal liaison officer with the host government's cyber defense units, so he was familiar with their programs. Now a retired naval intelligence officer with twenty-three years of experience, he had been recruited nearly eight years earlier by the NSA to serve as the deputy director for counterintelligence and cyber security for the Asia-Pacific Region. Michael had earned a name for himself in the cyber intelligence community because of his mathematical and computer engineering prowess. He had played a key role in disrupting the latest cyberattacks from the Chinese and North Koreans.

He'd also worked on several cross-regional teams to address recent attacks by Russia, North Korea, and Iran. Several months earlier Michael's team of cryptologists and cyber security analysts had discovered a code they'd rarely seen, and they were unable to decipher it. It was showing up in computer networks and industrial control systems across the country. It used circular text and a new type of mutation string, the partial origins of which they'd only seen a couple of times—in Matt O'Shea's MIT code and the Fawkes virus—which, unbeknownst to the authorities, Matt also had written under the hacker alias "Red Fox."

Michael and his team were conducting further investigations into a handful of recent technical glitches with computer mainframes at power plants across the country when they identified it. They realized the linkages between Matt's old program from MIT and figured the hackers were still using some of his foundational code for their new malware.

The power facilities had reported that their control monitoring systems designed to trip their alarms in the event of overheating or usage surges weren't activating, resulting in grayouts or black-outs in local rural areas. Most of those events didn't draw much concern at first.

The power infrastructure within many U.S. cities was designed decades ago with a fifty-year lifespan, and many places had exceeded that. As a result, it was presumed that those events were simply part of an outdated energy grid. But as they began to occur more frequently and were more widespread, the trends caught the NSA's attention. One of the first occurrences where they'd seen a similar type of malicious code and malware used was in the Northeast blackout of 2003. The authorities discovered afterward that there had been a software bug that had kept the system alarms from triggering, resulting in the power transmission lines overloading and, eventually, overheating and taking out the entire system. But because it had been a one-time event, no one had thought much of it—until now.

Recently, the U.S. Department of State had reported having network issues, and it suspected its systems had been compromised. Michael and his team investigated and deduced that a phantom malware had somehow been loaded into the computer systems and that a remote access tool was being used to bypass the computers' central systems through a backdoor. They'd seen similar approaches before, but Michael sensed there was something different this time, and he had a bad feeling about it. He knew that this, along with what they'd discovered with the Fawkes virus, was an indication of an imminent cyberattack; they just didn't know when, where, or by whom.

Michael and his team assumed that the source of the code and the attacks were coming from China or North Korea—and possibly Russia. The transmissions were encrypted, and the signal paths and locations changed frequently. From what he and his team had assessed, foreign government entities were attempting to access the U.S. government intelligence and Defense Department's mainframes. The Chinese military was a likely suspect because it had long been trying to hack U.S. systems and had done so successfully on some occasions. In recent years there was the incident in which the Chinese gained access to the U.S. Defense Department's files and designs for the latest F-35 stealth fighter. It was then that Michael had his first real taste of what the United States was facing.

Over the past few weeks, as Michael and his team researched further, they realized that government computer systems and power plants weren't the only targets of the malware. The malware had shown up in computer networks and industrial control systems for banks, stock exchanges, flight navigation systems, airports, hospitals, utility companies, dams, and satellites.

The NSA had the best and brightest cyber team in the world working in its TAO. Matt O'Shea at Lucigen was one of them, and Michael was one of the few people within the NSA and the White House who knew of Matt's dual role. Michael and his team had been racking their brains for months, but they weren't making much headway. He hoped that O'Shea's experience would help. From what they surmised thus far, no malware had shown up in Lucigen's computer systems.

Michael would be glad to get away and leave all this behind for a weekend, so he sent his last email and shut down his computer. The fall sun was setting over the trees as the orange-red sunlight drifted through his office window. With his computer screen blank, he whirled around in his chair, grabbed his work bag, and headed for the door. This was the earliest he'd left in months, and the long hours were taking a toll on his marriage. He'd barely seen his wife since this project had begun, and this was going to be their weekend away.

Michael hurried to the door but, just as he grabbed the handle, the phone rang. Turning around he saw the flashing red light. *Just my luck. Who would be calling me?* He stood there considering what to do. *It can wait until next week.* The phone stopped ringing, and he opened the door and left, locking it behind him. As he strolled down the hall, the phone rang again, though this time out of earshot. He didn't know it was Godfrey, the Director of National Cyber Security, his boss, who was calling.

5

Matt sat at his dining room table finishing the last of his dinner. It was his regular Friday night ritual—Chinese food, a six-pack of beer, video games, and betting on the weekend's sports. Matt also played poker from time to time, but he kept it quiet because they sometimes played high stakes, and he didn't want to get caught, again.

Matt was nearly twenty-three years old. He was five foot eleven with broad shoulders, heavyset with a pudgy belly, and trunk-like legs. He wore nerdy, thick, dark-rimmed, tinted glasses that hid his hazel eyes. He kept a constant five o'clock shadow that he'd grown to cover his baby face. His dark brown hair formed a fuzzy cotton ball that hung down near his shoulders and complimented a set of bushy sideburns that extended halfway down his cheeks.

Matt didn't own a business suit. His daily attire consisted of ratty jeans or cargo shorts, tennis shoes or flip-flops, and whatever old-school comic, *Star Wars*, Atari, or other video game T-shirt he could find at the local Goodwill thrift store. Matt considered jeans, tennis shoes, and a solid-colored polo shirt formal business dress. Matt was never one for style because he spent nearly every waking hour in front of a computer. Never knowing who might recognize him from his days at MIT, he did what he could to change his appearance and be more inconspicuous. Moving out of Boston had helped.

As a kid, Matt had tried to play sports, but he wasn't any good. Because of his size, he attempted football in junior high, but he lacked speed and coordination. Matt spent most of his time riding the bench when the coach didn't have him serving as a tackling dummy during practice. His attempts at basketball weren't much better. He only played one season, and his team lost every game but one. Sports were a lost cause, so he turned to something he was much better at—computers and video games.

Matt lived in an efficiency apartment near Capitol Hill. He and his younger brother Charlie shared the place. Charlie had dropped out of college and moved in after Matt left Boston. Charlie never knew the full story of what happened to Matt at MIT, but he always looked up to Matt as a role model and father-figure, so Matt didn't want to say anything to disappoint him.

At times the apartment was cramped, but they made it work. The entrance to their place was Matt's bedroom where a Murphy bed pulled out of the wall to save space. The living and dining room were combined into one small room, and the kitchen wasn't much bigger than a handicapped- accessible stall in a public restroom. The kitchen was a mess, along with the rest of the apartment. The dishes were piled in the sink, and Matt hadn't taken the trash out all week. The smell of days- old take-out food permeated the air. Newspapers and video game magazines blanketed the living room floor and coffee table. It was hard to believe that someone lived in such squalor.

At first, Matt had attempted to keep the place clean, but after Charlie's tragic death about six months earlier when his car was hit by a dump truck, nothing else seemed to matter. The driver of the truck was drunk after spending happy hour with his construction buddies. The driver also was speeding and texting when he ran a red light and broadsided Charlie's car in an intersection. Matt was surprised Charlie hadn't died on impact. Instead, Charlie ended up in a coma. The truck driver staggered away from the accident without even a scratch. The emotional and financial distress of the situation wore Matt down. The truck driver's company dragged out the legal proceedings for months claiming negligence on Charlie's part for not yielding as he entered the intersection, even though Charlie had a green light. The legal and medical fees piled up. The company's highly-paid lawyers made Matt's life miserable by drowning him in paperwork and court proceedings.

Their parents had left Matt and Charlie on a doorstep when the boys were young. At three years old, Charlie was a toddler at the time, and Matt was just seven. Matt remembered the experience as clearly as if it were yesterday. His parents had driven to a farm in rural Shenandoah Virginia. His mom waited in the car as his father dropped the boys off on the porch, rang the doorbell, and then ran back to the car. His parents waited for someone to come to the door before they drove off, the dust cloud billowing up behind their car on the gravel road. As he stood there, Matt wanted to chase after them, but his feet felt nailed to the porch. The tears welled up in his eyes as he realized he and Charlie were abandoned and alone. But then he heard Charlie crying, so he knelt to comfort him. Matt promised himself that day that he would never desert Charlie, and he never did.

After the car accident, as Charlie lay in a coma and on life support in a D.C. hospital, Matt stayed by his side nearly every moment. Charlie was only nineteen. The doctors told Matt that Charlie would never fully recover from his injuries and that he had suffered significant brain damage. Matt made the decision to take him off life support, which tore Matt apart down to his soul. Matt had never felt as alone as he did that day. It was the worst moment of his life. Matt kissed his brother goodbye on the forehead before he left the hospital room.

After Matt went home to get cleaned up and changed before returning to Charlie's side, he received a call from the hospital informing him that Charlie had passed. The trauma was too much for Charlie's battered body to handle. Matt wished he'd been there with him. It broke his heart that Charlie died alone. He hoped at least a nurse or doctor had been present.

The funeral was held a week later. It was small and brief. A handful of Matt's work acquaintances attended to show their support and respect. And a strange older man who stood in the distance watched from beneath the shade of a tall oak tree. Matt wasn't sure, but he swore that the man looked familiar. There was something about his demeanor. Matt shook his head and dismissed it. He had other things on his mind.

■ ■ ■

Matt was finishing his final bites of rice when his phone rang.

"Hey, John," Matt said, pleasantly surprised. "I didn't expect to hear from you tonight. I thought you had a hot date with that so-called girlfriend of yours that I've never met. What gives?"

"Yeah, that's what I thought too, but she called a little bit ago to tell me she's doing a girls' night instead. I haven't talked to her all week. Can you believe that nonsense?"

"That's a bummer. I'm sorry to hear that," Matt responded half-heartedly. He had selfishly hoped that something like this would happen so he and John could go out.

John was in his late twenties, socially awkward, but brilliant. He was an only child and came from a broken home. John's parents separated when he was eight, and his dad had died when he was ten. The doctors said it was due to a heart attack, but John always believed his dad had overdosed. It wasn't a secret that his dad had been an alcoholic and drug addict. His mom remarried another deadbeat. John didn't care much for his stepdad and avoided any interaction by busying himself behind closed doors with his computer.

John was a scrawny five foot seven and one hundred and thirty four pounds. He had thin blond hair and a buzz cut because he hated having to brush his hair. It also didn't give his stepdad or others anything to grab when they bullied him when he was growing up, so he still kept it short as an adult just in case. His wire-rimmed glasses framed his narrow face, which was scarred and pockmarked from years of untreated acne.

As a kid, John's parents forged doctor's notes to excuse him from recess. He supposedly had a heart condition and a blood disease that caused him to bruise easily. That's the story his parents told the school as a front for their abuse. Apparently, no one ever questioned it. John also had a speech impediment as a kid, so he was bullied most of his early childhood, keeping quiet so kids wouldn't make fun of him. He'd never learned to fight back, physically or otherwise, so he built up anger and resentment that he tended to unleash through video games. John was unpredictable when he drank, so Matt never knew if he'd encounter happy John or angry John.

John's parents forced him to play organized sports as a young teen in an attempt to toughen him up, but with little success. As John withdrew and avoided his parents by spending more time on the computer, he discovered in junior high that he was incredibly capable with writing programs. If there were an Olympic competition for computer programming, John would have won hands down.

To Matt's knowledge, John had never had a real girlfriend. The only women John had ever supposedly "dated" were ones he met online through chat rooms and dating sites. At times, Matt felt sorry for him, but Matt didn't have any other friends, and given his past, he needed indiscreet people like John who wouldn't draw much attention or ask too many questions. Besides, John was a loner like Matt and had a dry sense of humor that Matt appreciated. Fueled by his attempt to forget his dysfunctional, abusive childhood and lonely existence, John drank like a fish. John had severed contact with his mom after he turned eighteen and moved out, a decision he had never regretted. He was a good person despite his social awkwardness and occasional drunken outbursts.

Despite many of their apparent differences, Matt felt a strange connection to John's broken past. They could spend hours hanging out playing video games and never talk. Most of the time, that's what Matt preferred. He didn't want anyone knowing his personal business. John never asked many questions of Matt. If he did, it was about work or the latest video game or a comic book. They filled a companionship void for each other.

John's elusive "girlfriend" tended to be a flake. Matt had never met the woman in person even though John had known her for over eight months, and she lived locally. Aside from a handful of online photos of a sexy, petite college-aged Hispanic girl in a bikini or close-up selfies, that's all that Matt had seen of her. John never met her in person or even video-chatted, which further raised Matt's doubts. Matt always suspected that John was getting fooled by someone pretending to be an attractive woman—"catfished," as they call it.

"Yeah, it stinks, but what can you do?" John sounded disappointed. "I was calling to see if you wanted to grab a drink tonight. Are you free?"

"Sure. What time? I'm just finishing dinner."

"Let's meet at nine thirty at the Lounge."

"That sounds good, but I don't want to be out too late; I have to work tomorrow." The words made Matt cringe. He'd almost forgotten that he had to work on Saturday and Sunday.

"Oh, that's right; the boss caught you before you could escape."

"Go ahead and rub it in, you ass."

"Hey now, I'm just kidding. I'll see you at nine thirty. Dress half-way decent, would you? And I don't mean those ratty jeans and nerdy T-shirts you typically wear. Try something else for a change. I swear, you kill me sometimes with the clothes you wear. How are we ever supposed to impress the ladies if you dress like a nerdy, homeless bum?"

"Whatever. Like you should talk. You don't dress any better. Besides, it's chilly outside, so I won't be in a T-shirt. I'll be in my ratty hooded sweatshirt." Matt smirked. He wasn't worried about his appearance or impressing anyone. "I'll see you later."

The more he thought about having to work in the morning, the more annoyed he became. Matt had been looking forward to a weekend off. Instead, he'd be stuck in that stuffy office all weekend. At any rate, Matt was glad John had called. Some drinks and a night out were just what he needed.

6

While Michael Stevens was leaving his office at NSA head-quarters, his wife Kate was at home preparing dinner when the phone rang.

"Hello, Stevens' residence," she answered in her soft, sweet voice. She was an attractive woman in her early forties with shoulder-length wavy dark-brown hair, brown eyes, smooth olive skin and a slender yet curvy figure. She had lusciously shaped lips that could hypnotize when she spoke yet spit fire just as potently. Although petite and unassuming at five foot six, she had a passionate attitude that suited a salty former naval officer like her husband well.

"Mrs. Stevens?" the voice on the phone asked.

"Yes. May I ask who is calling?"

"This is Director Godfrey. Is Michael there?" There was a sense of urgency in his voice.

"No, not yet. Michael called over an hour ago to say he was leaving the office. He should be home any moment now." She was puzzled as to why the director would be calling. It was after 7 p.m. on Friday evening of Veterans Day weekend. What could

Director Godfrey possibly want? She knew Michael had been working long hours for months on a top-secret project, which most of his assignments were. Michael never talked about his work, and Kate had learned not to ask. She especially knew not to ask the director, but her curiosity got the best of her.

"Director Godfrey, it's such a pleasure to hear from you. You haven't called the house in months. It must be a national crisis, or perhaps you're calling to tell Michael that since he's been working such long hours, you'd like to give him Tuesday off so he can spend time with his wife." Her tone was cynical, but there was truth behind it. Michael had been working extremely long hours for months and was seldom home. Their marriage was beginning to suffer, and the thought of it infuriated her.

The director picked up on her anger and resentment. He had no time for her attitude and sought to appease her, if only momentarily.

"Kate, your husband has been doing a tremendous service for our country. I realize he's been working long hours and that it has impacted your personal life. When this project is over, I promise you his hours will scale back, and I'll give him more time off. In the meantime, he's working on a national security matter. There's something critical that I need to discuss with him. I called him earlier at his desk, but I must have just missed him."

"Have you tried his cell?" she asked, stating the obvious.

"I did, but there was no response. It went straight to voicemail."

Kate was puzzled. Michael rarely turned off his phone and almost always answered it promptly. *Why would he have his phone off or not be returning the director's calls?* She wondered if something was wrong as she glanced at the clock on the kitchen wall. He was running late, but that was typical. He'd call to say he was leaving work, and then he'd spend another hour or two in the office.

"Director Godfrey, as I said, Michael should be home soon. Would you like me to have him call you?"

"Yes, please do."

"Should he call your office?"

"No. Please have Michael call my cell. I'll be leaving here shortly." He sounded relieved that he would be going home soon too.

"I'll have him call when he arrives," she said, trying to sound pleasant despite being annoyed by the disturbance.

"Thank you. Enjoy your evening." His tone was soft and sincere. For the first time, Kate felt that the director might have somewhat of a caring heart.

"You too. Good night." Kate was puzzled by the director's call. She usually gave little thought to Michael's tardiness because it had become such a regular occurrence. But in light of the director's call, she began to worry, glancing again at the clock. She wondered where Michael could be. He probably stopped for a quick drink to unwind. He tended to do that more often lately.

Kate picked up the phone to call Michael's cell when she heard the front door open and close. She was still holding the phone when her husband dragged himself into the kitchen.

Michael was carrying a beautiful bouquet of two dozen red roses, a bottle of her favorite Cabernet, and an exhausted expression. His navy blue suit jacket was open, his tie loosened with the top button of his starched white dress shirt unbuttoned. He moved next to her and kissed her lovingly on the lips.

"I'm sorry I'm late again. I wanted to stop by the store and get you something nice."

Kate was upset, but she was moved by his sweet gesture and simply happy he was home. She hadn't had a pleasant evening with Michael in months, and she didn't want to ruin it. Then the thought of Director Godfrey's call jumped back into her head. Michael was setting his work bag down on the kitchen counter when she told him, "Director Godfrey called a little while ago. He said he's been trying to reach you; it's important." There was curiosity in her tone. She hadn't extracted much information from the director, and she was hoping that Michael might say more.

Michael looked at her, disappointed. *Am I going to have to work again this weekend?* "Did the director say what he wanted?"

"Not specifically—only that you should call when you got home. He was leaving the office soon. Did you want to call him now?"

Michael leaned over and kissed Kate on the lips again. "Whatever the director has for me can wait. I'm hungry, and it looks like you've prepared a fabulous gourmet dinner. You've dressed up, too. Shall we?" He motioned to the dining room table where the food was waiting with a bottle of wine and candles. Michael had missed her and was looking forward to spending some quality time with his wife.

"Yes, let's," she replied happily, glad their talk hadn't turned into another argument like it had on too many recent nights.

"Tonight is our night," Michael said, "and I don't want anything to interrupt that, not even a call from Director Godfrey."

She beamed with joy at the thought of finally spending a pleasant evening with her husband.

7

Matt and John sat at their local bar, the Lounge. They frequented it because the venue was not their usual scene. They dressed in jeans and T-shirts while everyone else was dressed more formally with button-down shirts, slacks, or suits for the men and elegant dresses or outfits for the women. Matt and John stood out like a pair of cowboys at the opera. It was a wonder they had never been thrown out for being inappropriately dressed. But it didn't hurt that John had known the manager for years, and they tipped the bouncers and bartenders well.

The Lounge had plush maroon seats around the perimeter walls with short cocktail tables and soft accent wall lighting. Patrons had to order bottle service to sit at a table, which had a minimum $200 charge, usually too expensive for Matt's and John's meager wages. That was why they typically sat at the bar that oozed a modern, sleek feel with frosted glass shelves behind and a high mirrored wall with small multicolored ambient lighting all around. There was cool house music or jazz playing in the background with a strobe light flashing at the side of the main room where there was a small dance floor toward the back.

John swung around in his swivel chair to scope out the scene. "Hey, I'm glad you came out tonight. You seem like you've been withdrawn and down lately." He sounded sincerely concerned.

"You know how hard things have been since Charlie died. He was the only family I had." Matt's voice trailed off as he gazed into his beer as if searching for something at the bottom.

"I know. I see how hard it's been for you, which is why I wanted to bring you out. All you do lately is work or stay home. It's depressing, even for me, and I should know. Honestly, I worry about you. I miss the goofy guy you used to be. Do you remember the times we used to have? We'd see how many women we could hit on and how many numbers we could get in a night. We used to get shot down like ducks during hunting season, but we had fun." John gently nudged Matt's arm.

"I remember." Matt's voice trailed off. "It's just been hard since Charlie died. I raised him since he was a toddler. I remember when my parents abandoned us on that doorstep of that stranger's farm home in Virginia when we were kids. I don't know why they left us, and I probably never will. I vowed never to leave Charlie like my parents left us."

"You don't get it, do you? You never abandoned him. You were the best brother anyone could ask for. You took care of him all those years, especially when he was in the hospital. No one could have predicted his accident. You did all that you could for him. Don't beat yourself up about it."

"I could have done more." Matt's hand was clenched tightly around his glass, and his other balled fist pounded away on the counter out of frustration and hurt.

"Perhaps, but you are a loyal person and brother. Don't you realize that?"

"Do we have to talk about this tonight? I'd rather not."

"No, of course not. I didn't mean to upset you."

"I know you're trying to reassure me. It's still really hard for me to talk about Charlie's death," Matt said sadly as he stared blankly into the bottom of his drink, hoping he'd somehow be able to escape into its depths.

John put his hand on Matt's shoulder. Matt looked up at John as his eyes began to well up with tears.

"Hey, let's get out of here and go someplace to let loose and have some fun. This place is too stuffy and pretentious anyways. I've got just the place."

Matt saw John's grin spread from ear to ear and thought: *This could mean trouble.*

8

Kate and Michael had enjoyed their romantic, candlelit dinner and were cleaning up the kitchen. Michael had cleared the dishes and was sitting at the dining room table watching as Kate moved as gracefully as a ballerina throughout the kitchen. She was wearing a loose, open back, mid-thigh, silky burgundy dress with a strap that tied around her neck. Her dress flowed eloquently around her as she danced about effortlessly. Michael gazed at her in admiration, taking in all of her beauty from head to toe.

Kate must have sensed him staring. She glanced over her shoulder and smiled invitingly. "Can you help me?" she said, batting her eyes as she motioned to the strap around her neck.

Michael eagerly jumped up from his chair. He hurried up behind Kate, putting his hands on her shoulders and rubbing her smooth, soft skin. Lovingly sliding his hands up and down along her back, he caressed the length of her spine, leaning forward and gently kissing her neck as he untied the knot. The dress straps had dropped in front of her when the phone rang.

Startled, she jumped and grabbed the front of her dress.

Michael turned around in fury as he looked for the phone. *Who the hell is calling so late on a Friday night? Don't people have anything better to do?*

Kate was already tying her dress back around her neck as she stood by the sink. How quickly the mood was ruined. Michael's heart sank. He missed spending time with his wife, and the past several months had been stressful on both of them. Michael grabbed his phone from the countertop and turned off the ringer. Kate wore a disappointed look. Her once beautiful and lively eyes had gone cold, and he could feel the heaviness in the air between them.

"What's going on, Michael? What aren't you telling me? Director Godfrey said he hasn't been able to reach you all night. Why are you avoiding his calls?"

"Honestly, I've just been overwhelmed lately, and I needed some quiet time."

The long hours at work had run Michael into the ground. He'd been talking with the director off and on all day. They were making major headway with their project and could expect a breakthrough any day. Michael was tired of listening to the phone ring and just wanted to disconnect for a while, so he'd turned it off to have some peace and quiet. Michael was late because he'd stopped by the jewelry store and florist. He wanted to surprise her with some new jewelry and a pleasant weekend away in New York. They had been talking about it, so he figured this was the best time.

Michael picked up his work bag, opened it, and pulled out a jewelry case and two airplane tickets. "Besides, I wanted to surprise you. I'm sorry if it seemed as though I was avoiding you or hiding something." His voice was sincere as he gazed caringly at her.

Kate returned Michael's loving gaze. "I know, Michael. I've never once doubted you." She paused a moment. "Oh, Michael!" she exclaimed, gliding over to him and throwing her arms around his neck, kissing him lovingly on the lips as he pulled her close.

"I'm sorry I got upset. I know you've been under a lot of stress." Her voice trembled as she cried softly.

Kate pulled away momentarily to take a long look at the man who'd stolen her heart years ago. "I love you."

"I love you too." Michael kissed her gently on the lips as he wiped the joyful tears from her eyes. "I believe we were rudely interrupted. What do you say we go upstairs?"

Kate glanced playfully at him with raised eyebrows and a coy smile. "Why bother going upstairs?"

As the words rolled off her tongue, he passionately pulled her close as she swooned in anticipation.

9

John surprised Matt by taking him to an improv comedy club, the Laughing Jack. John figured Matt could use some fun and cheering up, and they knew a number of the comedians.

John smirked and slapped Matt on the shoulder. "Come on. Let's go inside."

As they walked through the black tinted glass double doors, a handful of college-aged kids were lingering in the lobby. One of the tweed-sport-coat-wearing frat guys was being loud and obnoxious after too much to drink. Obviously embarrassed, his tipsy girlfriend was trying unsuccessfully to shut him up and get him to leave with her.

It was an older D.C. establishment, the floor covered with gray laminate that stuck to your shoes when you walked. The lobby was small, able to accommodate only a dozen or so guests. A handful of annoying drunken college kids currently occupied it. Sconce lighting adorned the bright red walls. Encased poster ad boards promoting the latest shows lined the wall behind the main ticket counter that looked like a large waist-high plywood box. The light blue paint had worn off where people had leaned against the top. There was an old cash register on each end of the counter. A dark maroon curtain concealed the entrance to the main showroom.

As they pushed their way through the other guests to the counter, they were greeted by warm smiles from the employees, particularly by an attractive, full-figured twenty-something brunette behind one register. She had a particularly inviting and friendly aura as she checked out John and then Matt. Matt was caught up in her voluptuousness, and his face lit up with eagerness. He preferred more full-figured women compared to the thin model type.

"Look at you, lover boy," John said as he winked at Matt. "Looks like someone is smitten." John was joking, but he was glad to see Matt's grin, a dramatic change from earlier.

The girl's sparkling blue eyes and long lashes greeted Matt and John as they moved to the counter. "Welcome to the Laughing Jack. How may I help you?" Her soft, angelic voice resonated in Matt's ears.

John stepped up to the counter and ungracefully pushed Matt out of the way. "Hello, my dear, we'd like two tickets. When does the next show start?"

"The show is continuous; you just pay a cover charge. Our theater nights are Monday through Thursday, but we have improv and stand-up on the weekends."

"Why, thank you, ma'am; that's good to know," John said in a butchered redneck accent, being intentionally obnoxious. He'd seen how the young woman was eyeing Matt, and he hoped that if he was annoying enough, Matt might man up and talk to her. John glanced at Matt and gave him a nod and a look as if to say, *"Well, what are you waiting for? Get to it."*

"Hey, mister money bags, you're paying for this, right?" John said, and then he slapped Matt's upper arm with the back of his hand.

Matt was getting annoyed with John's childish, drunken antics. Finally, he gently but firmly pushed John out of the way and blurted, "I should apologize for my jackass friend. He doesn't know how to behave in the presence of a lady." Matt stared at John who wore an astonished, tipsy expression.

The young woman looked at Matt with one eyebrow raised and her head cocked slightly to the side as she started to chuckle. "Aren't you feisty? And what makes you think you're not a bigger ass than your friend?" She leaned over and put both elbows on the counter with her hands propping up her chin. Matt could feel her x-ray vision piercing through him, and he couldn't look away. He felt trapped, but in a pleasant way. Then, without warning, Matt burst out laughing.

"I'll tell you what. Why don't we go out, and I can show you just how big of an ass I can be? What do you say?"

"Sure, I'm up for that, but I don't know if a nerdy-type like you can handle me." She looked at him with an intimidating yet flirtatious stare.

"I guess that's something we'll find out soon enough," he said, eyeing her head to toe, sizing her up.

"I suppose so." She was intrigued by his cockiness, especially for such a geeky guy. Matt looked like he was going to a comic book convention in his Superman T-shirt and blue-hooded, zip-up jacket.

"How much are the tickets?" Matt asked.

She flirtatiously leaned over the counter in her V-cut shirt. "Consider them on the house. You can make it up to me later." She blew him a kiss and then floated away like a feathery runway model to the end of the counter to help another guest.

Matt leaned over and followed her with his eyes. *Mmm . . . mmm . . . mmm . . .*, Matt thought, shaking his head. "That's nice," he mumbled under his breath before glancing at his watch. It was almost 11 p.m.

"Did you say something? Is it past your bedtime, little boy?" she asked mockingly.

"I just said 'that's nice.' And no, it's not past my bedtime. But I do have to work tomorrow." There was reluctance in his voice.

"What kind of work?"

John spoke up: "Matt here is a computer expert. They have him work on Saturdays because his work is top secret. He does network security." John nodded and winked at Matt.

The woman looked at Matt. "Oh, really? What kind of secret computer security guy are you? Out there saving the IT world now, are we, Superman?" she teased as she pointed at his T-shirt. Despite his thick-rimmed glasses, the long wavy hair and scruffy, unshaven look, behind all of the nerdiness, he had a cocky edginess to him. She could tell he might be pretty handsome if he managed to get a haircut and clean himself up.

John butted in again: "He's a damn good IT security guy." He then turned to Matt and nudged him with his elbow. "Ain't that right, buddy boy?" John said, still using his worst redneck accent.

"I'm not all that good. I'm just your average computer guy making a buck," Matt replied modestly.

"Average guy my ass," John blurted out as he threw his hands up to dramatize his objection. "Are you kidding me? You're the best," he hiccupped, his intoxication level apparent. John shouldn't have had the four shots before they left the lounge. Despite his binge drinking tendencies, he was still a lightweight.

Matt spun toward his friend and gave him a stare of death, his patience wearing thin. "You'll have to forgive my friend. He gets rather annoying when he's drunk."

"That's okay. I see guys like him in here all the time." Her smile showed she understood, but her focus had shifted to the drunken college kids who were finally leaving.

John piped up, realizing he'd somehow said something to set Matt off. "I'm sorry if I'm ruining your chances," he whispered.

"You turned on by my shirt?" Matt asked her as he pointed to the big "S" on his chest.

"Nah, it's cute—in a childish way," she said. "I've always dreamed of getting swept off my feet by Superman. Do you want to be my hero tonight?" Her response was pleasant and playful.

Matt stared quizzically at her, unsure if she was pulling his leg and not knowing how to respond. She spoke up before he could formulate an answer.

"Well, it's been fun talking with you boys, but I need to get back to work. You'd better get inside before the show ends." She motioned toward the door, though Matt didn't want to go. "Don't worry," she said, noticing Matt's reluctance. "I'll be here when you leave. I close tonight."

"Hey, Romeo," John said, slapping Matt on the shoulder, "are we going to watch the show or just stand here yapping all night?"

Matt gave John a spiteful look and shook his head. He'd been talking with her all this time and hadn't even asked her name. Matt turned and said, "I didn't catch your name."

"Perhaps that's because you never asked me for it," she said tersely.

"I apologize. I was so wrapped up in your beauty that the thought slipped my mind."

She rolled her eyes. "Of course it did. It's Nicole," she replied smugly.

"I'm Matt."

"Of course, your friend said your name already."

Matt felt foolish. Then he felt another slap on his shoulder, and that one hurt. "Are you coming or what? I didn't pay good money to come here only to have you jabber the night away," John sarcastically slurred as he swayed drunkenly.

Matt gave John a dirty, annoyed look before following him through the red-curtained door. Matt checked the time: the final act would start soon. The stage manager announced the final comedian as they made their way to the bar area. Luckily, they hadn't made last call yet.

It was an older dive, judging by its off-the-beaten-path basement location and from the overall décor and ambiance. It had a single long, dark brown wooden bar along the back wall to their left. Liquor bottles lined the shelves behind the bar, and there were beer taps at both ends. Surprisingly, the place was nearly full with more than a hundred people. They were sitting at the bar and around small tables scattered about the cement floor in the middle of the room. Semicircular booths lined the side walls. The place was dark except for a handful of strategically placed lights over the stage and around the bar. The alcohol spilled throughout the night by guests created a musty, stale odor that permeated the air. Their feet stuck to the cement floor as they walked. There was a stage up front on their right with a microphone, a director's chair, a round table with a glass of water, and a bright red curtain as a backdrop. The next comedian hadn't appeared on stage yet for the final act.

The tall, lanky, hipster-looking bartender greeted them with a friendly smile.

"What are you guys drinking tonight?"

"Do you have any specials?" John asked.

"Not tonight."

"That's okay. We'll take two beers. Whatever's cold and on tap," John said.

"Coming right up," the bartender said before turning and shuffling away.

Matt and John managed to find two empty stools at the far end of the bar. They plopped down and bellied up to the rail. The bartender returned a minute later with their beers and sat them down in front of them.

"How much do we owe you?" Matt asked.

"They're on the house, courtesy of the young lady." He motioned toward the door where they'd entered. Nicole was leaning against the wall with her arms crossed and her head tilted slightly to the right as she grinned at them.

John elbowed Matt in the side. Matt was getting used to it by now. "It looks like she has a thing for you," and he gave Matt an overly dramatic wink.

"Yeah, yeah, enough already. Let's just drink our beers and enjoy the show." Matt glanced at her and raised his glass. She cordially waved and walked back through the doorway, the curtain flapping shut behind her.

Matt and John continued talking, mainly griping about work and their boss while downing their beers. They lost track of time and paid no attention to the comedian who was performing. As they were busy trading work and video game stories, in the background they heard the voice of the stage manager. "Thanks for coming tonight everyone, and we look forward to seeing you again soon."

Matt and John turned their stools toward the stage. One of the staff had closed the curtain, and the patrons were getting up to leave. A few groups lingered to finish their drinks. The bartender turned the main lights on over the stage. Matt yawned and squinted at his watch, and his eyes burned. It was after 1 a.m. He shook his head. Matt had never meant to be out so late. He knew he'd be hurting in the morning with as much as he'd had to drink. Not wanting it to go to waste, he chugged the last of his lukewarm beer and signaled to John to do the same.

"Let's go," Matt said, and he motioned to the door.

They spun around and slid off their vinyl stools before strolling toward the exit door. As they made their way through the velvet red curtain, they saw Nicole closing out the register. Matt sauntered confidently over to her. She saw him coming but pretended she didn't. He walked up and tapped his fingers on the wooden counter to get her attention. Nicole glanced up with a callous expression.

"Can I help you?" she asked, clearly agitated about something.

"Yes, you can. I wanted to thank you for the tickets and drinks," Matt said with sincerity and gratitude.

"No problem," she replied dismissively as she turned away and continued her work at the next register.

"Nicole," Matt muttered softly.

"Yes," she said as she looked up again.

"I'd like to take you out sometime. Can I give you a call?" Matt's voice was shaky. It had been awhile since he'd asked for a date.

"You would, huh?" Her tone was skeptical as she looked at him inquisitively.

"Yes, of course. Can I get your number?" Matt asked even less confidently than before. Nicole was throwing him off with her icy, dismissive demeanor.

Nicole peeked up at him. "No," she said in a curt, abrupt tone. Then she smirked and turned away again.

"No?" Matt was baffled. Earlier she was flirting and making innuendos. Now she acted as if he didn't exist. "Well, okay," his voice trailed off as he shuffled away defeated, his shoulders hunched.

Nicole turned and looked up with a playful grin. "Hey, where are you going? I thought you wanted my number. Come here, Superman. You give up too fast."

"It's late, and I'm tired. I just want to go home." The exhaustion was apparent in Matt's voice and on his face where bags were forming under his eyes.

"If you want to wait, you could just come home with me tonight. I don't live far from here," Nicole said with a seductive look as she leaned over the counter in front of him.

Matt began to melt, though he wasn't sure if she was joking. "Are you serious?" he asked, his voice somewhat hopeful.

"Nah, I'm just pulling your leg. I'm not that kind of girl." Nicole smiled teasingly and paused a moment. "Now don't lie: you thought you had a chance, didn't you?"

"Kind of," he guiltily admitted as he shrugged his shoulders sheepishly.

"I bet," she said with her hands on her hips.

"A little over-confident, aren't we? I saw you staring at me from the moment you two walked in here."

"I suppose I was, but your beauty is just too hard to resist." Matt's tone was drenched with sarcasm. "Can I get your number or not? I don't have time to play games."

"Sure, come here." She reached out and scribbled her number on the palm of his hand with a pen. "There you go. Give me a call."

"I will." The excitement in Matt's voice was apparent.

"You'd better leave before the bouncers kick you out." She glanced at the two large gym-rat bouncers ushering guests out the front door.

"Good idea. I wouldn't want that. I'll call you next week." Matt turned and started to walk away.

"Or you can call this weekend, whichever you prefer," she said in an inviting tone.

Meanwhile, John had been standing by the front door reading an ad board for the upcoming shows, oblivious to his pal's conversation.

Matt tapped John on the shoulder, "Let's go. I need to be up early in the morning."

They walked outside and up the stairs. The street had quieted down, but there were still a few cars around, even at that late hour. It was raining, and the fall air was crisp. Matt zipped up his jacket.

The two stood under the awning of the comedy club and waited for a cab. Meanwhile, exhaustion overcame them. It had been a long week, and although it was liberating to get out, they both knew they'd been out too late and had drunk too much. They stood there swaying silently in a daze, hypnotized by the rain dropping off the awning.

Finally, a red cab rolled up. Matt turned to John and said, "You take this one. I'll catch the next."

"I see what's going on," he said, smiling. "You still think you have a chance with her tonight, don't you? Look, you got her number, and she seems interested. Give it a couple of days and then call her. Don't go back in there."

"You're right," Matt said begrudgingly. "I'll call her in a few days or so."

"Hey, it's protocol. I read it online somewhere. You have to wait at least two or three days before you can call Nicole. That way you don't come across as too desperate. That's the last thing you want. You don't want her to think that, do you? Besides, I bet a friendly girl like her probably gets hit on all the time, especially from drunk jerks like us."

"I know. I get your point," Matt said, slightly disheartened as he glanced at his watch.

"All right, I'm out of here." John gave Matt a fist bump and pulled his jacket over his head as he climbed into the back seat of the cab, closing the door before waving to Matt. There was a momentary pause, and then the cab accelerated down the dark, rainy street.

Matt stood quietly, oblivious to the world around him. His trance was interrupted by a ringing cell phone. It seemed so far away, but he snapped out of it and looked down at his screen. The call log read "Unknown Caller." He was perplexed as to who would be calling him so late. He put the phone back into his pocket and peered down the street to see if any cabs were coming. A moment later his phone rang again. The screen read the same: "Unknown Caller." He didn't get it. *It must be someone dialing a wrong number.* Then the phone rang a third time. Still, the screen indicated the same. Matt decided to answer anyway. He heard the sound of heavy, anxious breathing on the other end.

"Hello? Is anyone there?" Matt muttered.

Then the deep voice of an older man broke the silence: "Is this Matt O'Shea?"

"Yes, it is." Matt was confused; he didn't recognize the voice, but the stranger somehow knew his name.

"Is anyone else around?"

"No. It's just me," Matt replied, bewildered and drunk.

"Good, now you must listen very carefully to what I'm about to tell you."

"Who are you?" Matt asked, fumbling for words.

"There will be time for questions later, but for now you must listen. There's not a moment to lose. You have to go to your office right now and check your company's computer systems. It's important. It can't wait. Do I make myself clear?" There was urgency in the older man's voice, but Matt didn't care. He was exhausted and could barely see straight. Besides, he thought it might be a colleague playing a prank.

Matt murmured into the phone, "Look, I don't know who you are or what prank you're trying to pull, but it's late, I'm drunk, and I don't have time for this." Matt hung up and put the phone back into his pocket, shaking his head as he dismissed the call.

Director Godfrey tried calling a final time, but Matt's phone just rang and rang before eventually going to voice-mail. "Dammit, man, answer your phone," Godfrey said aloud. "There's no time for this." Then the director slammed his phone down as he fumed in anger.

Matt stood out front of the club for what seemed like ages before, finally, another cab pulled up. He flagged it down and climbed into the back seat as he mumbled his address to the driver. Sitting there, all he could do was stare aimlessly out the side window as the raindrops ran down the glass. As a feeling of numbness radiated through his entire body, Matt's mind drifted off, barely hearing when the cab driver told him he was home.

"Hey, buddy, we're here. Time to go." The driver turned around and slapped the top of his seat. "Hey, pal, you're home."

Matt snapped out of his drunken daze and responded, "Oh, yes. I'm sorry. How much do I owe you?" His voice was distant and groggy.

"That'll be $12.85."

"Sure thing." Matt reached into his wallet and pulled out a twenty. "Keep the change." He then stepped clumsily out of the cab and stood bewildered as the driver pulled away. He hadn't been out so late in months, and he knew from the beginning it was a bad idea. His feet felt like cinder blocks, but he looked forward to being in bed shortly, though his bedroom felt miles away. He looked up at the monumental steps before him. He gathered his strength, grabbed the railing, and started his climb. He reached the door, swiped his entry fob key, and shuffled inside the lobby.

The main corridor of the 1980s apartment building showed its age. It was quiet and desolate. The small Romanesque sculptures along the walls in the entryway seemed to take on lives of their own under the dull fluorescent lighting. As Matt trudged up another small flight of stairs, he could hear a stereo blaring behind one of his neighbor's doors down the hall. He felt better knowing he wasn't the only one up, yet he was dreading going to work in only a few hours.

He staggered over and pushed the elevator button. Although he typically took the stairs to the third floor, it seemed too much to handle tonight. Slouching against the alcove of the elevator, he waited for the door to open. There was a buzzing noise, then a jolt and a clunk as the elevator stopped. As the elevator door opened, he could barely stand straight as he staggered inside. He hit the third-floor button and stepped back, propping himself against the railing. The door squealed as it closed. Everything around him seemed to be moving in slow motion. Jokingly, he lifted his right hand and put his index finger to his nose as if he were doing a sobriety test. He swayed and then began to laugh as he realized how wasted he truly was.

The elevator jolted as it stopped, and the door opened. He rocked forward off the wall and lurched into the hallway, standing still for a moment as he gathered his senses. Everything was quiet except for the faint sound of a TV in the distance. The hallway was dark, and the air was musty. The laminate floor under his feet squeaked as he shuffled along. Finally making it around the corner to his apartment, he pulled out his keys as he gathered himself. Matt had a strange feeling, and a chill ran down his spine. He cautiously opened the door before creeping inside and shutting the door quietly behind him. Kicking off his shoes, he didn't bother pulling out his Murphy bed. Instead, he shuffled through his bedroom straight to the couch and plopped down, taking a moment to set his phone alarm. Sinking into the sofa, he closed his eyes and passed out.

10

A young professional couple had just returned to their hotel from a Friday night out in D.C. They were visiting from Florida. They entered the lobby in their rain-soaked outfits, scurrying past the reception desk toward the bay of elevators. They had been caught in the storm and were eager to get to their room and get out of their cold wet clothes.

They saw that one of the elevator doors was open and had started to close, so they rushed to catch it, calling out to "hold the elevator!" They giddily stepped inside, holding hands and chuckling to each other, both slightly tipsy from the night of bar hopping. The other two hotel guests looked on and tried to mind their own business, but they failed; their annoyance was unmistakable.

The young man pushed the button to the fifteenth floor. After a moment of awkward silence as the guests glanced at each other, the elevator lurched upward. The young couple held hands and stared at the numbers blinking above the doors to mark their ascent. Then, without warning, the elevator bounced to an abrupt halt, and the lights went out. They all waited in silence, but after a minute or so they began to get nervous. The young man reached into his pocket and pulled out his cell phone, activating the flashlight app so he could see well enough to locate the elevator's emergency call button.

"This is the operator. What's your emergency?"

"We're in the hotel elevator. It just stopped. I think we're between the eleventh and twelfth floors," the young man said anxiously.

"Sir, we'll send help as soon as we can. The hotel just lost power, and we're working to restore it."

"How long will it take?"

"We're not sure, but hopefully not long. We just ask that you be patient and remain calm; help is on the way."

The young man shined his phone light around and noticed his shivering girlfriend looked horrified. He shone the light on the two middle-aged men, and both were clearly concerned. The young man glanced back at his girlfriend and held her hand reassuringly as he leaned over and kissed her on the cheek. He shook his head in disbelief; he wished they were still in the lobby rather than confined in this dark metal box. He hoped they wouldn't have to wait long; the last two beers he chugged before they left the bar were catching up to him.

11

Back at NSA headquarters, it was after 1:30 Saturday morning. Godfrey was still at the office. He hadn't left because he was busy working on what he believed was a breakthrough in their project. Something was happening with the code they were monitoring, but Godfrey didn't know exactly what. He was frustrated that he was unable to reach Michael, having tried all of his numbers, and it had been hours since he had called Mrs. Stevens. *Why hadn't Michael called back?*

Godfrey had left a message with Kate, and he knew she would have relayed the message long ago. In desperation, the director dialed Michael's home number again, and then he called Michael's cell. There was no answer on either line. *He's avoiding me. I can't say that I blame him.* He had tried Matt O'Shea too, and he'd blown him off. He knew it was late, but what was wrong with them? This was a national security issue.

Godfrey got the sense that Kate wasn't happy that Michael had been working such long hours for months. *But how could Michael just ignore me now, particularly in a time like this?* He wrestled with his thoughts about the code they'd discovered. They knew it would be monumental, but they didn't know how it would impact the intelligence community or national security as a whole. All he knew was that there was a motive behind it. Their hunch was that the Chinese and Russians were driving it, possibly even the North Koreans, but they couldn't confirm it—at least not yet. If anyone could solve this puzzle, it would be Michael and his TAO team, which included Matt O'Shea.

Michael not only had extensive experience in Asia and Europe, but he was also a mathematical and statistical genius, especially with computer engineering and programming. He had a natural talent that the director recognized early while Michael was still studying at MIT. Godfrey was reflecting on the day he'd hired Michael as he looked at the clock on the wall. His stomach began to growl. Except for a bagel and coffee for breakfast, he hadn't eaten all day. He'd been so consumed by work lately that doing without meals had become a common occurrence.

Before they came across this new malware, Godfrey's life had been manageable. But since then his life had been turned upside down. After his wife of over thirty-five years had moved out months ago, he had dedicated himself to his work and his country full time. His job had become his refuge, but also his prison.

Godfrey peered out the window into the darkness, seeing his ghostly figure reflected in the glass. He looked and felt as though he'd aged ten years over the past twelve months. The wrinkles on his face and bags under his eyes were more pronounced, and he felt like an old man, although he was only sixty-two. He stared at the reflection of the unrecognizable stranger before him. *What has happened to me?* He had shaved his head bald hoping it would make him look more distinguished, but it had the opposite effect. His raccoon eyes were wrinkled and had lost their vibrant sparkle from hours of staring at a computer screen. He had packed on more than twenty pounds, and he looked down at his pudgy belly that bulged over his belt. Once an athlete and physically fit, it bothered him that he'd let himself go. His back ached from sitting hunched over in a chair most of the day. As he stared at his hands that were resting on his thighs, he noticed that they, too, looked older than their years. The weight of the world rested on his shoulders. Gone were the early days of his career when he was able to go home to meet his wife for dinner. The simple things—going to the gym to work out, taking walks, reading a book at lunch—all were distant memories.

Godfrey would be glad when all this was over, though he feared it was only the beginning. He had contemplated retiring in recent years, but he had more to accomplish, and he certainly didn't want to leave before he finished this final project. It was what Godfrey had worked so hard for over the years. He felt responsible for what was going on in the cyber world, but he couldn't tell his team the truth behind their project. After all, Godfrey had modified O'Shea's code and was using it for his own private surveillance program at the NSA. But he had recently realized that he wasn't the only one using O'Shea's program, and he needed Michael and his team to help figure out who had usurped it and what they planned to do with it.

Godfrey glanced at the clock on the wall as he slumped in his chair and sighed deeply. *I suppose there's nothing more I can do tonight.* He sluggishly spun around in his chair to face the computer. The screen was a sea of red text, his inbox full of unread emails. He tiredly shook his head. *Never a break.*

Godfrey closed his email and shut down his computer. He grabbed his suit coat and jacket and took one last look at his desk before heading for the door. The red message light was blinking on his desk phone, but Godfrey didn't remember missing any calls. Wondering why he hadn't noticed it before, he checked his watch. It was late. Whatever the issue was could wait until the morning. Godfrey left the office and entered his code on the keypad to lock the door.

His receptionist Alexis had left hours earlier along with everyone else. They were well on their way to enjoying the long weekend. Most of the lights in the hallway were out, so the motion-sensing lights flickered on as he walked past the other office suites down the long corridor. Arriving at the main door at the end of the hallway, he scanned his badge and put the palm of his hand on the digital screen reader. The green light on the security pad by the heavy metal door lit. There was a click, and the door hissed. Grasping the handle, he pushed it open. He wound his way through a series of maze-like hallways, passing through several secure access doors as the pounding of his dress shoes on the hard tile floors echoed.

He made his way to another set of elevators where he approached the panel between them, scanning his badge before pushing the down button, waiting patiently. The door opened, and he stepped inside, swiping his badge again over a scanner panel and pushed the button for the first floor. *They don't make it easy for us to get in or out of this place,* he thought as he leaned against the wall. His mind was a blur, and he couldn't think straight. The elevator came to a stop, and the door opened with a ding. He had passed by a couple of security desks before he reached the main lobby. The guard station was in the center of the entrance with security checks on each side. There were two guards working, with one sitting at the desk and the other leaning over the counter. It appeared the two of them were having a heated discussion, probably about the upcoming Redskins football game. Godfrey approached them.

"You're working late tonight—or early this morning—sir," said the guard who was leaning over the counter, "especially on a holiday weekend. It must be something important." The guard forced a smile, trying to be cordial.

Godfrey shrugged and replied, "Yeah, it's always something important around here."

"Do you have any plans for the long weekend?" the other guard asked.

"I'll be working. You gentlemen enjoy your weekend." He then hurried by, not in the mood for further small talk.

"Thanks, we will," they replied almost in unison.

Godfrey exited the building into the chilly, brisk air. It was refreshing to be outside. It was pleasant and quiet, and the parking lot was empty except for a couple of dozen cars scattered here and there. He could hear in the distance the sounds of the traffic on the Baltimore-Washington Parkway.

Godfrey spotted his charcoal gray Mustang GT500, a welcome sight. It was two years old and featured tinted windows, shiny chrome wheels, louvers on the side rear windows, and a custom hood with air intakes that looked like two flat narrow nostrils. The car sported aftermarket features under the hood that he'd added for more horsepower. It included light gray leather seats and top-of-the-line sound system. With its exhaust system, you could hear it coming down the street, and it turned corners like it was on rails. It was sleek, and in a way, it represented a sense of freedom. He'd wanted one since he was a kid, but not until he gave it to himself for his sixtieth birthday was that desire realized.

He unlocked the car, opened the door, and slid his briefcase behind the driver's seat before hanging up his suit coat.

He climbed into the front seat and pushed the ignition button. Nothing. He pushed it again, but still the engine refused to turn over. There wasn't even the clicking sound of a dying battery or a struggling starter. The car was dead. Too tired to complain, he sat there shaking his head. *Did I leave the lights on?* He couldn't remember, but this was the last thing he needed, especially at such an hour. Godfrey leaned his head against his hands on the steering wheel and silently prayed: *Please start.* He pushed the ignition button again. His prayer was answered: the engine turned over and revved up.

Godfrey's drive home was a blur of physical and mental exhaustion, so much so that he didn't even stop to grab something to eat. Even in all the months that they'd been working on this project, he couldn't recall being home so late. He staggered into the house and plopped onto one of the stools at their breakfast bar counter.

The six-bedroom, four-bath house was dark and eerily quiet. It had been that way since his wife had moved out. It was especially lonely on nights like this with not even his black Labrador Lexy to comfort him—his wife had taken her, too. Godfrey remembered the nights when he would come home and Lexy would be excitedly wagging her tail as she stood at the door. Now, he faced only the solitary void of a house that seemed much too large. They had bought all that space in case the kids wanted to move home after college and so they could entertain in a manner befitting his lofty NSA position. But neither had happened. His son and daughter were both grown and married with families of their own. They lived in Northern Virginia, not far from Bethesda, yet with the Beltway traffic it made for a daunting journey that was seldom attempted. He didn't even have time to phone. He justified everything by telling himself he was serving his country and that was the sacrifice he had

to make. As for entertaining, he spent so much time with colleagues that the last thing he wanted to do was party with them
at his house.

Godfrey sat staring at the microwave clock, the heaviness
of his eyelids weighing on him as he struggled to keep his eyes
open. It seemed so far to his bed. Shielding his eyes, he turned
on the hallway light before sluggishly climbing the steps, cling-
ing to the railing all the way.

After what seemed like an eternity, he made it to his bedroom, stopping to stare into the shadows. He looked vacantly
at the bed, remembering the silhouette of his wife lying there
asleep, and a wave of sadness washed over him. Despite all the
problems, all the arguments, he missed her deeply. She couldn't
stand that he was married to his work and absent so often. She
couldn't understand why he had become so unhappy and so difficult to be around. He had shown such tendencies early in their
marriage, but his attitude had only grown worse over the years
as he became more cynical and jaded. In his mind, everything in
the country was going to shit. America's foundational values and
principles were fading, and U.S. politicians and business leaders
were selling out their country for personal gain. He had become
aloof from almost everyone, so she decided it was best to move
out to give him time and space to figure things out. Initially, he
had agreed and thought it would be healthy for both of them, but
at times like this, he wasn't sure it had been the right decision.

Godfrey scanned the disheveled bedroom and muttered a
few profanities. His clothes and papers were scattered, and the
sheets and blankets of the unmade bed were strewn about the
floor like a used parachute. Godfrey loosened his tie and attempted to throw it on top of his dresser but missed. He didn't
bother picking it up. He then plopped down on the end of the

bed. Staring blankly at the wall in a mindless stupor, he untied his shoes before kicking them off. Godfrey scooted back onto the bed, laid down, and looked up at the ceiling fan where the shadows and lights from outside danced around the room. He clasped his hands behind his head and closed his eyes. He quickly dozed off, the whirling of the fan helping lure him to sleep.

12

Saturday morning at his apartment, Matt was startled from his slumber on the couch by the ring tone of his cell phone. The phone was wedged between the seat cushions, but he managed to dig it out.

"Hello?" he croaked.

"Matt, it's John. I thought I'd call to see how you're doing this morning. Did you just wake up? Aren't you supposed to be at the office by now?"

Matt sat up quickly. "Son-of-a. . . What time is it?"

"It's after ten."

"Uh-oh." John could hear Matt ranting and cursing. "I was supposed to be there by eight thirty."

"What are you going to do?"

"The only thing I can do—get there as soon as I can. I need an excuse. Think of something."

"Why not call and tell them the truth?"

"What? That I was out late, got drunk, and overslept? That would go over really well."

"No. Tell the boss your alarm didn't go off, but that you're on your way. You don't live far from the office."

Matt glanced at his alarm clock. It was blinking 12:00 a.m. "Hey, John, did the power go out last night with the storm?"

"I don't know. Everything seems fine in my neighborhood. Why?"

"Just wondering. It looks like the power might have gone out here."

Matt quickly focused on getting to work.

He and John were both contractors for Lucigen, but they were expendable. The economic crisis and the recession that followed had resulted in the unceremonious layoff of a number of their colleagues. Although Matt was undercover for the NSA, he was treated like any other employee. No one at the company knew of his dual role. Given his issues with authority, he'd been reprimanded for insubordination and his cavalier ways. Part of the deal with the NSA was for him to keep his nose clean and stay under the radar. He was explicitly told not to draw attention to himself. Matt hadn't been doing too well at that, and he couldn't afford to blow his cover.

"Hey, I just remembered, the boss isn't working today," John blurted.

Matt felt a brief sense of relief. "Who's covering the office then?"

"I'm not sure. I can call Tom and find out. I think he's working."

Tom was the team leader for their division. He was an African American male in his mid-forties, over six feet tall and lanky as a light pole. He was always well dressed—or overdressed— usually in button-down shirts and slacks with the occasional suit while everyone else was in jeans and a polo or T-shirt. A good looking guy with a well-groomed goatee and shaved head, Tom was missing an upper front tooth on the right side. Apparently, he'd taken an elbow in the mouth while playing pick-up basketball, and he'd never bothered to have the tooth replaced. He held a degree in Management of Security Information Systems from George Mason University. He was married with a four-year-old son. Tom was personable and always tried to keep the workplace environment light-hearted with his sense of humor despite the intensive workload and schedule. He balanced out their boss' autocratic management style. Like most of the other guys on their team, Tom refrained from sharing too much about his personal life.

"Would you find out for sure if the boss is coming in? I need to get ready."

"Sure. I'll call you right back."

Matt felt less panicked.

John ended the call, searched for Tom's cell number, and hit the call button. The phone rang, but there was no answer. John hung up and called Tom's office. The phone rang and rang, but still there was no answer.

"Come on, pick up the phone," he pleaded aloud.

Someone finally did.

"Hello."

"Tom, it's John from the office. Are you working today?"

Tom was agitated that John had interrupted him, "Obviously I am since you're calling me at my desk. Did you call just to rub it in or what?"

"No. Listen, Matt's alarm didn't go off. He overslept and he's running late. I need you to cover for him."

"Matt was supposed to be here at eight thirty. I was wondering if he was going to show up. Is he on his way?"

"Yes, but he won't be there for another thirty to forty-five minutes. Do you know who's managing the office today?"

"Well, it's just me for now." There was disdain in Tom's voice.

"No other team leaders or managers are in today then?"

"Not unless the boss comes in, which is highly likely at this point?"

"Is anyone else there?"

"Just the weekend crew."

"Great. Hey, you're not going to snitch on Matt, are you?"

"Of course not."

"Sorry, I had to ask."

"I'll cover for him, don't worry."

"That'd be great."

"I'll catch you later. I need to get back to work. We've got a situation on our hands."

Tom ended the call and rocked back in his chair. It was going to be a long day. They were trying to validate what appeared to be a network system security breach that had happened overnight.

John was about to call Matt when the phone rang.

"Matt, I was just going to call you back. I've got good news: the boss isn't at the office, and Tom will cover for you."

"Great. I'm on the road and will be there soon. I'll call you later."

"Sure thing. Let me know how things go."

"I will."

With that Matt focused intently on the road. He was now two hours late. Finally, he raced into the building.

"Hi, Edith, how are you doing this fine Saturday?" He tried to sound upbeat despite having to work on Veteran's Day weekend.

"You don't have to pretend. I don't want to be here either," Edith chuckled warmly.

"Is it that apparent?" he asked with a guilty look.

"I could be blind and see how miserable you are."

"Yes, but I overslept. Luckily, I don't think my boss is in today."

Edith was a slightly heavy-set, soft-spoken African American woman in her late forties. She was friendly, caring, and pleasant to talk to most days. Matt appreciated her words of wisdom when she would impart them. She had a grandson in high school who played football. He would talk with her about her grandson's sports, and she would say how talented and proud she was of him. Her gentle demeanor reminded him a little of his mother. The thought of her briefly opened painful wounds that he preferred to forget.

Matt was approaching the elevator when his cell rang. "Hey, John, what's up?"

"You at the office yet?"

"What are you, my mother? I swear . . . I just got here. I'm waiting for the elevator."

"Why don't you just walk to the third floor?"

"I suppose I should." Matt had grown lazy and had made it a habit to use the elevator. Besides, his legs ached, and his head was pounding from his hangover.

"Is everything okay?"

"I just have a lot on my mind."

"You need to relax more."

"I will."

Just then the chime sounded, and the elevator door opened. Matt stepped inside and hit the button for the third floor. The elevator surged upward until it stopped, and the doors opened again.

He stood there momentarily staring into the empty corridor before he cautiously took a few steps, looking first to the left and then to the right. There was no one to be seen or heard, so he turned and headed down the long hallway. All of the doors were closed, and most of the lights were off. The sounds from the air vents buzzed overhead. The tile from the low-hanging ceiling was brown with water stains. Many of the doors were solid metal, and others featured frosted glass. It was a dingy building with off-white walls and waxed, speckled floors. It was evident that the building needed to be renovated. Matt would have expected more from a private energy company, but he figured they were saving money. *Cheap bastards.*

Companies were always more concerned with fattening their pockets than taking care of their people or doing right. Matt didn't care for big business, corporate America, or "the man." He was a fan of the little guy, the underdog, because that's what he'd been all his life. From what he could recall, his dad had been laid off years ago, and his parents argued regularly about finances. Their mom stayed home, so their dad was the sole source of income. Maybe that's why they had abandoned their boys; they couldn't afford to take care of him and Charlie. Either way, Matt would never know.

Matt arrived at his office and, as he reached for the door handle, he paused at the sound of voices . . . loud, familiar voices. One of them sounded like his boss raising a ruckus. Matt put his ear to the door and listened intently to see if he could make out anything.

Just then Matt's phone rang; it was Tom. Matt scrambled to silence the phone. The voices behind the door stopped talking. Before Matt could think, he sped down the hall, hoping he could make it to the stairwell in time. As he rounded the corner, he heard the door open. Matt leaned against the wall, breathing heavily. The stairwell door was just out of reach, but he hoped that whoever had just come out of the office would walk the

other way or go back inside. Matt stood there, his heart pounding
as sweat ran down the sides of his brows. After a short time he
heard the door close and footsteps move quickly in the opposite
direction. He cautiously peered around the wall in time to catch
a glimpse of someone rounding the corner at the far end of the
corridor. It didn't look like the boss, but he couldn't be certain.

The boss cut a distinct physical figure that complemented
his Napoleonic inferiority complex. He was about five foot six
with broad shoulders and chest and a beer belly to match. At
nearly two hundred and fifty pounds, he had the wobble of a
penguin due to a gimpy knee. He had the rugged look and demeanor of a construction foreman. The man was shrewd and
rough around the edges, a real scrooge. He had a whip for a
tongue and was never at a loss for profanities when he got upset,
which was most days. His deep, raspy voice was due to years of
chain smoking, and he always smelled like cigarettes. No one
knew if he was married or had kids. Matt figured he wasn't and
didn't because no one could stand to be around someone so vile.
The only thing Matt respected him for was that the man knew
computer engineering and network security inside and out.
That's probably why he was such an arrogant, outspoken prick.

Matt and the others would impersonate him when he was
not around. One day in the breakroom, while with John and a
couple of the other network systems guys, the boss happened to
walk up behind Matt when he was in the middle of his skit. Matt
tried to play it off, but the boss wasn't having it. And he never
forgot that performance.

Matt stepped into the stairwell to call Tom. The phone rang
and rang. "C'mon, Tom, answer the damn phone," Matt pleaded
aloud. When no one answered, Matt called John, knowing he'd
pick up.

"Hey, Matt, how's it going?"

"I'm not sure," Matt replied.

"What do you mean? I thought you'd be at your desk by now. Where have you been?"

Matt glanced at his watch and then put the phone up to his ear again. "I think the boss might have come in today after all."

"What gives you that impression?"

"Well, just outside the office door a few minutes ago I heard loud voices; one of them didn't sound happy at all. The voices were muffled, but I could have sworn I heard the boss. You know his distinctive raspy, bark. My phone rang while I was listening. The voices grew quiet, and I ran for the stairwell. Tom just called me, but when I called back, he didn't answer."

"Did he leave a message?"

"I haven't looked." Just then Matt's phone began to vibrate. He gazed at the screen. "Hey, John, I need to answer this. It's Tom. I'll call you back."

Matt clicked over and asked, "Tom, what's up?"

"Where the hell are you? You should be here by now."

"I'm in the stairwell. I was just talking with John on my way to the office."

"Well, while you're sleeping in and taking your sweet-ass time getting to the office, we're busy working."

"I'm sorry I'm late. I came by the office and heard loud voices arguing. I ran away to be on the safe side. Who was that?"

"It was the boss. We were getting chewed out because there was an incident last night."

"An incident?"

"Yes. You know, a systems security breach."

There was a long silence.

"Really? What happened? Did he ask about me?"

"We're not sure what happened yet, but we're looking into it. I'll fill you in later. Honestly, I think the boss forgot that he asked you to work, but we're all hands on deck right now anyway."

"Thanks for letting me know." Matt ended the call with a huge sigh of relief.

Matt didn't know many people at the office who would put their necks out for anyone. Tom was one of the good guys. As the pounding of Matt's heart slowed, he headed down the hall back to his office. When he arrived he swiped his badge, entered his code into the keypad next to the door, and finally was granted entry.

The open cubicle environment was just as he had left it the night before. The commercial- grade, beige modular cubes were all interconnected with shoulder-high walls on two sides and limited storage shelves above the desks. Horse trailers had more room than those cubicles. People who were tall enough could see into their neighbor's cube, so privacy was nonexistent.

Plopping into his chair, Matt glanced at his screensaver as it danced about. He grabbed the mouse and moved it side to side to activate the login prompt. After Matt had logged into his computer and the screen had refreshed, he stared in horror at the words on the monitor. His heart raced, dreading the thoughts that rushed through his mind.

13

Michael and Kate had enjoyed their quiet Saturday morning together. It had been months since they'd been able to take their time getting up. Michael had scheduled an early afternoon flight to give them time to have breakfast, pack, and drive to the airport.

As they waited in the terminal, they sat and watched the people scurry between gates. Michael smiled, enjoying the people-watching. Since joining the NSA, he hadn't traveled as much as he used to. When he was in the navy he traveled all the time. There were advantages and disadvantages to both. The trips were enjoyable most of the time, but it meant being away from his friends and family. His mind wandered as he took in his surroundings. The smell of warm cinnamon buns in the nearby food court permeated the air, tantalizing his nostrils.

Kate leaned over and nudged him. "What are you thinking about?"

"I'm just people watching." He smiled warmly at her, an airy feeling about him.

She smiled back and said, "I'm glad we have a weekend to ourselves. We've hardly had a chance to spend any time together.

Last night was our first date night in a while, and that almost got ruined. It ended well though." She spoke lovingly as she nudged his side.

"I know. I'm sorry. I've missed being able to spend time with you."

Kate leaned over and kissed him gently on his cheek. His heart began to throb as he felt her soft lips, warm and moist, against his flesh. Michael remembered how much he loved his wife despite all the challenges they had faced over the years. She was an angel. It was the simple gestures that reminded him of how lucky he was to have her in his life.

Michael leaned over and whispered in her ear: "I love you." Kate's radiant face glowed with joy as she snuggled against him.

Just then Michael felt his phone vibrate. He checked the screen and saw he had a missed call. *Who'd be calling me on Saturday afternoon?* Michael unlocked his phone, opened the call log, and recognized the number immediately.

14

Godfrey hadn't gotten much sleep, and he took his time arriving at his office late in the morning. After all, it was the Saturday of a holiday weekend, and he hoped for a quiet day at NSA headquarters. Sulking in his chair, he stared at his computer screen thinking that he should have been vacationing with his wife or family. It wasn't like he would get much done. Most of the staff had left for the weekend, leaving only a skeleton crew.

He still couldn't figure out why Michael hadn't returned his call; the matter was important, and Michael was the only one he could confide in. Godfrey stared at his screen as he rocked in his chair. It was such a beautiful day. There was hardly a cloud to mar the blue skies, so he spun to fully enjoy the view out his large window.

Godfrey tapped his fingers on his desk and huffed to himself as he reviewed his achievements memorialized on the wall that now reminded him how vain he'd been. *What were they all for?* His life was empty. It had all been for nothing—at least that's what he thought. Empty on the inside from the years of toil and stress, his passion and vigor were long gone. His wife, the love of his life, was gone too, if only temporarily. Closing his eyes, he felt the warmth of the sun's rays radiating through his windows as he gradually dozed off.

15

Back at his cubicle, Matt fumbled about desperately as his heart pounded, and he started to sweat. Horror covered his face as he stared at the words flashing on his screen:

SYSTEM TERMINAL COMPROMISED
NETWORK FAILURE ALERT

"What the—" he blurted. "Could today get any worse?" If the system went down, parts—if not all—of D.C. would lose power. He paused, thinking back to his conversation earlier with Tom. *Certainly my computer wasn't the access point. I've got to let Tom know.*

Then the strange phone call from the night before suddenly raced into his head. *Son-of-a . . . That call can't be a coincidence. But who? The voice sounded vaguely familiar and told me to go back to my office.* Matt didn't have time to think about it further. Springing from his chair, he darted for the door as he sprinted a short distance down the hall to Tom's office and flung open the door.

"Tom! Tom! Where are you?" He ran to the other side of his cube. The chair was empty, and the computer was off. *What the hell? Where is he? Maybe he'd stepped out for coffee.* He'd just talked to Tom minutes ago. At any rate, Matt needed to notify someone that his computer had been compromised.

Matt considered his options. *How could this have happened?* Matt had turned his computer off last night—at least he thought he had. He remembered hurrying to get out of the office before the boss caught him, but he was almost certain that he'd turned the computer off, just as he did every time he left the office. Did he mistakenly abort the shutdown somehow? If that was the case, his computer could have been exposed for hackers to access the network. That thought put him in a panic. The Chinese, Russians, North Koreans, and other foreign entities were constantly trying to hack U.S. systems to get information and cause power disruptions, but they had enjoyed little success. If they had evaded the firewalls this time, it could be a nightmare for D.C., and Matt knew it. He'd need to gather any evidence he could.

Matt pulled out his phone and called Tom. Seconds later, Matt heard a phone vibrating in the bag near Tom's desk. Matt reached in, grabbed it, and saw his number on the screen. Tom had left his phone behind. Matt shook his head and muttered, "Great." He then stepped out of Tom's office and ran down to the end of the hall to the boss's office. The door was unlocked, and he felt a glimmer of hope, but once inside the office suite, he saw it was empty.

"Where the hell is everyone?" he said aloud. "He stood with his hands on his hips, perplexed. After a moment, he turned and raced back to his desk.

"What the . . . ?" The desktop screen had returned to normal. *Is someone playing a trick? Are they running network tests or something? If so, no one told me about it.*

If there had been an actual network system security breach, there's no way his screen would have returned to normal just like that. The only way to deactivate the notification alert was at the administrator level, and there were only a handful of people with that degree of system access. Matt was stumped. He pulled up his system controls and typed some commands to research the logs that tracked all activity on his computer network. It would show if there had been a breach or any other abnormal connections. Scrolling through the diagnostics reports and files, he found nothing unusual.

What's going on? He hadn't imagined that text on his screen. In frustration, he buried his face in his hands and then shook his head. Startled by the sound of his computer beeping, he slowly raised his head and stared at the screen again.

"You've got to be kidding me . . ."

16

In the terminal at Reagan National Airport, a short distance from his gate, Michael stood outside the men's restroom and stared at his phone. Godfrey was still trying to reach him. *What could be so important that he'd be calling so much?* Since his wife had moved out, Godfrey had become consumed by and obsessed with his job. Michael knew he would only call in an emergency, but surely this was not the weekend for that.

Michael had planned everything for the weekend down to the last detail. It was going to be special for him and his wife. Although dedicated to his job and his country, Michael was not going to let work interfere with this long-awaited and well-earned weekend. When he returned to the gate, Kate was standing by her seat looking uneasy as the final group of passengers was boarding. He touched her softly on the arm.

She turned abruptly, startled. "There you are. I was beginning to worry."

"I'm sorry. I lost track of time. The director called me again."

"You were gone for almost twenty minutes. Is everything all right? What did Director Godfrey want to talk to you about?"

"Honestly, I don't know. There was just a message. I didn't bother checking it." Michael's tone was indignant.

"What if it's something important? He's tried you several times since yesterday."

"Whatever it is can wait," he replied defiantly.

Kate gazed at him curiously. "This doesn't sound like the Michael I know."

"I've been breaking my back for nearly six months straight, and you would think I could get three days away without being bothered."

Kate recognized that he was frustrated. The grueling schedule had taken a toll.

"I know Director Godfrey can overdo things, but he's never been this persistent, certainly not since you started this project. There must be something going on."

"There's nothing so important that it can't wait until next week."

"Aren't you just a little curious?" She lovingly grabbed his hand.

Why would Godfrey be trying so hard to contact me? Michael thought. *Perhaps there was something wrong. Godfrey did say they were getting close to a breakthrough with the code they'd discovered. Could this be it?*

"Do you think I should call him?" Michael's eyes searched for her approval. This weekend was supposed to be about her. But before Kate could respond, the gate attendant interrupted.

"Excuse me, folks, but if you're on this flight to New York, this is the final boarding call," and she gestured to the gate where the stragglers were filing through.

Michael looked caringly at Kate and smiled. "New York City, here we come."

"Are you sure about the director?" she asked again.

"I'll send him a quick text once we're on the plane. If we want to catch this flight, we have to go now." With that, he grabbed their bags and headed to the gate. Kate handed the attendant their boarding passes, and they hurried down the ramp to the plane.

17

Godfrey slowly opened his eyes, not realizing he had dozed off for a little over an hour in his desk chair. The lack of sleep was catching up to him. He shook out the cobwebs and rubbed his eyes. He still didn't know why Michael hadn't returned his calls, but he needed him in the office. Michael had to be located immediately. He reached down and unlocked the bottom right drawer of his desk, opened it, grabbed a silver metal box, and placed it on his desk. Godfrey looked around to make sure no one was watching, though he knew someone was *always* watching. At the NSA, the walls had eyes and ears. He took a small electronic chip key from the chain around his neck and inserted it into the keyhole on the side of the box. Placing both thumbs against the front of the box on two thumb-sized indentations, he waited for the scanner to read his fingerprints. There was a click, the locks opened and, after raising the lid, he peered inside.

A soft, gray foam lined the interior. He removed the top layer of padding. Under it was something that looked like a thin USB drive. There were grooves etched into the edges of it like a key. Then he opened a hidden compartment on the side of the box. He peeled back part of the lining to expose a glass case about the size of five quarters stacked on top of each other. Godfrey picked up the case. Inside the middle of the small petri-dish-shaped container was a minute cylindrical electronic device roughly the size of a sesame seed, and that led him to recall the riddle they had him recite when he started his new role:

The seeds of trust are sown; across the earth they're strewn.
Tend your flock each day, and cast your net lest they stray.

The words echoed in his head. *Lest they stray, the seeds are strewn . . .*

The device he held was a prototype of a nanotechnology microchip that they embedded into certain employees. This was their latest version, the design of which he had personally overseen. They were still testing for any adverse effects on humans, so the microchip had only been used on a handful of test subjects, including Michael Stevens and Matt O'Shea, though neither knew it.

The chips contained all of their personnel, medical, and financial records, and it also monitored their vital signs and physical location. The devices were implanted under the skin of the employees so they could be tracked and monitored as necessary, especially for covert programs. It was one of the NSA's special operations surveillance programs that Godfrey oversaw. The Agency used the chips in assignments when there could be little to no contact with an agent or staff member. The device had been embedded when Michael had visited the Agency's health unit for his required "immunizations." It was one of the secret government programs started after 9/11 under the auspices of the Patriot Act. The Agency knew if human rights and other interest groups found out what they were doing, their operations would be severely compromised. The defense and intelligence communities had used similar devices and systems with their employees for years, particularly with the Special Forces and Special Activities Divisions with operations in foreign countries.

The NSA had already suffered some public relations debacles over tapping and recording phone and email communications as well as intercepting computer shipments to questionable persons in order to bug their equipment and conduct surveillance. Godfrey knew they couldn't afford further negative media attention. If the public knew the true extent of the NSA's monitoring programs, it would cripple his program and its funding and, perhaps, even land him in prison.

Godfrey turned in his chair to face the surreal painting on the back wall that featured a cloudy sky with the sun's rays piercing through. An elderly, sun-dried fisherman stood in a small, rickety wooden rowboat that floated on a sea of golden wheat fields. The fisherman was casting a net of metal chains and shackles toward a small flock of half-sheep, half-fish creatures alongside the boat. That poem resonated in his head again as he gazed at the painting: *The seeds of trust are sown; across the earth are strewn. Tend your flock each day, and cast your net lest they stray.*

He stared at the small glass case before whirling around in his chair to face his computer. He entered his login information before navigating to a secure surveillance system. From there he'd be able to locate Michael. Godfrey pulled out his journal and thumbed through the pages to find his password before entering his user access information. *Now let's see where you are, Michael.* Navigating through a series of prompts and menus, a satellite image of North America eventually appeared on the screen. Godfrey zoomed in on the Eastern Seaboard of the United States until he was able to distinguish the image of a long island with a large, green rectangle toward the north end. Zooming in closer, he was able to see a tiny red dot blinking. *There you are: New York City.*

Godfrey called the Agency's central travel line. There was always someone there because the NSA was a 24/7 operation.

"Central travel booking. This is Tina. How may I help you?"

"Hi, Tina, this is Director Godfrey. I need a seat on the next flight to New York City from D.C."

"Today?"

"Yes. I need to get to New York by this evening; it's urgent." He always kept a travel bag in his office with a spare suit and change of clothes in the event he had to make a last-minute trip. "When is the next flight?"

"Sir, there's a 4:25 flight leaving Reagan National and arriving at LaGuardia at 5:38 p.m."

"Are there any other options from BWI?"

"I checked, sir, but the flight out of Reagan is your best bet. That gives you a couple of hours to get through security and make your flight."

"Great. Please book it and arrange a hotel near Madison Square Garden. Also, please arrange for a driver to meet me curbside at the airport outside of baggage claim."

"Sir, I'll text and email you the confirmation details shortly."

"Thank you." Godfrey ended the call and checked some details on his computer before heading for the airport.

18

Matt stared blankly at the words that kept appearing and disappearing on his computer screen:

CRITICAL SYSTEM ERROR
NETWORK FAILURE ALERT

The beeping from Matt's computer echoed in his ears as he sat there, baffled. *What's going on?* There still was no indication of what was triggering the notification. Each computer was equipped with a customized, hardware-based firewall so that if network traffic patterns appeared abnormal, the hardware system would detect it and shut down the attack. But it wasn't foolproof. If there was a breach and someone had broken through and installed malware, then that could explain why the system was acting so strangely. A hacker might have been trying to cover his tracks but couldn't do so cleanly. *Amateurs,* Matt scoffed. *Perhaps someone wanted to be found, but why? Maybe this was a decoy.* That often happened in cyber warfare. There would be an attack in one or more locations to draw attention away from a more devastating attack elsewhere. The real attack would get lost in the noise. Matt had used various diversion tactics in his own hacktivist activities, so he was familiar with the methods. The only way for him to find out what was going on would be for him to go to the Systems Operations Department and disassemble his computer. From there he could run tests on the internal drive directly in case some rootkit was installed that was trying to prevent him from finding the malware's source. He needed to figure out why it was on his computer and how it got there.

Matt rushed out the door and down the hall to his boss's office. He knocked before entering, but the boss wasn't there.

Matt then hurried to Tom's office and, opening the door, he groaned. Tom still wasn't back. "Where the hell is everyone?" he said aloud, annoyed. He grabbed some paper and a pen from Tom's desk and wrote quickly:

> *Tom,*
>
> *I have an urgent matter that just came up. We need to talk. I'll either be at my desk or in the SysOps room downstairs.*
>
> *Call me.*
> *Matt*

He left the note on Tom's keyboard before he raced out the door and back to his office. Matt logged back into his computer so he could close out the command prompts he'd opened and properly shut down.

Matt had checked the server systems, and there was no report whatsoever of a network breach or system failure. That surprised him, especially with the notifications that had appeared and disappeared on his monitor earlier. If anything, the Systems Operations room would allow him to run the necessary tests that he couldn't from his desk. He also would be able to use his access codes the NSA had given him to remote into their Black Viper network and conduct malware scans using their supercomputer. The NSA's systems were highly advanced and were designed to conduct protocol checks to identify exceptions that most standard commercial systems checks would miss, particularly with the outdated software that Lucigen was using. The Black Viper system processed ten terabytes per second, so he knew he'd find the problem quickly. Matt had to be extremely careful not to get caught. He didn't want anyone at the energy company to know what he was doing or who he was actually working for.

As he was about to close the command prompts and shut down, Matt noticed his cursor jumping back and forth across the screen. He paused before moving the cursor, but it seemed as though his wireless mouse wasn't responding. He turned it over and opened the bottom to check the batteries. As he did so, his cursor started to move across the screen. The arrow clicked the "close" icon on the command prompt he'd been typing in, and another prompt opened.

"What the...?" Matt shook the mouse on top of the desk. The cursor didn't move. As he watched, commands were entered into the prompts to shut down electricity to parts of the city. In a panic, he immediately reached behind the computer and pulled out the network cable hoping that would stop it. Seconds later the typing resumed. *"Shit. This is bad."* Someone was remotely controlling his computer to access Lucigen's systems, but he didn't know who or how.

Frantically, he pulled the power cable from the back of his machine and, thankfully, the screen went blank. He grabbed the equipment cart that was next to his cubicle and loaded his computer system onto it. He gave his workspace one last look to make sure he had everything he needed before heading downstairs.

The squeaking wheels on the cart echoed down the corridor as he made his way to the elevators at the far end of the wing. He entered the elevator and hit "B" for the basement. After a short ride, the elevator doors opened, and he pushed the cart into the hallway. The motion-activated lights illuminated as he rushed down the corridor. He entered the service entrance and rushed past the swinging doors that led to the loading docks. Finally, he came to a solid metal door with an electronic keypad and a badge recognition device. Matt swept his badge and entered his security access code. The red light on the panel turned green, and the door to the SysOps room unlocked. Matt pushed it open, pulling the cart inside. After switching on the lights, he locked the door behind him. The incandescent lights flickered on in the air-conditioned but stuffy room. He looked around. Heavy duty metal shelves stocked with electronic network equipment and computer parts lined the exterior walls. He would have plenty to work with. The room housed several of the company's smaller network servers that controlled power to the city. With the network breach through his system, he needed to find out any details about the malware being used and what damage might have been done. The consequences for the city could be dire because power could be completely knocked out across downtown D.C.

Matt pushed the cart to one of the work areas. He then lifted his computer, set it on the countertop, and turned on the diagnostic systems to let them boot up. While the system was loading, Matt attached his computer cables and hardware to the control panel, but he intentionally didn't connect the network cable. Once everything was hooked up and the malware scanning system was running, he sat down and keyed in his access information. The scan would determine what malware was being used and might yield important clues as to how the hacker had entered the system. If Matt had to guess, he would bet money that someone used a backdoor or a Remote Access Trojan, or RAT, as they were called. He had used them himself. The only trick was locating them. Not knowing how long their network systems had been exposed, the damage to their control systems could be significant. Even with all of the technology assurances, protection of their information and systems was never 100 percent.

Matt navigated through a series of command prompt screens and identified and selected the malware scans he needed before proceeding.

19

Michael and Kate peered out of their airplane window as their flight touched down at LaGuardia. While the plane taxied, Michael peeked out the window over Kate's lap to watch the bustling activity on the tarmac.

"What are you thinking?" she asked kindly. "It looks like you're in deep thought again." Her eyes sparkled.

"Nothing, really; I'm just thinking about the usual: you know, life, work, the weekend." His tone was soft but distant.

Kate gazed into his eyes. Michael could see her love radiate from every ounce of her being. "If I only get to do one thing with you this weekend, I know what that will be." She winked playfully and puckered her lips seductively as she slid closer to his side.

Michael laughed lightly and shook his head. She always had a way of making things better by lightening the mood. He loved how, despite whatever was happening, Kate always had a great sense of humor. She brought that out in him too, which was another of the many things he loved so much about her. It was also one of the main reasons he was able to keep his sanity and make it through work the past six months. She was an amazing woman, and he realized how lucky he was.

"There you go again, off into Michael's world. When are you going to invite me to join you?" she asked and then grinned, playfully prodding his side.

Just then a flight attendant advised, "Please wait until the aircraft has come to a complete stop and the captain has turned off the seatbelt sign before getting out of your seats."

Soon after a ding was heard, the seat belt sign went off. People hastily stood up and grabbed their bags from the overhead bins and beneath their seats. But Kate and Michael were in no hurry. They stayed in their seats holding hands, waiting for the people ahead of them to clear out. When the row in front of them had departed, Michael and Kate stood and removed their bags from the overhead bins. They made their way off the plane, through the terminal, and toward baggage claim and ground transportation. Out on the sidewalk they found a taxi booth and a row of Yellow Cabs.

"Do you need a taxi?" a young man asked politely.

"We sure do," Michael replied.

"Where are you going?"

"Midtown."

The attendant handed the couple a brochure with the rates and other taxi information as he waved to one of the driver's to pick up his next fare.

"Where to?" the cabbie asked as he stood by the open trunk.

Michael replied, "We're going to midtown near Madison Square Garden—the Manhattan Midtown Hotel."

"Sure thing." The cabbie reached down, grabbed their bags, and tossed them into the trunk.

Michael and Kate climbed into the back seat, and the cab sped off toward the city.

20

Godfrey checked the clock on his computer. He needed to leave for the airport soon. After verifying Michael's location in Manhattan, Godfrey decided to check his personnel records in the surveillance system. He located them, but he didn't know how to react to what he found: Godfrey was staring at an image of himself. Beneath his photo the words on the screen read:

Under Surveillance . . . Monitor for Threat Level . . .

"What the . . .," he said as he stared at his monitor. He couldn't believe what he was seeing. *Under surveillance? But why, and by whom?* Looking through the access log, he searched for the last entry into his system. It had been after midnight the night before, only a short while after he'd left his office. *Had someone entered after I left? That didn't make any sense. Who would or could do that, especially at that time of night?*

Godfrey wanted to know who else was being monitored, so he pulled up a directory with his team and searched first for

Michael's full profile. He eyed the screen and read the words under Michael's photo:

Under Surveillance . . . Monitor for Threat Level . . .

There was a small icon in the upper left of his monitor. Godfrey clicked it, and various video surveillance feeds appeared. He recognized Michael's office and his house and what looked like the inside of a car. *What is all of this? Why is Michael under surveillance? I didn't approve this.*

Aiden, his chief of staff, was the only other person who had access to his office and the surveillance system. Not even his secretary had access. But why would Aiden be snooping around in his office? And if it wasn't Aiden, who was it?

The director had hired Aiden over five years earlier. Aiden was in his late forties with short, wavy, auburn hair peppered with gray and styled to the side. His thin, weasel face and rounded chin encased his hawkish eyes and pointed nose. An avid tennis player and golfer, he had a narrow build and was as swift and agile on his feet as he was with his words. A shrewd, calculated man, the director respected his analytical and strategic abilities. He had remained loyally by Godfrey's side through a number of public relations debacles and worked closely with Godfrey on countless secret projects. Godfrey believed he could trust him with his utmost secrets, yet this latest revelation caused him to question that belief. Godfrey knew years ago that he would need a successor at some point, and he had long considered Aiden his protégé.

Godfrey was concerned about the other members in his TAO cyberterrorism unit and if their mission might be compromised. He conducted a quick search for the others on his task force. It was the same result for each one; all were under surveillance, including David and O'Shea. *Could this be tied to the code and his classified national security project? Was there something that someone didn't want them to know? Surely it was no coincidence.* His mind overflowed with questions for which he had no answers. He needed to get to Michael, and soon. Godfrey worried something might have happened already, which was why Michael wasn't responding to his calls.

Godfrey shut down his computer, grabbed his travel bag from the closet, and headed to the airport.

21

When Michael and Kate arrived at their hotel in midtown Manhattan, their taxi driver unloaded their bags onto the curb, and Michael paid him, including a generous tip. The bellhop, dressed in his long red uniform coat, took their bags and followed Michael and Kate as they strolled into the lobby. Welcoming smiles greeted them at the reception desk.

"Good afternoon," the young woman behind the counter said. "Is this your first time to our hotel or New York City?"

"This is our first time at your hotel," Michael responded, "but we've been to New York before."

"Great. Welcome back. Do you have a reservation?"

"Yes."

"Under what name?"

"It should be under Stevens, Michael Stevens."

"Give me a moment, and I'll check that for you, sir," she said, and she looked intently at the screen as she typed away on the keyboard. She looked up from the computer, a hint of regret on her face, and said, "I'm sorry, sir, but I don't see your reservation."

"What do you mean?" he replied curtly, his voice rising.

"I'll be happy to check again. When did you book it?" the young woman asked politely.

"I booked it over a month ago through your eight hundred number."

"Okay. And do you spell Stevens with a 'v' or a 'ph'?"

"With a 'v.'"

"Okay, let me check a couple of things for you and see what I can find."

Michael and Kate waited. Michael leaned anxiously against the reception desk as he tapped his fingers on the counter. It was a nervous habit. Losing his reservation was the last thing he would have expected. Finally, the young woman looked up from her computer.

"Here it is. It was misfiled under 'ph' instead of 'v.' My apologies. Your reservation has you arriving today and departing on Monday. Is that correct?"

Michael sighed, relieved. "That's correct."

"Terrific. I'll go ahead and check you into your room. I'll just need an I.D. and your credit card for incidentals. Will you need any special services or accommodations?"

"Not right now, but thank you."

"And will you need any help with your bags?"

"No, I believe we're good. But if you have a city map, that would be great."

"Certainly." The woman reached beneath the counter and grabbed two brochure maps of the city. "Are you interested in any of the city tours or Broadway shows?"

"Perhaps; we'll have to see what's playing," he said as he took the brochures from the young woman.

Michael was ready to get to the room and relax before dinner. He grabbed their wheeled bags and headed toward the elevator. Once inside, Michael eyed Kate, excited to get her up to the room. She noticed him looking her up and down and gently slapped his arm. "Stop that. I'm not a piece of meat."

"What?" He stepped playfully away, pulling his arm back. "I'm just admiring your beauty."

"I know you're doing more than that."

The elevator took them to the top floor. The door opened, and they headed toward the suite at the end of the long hall. Michael hadn't told her that he'd reserved a special room; he wanted to surprise her.

When they reached their room, a sign on the door greeted them:

Honeymoon Suite

Kate was ecstatic. She turned and wrapped her arms lovingly around Michael's neck and kissed him passionately. Kate pulled away momentarily. "Oh, Michael, this is going to be an incredible weekend. I love you so much." Then she looked deeply into his eyes as they held each other tightly.

"I love you, too. Shall we go inside?" Michael said, motioning toward the door.

"Absolutely."

A bottle of champagne on ice, a hors d'oeuvres platter, and a card on the table welcomed them. Michael picked up the card, opened it, and read it quickly. He wanted to make sure they'd gotten it right. He then put it back into the envelope and handed it to Kate to read:

To my amazingly beautiful and supportive wife whom I love so much. My life would not be what it is today if it wasn't for you. Thank you for all of your unconditional love, patience, and all that you do. You make me want to be the best man possible. You've made me the man I am today.

Love Always,
Michael

Kate melted as she read the words, and Michael could tell she was moved.

Kate turned and wrapped her arms around him as she looked longingly into his eyes. "What do you say we open that bottle of champagne?"

"Already? Don't you want to wait until we come back from dinner?"

"No. We're on vacation. I'm ready to open it right now," she pouted playfully.

"It's a little early. If we start drinking now, we may not make it out for dinner."

"And your point is what, exactly?" She displayed a mischievous grin. "Isn't that why they have room service?" she asked as she caressed his arm and hand.

"I suppose you're right."

"Now open that bottle while I change into something more comfortable," she said as she flirtatiously pinched his side. "I'll be right back. Don't go anywhere." She strutted seductively into the bedroom, taking her tote bag with her.

Michael watched her disappear. He then placed the *"Do Not Disturb"* sign on the door before opening the champagne and pouring two glasses. He was enjoying a sip on the couch when the bedroom door opened. He smiled broadly as he stared at Kate.

"Do you like it?" She curtsied slightly and did a full turn in a silky, bright red, mid-thigh satin and lace low-back slip.

"I do," he said, fumbling his glass as he tried to set it down.

"Are you going to stand there gazing, or are you going to bring me my drink?" She swayed side to side, teasing him.

Michael admired how incredible she looked. She taunted him, but that was part of the fun. He figured two could play that game.

"Why don't you come join me here on the sofa?" he said as he patted the seat cushion.

Kate strutted toward him and leaned over him, putting her hands on the back of the sofa, her chest bared before him.

She then reached down and took the champagne glass from his hand and put it on the end table.

"What did you do that for? I was going to drink that."

"You're going to need both hands for something much better." She tilted her head and gave him an inviting look. She gazed longingly into his eyes as she straddled his legs, leaning forward to whisper something in his ear. That was all he needed.

22

In the Systems Operations Room, Matt sat in front of the diagnostics computer terminal patiently awaiting the results of the malware scan. He was getting bored, so he walked around. Perusing the various computer parts on the shelves, Matt noticed all the blinking lights on the network servers. He pitied the poor person who had to keep track of that inventory and keep the servers running. It wasn't an easy job. He grabbed a new USB drive off the shelf and took it out of the box. Matt wanted to make sure he saved whatever report his scans generated. Then he returned to the computer where he plugged the thumb drive into the USB port on the main panel. No results had shown up thus far. The numbers indicated the percentage of the scan that had been completed:

28% . . . 31% . . . 34% . . .

Matt stepped away from the computer again and moved to the other side of the room as his mind wondered. His lack of sleep and the headache from his hangover weren't helping.

Finally, Matt's trance was broken by a loud beeping alarm. The screen was flashing red.

"*Son-of-a—*" He darted to the computer, stared at the screen, and read the flashing words on the monitor:

CRITICAL SYSTEM ERROR DETECTED

"How can there possibly be an error?" he blurted out in frustration. "This isn't supposed to happen."

Matt desperately clicked the mouse and pounded at the keyboard. Finally, he slouched back into his chair. Then both the notice and the alarm stopped abruptly, and the screen returned to normal. His heart raced. He was sweating despite the cold air in the room. *What's going on? This response isn't typical. There must be something wrong with the systems, but that would be nearly impossible—unless someone was toying with him from inside NSA headquarters' systems.*

Matt pulled up the diagnostics report and scanned the results to see what information he could find, but there was nothing. Matt checked the progress display again, but it still showed only 37% complete. The partial code that the report had identified didn't indicate anything, and so he quickly reviewed the lines of text but, again, he didn't see anything. All seemed normal.

Matt looked back at the progress indicator, but the numbers weren't advancing. The system error must have disrupted the malware diagnostic scan. He pulled up the menu to see if he could continue the search where it had left off. He clicked through the various prompts on the screen until he reached "Resume Diagnostics Test." After he clicked "Proceed," he waited. The screen flickered, and then the numbers began to advance: 40% . . . 43% . . . 47%. He was satisfied things were back on track. But no sooner had he stepped away than the alarm sounded again. He spun and glared at the screen message:

CRITICAL SYSTEM ERROR DETECTED

Matt tapped away at the keyboard in an effort to override the error. "What the hell is going on here?" he blurted out, frustrated. Such errors were not supposed to occur, especially not with the new state-of-the-art Black Viper system.

Matt couldn't even manage to stop the annoying alarm. Then he noticed a faint metallic burning smell. *The processor.* Matt realized the cooling fan was no longer spinning; the computer was overheating. The burning smell was getting stronger. He didn't know whether to unplug the computer or not. If he didn't, it could overheat and destroy the hardware along with the information he needed.

The alarm continued to sound, so Matt made his decision and unplugged his computer. The beeping noise from the diagnostics machine stopped, and the screen froze. There were only two phrases that remained:

CRITICAL SYSTEM ERROR
DIAGNOSTICS TEST MANUALLY
ABORTED

Matt stared at the computer monitor as the faint smell of burning silicon and metal tingled in his nose. His heart was pounding, and perspiration dripped from his brow. *What a mess.*

He exited the diagnostics test portal and returned to the main screen, hoping he could identify the source of the problem in one of the partially completed diagnostics reports. Matt searched the menus and found a half-completed report that he saved to his USB drive. Then he skimmed the reports for any indication of what could have gone wrong that he hadn't noticed before, but there were still no apparent anomalies.

According to the report, both errors had happened about the same place in the scan, which could only mean a couple of things. It was possible that some corrupted data was causing things to crash whenever anything tried to read it, possibly due to a hardware failure. It also seemed as though someone could have used a backdoor to get into the system and was intentionally causing the errors as a means of hiding their activities or concealing their attack vector. Either one wasn't good. The processor was being rigged to overheat, causing it to burn and cover any traces. If that happened to all of the company's control systems, the power to D.C. would be knocked out, at least those parts of town controlled by the impacted network servers. But whoever was behind this would have needed a software program to open the backdoor into the system. Trying to access it directly from the outside wouldn't have worked. The network's security system was designed to prevent that exact scenario, so they must've used some means of transmitting a signal out from inside the network.

Matt sat perplexed. *How could the software have been installed on his computer without anyone knowing, including him?* There would need to be a separate set of tests run to find out. He didn't know the extent to which the hardware had burned, but he knew damage had been done. He examined the metal box in front of him and huffed. The heated vapor from his breath was visible in the cold basement air. Grabbing the system, he carried it to a large, stainless steel table covered in a black antistatic mat in the middle of the room. Overhead spotlights illuminated every square inch.

Matt removed the tool box from under the table. He pulled out the screwdriver and began taking off the casing. Grabbing one of the small flashlights, he shined the light inside to check the damage from the overheating. It appeared to be less serious than he'd feared. He wouldn't know more until he was able to dissect the hardware further, so he rolled up his sleeves and went to work.

After disassembling the motherboard, being careful not to damage anything, he carefully held one of the custom circuit boards. He grabbed the magnifying headset from the toolbox, similar to what jewelers use, and examined the memory card to see if there was any damage. For comparison he walked over to one of the supply shelves, opened the lock on the door, and grabbed a new circuit board. He placed both of them on top of the table and examined them meticulously. He wanted to physically compare them before he plugged the old one back into the machine to run a new test. He found nothing unusual, so he figured that when he ran the test, it would help him isolate the problem. Matt grabbed both of the circuit boards and returned to the diagnostics machine.

Matt carefully hooked up both circuit boards to run simultaneous tests. The new one was going to be the control to help him determine where the error had occurred. Once both were plugged in, he fired up the diagnostics machine again.

Matt returned to the center operating table and proceeded to disassemble the computer, removing all of the internal parts and placing them neatly on the table. It wasn't long before he heard a familiar sound; the error alarm was sounding. He dashed to the computer where the screen was flashing error warnings.

"*What the*—." He stopped the scan, and the alarm ceased, but the buzzing continued in his ears as he stared at the screen.

Matt scrolled through the menus and pulled up the partially completed diagnostics report. It should tell him what was wrong and if the security breach had done any damage.

As he scrolled through the report, he found his answer. He wasn't sure what it was, but there were exceptions in the information sequence and abnormalities in the coding. *Something built into the motherboard or on the computer itself must be manipulating the information flow and causing the problem, but what, and why?*

Matt knew that since 9/11 the NSA had helped intelligence agencies intercept computer equipment shipments to potential terrorists and other questionable persons. Word had reached the public through news reports only a few months earlier, but he had known for some time. Unbeknownst to the end-users, the FBI and CIA—with the help of the NSA—would intercept and bug the equipment before sending it along. They did this routinely to gather intelligence. *But could the same have been done with his company's computer?* Was it an inside job by the U.S. government, or was it an act by a foreign country or organization?

Ironically, despite the push for highly resilient security systems within the public and private sectors, most of their equipment was still manufactured in China or elsewhere overseas. There would have been ample opportunities to manipulate the hardware or software on the computer and network systems. Matt was well aware of the cyberwar going on with China and Russia. North Korea and Iran also had their fair share of involvement. The only logical explanation he could think of was that a malware agent had been installed, but he had no tangible proof. Matt needed more time to collect evidence, but that was time he didn't have.

Matt wanted to check one more possibility in the hardware before calling Tom. He partially disassembled the computer on the table. Then he grabbed the magnifying headset and examined the wires connected to the motherboard, tracing them to see where they ended. Finally, he found a stray wire trailing out of the hard drive cage that was connected to one of the computer ports on the motherboard. It was an unusual wire that he didn't recognize. Matt followed the wire until he saw what it was connected to, a device about the size of a small stick of chewing gum. He knew immediately what it was—a cellular network microcard, and it didn't belong there. Someone had physically installed it on his computer, but the questions remained: who, how, and why?

His hunch about his computer being tampered with was right. He guessed it could have been the NSA keeping tabs on him while he was undercover, but they wouldn't shut down power to D.C. It didn't make any sense. He was certain now as to how they were remoting into his computer and his company's network to bypass their security measures, so Matt carefully disconnected and removed the card from his motherboard and carried his partially disassembled computer back to the main panel. He reconnected it to the computer mainframe network. *Let's try running those malware scans now that this has been discarded* he thought as he held up the cellular network card and looked at it before setting it down on the tabletop.

Matt figured it was a good time to call Tom. But before he could reach for his cell, the landline on the wall rang. Matt checked the caller I.D., but it showed the caller as "Unknown."

Hmmm . . . Who would be calling other than Tom? He's the only one who knows I'm down here, unless someone else saw my note on his chair. Matt answered.

"Matt, is that you?" It was Tom.

"Yes, Tom, it's me."

"What are you doing?"

"What do you mean what am I doing? Where is everyone? I looked, but I couldn't find anyone."

"The boss called us all into a long meeting, and then we went to grab a coffee and a bite to eat. We're going to need it."

"Well, that explains why I couldn't find anyone. But why the long meeting?"

"Did you not hear what I said earlier about there being an incident? There's a lot of work to do." Tom's voice was filled with resignation.

"Really? What incident? When?"

"The boss was doing his daily scan reports and system review updates this morning on the network. It appears we had a security breach sometime after midnight. He's having us drop everything and get on it. He's concerned that our network may have been impacted. He believes the penetration of our systems caused scattered blackouts last night across the city, *not* the thunderstorm as the public is being told. We've been able to restore power to most of those affected. But if another, more devastating attack happens, even more parts of D.C. could lose power for a longer period. The boss already called the Department of Homeland Security and FBI for help. They arrived on site less than an hour ago."

There was a long silence as Matt stood in the cold room, speechless.

"Matt, you sure got quiet all of a sudden. What was your note all about? Do you know something about this?

Matt glared at his disassembled computer.

"Matt, what's going on?

"Tom," Matt's voice was faint and distant.

"Yes, what is it?" Tom replied. There was another long pause. "Matt, please tell me you didn't have anything to do with the breach."

"It happened through my computer terminal sometime between when I left work yesterday and when I arrived this morning." Matt's voice was lifeless. His thoughts flashed back to the mysterious call from the night before. The stranger had told him to go back to his office immediately to check on his computer systems. But who had called him?

"What happened? How? Why didn't you tell anyone about it?"

"I did! I tried, dammit! I called you! I stopped by everyone's desk, and no one was around. I've been trying to figure out if it was a real breach or just a system malfunction. Nothing showed up on the initial system scan when I ran a report earlier today. I could have sworn I shut my computer off."

"Just calm down. I didn't mean to seem as though I was interrogating you."

"It did seem a little like that," Matt snapped back. "Tom, I don't know what do."

"First of all, where are you?"

"What do you mean where am I? You called me down here in the SysOps room."

"Oh yeah, that's right. Sorry about that. I just had a memory lapse. A lot is going on."

"Listen, Tom, I think I'm going to be in a huge mess over all of this. I need your help. I've tried everything and can't seem to figure things out. Not only that, I found a cellular network micro-card installed in my computer that was connected to the motherboard. I sure as hell didn't put it there. I think that's what enabled the malware agent to penetrate our systems. Someone was using the cellular network card as a remote access tool to enter through a back door and get inside our systems to disable them."

"You found a cellular network card attached to your motherboard?" Tom asked in disbelief. The company's computers were routinely scanned, physically inspected, and tested. To compromise a computer as Matt was describing without being detected was all but impossible. "What all scans have you tried?"

"Everything," Matt said with a sigh. He had run the localized tests that the company used, but he wasn't going to tell Tom that he'd also used the NSA's systems to do subsequent scans. Only NSA cyber defense specialists with compartmentalized clearances had access to the classified systems, and Matt was one of them. But Tom didn't know that.

"And nothing worked?"

"Nope. I keep getting system errors when I run the diagnostics malware scans."

"Hmmm, don't go anywhere. I'll be right down."

Meanwhile, Matt spaced out and stood with the phone in his hand listening to the dial tone for almost thirty seconds. The lack of sleep was making him loopy.

After about five minutes, Matt heard the sound of the keypad for the door lock activate. Matt turned as Tom entered the room

"Is everything okay? You look like crap," Tom said as he looked at Matt in his disheveled state.

"Yes, I'm fine, but this is a mess." He ran his hands through his ratty, wavy hair.

"It'll all work out, Matt. We'll get to the bottom of it. Remind me again what all you've tried. Aside from your strange theory about malware agents and backdoors on our secure computer network, do you have a sense of what else might have happened?"

"I don't, honestly. But what I do know is that the card is not just a theory—look," Matt said as he held up the cellular network card.

"You weren't kidding."

"Absolutely not. I know it sounds far-fetched, but I have no other explanation."

"I don't know where you come up with these ideas." Tom remained skeptical despite seeing the cellular network card for himself.

Given Matt's background as a hacker and programmer, he knew these things happened, so it wasn't too much of a stretch for him. He'd also been involved in some projects using similar technology and approaches, so he knew it was possible. Tom, on the other hand, was an old school IT systems administrator and not up to speed on the latest in cyber security.

Tom had no idea of Matt's extensive hacking and computer engineering experience—from both sides. The story Tom heard from the boss was that Matt had dropped out of a four-year college and had only recently been hired out of some unknown computer trade school. Unlike Tom, who was a full-time Lucigen employee, Matt was an independent contractor, and as such he was viewed as a second-class citizen. Independent contractors were expendable, and turnover was high. There was often tension between the career employees and the contractors, partially because of the job uncertainty but also because the contractors tended to make significantly more than the career employees for doing the same work. Although Tom liked Matt personally, he didn't think too highly of his computer skills, at least those he'd demonstrated. Matt also had to play the part of a new, inexperienced computer techie and not let onto the fact that he was a computer engineering genius. That was difficult because Matt's arrogance could get the best of him, so he wasn't good at hiding what he knew.

Tom noticed that Matt was preoccupied. "Listen, don't stress. Just run me through what you've done up to this point."

"Everything?" Matt responded flippantly. "You want me to recount everything? You're kidding, right? I've been running tests since I got here," Matt said, glancing at his watch. He didn't realize he'd already been at work for hours.

"You don't have to give me all of the details, just the relevant points. Did you do a systems check when you first discovered the problem? What diagnostics scans have you run? Did anything show up in the control diagnostics and monitoring systems? Were there any abnormalities?"

Both Tom and Matt took a moment to sit. Matt went through everything he could think of, except the NSA Black Viper systems part. He walked Tom painstakingly through all the steps he had taken to try to diagnose the problem and what, if any, damage had been done.

When Matt finished telling Tom all that he'd done, Tom fell silent. Matt's question finally broke the long silence. "What are you thinking?"

Tom still said nothing.

"Tom!" Matt said, raising his voice to get his attention.

Tom had been staring at the floor, apparently in deep thought, when he gradually lifted his head and stared at Matt. There was confusion on his face.

"I don't get it, Matt. Everything you said you did appears to be correct. It doesn't sound like you missed anything. I don't know why the reports aren't showing anything and why you keep getting those critical network system errors. This is all so odd, especially when you said you ran the initial scan in your office and nothing came up. If the boss was able to pull the report and find the breach, then how come you weren't able to find anything? You should have been able to identify the breach and pull a report from your computer just like the boss, especially from here. Something isn't right."

"You're telling me. This is the craziest thing. I think hackers were trying to cover their tracks. But I figured I would have had some answers by now." Matt leaned against the counter, trying to think of other options. "Hey, why don't we ask the boss for a copy of the report? He has everyone coming into the office to work this security breach, so I don't know why he wouldn't share it, unless he's trying to hide something."

"You want me to ask for a copy?" Tom's reply was bathed in skepticism.

"Sure, why not? You were just meeting with him. Couldn't you just grab the report and bring a copy down here for us both to examine? Why would he object to that? You're one of the team leads. What did he say earlier today in your meeting?"

"He only told us there had been a systems security breach during the night and it possibly contributed to the power outages across the city. He said we would need to put in extra time to assess the damage and address it based on what he identified in his daily systems report."

"Did he give any specifics?" Matt asked.

"He just spoke in generalities and didn't give us any details to work with. Members of Homeland Security and the FBI are already on the case." Tom's voice trailed off.

"Track down the boss and see if you can get the report. In the meantime, I'll stay here and see what more I can figure out." Matt stared intently at Tom. "That sound okay to you?"

Tom gave Matt a half-cocked, quizzical look and asked, "Are you serious?"

"Of course I am. Listen, we need to figure this out, especially because it involves our network infrastructure and my computer. It could be catastrophic for D.C. if all our power systems were taken offline. It's apparent that what we've tried isn't working, and we still don't have any answers. I think the boss knows something that he's not telling us."

Tom looked at his young, somewhat hysterical colleague, not knowing how to respond. He'd never seen Matt like that before.

"Tom, I need your help to figure this out. I'm sure the boss knows that my computer was the access point for the intrusion. That would have shown up in the report. My IP network address would have been all over it. If he finds me here he's going to wonder what I'm doing, especially with that." Matt pointed to his disassembled computer on the table. "I know he doesn't trust me. He's told me that."

"I suppose you're right. Let me see what I can find out. If anything comes up, I'll give you a call. In the meantime, don't go anywhere, especially not back to your office."

"You don't have to worry about that. What if someone comes in and finds me here? I don't anticipate that happening, but it's a possibility."

"Just be as discreet as you can," Tom said.

"Well, given that I'm in here and there's been a security breach that may have involved my computer, I don't know how discreet I can be with a half-assembled computer in a systems diagnostics room surrounded by secure network servers. That'd be kind of hard to explain," Matt said smugly. The more he thought about the situation, the less he liked it. Depending on the level of damage, they would undoubtedly come after him. He paused a minute and shook the thoughts out of his head. He was always overanalyzing things. Matt was instructed to maintain his cover at all costs. If anything bad happened, he was sure the NSA would bail him out. They couldn't have one of their undercover cyber specialists get into trouble. He wondered if his colleagues at the NSA knew the full extent of what was happening. He'd accessed their systems to run the scan, which he tended to do from time-to-time, but this was the first time he'd used the Black Viper supercomputer. The NSA had to know more about the breach. His instructions not to contact the agency under any circumstances were clear, so he was going to have to figure this out on his own, at least for the time being.

23

Director Godfrey arrived at LaGuardia without his usual security detail. Given the last-minute nature of his trip and the fact that he was under surveillance, he thought it was best to go alone.

Godfrey found his driver, confirmed the security code that only his driver would know, and then they headed for downtown Manhattan. Godfrey was in the back seat on the phone, so he didn't notice the route the driver was taking until he finally looked up.

"Which way are you taking into the city?"

"The usual," the driver replied nonchalantly.

"It doesn't look familiar. I don't think I've ever gone this way before," Godfrey said.

"Don't worry. I sometimes think that too at night. There are some bottles of water in the center console if you're thirsty."

Godfrey reached for a bottle of water, not thinking to check the seal to make sure it hadn't been tampered with. Godfrey opened it and took a long gulp. Parched from not having had much to drink all day, he finished off the water and set the bottle off to the side. Minutes later Godfrey had an uneasy feeling in his stomach. He also was light-headed, and his vision was blurry. As he reached for the water bottle to examine it, he passed out. The driver, grinning deviously, glanced back at Godfrey through the rearview mirror.

24

In their Manhattan hotel room, Kate and Michael laid naked in bed wrapped lovingly in each other's arms. Kate was tucked against his shoulder with her head propped up on his chest as she lay sleeping. Michael was lying on his back, his right arm wrapped under Kate, his left arm resting on his chest. His eyes were wide open as he stared at the ceiling. It was time for dinner, but he turned over to gaze lovingly at his wife's body, her arms and legs draped around him. He couldn't remember the last time he had enjoyed such an intimate time with her, and he didn't want it to end.

Michael hadn't eaten since they had left D.C., and his stomach was rumbling with hunger pangs. The noise caused Kate to stir in her sleep. As he attempted to slip away and grab a snack from the other room, each time he made even the slightest movement, she would hold him tighter. Michael decided to let her sleep a little longer. He closed his eyes and tried to sleep, but his thoughts churned feverishly.

As his mind returned to the phone calls from Director Godfrey, a flash of anxiety came over him. He was supposed to have called the director as soon as they landed. *Why had the director called so many times? It wasn't like him. Something must be wrong.* Michael's heart pounded as the thoughts spun in his head. *What if something was horribly wrong and I did nothing?* The achy feeling throughout his body started to form a knot in his stomach. He felt trapped. He gently rolled over and gazed again at Kate before peering at the clock.

Stealthily, he slid from under Kate's loving grasp. As he did so, he watched her intently. It tore at him to sneak away as she stirred in her slumber.

Michael stumbled along the wall and into the bathroom until he found the robe hanging on the door hook. He put it on and tiptoed toward the bedroom door, hoping the sound of his footsteps wouldn't wake Kate.

Michael stepped into the living room and quietly closed the bedroom door behind him. He checked his phone and saw two new messages, so he dialed his voicemail. The first message was from Kate last night, but the second was from Godfrey.

"Michael, this is Director Godfrey. We need to talk. Call me as soon as you get this. It's about something 'eminent.'" His message was cryptic, but there was a sense of urgency in his voice.

Michael checked the time of his call. It was around the time they were boarding their plane in D.C. Michael wondered if he should even bother calling back now. He was in New York City and couldn't do anything until he got back to D.C. He paused for a moment before finally calling. The phone rang until it went to voicemail. He hung up and tried again. There was still no answer. *What's up?* he wondered. Godfrey always picked up the phone. Godfrey's wife had left him months ago, and all he'd done since was work. He had to be available. Michael hung up and tried one last attempt, and this time he left a message.

"Director Godfrey, it's Michael. I'm in New York City. I got your message that you needed to talk. I'll be here until Monday morning. I don't think I will be of much help until I'm back at the office on Tuesday. Kate and I are up here for the long weekend. Feel free to give me a call on my cell when you get this message."

Michael ended the call and sat silently, feeling more at ease knowing that he'd made the call. Now all he could do was wait. Michael set his phone down on the table and slipped back into the bedroom. Kate was sitting up in bed with the blankets wrapped around her.

"Who were you talking to?"

"I gave Director Godfrey a call. He left me a message that there was something important he needed to discuss."

"Did he say why he's been trying to track you down all last night *and* again today?" Her tone was resigned and cynical.

"He didn't answer, so I left a message."

"He didn't answer his phone?" she asked, surprised.

"No. No response at all. It's not like him. At any rate, he'll get back to me soon enough. He's always working."

"I'm sure he will. I hope whatever it is can wait until Tuesday."

"That's what I'm hoping too. I was reluctant to call, but Godfrey sounded concerned. I didn't want to worry and have that distract me from enjoying our weekend."

"I don't want that either." She reached out to invite him back to bed.

"For the time being there's nothing I can do but wait until I hear from him."

"Why don't I help you get your mind off things?" she asked as she patted the bed and pursed her lips.

Michael grinned and asked, "Woman, what am I going to do with you?"

"I don't know, but I can't wait to find out." She rolled over and laid on her side, her left hand propping up her head. She patted the bed again with her right hand as she gazed at him, playfully pouting as she slowly caressed her hips and thighs. His eyes followed her every movement.

"How's this for a distraction?" she teased.

There she goes again. "Work what? Godfrey who?" He chuckled and jumped back into bed.

■ ■ ■

Meanwhile, in another part of Manhattan, in the backseat of an SUV bound for an undisclosed location, Godfrey lay unconscious. In his pants pocket, his phone began to vibrate. There was an incoming voice message from Michael.

25

After Tom left, Matt moved to the diagnostics computer and waited for the scan to complete its run through the NSA's secure Black Viper system. He hadn't experienced any more errors, at least not yet, and the scan was 73% complete.

Progress. Almost there. Just a little longer, and I should have what I need.

Matt returned to his hard drive and continued to examine it. After what seemed like only seconds, the diagnostics computer began to beep, and he looked over to see why. A message flashed on the screen that read:

> Scan Halted – 95% complete – Unknown
> Process Detected

A pop-up box appeared on his screen that read:

> Would You Like to Save the Current Scan
> Report?

Matt didn't know what was going on, but he needed to preserve whatever information the scan had generated to the thumb drive. He could analyze it later, so he clicked "Yes" and then "Continue."

An hourglass icon showed up in the center of the screen, indicating the computer was processing the action. Matt waited briefly, but the hourglass image didn't go away; it just kept spinning in the middle of his screen. He shook the mouse and clicked it a few times, hoping to get a response. *This is taking unusually long to save.* Seconds later he got an indication of why; another pop-up box appeared on his screen:

Administrator Profile Recognized

What's this all about? He tried to take control of the computer, but when he moved the mouse and hit the keys on the keyboard, he didn't get a response. Then another notice popped up:

Administrator Remote Access Approved

What the . . . Someone knows I'm on here, and they're accessing the system. But who? Someone within the agency was accessing his terminal in the SysOps room and could see that he was running a scan using the NSA's computers.

Matt watched the cursor move back and forth across the screen as it checked the different menus. That was very problematic. Who was on the other end? He was going to have to act fast.

Just then the phone on the wall rang. Matt jumped as the sudden ring startled him. He checked the caller I.D. and saw the call was coming from inside the building. *Could it be Tom?* He did say that he'd call to let him know what he found out. *How long had he been gone?*

Matt glanced at his watch. Tom had left nearly an hour ago. *Could he have found something?*

Matt was reluctant to answer the phone, especially given that someone was remotely accessing the computer again, though this time it was within the NSA's systems. He had to chance it because it could be Tom with vital information. Matt cautiously picked up the phone, but he didn't say anything.

"Matt, are you there?" It was Tom, out of breath. Matt paused to make sure it was Tom.

"Matt, it's me, Tom. Are you there? If you're there, answer." There was urgency in his voice.

Matt took a deep breath. "Yes, it's me. What's up? Why are you so out of breath?"

"Get out of there now!" There was no hesitation in Tom's voice.

"What are you talking about?"

"You've got to leave now. Security is on its way. They just left the boss's office with the FBI minutes ago. They'll be there any moment."

"Do they know I'm down here? Why are they sending security?" Matt asked in a frenzy.

"They don't know it's you down there, but they know someone is in that room and running tests. They got an anonymous tip that the breach was possibly an inside job. Security is locking down the building. Anyone trying to cover up or get more information on the network breach can only do it from one place in this building, and you're there."

A wave of fear swept through Matt's body. *What will they do if they find me here?* They would implicate him, even if it weren't his fault. *My cover could be blown.* He couldn't risk it.

"Tom, someone is remotely accessing the diagnostics computer and reviewing the scans I was running."

"I thought you removed that cellular network card from the computer."

"I did. There must be others, or they're accessing it another way. I don't have any control over it anymore. I don't know who it is. It looks like they're trying to turn off other power systems in the city. We've got to do something."

"That's a secure system. No one is supposed to be able to remote into it, not even tech support staff . . . Matt, don't go anywhere. I'm coming down right now. I'll help you explain it to the authorities. Stay put. Running will just make you look guilty."

"Okay," Matt reluctantly replied as Tom hung up. *Is Tom crazy? I'm not sticking around to find out what will happen to me. I'm getting out of here.*

Without hesitation, Matt darted for the door. But then he stopped and leapt back over to the table by the computer. He watched the screen as someone was still controlling the computer. Matt yanked the thumb drive from the computer without bothering to eject it correctly and unplugged the computer. He grabbed the loose computer parts and paperwork he needed before rushing from the room, leaving his disassembled computer behind.

Matt poked his head out the door to see if anyone was coming down the hall. He heard no footsteps approaching from either direction, only the buzzing and rattling of the ventilation system in the ceiling. Matt was unsure which direction security would be coming from. They could be coming from all sides for all he knew. Matt had a better chance if he could get to the stairwell around the corner unnoticed. He needed to go back to his office to get his things, but should he chance it? It was likely that they'd already been by his office and knew he'd been there. It'd be obvious that his computer was gone. Reluctant to go back to get his bag, it was a risk he'd have to take.

Matt sped around the corner and bounded up the stairs to the third floor. He cautiously opened the door and peered out of the stairwell to see if there was any sign of anyone, but it was clear. His office was just around the corner. If he could make it there and back without being seen, he'd be in the clear, at least until he needed to exit the building. If they were looking for him, then all the guard stations would be on alert. No one would be allowed to leave.

Matt stepped out of the stairwell when his phone began to vibrate, the caller I.D. showing it was John. "John, I can't talk. I'll call you later." John didn't even have the chance to respond before Matt ended the call and turned off the ringer. The last thing he needed was for his phone to ring and give him away. He peeked into the hallway again. It was still clear.

Matt hurried to his office and put his ear against the door to listen for any indication that someone might be inside. Not hearing anything, he knocked just in case, but there was no response. He knocked again and waited before quietly entering the keypad code to access his office.

Matt was speechless at what he saw. Someone had overturned his workstation. There was a brief flashback to his college apartment in Boston where the authorities had ransacked his place. There were papers and files all over the floor, and his cabinets and file drawers were open. His chair was lying sideways on the floor, and his entire cubicle was a mess.

Matt searched for his backpack, hoping the intruders hadn't taken it. He had been careful to tuck it into the narrow nook behind his file cabinets along the wall. By chance, they hadn't found it. Whoever had searched his office was in a hurry. Matt didn't know what they were looking for nor did he have the time to hang around to find out. He took one last look at his desk, grabbed his bag, put the items in it from his computer, and headed for the door. Glancing into the hall, he'd managed to sneak throughout the building without being seen, though he knew they'd be monitoring the security cameras. He had to hurry if he was going to get out.

Matt's best bet would be to exit through one of the loading dock entrances in the basement that opened to the back alley. Security wasn't as tight there on the weekends, and he'd have more places to hide among the shipping crates and boxes. Then he could slip out through the alley and make a run for it.

Matt sprinted to the stairs and leapt down toward the basement. Once there he only had to navigate about a hundred feet along a couple of zigzagging corridors before reaching the loading docks. Once at the bottom of the stairwell he slowly opened the door and was letting it close behind him when he heard voices around the corner. He froze, hoping they would stop to take the elevators and not come around the corner.

Matt tried to slow his breathing, but his heart was pounding too hard. It felt as if it were going to burst out of his chest. He listened intently to what the men were discussing.

"I can't believe we have to work overtime today because of this security breach. Nobody is getting any breaks until we track this guy down. He's probably not even in the building. If the incident happened last night, I seriously doubt anyone in their right mind would still be around, let alone come to the office. That would be crazy."

"You're telling me. I was supposed to be watching a movie tonight with my girl, and that doesn't look like it's going to happen. You know, this nonsense always happens to us. Everyone is out enjoying themselves, and we're stuck here trying to locate some chump. At least we know what he looks like. If he's still around, I doubt he's getting out of here. This whole building is locked down."

"Yeah, whoever this O'Shea guy is, he's got a slim chance of escaping."

"You never know. He seems like a smart guy. I bet he'd have an exit plan, especially if this was an inside job."

Exit plan. I wish.

"I suppose you're right. What do you think the feds will do to him?"

"I don't know. They don't even know for sure if he's involved."

Just then the elevator bell dinged, and Matt could hear the doors slide open. He waited momentarily for the doors to close. He heard the voices drift away, and then there was silence.

Matt looked at his watch. It was early evening. If it wasn't dark yet, it would be soon enough. The cover of night would help his chances of escaping.

Matt rapidly made his way down the corridor and around the corner, sneaking through the double swinging plastic doors and into the loading dock area. It was Saturday, and deliveries were made during the week, so there were no guards.

Matt checked the loading dock to see if the main bay door was open, but it wasn't. Climbing down from the platform, he hurried to the large, corrugated metal door. There was a standard size door built into the larger door. With any luck he'd be able to open it without having to activate the main bay door. The loud clanking metal would certainly draw attention. He grabbed the handle of the small door and pushed, but it didn't budge. He tried again, this time leaning against it with his shoulder. Still nothing. Any minute someone could walk in on him, and he'd be trapped. He couldn't think about that now. Leaning his back against the door, he sighed in frustration. The door rattled as he shook it.

Matt looked around for anything he could use to pry the door open. Finally, he saw a crowbar lying beside some wooden

crates on the other side of the loading dock. It might be all he
needed, and his time was running short. If security was doing
a full search of the building and was on the way to the SysOps
diagnostics room, it wouldn't be long before they found his half-
disassembled computer and came looking for him.

Matt ran over and climbed onto the platform. He was bend-
ing over to pick up the crowbar when the double doors opposite him swung open and a security guard walked through. Matt
swiftly ducked behind the crates. Fortunately, the containers
were large enough that he remained out of sight.

In his fumbling around though, Matt accidentally bumped
some cardboard boxes. The guard stopped to take a look and
headed in Matt's direction. Matt's heart pounded. Then he heard
a little squeak and some rustling noises as he looked to his side
to see what was perhaps his saving grace. As he tried to remain
calm, an enormous rat the size of a squirrel scurried onto the
platform behind him. Matt held his breath before gladly letting
out a soft sigh as it ran away. He hated rats.

"You've got to be kidding me. It's only a stupid rat," the
guard muttered. Matt heard the guard's footsteps as he departed
through the loading dock doors, the swinging doors flapping
against each other before they eventually came to a stop.

Matt waited before peeking out from behind the crates to
make sure the guard had gone. He grabbed the crowbar and ran
back to the door, putting it in by the door lock as he began to
pry. No luck. Next, he rammed the point of the crowbar into
the side of the lock and shoved, but the door barely budged.
Apprehensive as he pushed harder against the door, he stopped,
realizing that the sound of the shaking metal was echoing loudly
throughout the loading dock.

There had to be an easier way. He glanced at the guard booth
on the platform. Perhaps there was a set of door keys. His guess

was right. On a hook about waist high was a set of keys. The only trick would be to find which of the dozen or so keys opened the door. He snatched them and hurried back to the door. One by one he tried the keys, feeling a sense of hope as he only had a few more to go. Certainly, one of them had to work.

Just then the loading dock door swung open, and two security guards and an FBI agent stepped through. "You! Stop right there!" one yelled as Matt was turning the last key.

They ran toward him and commanded, "Put your hands in the air!" as they drew their guns.

Matt wasn't about to be caught. He had too much at stake, so he shoved the door, and it flew open. He stumbled forward through the threshold and into the cold evening air. Flinging the door shut behind him, he took off running, not bothering to look back.

Matt heard the men yell again as the metal door flew open with a bang. "Stop or we'll shoot!"

Matt wasn't going to stop, and as he sped down the alley, gunshots rang out as bullets ricocheted around him. Determined to get away, he ducked and dodged, keeping his head down as he sprinted as fast as he could. As he rounded the corner from the alley entrance, he saw a police car parked about thirty yards away on the side street. Having heard the gunshots, the officer had exited his vehicle and drawn his gun as he crouched behind the driver's door for cover.

Matt screamed and waved his hands in the air as he ran. "Don't shoot me! They tried to rob me, and now they're trying to kill me!" Matt motioned behind him as he sped down the middle of the road.

As Matt approached the squad car, the FBI agent chasing him passed the corner of the building and fired another round, the other guards fast on his heels. The police officer ahead of Matt wildly motioned for him to get out of the way. The officer immediately opened fire as Matt ducked and ran past him. It was getting dark, and amidst the flurry, the officer didn't notice in the distance the badge flailing around the neck of the plain-clothed FBI agent. The agent dove to the ground and scrambled behind a trash can on the sidewalk. The two guards who were quick on his heels also took cover when they heard the shots. A brief standoff ensued, which created enough of a diversion for Matt to escape down the street, around the corner, and out of harm's way.

Matt ran several blocks before stopping to catch his breath. As he bent over gasping for air, he heard police sirens and saw a half dozen D.C. police cars and black SUVs speeding down the street in the direction of his building.

Matt gathered himself, knowing that he had to act fast. He needed to get to his apartment but wondered if the authorities were already there. Matt had to get cash, and plenty of it. Knowing what he did about surveillance, he knew that as soon as he used his credit card, the authorities would pinpoint his location.

But the authorities were only now discovering that he was on the run, so perhaps he had a head start, if only for a short time. If he made it to an ATM soon, he could at least get enough cash to last him until he could get out of town and figure things out. He searched for an ATM but didn't see one. Chinatown was a short distance away, and he knew there would be plenty of ATMs there. Besides, it was Saturday night, and the streets would be crowded with hockey fans because the Capitals were playing. He'd also have a better chance of hiding among the crowds if the police were looking for him.

As he took off at a brisk pace, he called John. The phone rang a couple of times before John picked up.

"Matt, it's you. What the hell is going on? Tom called me from the office. What's all this I hear about a security breach and the network being compromised? It sounds like all hell is breaking loose. The boss called all of us into the office to work."

"First, I'll tell you that I'm innocent. There was a security breach last night around midnight. When I got into the office today I found out about it. I was trying to figure out the source and the extent of the damage to our networks. God forbid our systems would go down, and the city's power would go out. I was in the SysOps diagnostics room running scans when all of this madness started. I can't talk long. I need to get out of town to a safe place. What did Tom tell you?"

"Tom mentioned the security breach and that you had been trying to diagnose the issue," John said. "And he said that when he went to talk to the boss, the FBI was already there waiting to search the building. He stalled them as long as he could, but you were gone by the time the authorities arrived. Where are you now?"

"I can't tell you, but I'm going to need your help. I've got to get some cash, and I'm going to need you to go to my apartment and pick up some things for me. Do you still have your spare apartment key?"

"Let me check." John fumbled with his key chain. "Yeah, it's right here."

"Great. I need you to go over there right now. Pack some clothes and grab some money for me. In the nightstand to the right of my bed there's a small box in the top drawer. It used to be for checks. I have at least five hundred dollars cash in there, maybe more. When you get to my apartment, call me. When we talk next, I'll set up a time and place for us to meet. What time do you have now?"

"It's just before five thirty."

"Great. Call me when you get there."

"Are you all right?"

"I'll be okay. Right now I'm just trying to calm down after having been shot at."

"What?" John gasped. "They shot at you?"

"Yes, as I was running from the building the guards opened fire."

"Why would they shoot at you?"

"I don't know, but I'll give you the details later."

"But what about . . . ?" Matt ended the call before John could finish his question.

John had been lying on his sofa watching TV in his living room when Matt had called. The conversation had gotten him on his feet, so it didn't take him long after Matt hung up before he was out the door. John only lived a short distance from Matt, so he'd be at the apartment in no time.

John ran down the hall to the elevator. As he waited, thoughts filled his mind, making him uneasy. *If Matt was a fugitive, would they be sending people to his place to find him? Would the police or FBI be there already? What will I be walking into when I get there?*

Meanwhile, Matt walked speedily through the streets looking for an ATM. Finally, he found one. Pausing a moment, he decided whether he should get the cash. He knew it wouldn't take the authorities long to find his location, and he hoped John would arrive at his place before the FBI showed up. He needed cash either way; it was a risk he had to take.

26

In their hotel room, Michael and Kate had worked up an appetite. They had dressed for an evening out, Michael sporting one of his favorite sleek, charcoal gray suits but no tie. After all, he was on vacation and was in a casual mood. His black dress shoes were newly shined as he stood in front of the living room mirror checking himself out. As he did, he saw Kate leave the bedroom. She looked spectacular in a three-quarter length silky black spaghetti-strap dress with a v-shaped front, low-cut back, dark pantyhose leggings, and black, shiny high heels. She wore her brilliant diamond bracelet and necklace that he'd bought her for her birthday. Her make-up was freshly done, and her long, soft brown hair was styled and curled. It playfully bounced as she strutted like a runway model out of the bedroom. Michael took a moment to admire her. Her custom-tailored dress fit her exquisitely, every curve and line of her body accentuated as she moved, the silky dress sliding back and forth over her hips. She eased up behind him and kissed his cheek. His heart began to speed up again as the smell of her sweet perfume tantalized his nostrils.

Michael turned and kissed her, running his hands up and down her hips, eagerly lifting up her dress. "Mmm . . . you look marvelous," he said as he tried to slide her skirt higher.

Kate gently slapped his hands away. "Thank you. But you can't have dessert until after dinner." She puckered her lips seductively before turning away and gliding toward the closet to grab her coat.

Michael had fallen in love with her many years earlier, but it was moments like this that reminded him how phenomenal a woman she was. He was a lucky man, and despite all their hard times, she was always loving and supportive. He had never known another woman like her.

They had met in a café in New York City years earlier when he had been up from D.C. visiting friends from college. His best friend Paul had asked him up for the weekend to hang out with Rebecca, the girl Paul had dated in college and whom he had started dating long distance again. Paul wanted Michael's opinion because he was starting to think she might be "the one." Michael hadn't seen Rebecca in years. Michael and Paul had played football together at the Naval Academy while Rebecca had attended the University of Maryland in Annapolis. Paul later reconnected with Rebecca when she moved to New York for work. Paul was living in Maryland and stationed in Annapolis at the time, so they saw each other regularly.

Michael met Kate for the first time on a cold Saturday evening in March when he was hanging out with his friends in New York City. Michael and his two friends had wanted to go to one of the trendy steakhouses in Midtown. When Paul and Rebecca arrived at the restaurant to meet up with Michael, they discovered it was going to be over a two-hour wait, so they all decided to go for a walk around the neighborhood. The three of them came across a quaint café just down the street. It was chilly, so they decided to go inside and warm up with a hot drink while they waited.

At the time, Michael had a sporty, clean look with his military haircut. He was wearing a long black wool coat with his collar turned up and a scarf around his neck. Michael walked with a particularly confident yet quiet aura. As he strolled about the café viewing the gallery of photos on the wall, he noticed Kate sitting alone. She was wearing a dark blue sports fleece jacket and fitted jeans. Kate was sitting at a counter overlooking the downstairs part of the café. Although she was alone, she wore a broad smile. Despite being dressed in plain casual clothes, there was an elegant presence and radiance about her that Michael couldn't quite put his finger on, but it captured his attention.

As he waited in line, he noticed her smiling warmly at him. He began to get nervous, and his stomach churned. He looked around at the artwork on the walls, acting as though he hadn't noticed her. But every time he looked up, she was staring directly at him. *Who is this woman?* Her eyes sparkled, and she seemed so alive and happy.

After getting his hot chocolate, he admired more of the artwork and photos. His friends had grabbed a table toward the back, but Michael decided to give Paul and Rebecca some time alone. Eventually, he worked up the courage to approach Kate. As he did, his heart throbbed, and his palms started to sweat. Michael had never been so nervous, particularly with a woman. As a college athlete he'd never had a problem with the ladies. They usually approached him. He didn't know what it was about her, but he was sheepish and at a loss for words. His nerves were driving him crazy, and he felt like a million butterflies in his stomach were all trying to get out.

Michael turned to say something to Kate, but he wimped out. He quickly looked away so as not to draw her attention. Then he heard a pleasant, friendly voice.

"You look lost," she said, chuckling slightly under her breath. Michael wasn't certain she was talking to him, so he turned around. Sure enough, she was staring right at him.

"Excuse me?" he asked, surprised. "Did you say something to me?"

"You heard me. You look lost."

"How do you figure?" he replied, challenging her.

"Well, I've been watching you. You keep walking in circles."

"I was looking for you," he grinned flirtatiously. He often used humor in uncomfortable situations.

"Very cute. I bet you say that to all the ladies." She winked at him, amused by his wit.

"Nah, just those I find intriguing," he said as he moved his eyebrows up and down. "What about you?"

"What about me?" she asked, shrugging her shoulders.

"What's your story?"

"I'm waiting for my friends. They took their daughter next door to the toy shop to keep her busy while we wait for our dinner reservation."

"Where are you going for dinner?"

"Why do you want to know? Are you going to follow me there?" She was joking, but he couldn't tell from her stern expression.

"Relax. I'm just messing with you." She grabbed his forearm and shook it gently.

"Would you like to join me? Your friends look preoccupied." She subtly motioned toward Paul and Rebecca who were sitting at a small table in the back of the café holding hands across their table and gazing deeply into each other's eyes.

Michael peeked back at his friends and then at Kate. "I'd love to," he said, sitting down on the round stool next to her at the counter.

They talked and laughed until Kate's friends returned from next door. She graciously introduced Michael to them. They exchanged friendly banter before her friends signaled that they needed to go. As they said their goodbyes, Michael got Kate's number before he rejoined his friends. Kate waved to him through the window as she passed by on the sidewalk. He waved back. He wasn't going to let her get away.

Michael's best friend pushed him on the shoulder, nearly knocking him over a stool. "Looks like someone is in love." Michael didn't know Paul and Rebecca had been watching him from a distance.

"Whatever," he said, trying to play it cool, but he couldn't fake it.

"I've known you for years. You can't hide things from me. I'm happy for you. Just don't screw it up. She could be good for you." Paul patted Michael on the shoulder.

Michael called Kate later that night to invite her to join him and his friends for drinks, but she already had plans, so they settled for breakfast on Sunday instead. They had an enjoyable time talking and laughing all morning. He felt as though he'd known her forever. Their conversations and interactions flowed effortlessly. Later that day, he flew back to D.C.

Kate and Michael talked every day the following week, and she invited him to come up the next weekend. Michael was surprised things were happening so quickly, and he wasn't sure how to respond to her invitation. Against his usual conservative approach to life in general and women in particular, he followed his gut and took a chance. His friends and family were astonished because it was so out of character for him.

After a few months, Michael had fallen head over heels in love. Hardly a week went by that he and Kate didn't see each other. He would take the train or bus up from D.C., or she would come down from New York. They felt as though they were soul mates. Paul even told Michael later that, after that first meeting, he thought Kate could be the one for him. Michael didn't believe it at the time, but as he got to know Kate, he began to think so too.

The long distance relationship and their careers were challenging, but Kate and Michael made it work. They dated for a year before they became engaged. Six months later they were married, Kate moved to D.C., and the rest was history.

"Michael," Kate quietly said as he stared off in a daze, reminiscing about how they had met.

"Michael?" she whispered again in his ear as she kissed him softly on the cheek.

With a slight twitch, he snapped out of it and turned to gaze into her beautiful eyes.

"What were you thinking about? You look happy. You have that smile I fell in love with the night we met."

"I was thinking about that first meeting here in New York too," he said lovingly.

"That was a magical evening," she said. "I felt as though we'd known each other forever."

"It did seem that way. I'd never met anyone like you before. We just connected so effortlessly. I don't know how to describe it."

"It was special." She kissed him on the cheek. "But before we reminisce all night, I'm getting hungry. We can talk more over dinner."

Michael could tell by her tone that she was getting edgy. He knew her well enough to know that she still could be cranky. It was time to get going.

She saw his quirky smirk and nudged him in the side. "What were you thinking?"

"I was thinking about how I need to feed you to keep you happy. Happy wife, happy life."

She poked him playfully.

"Hey now, I was only kidding, but you know how you can get when you're hungry."

"I know. I can be such a bother, but you love me all the same." Kate glanced up at him with her pouty lips and her puppy dog eyes before bursting into laughter.

Michael took her arm in his as they strolled out of the room and down the hall toward the elevators.

27

Awakening to the smell of sweet cigar smoke, Director Godfrey found himself blindfolded with his hands and legs bound to a chair. He wiggled to test the ropes, but they barely budged.

Godfrey wasn't gagged, so he called out, "Hello? Hello? Is anybody there?" He couldn't tell where he was or how long he'd been unconscious. His head hurt from whatever drug he'd ingested. He tried again to shake himself free from the chair, but with no luck. Again, he called out hoping to get a response, this time a bit louder: "Hello?"

Godfrey heard a door open behind him and someone entered the room. The door closed, and he heard footsteps approaching as he sat in anticipation, not knowing what they would do to him.

Godfrey spoke again. "Who's there?" he asked as he squirmed in his chair. Then he heard what sounded like a familiar voice.

"Relax, Director Godfrey. You have nothing to fear. We don't intend to harm you. That is, of course, unless you don't cooperate."

"What do you mean? You kidnapped and blindfolded me. What do you want with me? Why am I here? Why is my team under surveillance?" The only initial response was silence, except for heavy breathing just behind him.

"Who are you and what do you want?" Godfrey asked again.

"All in sufficient time, director. You will have all of your questions answered, I promise you," the voice said calmly. Godfrey struggled to recognize the deep, Russian-accented voice. It sounded familiar from a distant past. *But from where and when?* Then it hit him. The Russian stranger must have noticed the change in Godfrey's expression.

"I see you may finally recognize me."

"Yes," Godfrey said, "I believe so."

28

Matt stood at an ATM near the Chinatown metro stop waiting for his cash. He made sure not to let the camera capture his face. Even though it was dark, Matt put on sunglasses and covered his head with a baseball cap. He put on his gloves before inserting his card and keying in his PIN in the event the authorities might try to collect his fingerprints from the machine. He knew that once he inserted his card and typed in his PIN number, the clock would start ticking. If the FBI were searching for him, it wouldn't take long to find him.

Matt's mind filled with myriad thoughts. *Where can I go? Who can I talk to? Who can I trust?* He hoped his NSA colleagues were aware of what was going on and would come to his rescue.

Matt snatched his money from the ATM and walked calmly yet briskly down the street, not wanting to draw any attention by running.

Meanwhile, at FBI headquarters nearby, the Strategic Information and Operations Center (SIOC) was bustling. The center operated around the clock to monitor incidents and serve as an information clearinghouse to provide real-time updates on investigations and tactical operations. Because they'd received word about the network security breach at Lucigen, they'd been carefully monitoring the situation.

Director Donovan, head of the Counterterrorism and Cyber Defense Division, was awaiting an update from his tactical team about Matt O'Shea. Donovan was a clean-cut African American man in his early fifties. A former marine and Iraq war veteran, he prided himself on keeping fit. Though not a towering figure at just under six feet, his stocky, muscular presence and stature commanded authority. With a hardworking, no-nonsense personality, he was known across the Bureau as the go-to man to get things done. Having spent his fair share of time digging trenches and cleaning latrines while in the military, no job was beneath him, and he usually took on the less desirable tasks with vigor. He'd earned quite the reputation over the years and was well respected despite his direct and abrasive attitude. He never tolerated excuses and pushed his agents and staff to be the best.

"Sir, we have activity at an ATM near Chinatown," reported one of the dozen agents working in the event monitoring room.

"Where'd you say that was again, Hawkins?" the director asked.

Hawkins was in his mid-thirties, about five foot eight and skinny with brown hair, blue eyes, and a faded haircut on the sides that was textured on top. His tan skin was a blend from his European immigrant grandparents. He wore tan slacks and a black polo shirt. Because he was still new to the Bureau, he spent most of his time at a desk learning the ropes and working with the analysts.

"It was near Chinatown," Hawkins replied in his thick Boston accent.

"Are you sure it was O'Shea?"

"I can't be certain, but it was his credit card."

"Can we get a visual from the ATM's camera?"

"We sure can, just give me one minute." Hawkins tapped away at the keyboard as he accessed the bank's security system to view the ATM footage.

"Sir, we have it ready," he said as he pulled it up. The video footage showed a man in a ball cap and sunglasses walking up and taking out money.

"Let me see." Donovan stood behind Hawkins as he replayed the footage. "Put it up on the main screen." Hawkins complied quickly.

"Can you pull any footage from the cameras on the surrounding buildings before or after he was at the ATM? Perhaps he put the hat on just before he got there. Maybe we can get a better look at his face. From that footage it could be anyone." Donovan glared intently at the large screen on the front wall.

"I'm checking the other surveillance cameras now . . . There's nothing, sir. That's all we have."

"That's not sufficient," Donovan blurted out. "I need to know if that was him, and I need to know now. I need agents on the site immediately. Do we have any nearby?"

"Let me check." He searched quickly on his computer. "Today is your lucky day."

"Cut the sarcasm, Hawkins. Who's out there, and where are they?" Donovan snapped.

"Fortunately, that ATM is not that far from our building."

"I don't need your commentary; just tell me who our nearest agents are!" Donovan insisted.

"Yes, sir," he said as he sank slightly in his chair and searched the system.

"Hawkins, do you have those names for me yet?"

"Yes, sir. Burton and Perez are only a few blocks away. I believe they are both still at Lucigen investigating the security breach."

"Get them on the phone."

"Yes, sir, right away." There was a brief moment of silence before he added, "Sir, I've got them."

"Both of them?"

"Yes." Hawkins put the phone on speaker.

"Attention, Agents Burton and Perez, this is Director Donovan. We are in a code red status and tracking a target in your vicinity. We believe the target is involved in the network security breach at Lucigen. This event is a local security risk. The target was last spotted at an ATM on 7th Street near the Chinatown metro stop less than five minutes ago. I need you there immediately. We're texting you an image of him now. The suspect goes by the name Matt O'Shea. He is a white male, mid-twenties, approximately six feet tall, a little heftier than average build. He has about shoulder length brown hair and hazel eyes. He was last seen wearing a dark ball cap, sunglasses, and a mid-length black jacket. We don't know if the suspect is armed or not, but we need him alive. I repeat: we need him alive for questioning."

"Roger that, sir," the agents said almost in unison. "We're leaving Lucigen now."

Donovan turned to the vast team of analysts who were working diligently at their computer terminals. "What do we know about this Matt O'Shea character? I want to know where he lives, where he hangs out, who his friends are, where his relatives live. I want his phone lines tapped. If he's on the run, he's going to contact his friends and family for help, if he hasn't already. We need to cut off his support. I want this guy caught immediately; do I make myself clear?" Donovan looked around. The staff looked up sheepishly and nodded quietly in agreement. "Great. We'll regroup in thirty minutes for a status check." There was silence as Donovan spoke. Once he finished, the facility broke into commotion with everyone typing away at their keyboards and making phone calls to coordinate surveillance efforts with the FBI field teams and D.C. authorities.

Matt was standing just down the street and around the corner from the ATM. He was about to take off running when two black, unmarked squad cars came screeching around the corner. Matt wanted to see where they'd stop, so he glanced around the nearby wall as they sped by him. They came to a screeching halt in front of the bank where he'd just taken money from the ATM. The doors flew open and armed men in FBI jackets jumped out.

Matt looked at his watch. *Holy— they didn't waste any time.* He'd only withdrawn the money minutes ago. It wouldn't be long before the D.C. police and FBI would be all over the place. They certainly would find where he lived if they hadn't already. *John! I've got to get ahold of him and see if he's made it to the apartment.*

Matt pulled out his phone and called John, but then he realized the problem. *They're probably tracing this call right now, but I have to take the chance.*

The phone rang. John picked up.

"John, is that you?" Matt asked. There was heavy panting on the other end.

"Yes, it's me," John replied, trying to catch his breath.

"Where are you? Are you at my apartment yet?" Matt asked impatiently.

"Yeah, I'm just finishing up here." Matt had interrupted him as he was in the middle of stuffing a bag full of clothes.

"Did you find the money?"

"Yes. Do you need anything else while I'm here?"

"Grab a change of clothes, and make it quick. The FBI is probably on the way there if they're not downstairs already."

"What?" John responded in shock. "Here? Already? How'd they find where you live so fast?"

"I don't have time to talk. Just grab what you can and get out of there."

"You don't have to tell me twice."

"And John, they've probably tapped our phones and will be tracking us. Next time we meet, it'll have to be in person, or you'll need to call me from a burner or a pay phone."

"Won't they be able to trace those too?"

"Possibly, but it won't be as easy."

"Where are you now? I can come to you since they're not looking for me—at least not yet," John said apprehensively. He knew that by helping Matt, he would become a target as well.

"Meet me in Georgetown. It's Saturday night, and there will be a lot of people out. Meet me at the corner of M Street and Jefferson. I believe there's a bookstore on the corner. Can you be there in less than thirty minutes?"

"Yes."

"If you're not there by six thirty, give me a call. If I can, I'll call you about six fifteen."

"Got it."

"Now get out of there. The authorities will be there any instant."

John hurried to pack the rest of the clothes and items Matt requested. He'd just closed the door and was halfway down the hall when he heard the stomping of footsteps hustling down at the other end of the hallway near the elevators.

John had decided to take the far back staircase because it would bring him out onto a side street alongside the building.

John ducked swiftly into the stairwell and slightly opened the door to peek down the hallway. *Geez . . . Matt was right.*

At the end of the hall a SWAT team was lining up outside Matt's apartment. They were all dressed in black protective gear and helmets, and they had their weapons drawn. Two of them approached the door with a battering ram. They didn't even knock before they smashed in the door.

You've got to be kidding me. John wasted no time getting out of there. Closing the stairwell door, he bounded down the stairs until he reached the first-floor exit. The pounding of his shoes echoed throughout the staircase. He opened the large metal door and stepped out onto the street, the crisp, fresh fall evening air filling his nose.

John looked around to see if anyone had seen him exit the building, but other than a young couple walking their German Shepherd, he didn't see anyone. He walked around the building and down the street toward his car. Unfortunately, the streets were blocked off with cop cars, so he wasn't going to be able to drive. His only option was to take the metro or a cab. Either way, he needed to get to Georgetown, and he didn't have much time.

As he neared Union Station he decided it was better to take a cab. If he and Matt were under surveillance, the FBI would be watching the public transportation routes, especially if he was trying to make it out of town.

John stepped into the street and flagged down a taxi.

"Where to?" the cab driver asked.

"Georgetown, the corner of M Street and Jefferson."

"Sure thing."

John sat in the taxi in silence. His mind drifted off as he stared out the side rear window. John thought about Matt and what would happen to him if and when he was caught. He didn't know what all was going on, but he knew Matt needed his help.

Then the cab driver broke the silence. "Where are you off to tonight? For a Saturday night, it doesn't look like you're dressed to go out and pick up the ladies." The driver was a middle-aged man in his late forties with dark brown skin and a short, well-groomed beard. His accent was foreign, but John couldn't quite put his finger on it. John guessed he was probably Southeast Asian or Middle Eastern.

The driver asked again, "Where are you off to tonight?"

John wasn't thinking clearly, "Oh, I'm going to the intersection of M Street and Jefferson."

"Oh, I know. I mean, are you going out tonight? You know, the bars, clubs, looking for ladies, all of that."

John shook his head and replied, "Not tonight. I'm just meeting a friend."

"That's good. You all going out to eat? Georgetown has lots of places."

John was not in the mood for small talk. The barrage of questions was making him paranoid. Perhaps they were already following him, but he shook the thought from his head.

"I know some nice places if you'd like me to recommend one," the driver said in a friendly tone. "Do you like Italian food? There are some great places on M Street. I only wish I could remember their names. I think one of them had a green or black or red awning over the front door, something like that," he said, scratching his head in thought.

John smiled and nodded. The cabby was describing any number of restaurants in Georgetown. "Yes, I like Italian."

"Me too," the driver responded in a cheery voice. "What's your favorite dish? I like lasagna, but sometimes I'm in a spaghetti kind of mood, ya know?"

"Oh, for sure. I get like that sometimes." John was annoyed, but he was trying to be polite. Never in his life had he met a cab driver that was so talkative. Usually they minded their own damn business. John wished his driver would just shut up and drive, but he couldn't say that out loud.

"Hey, what's going on up there?" John pointed ahead of them over the front seat. "What's with the traffic lights?" All of the traffic lights and streetlights were out in front of them. For as far as he could see, there was a sea of red brake lights on Pennsylvania Avenue, and horns were honking.

"I don't know. The traffic looks stopped ahead. The lights are out for some reason."

There was utter confusion and gridlock. John saw all the people lined up and down the sidewalk. Others stood outside of their cars in the middle of the road trying to figure out what was happening. Horns blared, and people rolled down their windows to yell at the cars in front of them.

"I'll just get out and walk from here. How much?"

"That'll be $9.85."

John reached into his wallet and pulled out some bills to pay him. "Keep the change. Good luck getting out of this mess."

"Thanks."

John climbed out of the cab and looked at his watch. It was almost 6:30. John had a half mile or so to walk before he reached Jefferson Street. Hurrying, he dodged the swarm of pedestrians on the sidewalk.

John arrived at the corner where Matt told him to meet. John looked across the street to see if he could spot Matt, but he couldn't see him with all of the people passing back and forth and the cars and trucks stopped on M Street. Traffic still wasn't moving, so John crossed the road. As he walked, he checked out the storefronts, but there was still no sign of Matt.

John stepped onto the curb and waited anxiously. There was a bookstore on the corner a short distance away. As John approached the entrance, he noticed a young man reading a book inside the bookstore near the front window display. The man wore a black or navy blue ball cap and peered subtly up at John. John pulled out his phone and pretended to be talking to someone as he walked by the front of the store, stealing another look at the man inside. John couldn't see his face, but as the man turned slightly to the side to put a book back on the shelf, John recognized the red backpack with the comic patches. *It must be Matt.* John stepped into the bookstore and walked over near where the young man was standing. John stopped about five feet away, acting as though he was searching for a book when he whispered, "Matt, is that you?"

Initially, there was no response. The young man seemed not to hear him or was ignoring him, so John tried again, this time slightly louder. He cleared his throat, drawing attention from the other shoppers.

"Matt, is that you? It's me, John."

The young man peeked up from under his ball cap with a subtle smirk. Matt sidestepped to get closer, nearly shoulder to shoulder with John, but kept perusing the bookshelves. Matt then squatted down and grabbed a book off one of the lower shelves. John took that as a cue and knelt on one knee.

"Matt, is that you?"

"Yes, it's me."

John looked at his watch. It was just after 6:30.

Matt cocked his head slightly toward John and said, "You're right on time. Did you get everything?"

"Yes." John motioned to the backpack he was carrying.

"Thanks. I appreciate that."

"No problem. That's what friends are for, right?"

"Indeed. Did you have any problems? Had the authorities shown up yet?" Matt asked, hesitant to know the answer.

There was a long pause before John responded. "Nope, nothing to worry about." His tone was off, and he couldn't manage to look Matt in the eyes.

Matt turned his head slightly more toward John. "Are you sure there's nothing you want to tell me?" Matt insisted. "John, what is it?"

"The cops or the FBI came to your place as I was leaving. They were arriving at your front door as I was exiting down the stairwell."

"Did anyone see you leaving?"

"I don't think so. I made sure to double check."

"So what happened?"

John paused before he replied. "I don't know how to put this."

"What?" Matt grabbed John's upper arm.

"Umm . . . They knocked down your door." John pulled his arm away from Matt.

"What!" Matt blurted out, loud enough that the other shoppers looked over to see what was going on. When they saw it was nothing, they returned to their own business.

"They did what?" Matt asked in a calmer voice after the words registered, rubbing his hand across his face in disbelief.

"Yep, they knocked down your door." John hated to be the bearer of bad news.

"Did they even bother knocking first?" Matt asked, disturbed.

John didn't want to belabor the point, but he felt he needed to say more. "There was a SWAT team with a battering ram. I heard the door smash and the men yelling as I ran down the stairwell."

Matt's body slouched down. *How'd this all get started? This situation was a total mess.* Apparently, his colleagues at the NSA hadn't intervened yet.

John sensed his dismay and tried to cheer him up. "Hey, don't worry. We'll figure this out."

"I hope so."

"We will, but we're not going to resolve anything if we stay here. We need to get out of town soon. The authorities aren't wasting any time trying to find you. They're right on your heels, and it won't be long before they find us."

Matt was reluctant to admit it, but they couldn't stick around. They needed to keep moving until they were some place safe and had time to work things out. Right now, they couldn't afford to be caught, and he couldn't rely on his NSA colleagues to rescue him. He had to handle things on his own as best he could.

"Where do we go from here?" John asked.

"I'm not sure, but we can't wait here. If the FBI already busted into my place, they've probably identified all of my immediate friends and family and are either following them or have their phones tapped to see if I'll contact them."

"What do we do then? Who do we contact?" John asked.

"Let's assume they're not on to you yet."

John interrupted him. "Let's not assume that. I'm probably one of the last people you've called recently, yes? If they're checking your phone records, they would know we've had contact after you fled the building, so they're for sure on to me."

"You're right."

"How are we doing on cash?" John asked.

"I withdrew three hundred dollars from the ATM, and you grabbed the cash from my place. It seems like a good amount to last until next week. Would you take money out of your account?"

"I suppose so." John's voice trailed off.

"What's wrong?"

"The authorities are looking for us, but they don't have us pinned down here. I'm afraid that if I pull out money they'll locate us and make it harder for us to get out of town."

"I know, but if we're going to get money out of your account, now's the time. Otherwise, the authorities would have had time to track down and monitor any of my friends, not that I have many. I have no family or next of kin," Matt stated begrudgingly. "Listen, we've got to do it. We don't know how long we'll be on the run, and this might be our only chance."

"I suppose you're right, but we'd better have an escape plan."

"We have the night on our side. We'll have more places to hide in the dark. Get the money, and then we'll catch a cab into Rosslyn. We'll work out our next move once we get out of the District."

"I don't think we'll be taking a cab anywhere. Remember the traffic jam? All of the stoplights are out, and everything's at a standstill. Things were fine on the other side of town though. I didn't hit issues until I got about a half mile from here."

Matt thought back to some of the discussions he'd had with his bosses at the NSA before he went undercover. They warned of a possible cyberattack on D.C. that could take out the city's power and industrial control systems. That was part of the reason he was working at Lucigen. They warned it could happen all across the country. Matt didn't believe it could be starting already, but given the network breach at his work, he wasn't ruling it out. Besides, the U.S. defenses were too good—unless it was an inside job. The fact that Matt discovered a cellular network card in his computer didn't give him much confidence. If Lucigen had been breached, who knew the extent to which power and other systems across the city and country had been compromised? It was possible that others were being hacked at that very moment as part of a larger attack. John interrupted Matt's thoughts.

"Are you going to wait here or by the bank? I think we should stick together."

"Fair enough. I'll wait near the bank while you use the ATM."

"Okay."

"Let's go. We'll make this quick."

As Matt and John were exiting the bookstore, something caught Matt's eye. He stopped momentarily to look at an out-of-place, middle-aged gentleman reading a book. The man didn't give the impression that he was shopping for books judging by the fact that he was constantly looking up from his book. The man must have sensed Matt staring and glanced up at him. His expressionless face then morphed into a smirk. It was an awkward look, the uncomfortable kind. The man then returned to his book.

Matt was feeling uneasy about the suspicious man when John tugged at his sleeve. "Come on. We've got to go. What's the holdup?"

"Don't turn now, but there's a man to my right who seems out of place. Something about him doesn't seem right. I'm just not sure what."

John started to turn and look, but Matt grabbed his arm to stop him. "Don't look, I said. Not yet . . . Okay, now."

John peeked to the right. The man was reading a book and then lifted his head. He was wearing a long black overcoat with a beige scarf and black beanie. John took a closer look and noticed a small transparent spiral cord coming from under his hat. It ran from behind his ear along his neck and into his scarf.

John peered closer, thinking that perhaps the man was just listening to a headset or phone. It wasn't until the man turned to walk down the aisle away from them that he noticed there was only one cord. *An earpiece? Secret Service? FBI? It can't be. Could they have found us already?* John's heart started to pound.

Matt sensed John's tension and lightly tapped him on the forearm as he asked, "What's up?"

"That man you pointed out . . . he has a cord running out from his ear."

"And what's so odd about that? Everybody's wearing headsets and earpieces these days with all of their phones and iPods."

John whispered, "That's what I thought. It wasn't until he turned to walk away that I saw there was only one clear spiral cord."

"Are you thinking he's a special agent? It could have been a cord to his phone. I find it hard to believe that they located us here so fast."

"I don't know."

"This is D.C., and we're in Georgetown. Perhaps there is some dignitary or diplomat who's shopping here, and we're just being paranoid."

"Maybe, but the way he looked at me made me very uneasy."

"So do we try the bank or not?" Matt asked.

"I'm not sure. The police could be waiting for us there."

"Well, we can't just stand around talking. We need to get going." Matt knew they needed to move swiftly. "Listen, John, let's forget the money. We need to get out of town," Matt said, looking out the front door as droves of people walked by. He turned toward the back of the store.

"I bet there's a back alley entrance." Matt motioned with his head to the rear of the bookstore.

"Wouldn't they be watching both doors?"

"I suppose you're right."

"I say we take our chances out front with all of the people," John said. "We can lose them in the crowds."

"All right, let's go." Matt eyed the store to see if the man was still there. *He couldn't have left; we're standing by the front door.* At last Matt spotted him by the register, but Matt couldn't tell if he was buying anything.

John tapped Matt again and said, "Come on; we've got to go now."

They walked hastily out the door, around the corner, and down the hill toward the Georgetown waterfront. As they exited, the man watched them leave. Hurriedly, he put down his book and followed them.

29

In the control room of the Hoover Dam, two engineers were checking the control panels that managed the dam and power plant operational systems. There was a wall of screens with a complete structure diagram that provided the real-time operating status of the entire hydraulic systems and power stations. The engineers were sitting at their computer terminals going through one of their routine afternoon peak-hour checks when one of them noticed a red flashing alert sensor light that had been triggered. The system hadn't been bench tested in over two years, and it had never been checked online in the event of a full power outage at the dam. The dam had been completed in 1936, and many of the original electrical components and mechanical parts hadn't been replaced or upgraded in over twenty years.

"Hey, Russ, do you see that alert on the screen for the number four generator?"

"I sure do, Don."

"How does the power load look coming out of that generator to the transformers and transmission lines?" Don asked as he checked a number of the other power system components.

"It's running a little high and heavy, so we'll need to adjust the control gate and trim the valves to slow the water intake and reduce the load. We don't want to blow a generator or transformer. Make sure you gradually lower the pressure in that penstock pipe; we can't afford to have those turbines buckle too much as we're reducing the load. We had that happen last year, and it was a nightmare to fix."

"I agree. I'm going to reduce the load on that generator right now." Don entered a series of commands into his computer and waited.

"Russ, it doesn't look like I'm able to reduce the load through my terminal; my computer isn't responding to the commands. Can you try on yours?"

"Sure." Russ pulled up the schematics and entered a series of commands to reduce the load across the system. He paused for a moment but noticed that the system wasn't responding to him either.

"Russ, any luck?" Don rolled his chair over to look at Russ' computer station.

"Nope." Russ scratched his head.

"I'm going to try something else." Don pulled up another set of diagnostic screens and entered some commands. "If this doesn't work we may have to reduce the load on that generator manually. Get one of the engine room technicians on the radio, would you?"

"Will do." Russ grabbed the walkie-talkie off the desk. "Powerhouse, this is Russ in the control room, copy?"

"Copy that control room; this is Eddie. Go ahead."

"We're getting an alert on the number four generator. What are you showing on your end?"

"Give me a minute and let me check." Eddie, the lead tech, moved to the operator's control panel that was on a platform overlooking the entire powerhouse.

"Control, everything looks fine on my end; I don't see any alerts."

Don grabbed the radio from Russ. "Eddie, this is Don. Can you please check again? We just reduced the load by fifteen percent; what's it showing on your end?"

"Don, everything is stable on my end."

Don and Russ looked at the control panel on the wall in front of them. The alert light had just gone off. "This is Russ again. The issue seems to be resolved. Thanks, Eddie."

"Sure thing. Let me know if anything else comes up."

"Will do." Russ set the radio down on the desk.

Don wheeled his chair back over to his computer terminal and looked at Russ. "Good work. I'm glad we got this resolved. We're lucky that's been the only issue all day."

Russ had turned his attention back to the control panel when he noticed the same alert light was flashing again. "I'm not so sure about that; look." He pointed up at the wall. Seconds later the warning alert lights for five other generators were blinking red. "Are you seeing what I'm seeing?"

Don jumped up and sped over to Russ. "Yes, I am. How did that happen so fast? We need to reduce the load on those five generators, or we're going to be in serious trouble."

Don snatched the walkie-talkie again. "Powerhouse, this is control; do you copy?" There was no response. "I repeat; powerhouse, this is control, do you copy?" Don tried a third time. Finally, he got a reply.

"This is the powerhouse, Eddie speaking, copy." He was out of breath. "Go ahead, control."

"This is Don. Generators one through five are running heavy and we've got alerts going off. We need to reduce the load."

"Control, recheck your systems. I've got alerts on all the generators down here. I've got techs scrambling to figure out what the hell is going on. I've never seen this before." Don and Russ could hear the alarms in the background. They looked up at the monitoring system display. It was still only showing issues with the five generators. "Eddie, are you sure you're having problems with all of the generators?"

"If you don't believe me, you can come down here and look. We've got red lights blinking everywhere with alarm sirens going off. What the hell is going on?"

Moments later Don and Russ saw the alerts for all of the generators on their control panel schematics, and the alarms started bellowing in the speakers above their heads. The situation was getting critical, and fast. "Don, we've got to hurry and reduce those power loads."

"I'm right there with you, pal." Russ, in all of his years, had never encountered an issue with all the generators at once.

"What do we do?"

"Give me a minute." Russ paused. "Okay, we need to do a controlled shutdown if the fail-safes don't shut the system down automatically."

They heard yelling on the radio. "Control, this is Eddie. The fail-safes aren't triggering down here on my end. What's going on up there? These generators are overheating."

"Eddie, what are you talking about? We don't see that on our screens!" Russ was yelling over the sirens.

"Check your damn computer program. I'm standing here in front of one of the generators, and I can tell you we have a major issue. We must have a software bug. It doesn't recognize the commands we're entering. It won't let me override the system from here."

"Russ, get over here. Look." Don pointed at the control panel where there were red blinking lights throughout the entire system.

"Holy shit, what's happening? I've never seen this before. Get the chief engineer on the line. We need to let him know what's going on."

Don called the main line and, before he could say anything, he heard yelling on the other end. "What the hell are you guys doing over there? Do you not see what's going on in the powerhouse and across the system?" It was the chief engineer.

"Sir, we're doing all we can, but there's something wrong with the system software. We've got a bug or something. It doesn't recognize our commands, and the fail-safes across the system aren't triggering. Not a single one is working, and the generators are overloading."

"Then manually shut them down, dammit! Do whatever you need to before they overheat and, God forbid, explode."

Don yelled to Russ, "Have Eddie shut them down manually from his end!"

"Are you serious? We may not be able to get them back online. We'd knock out power to most of the Southwest if we do that." Russ threw up his hands and then frantically tapped commands on his keyboard in an attempt to reduce the load across the system, but nothing was working. They were exceeding their load capacity for the generators that were beginning to overheat, and that was having a domino effect on the rest of the system downstream.

"Sir, are you sure you want us to shut everything down? We don't have time to do a controlled crash, which means we may not be able to get the system back online anytime soon."

The chief engineer was screaming through the phone. "I'm aware of that! Shut things down before the dam blows up and everything in that room goes up in flames!"

"Sir," Don said, "we're trying, but the system isn't responding. Russ is having Eddie and his team do it manually."

Russ was on the radio with Eddie. "Eddie, talk to me; what's going on down there?"

"It's not good, not good at all." He was panting on the other end of the line. "We just lost generators one through five. It'll be a matter of minutes before we lose the others."

Russ continued to tap away at his keyboard, entering different commands and doing everything he could to shut the system down manually. Russ looked over at Don, "I'm going down to the powerhouse right now. We've got to turn those generators off. Can you shut the control gates for the intakes?"

"No, they're opening further to let more water into the system."

"What? You've got to be kidding. Dammit, we'll need to close those manually too." Russ lifted the radio again to speak. "Eddie, this is Russ; I'm coming down. The control gates aren't closing, and we can't reduce the loads on the generators from our computers here. The RPMs for the turbines are spinning way too high. They're going to buckle and snap the rotors if we can't slow them down."

"What's going on?" the chief engineer hollered through the phone, hoping to get Don's attention.

"Sir, Russ is going down to the powerhouse to try and figure this out."

Eddie screamed through the radio, "Guys! Generators six through ten just went down!"

"Eddie, you've got to do what you can to save the rest. I'm coming down now." Russ handed the radio to Don.

"I know, I know." Eddie pulled the radio away to get the attention of a tech who was running by him. "You there, get to the control gates; we've got to shut them down manually to stop the intake flow valves."

"Yes sir." The tech whirled around and raced toward the far end of the powerhouse.

"Russ, are you there?" Eddie barked.

"Eddie, this is Don. Russ headed down to help you out."

"I'm at my principal diagnostics monitoring panel right now, Don. What do you see from your end?"

Don looked up at what resembled a holiday display with all of the red, orange, and green flashing lights. "Major trouble, Eddie. Everything is lit up like a Christmas tree. This whole power system is going down if we don't figure this out and act fast."

There was a beep on Eddie's radio. "Don, someone is on another channel. I've got to switch over. It's probably one of my techs." He turned the dial on his radio. "This is Eddie; go ahead."

"Eddie, we're in huge trouble." The poor tech on the other end was huffing.

"Calm down a second and tell me what's going on."

"We can't manually shut down the control gates or the generators. The gates for the intake pipes are stuck, and the crankshafts to disconnect the generators won't budge. Judging from the look of them, they haven't been tested or used for decades. They're probably rusted in place."

Eddie was standing on the platform that overlooked the powerhouse when Russ came bounding down the metal stairs.

"Eddie!"

"Russ! I've got techs trying to shut down the control gates and the generators manually, but they can't. And the automated fail-safes online still haven't triggered. The overload is frying the entire system."

"I know, dammit." Russ flailed his arms about, exasperated.

"What do we do?"

Standing on their elevated platform they could see to the most distant wing of the powerhouse. Some generators were beginning to spark and catch fire, the smoke mounting on the far end of the cavernous building.

Russ grabbed the radio from Eddie. "Don, are you there? Don?"

"This is control, Don here."

"Don, it's Russ. We have a hot mess on our hands. This whole place is overheating and starting to go up in flames."

"I know. The chief engineer said to shut it all down. Have you had any luck manually?"

"None whatsoever. You know what that means. Call the chief engineer and let him know that we've got to shut the entire system down and throw the main line."

"But that will knock out power to this whole region!"

"Dammit, don't you think I know that. We've got no other choice. This place is going to go up in flames, and the fire sprinklers haven't kicked on yet. The generators are already catching fire. Call the chief!"

Don had the chief already waiting on the other line. He'd heard the screaming back and forth. "Chief, are you there?"

"Yes, what the hell are you doing over there?" The chief was infuriated. He knew the severity of the situation, and there was little he could do from his office.

"Sir, it's bad . . . horrible. The generators in the powerhouse are overloading and catching fire. We lost ten of the generators already, and we've got to shut the entire system down before we lose everything. That means cutting off power to millions of people across Nevada, Arizona, and California."

"You don't have to tell me. I'm well aware of the consequences."

"Should we alert the governors in the region? This situation isn't going to go over well for their constituents."

"Hell, this isn't going to go over well with anyone, including the president. There's no time. Shut it down."

"Yes sir." Don lifted the radio. "Russ, Eddie, get your people out of there. I'm shutting the whole place down—chief's orders."

"What about you?"

"Someone has to stay behind and do it. You guys get your people out. You've got less than fifteen minutes. Now move!" Don rushed to the central terminal panel with the main shut-off switch. It was only to be used in major emergencies, and they'd never needed to use it before. Flipping the switch at the dam would cut off power to tens of millions, and he knew it could take several days or even weeks to restore that power, particularly given all the damage that had occurred to the multi-ton generators and turbines. Don stared at the system monitoring panel on the wall as more red and orange lights blinked. He shook his head as he lifted the protective casing over the main shut-off switch. Don looked up: *Lord, help us all. With luck, they'll be able to divert power from the Grand Coulee and John Day dams up north or from the local power plants nearby.* Don didn't know it then, but hackers were attacking other power plants and dams across the United States. Millions of Americans were already being affected, region by region, state by state, city by city. Don hit the main shut-off switch, and within seconds he was engulfed in darkness.

30

Michael and Kate grabbed a cab from their hotel to their favorite Italian restaurant, Il Romano, where they expected to enjoy a quiet romantic dinner. Situated only blocks from Times Square, it was subtly tucked away from the hustle. It was a basement restaurant with an obscure black awning marked with the street number in white. Unless people were specifically looking for it, chances are they would walk right by it. It seemed clear to Michael that it was intentional.

The couple had, in fact, come across the place by accident themselves. It had been a rainy spring evening as they strolled back to Kate's apartment from a Broadway matinee. The skies had opened, and they didn't have an umbrella. Il Romano was simply the closest cover they could find. As they watched the rain from under the awning, they decided to go inside and wait out the storm. A nicely dressed little old Italian woman with a thick accent welcomed them to the quaint, third- generation, family-owned restaurant. There was a bar along the left wall that ended at the hallway to the kitchen. The bathrooms were in the back. Covered in red-and-white checkered tablecloths and with candles encased in dark red glass holders, a dozen or so tables were peppered about the middle of the room and along the walls. Picturesque paintings of the Italian coast and Tuscany covered the walls, and the faint romantic lighting was accented by street lantern sconce lighting. The aroma of homemade pasta and freshly baked garlic bread filled the air while classic Bocelli and Pavarotti music played softly in the background. They instantly fell in love with it, and it had become their restaurant of choice for special occasions.

After the cab from the hotel dropped them off and they were inside, they were pleased to see the place hadn't changed even though the father had passed away a few years earlier, and his two sons were in charge now. They were both successful businessmen and enjoyed the restaurant, but Antonio, who went by "Big Tony," was more akin to running the restaurant than his older brother Roberto, who preferred the other family businesses.

Michael and Kate walked in and were greeted by an old woman wearing a familiar warm smile. It was Mrs. Fazio, the late owner's wife. She recognized them and shuffled toward the couple with open arms.

"Hello, hello, my dears," she said with her thick Italian accent. "It's so good to see you both again. It's been so long. How have you been?"

Michael looked at Mrs. Fazio and couldn't help but chuckle. She was a slender tiny woman, about five foot four. Her fashionably styled hair that was done up in a bun had turned light gray, and her olive skin had aged well despite her wrinkles. She wore a flashy, bright blue sequined dress. Her neck and ears were adorned with shiny diamonds; her outfit spoke as loudly as she did.

"Come here, my dears, and give me a hug," she said as she jogged up to Kate and gave her a big hug and kiss on the cheek. "You look radiant."

"Thank you, Mrs. Fazio. I'm doing well. It's so good to see you looking so beautiful."

She laughed lightly and turned to Michael. "And you—are you taking care of my girl?"

"I'm doing my best."

"I see. Come here and give me a hug."

Michael leaned down and wrapped his arms around her tiny frame. She pulled back and looked up at him with that big, warm smile of hers.

"Come now, please take a seat. You must have your favorite table." Mrs. Fazio turned and hurried to the back corner of the restaurant as she yelled out in Italian. Michael could hear the excitement in her voice. Almost immediately, Big Tony emerged from the kitchen. He wore a white apron splattered with tomato sauce and flour.

"Hello!" he bellowed in a thick New York-Italian accent. "How you doin'? Since you've moved to D.C., you neva visit us." He looked as disappointed as he sounded.

He then wiped his flour-covered hands on his apron before he shook their hands and kissed Kate on the cheek.

"It's great to see you both. It's been too long." Tony's voice was gentle and sincere.

"Yes, it has been too long," Michael replied.

"What brings you to New York?"

"We had a long weekend, and I wanted to surprise Kate by getting her out of D.C." Michael turned and gazed lovingly at Kate. She reached down and grabbed his hand.

"What can I get you folks tonight?" Tony asked, elated to see a pair of his old regulars.

"We're not sure, but since this is one of our favorite places in New York, I'm sure anything we choose will be great." Michael looked at Tony and grinned.

Tony gave him a cockeyed look and put his hands on his hips in an intimidating fashion. "What do you mean this is one of your favorite restaurants in New York? This is supposed to be your favorite place to eat." Tony then stepped closer to Michael.

Though Michael was about half a head taller than Big Tony, he was about one hundred pounds lighter. Big Tony had dark black hair and a rugged, scruffy face from having not shaven for a couple of days. He was built like a linebacker and, in fact, had played high school football. Michael had played in college, so they always had something football-related to discuss.

Big Tony wore a stern look as he stared at Michael. His glare cut like a knife. He assumed Big Tony was joking, but he couldn't be sure. He used to joke with him about being in the mafia; Big Tony never thought it was funny, but he went along with it. Michael knew from his line of work not to probe too much.

Big Tony stepped closer while Michael stood his ground. Then Big Tony burst out laughing. "I still can't make you crack, my friend. You're a rock. Let me treat you both to dinner. It would be my pleasure." He gave them both a warm bear hug. "What do you say? Let me get you some menus."

Michael and Kate took a seat at the table as she giggled to herself.

"What's that about?"

"Everything: you, us, Il Romano, New York . . . I realized how much I miss it."

"I suppose so." But Michael had never been that fond of New York City. He found it suffocating. He preferred the outdoors and wide open spaces. But there were aspects of New York that he enjoyed—Central Park and Broadway and, yes, the food. For him, New York City was a place to visit, not to live.

"You don't sound too certain about that."

"You know how I feel about New York."

"I know, but I figured the city would grow on you."

"It still might, but right now I'm content with just visiting. Do we have to talk about this now? I'd rather that we just enjoy our dinner. We have discussed this at length before."

Kate had always wanted Michael to move to New York, but he was adamantly against it.

She sensed his walls going up as he withdrew. "You're right. Let's just enjoy dinner."

"Thank you." Michael felt a sense of relief. He didn't like these kinds of conversations with Kate because he felt he never could win. He avoided them if at all possible.

"What are you in the mood to eat tonight?"

"I'm not sure. I may just go with my usual."

Kate often went with the lasagna or the chicken parmesan. Michael liked the fettuccine Alfredo and the chicken parmesan as well. It was all delicious. You couldn't go wrong with anything they served. It was all fresh and homemade. They were reviewing the menu when Big Tony reappeared.

"Could I get you both something to drink? Some wine perhaps."

"We would love some wine," Kate replied. "What do you recommend?"

"It depends on what you order, but you can't go wrong with the Cabernet."

"Okay, let's take a bottle of that."

"Comin' right up. And could I get you both some water and bread as well?"

"That would be great."

They enjoyed the most delicious Italian bread, crispy on the outside and chewy on the inside. It came with soft butter and a small bowl of olive oil with spices for dipping.

Michael and Kate sat holding hands and staring deeply into each other's eyes until Tony returned. He put the wine glasses and bottle on the table and popped the cork, pouring them both a drink.

"What can I get you to eat?" he asked cordially.

Michael motioned for Kate to order first.

"I'll take the lasagna," she said, handing her menu to Big Tony.

"And for you, Michael?"

"I'll take the chicken fettuccini Alfredo."

"Excellent. I'll have that right out to you. Can I get you something in the meantime . . . perhaps an appetizer?"

"Some mozzarella sticks or calamari would be great," Michael said.

"Certainly. I'll get that right now." As Big Tony hurried away, Kate and Michael reached across the table again to hold hands, entranced in love.

Their gaze was interrupted by Michael's cell phone ring. He was immediately annoyed with the untimely interruption. He silenced it and refused to answer as the phone vibrated.

Kate looked at him, bewildered. "Aren't you going to answer that? It could be the director calling you back."

"Not right now. It can wait until we finish dinner."

Kate had known him long enough to read his nuances. "Are you going to let this ruin our meal?" she asked softly.

"No, but I'm annoyed because it always seems that when we're having quality time lately, it gets interrupted at the most inopportune moments. All I want is to have a quiet night out with you. Everything was going so well until that damn phone rang."

"I know, I know," she responded in an understanding tone. "Can we put the call aside and enjoy dinner?" She leaned across the table.

Michael's head was bowed in disappointment. He slowly lifted his head, and she beamed with love.

"I suppose I can."

"Would you feel better if you looked to see who called? That might put you more at ease."

"I could do that." He unclipped the phone from his belt and checked the screen.

31

In the unknown room filled with cigar smoke, Director Godfrey sat strapped to a chair, blindfolded. His wrists and hands began to ache from having been bound so long. His mouth was dry, and he licked his lips to wet them. He squirmed in the chair, his body weak and powerless.

"Is there anything we can get for you?" the Russian stranger asked.

"My mouth is dry. I sure could use some water." Godfrey heard movements to his right, and then he heard the sound of someone pouring liquid into a glass.

"Where am I, and what do you want with me?"

"You believe that you recognize me," the Russian-accented man said in a deep voice.

"You're Dimitri Kruchevko."

"How do you know?"

"It was something in your voice, your presence."

"Well, I never thought we'd meet like this again," Dimitri said solemnly.

"Nor I," replied Godfrey. "It's been a long time."

"Yes, it has." There was melancholy in Dimitri's voice.

Dimitri and Godfrey had worked together for many years on U.S. intelligence projects. Each had led a regional team while they worked for the CIA before Godfrey joined the NSA. Dimitri headed special projects targeted at Russian intelligence and the former KGB, which the FSB state security organization had replaced. Godfrey focused on the Western Hemisphere and Asia, mainly China and North Korea. They worked on a joint project investigating a series of blackouts across the United States and other countries from the 1990s through the early 2000s. They believed the blackouts were the result of cyberattacks that could be the precursors to attacks against the power grid and industrial infrastructure. They were making significant progress when Dimitri disappeared while overseas on vacation. The news media reported that the boat he was sailing off the coast of Portugal had been caught in a storm and sank. The boat and those on it were never found. The other men on the boat were some of his childhood friends from Russia. But within intelligence circles, word spread that Dimitri had either defected or been killed by the Russian mob, and the boat had been destroyed.

"They told me years ago you defected back to Russia and sold U.S. secrets to American enemies. I never believed them. Now I see that my judgment was flawed. How did you get back into this country?"

"Your judgment was not flawed. I had to defect to protect my family. The Russian FSB threatened to kill them if I didn't spy for them against the United States. My only option was to leave my wife and children and go underground. I did what I had to do. You would have done the same for your family. In the end, it didn't matter. Those bastards tortured and killed my family anyway, hoping that I would come out of hiding. They never believed that I'd died. I made it my life's work to find out who was responsible and hunt them down like the savage dogs they are."

"Where have you been all of these years?" Godfrey asked.

"I've been keeping busy serving the country, the United States, and myself in my way." He spoke in a defiant tone. He often operated autonomously and wasn't one to obey authority, especially if he didn't agree with those in charge.

"What do you want with me? Why am I here? You could at least take off the blindfold now that I know who you are."

"Not yet. You may know me, but you don't know my associates. They don't want you to see them. That would be very problematic for you."

Godfrey got right to the point. "Why is my staff under surveillance? Why are they being targeted? What the hell is that all about? They're no threat."

"The surveillance is a precautionary measure by my associates on the inside."

"Precautionary against what? The NSA, CIA, and FBI have many secret projects combating cyberterrorism and working on cyber defense. Why has my team been singled out?"

"Easy there, Godfrey. You will have all of your answers in time."

"Enough of this nonsense. Why all the charades?" Godfrey shook back and forth in the chair, nearly falling over.

"Patience, Godfrey."

"Why don't you just tell me why I'm here so we can get on with it already?"

"I could, but it's not my place." Dimitri had his orders from Aiden.

"Does this have anything to do with the project my team has been working on?"

There was a long pause. "No, it doesn't." There was uneasiness in Dimitri's voice.

"It doesn't?" Godfrey was skeptical. "The fact I've been kidnapped and you have me here makes me believe otherwise. I know it has something to do with the code we identified. We were getting close to cracking it and finding the source. It was only a matter of time." There was a hint of pride in Godfrey's voice.

"Honestly, it does have something to do with the code, but not entirely. It's more extensive than that."

"I knew we were on to something. Why is Russia involved?"

"You will find out soon enough."

"Enough of this, Dimitri. Tell me why I'm here!"

"Listen, I've said all I can for now." His friendly tone turned harsh.

"Then why do you still have me here? Who do you work for?"

"I have my employers, but I work for myself."

"You're a mercenary now; is that it?"

"Not quite. We have our own independent intelligence operations group, but we work with many organizations around the world."

"Who?" The vagueness and generalities were getting on Godfrey's nerves.

Dimitri changed topics and, with a serious tone, asked, "What do you know about Michael Stevens and Matt O'Shea?"

"What do they have to do with anything?"

"They have everything to do with the current situation."

"And what might that be?"

"The one you and I are facing with the code your team found. Michael is your program lead, is he not?"

"Yes, he is."

"Was he the one who discovered the code?"

"Not specifically. Michael's team found it."

"And what is O'Shea's role? He works for you, doesn't he?"

"Not directly. Michael recruited him."

"I see."

"What do you know about how Michael and his team discovered the code? Did he give you specifics?"

"They discovered it while they were doing some counter defense measures. Something had bypassed our NSA systems, and we didn't know how it could have happened. We looked to identify the code in the computer systems. They tried to track the source, but it was a moving target."

"What do you mean?"

"They couldn't find the source of the code. As soon as Michael and his team thought they'd traced it, it would relocate. It was continually moving and mutating."

"Did you search for any patterns or abnormal connections that might allow you to pinpoint it?"

"We did, but we had no luck. We were able to isolate potential locations in a few countries, but nothing definite."

"And what locations were those?" Dimitri asked. *Now they were getting somewhere.*

"There were several throughout Southeast Asia and other areas of Asia."

"I need to know what you know about the code." Dimitri was direct. "Listen, I can't tell you everything: one, because I don't know everything, and two, because this is a highly secretive matter."

"You don't have to lecture me on secrecy," Godfrey retorted. "What do you know that you're not telling me? Russia is involved, right? That's why you're here. You're working for the Russians."

"Just know that we need your full cooperation." Dimitri was speaking forcefully. He was tired of the back and forth. Aiden had given him specific orders to get as much information from Godfrey as he could.

"Dimitri, how do I know I can trust you with what I know? Trust is mutual, and you've shown me none thus far. You can start by untying me and taking this blindfold off."

Godfrey wasn't about to tell Dimitri what he wanted—not while he was still a hostage. Who knew what they'd do to him. Godfrey realized there was more to what Dimitri wanted, and he was also aware of the incident that had happened at Lucigen in D.C. He had tried to reach Matt on Friday night. Godfrey had seen the reports before he left for the airport that Matt had used their NSA Black Viper system to run diagnostics tests from his company's systems. Matt knew more about the code than Michael or his team did. After all, Godfrey was the one who had modified O'Shea's original code in the first place to use for his cyber defense surveillance program, but only he knew that. No one else in the NSA or White House even knew about it. Matt was going to be his scapegoat if he needed one. That's why he agreed for Michael and Aiden to hire O'Shea to go undercover.

"You can't trust me," Dimitri said, "and there's no way I can trust someone who sold me out to the Russian mob, so it looks like we're at an impasse."

"I sold you out? That's bullshit, and you know it, Dimitri. I never sold you out." Godfrey was being honest. "If you would stop all of this nonsense and tell me why you have me here, we could move this conversation forward rather than dancing around like we've been doing." Godfrey was becoming more annoyed with Dimitri's antics.

"We're at war, Godfrey." Dimitri's tone was strictly matter of fact.

"Yes, we are. We've been at war for years with a number of countries. Tell me something I don't know."

"This is a new type of war, Godfrey, one I'm sure you're very familiar with. It's one in which there are no traditional battle-fields or armies. Instead, a single man or a small group of indi-viduals can attack a country, perhaps even cripple it, with a few strokes of a keyboard and clicks of a mouse."

Dimitri was about to continue when someone entered the room. Godfrey heard the footsteps, and then he heard whisper-ing before more footsteps moved toward him.

"Hello? Dimitri? Who's there with you?" Godfrey called out. Suddenly, someone covered his mouth, and he could barely breathe. He fought from his chair but quickly lost consciousness.

32

Back at FBI headquarters in Washington, the SIOC was alive with activity. The agents and analysts were busy preparing the latest information on O'Shea and the isolated blackouts across the city. Director Donovan stormed into the center for an update.

"Listen up, everyone, listen up! I want an update on where we stand with tracking down this Matt O'Shea character and with securing the city. Do I make myself clear?"

There was an echo of "Yes, sirs" and a wave of nodding heads.

"Great. We'll meet in the conference room in fifteen minutes. I want everyone there."

Donovan walked out of the room and through the hall to his office. He sat at his computer when he noticed that the red light on his phone was blinking to indicate a missed call. As he reached for the phone, Agent Burton flew into the office like a goose landing on an icy lake.

"Sir," Burton said, catching his breath as he stood in the doorway. The chocolate colored skin on Burton's forehead beamed with beads of sweat. His narrow chest expanded and contracted has he panted, and the sleeves of his gray suit coat flapped around his arms as he caught Donovan's attention.

"Slow down Burton. What is it? Can it wait? We have our briefing in a few minutes."

"I know, sir, but no, this can't wait. We've found him," Agent Burton announced excitedly.

"Where?" Donovan asked, and then he jumped out of his chair and leaned intently over his desk toward the flustered agent. "Where is he?"

Agent Burton tried to get the words out, but Donovan interrupted him. "Out with it man!" he yelled as he slammed a hand down on his desk.

"He was spotted in Georgetown near M Street a short while ago, or at least a man that fits his description was," Agent Burton said, relieved he was able to get the words out.

"What the hell is he doing in Georgetown? I thought he'd be out of town by now. Why is he sticking around?" Donovan was baffled.

"He's probably been traveling on foot this entire time. In case you haven't heard, the traffic lights are out across the west and northwest parts of the city. It's one giant gridlock. Nobody can get anywhere. It's a mess."

Donovan paused to think, shaking his head.

"What is it, sir?"

"Nothing," his tone softened as his voice trailed off. He looked up with a partially content grin. "Good work, Burton. Get everyone together in the conference room. We'll meet now. We don't have a minute to lose."

"Yes sir." Agent Burton whipped around and rushed out of the office. As he ran down the hall, he yelled to everyone. "All hands in the conference room, now! Let's move it, people! We don't have all night!"

Arched over his desk, Donovan watched the staff running back and forth down the hall. He chuckled to himself, recalling the days when he was a field agent. Burton then swung back into his office.

"Sir, everyone will be ready in a minute," he said, out of breath again.

"I'll be right there."

"You got it." Burton turned and ran back down the hallway.

Donovan reached down and grabbed his notepad and pen. He walked around his desk and headed for the door. He had forgotten about the blinking red light on his phone indicating that he had missed a message.

33

Matt and John took off on a brisk walk down the street toward the Georgetown waterfront, staying vigilant to spot anything suspicious. There were more people out than when they'd arrived at the bookstore. The disabled traffic lights were causing mayhem with people yelling, cars honking, and police sirens blaring.

As they sped along, John turned to Matt. "Which way do we go out of town?"

"I'm thinking we head across the Key Bridge into Rosslyn and catch a cab out of the city from there. What do you say?"

"I'm not too keen on the idea. You've seen the traffic. It's still gridlock around here. Who knows if it's like that across the bridge or not."

"You're right. We've got to find another way to get into Rosslyn. We may have to walk across the bridge."

"Fair enough."

They slowed their pace as they neared K Street under the Whitehurst Freeway Bridge. They looked around for questionable people but didn't see anyone, at least not initially.

John turned to Matt and asked, "Do you get the feeling we're being followed?"

"Yeah, I do."

As they walked, Matt took in the surroundings. Finally, someone caught his eye. There was a Caucasian man, average build, about six-feet tall. He appeared to be talking on the phone. Matt couldn't see his facial features because he wore a hat, and it was dark under the bridge. He kept walking in and out of the shadows while on the phone. There was something off about him.

"There's a man with a black jacket talking on the phone behind us," Matt said.

"Are you sure he's following us?"

"Do you recognize him?" Matt asked.

"Not really, but I haven't gotten a good look at the man yet." John started to turn to look, but Matt grabbed his arm.

"Don't turn around. That'll be too obvious."

"Who could he be?"

"I swear he was the man we saw in the bookstore."

"It can't be," John said in disbelief. "The man in the store seemed much older. This guy looks like he's in his thirties. Besides, wasn't the other guy wearing a brown scarf? Do we make a run for it or what?"

"We can't draw any attention to ourselves. We have to lose him somehow," Matt said.

"What do you have in mind?"

"We can lose him in the movie theater or in one of these parking garages or restaurants," Matt said as he motioned subtly toward the buildings in the next block.

"But if he's got colleagues, couldn't he just radio them to close off the exits? If there's one, there must be more."

"Good point." Matt had a quizzical look as he mentally explored their options.

Matt and John continued walking down K Street. Matt knew there were some parking garages and side streets that they might be able to use for cover. John tapped Matt's arm. "In a second, I want you to stop and bend down like you're tying your shoe. I'm going to take a look to see if that guy is still following us."

They took a few steps and then Matt stepped off to the side into an enclave of a restaurant door entrance to tie his shoe. While he squatted, John looked around. The man was still trailing them.

Matt whispered, "Do you see him?"

"Yes. He's about thirty yards away on the other side of the street. He's slowed his pace and is looking in another direction."

"Has he looked at us at all?" Matt asked, looking up at John.

"No. He's just walking, minding his own business."

Then John saw the man fumbling with something in his pocket as he approached. It could be a gun. *Surely he wouldn't shoot them in plain sight with so many people around.*

"Where is he now?"

"He's a few doors down. He's on our side of the street now. He can't be more than twenty yards away. Wait. He just stopped." John saw the man hold his hand up to his ear and then lift his hand to his mouth as if he were about to cough.

Matt couldn't squat much longer. It would be awkward taking that long to tie his shoe, so he stood. Matt looked back but didn't see the man. "Where'd he go?"

John searched as well. "I don't know. He was right there. I think he must have stepped behind that cargo truck." John pointed to the truck parked near the curb.

Matt wasted no time. "We need to get out of here now."

Matt wasn't certain, but he figured that was a surveillance truck.

The unmarked moving truck was out of place. There weren't any residences nearby, and most shops were closed.

"Where do we go?"

Matt motioned to the restaurant door. "We'll go in here and out the back."

"And what if they're waiting for us?" John was worried that they might be walking into a trap.

"We can't just stand here."

"You've got that right. Let's go."

Matt opened the door and stepped inside. John took one last look at the truck. The man hadn't come out from behind it, so John followed swiftly behind Matt. They made their way to the back of the restaurant, stopping briefly at the end of the bar.

"Where are your restrooms?" Matt asked the waitress as she put drinks on her tray.

The young woman pointed down a hallway behind her and said, "They're toward the back."

"Great. Thank you."

They hurried toward the rear and past the restrooms. They couldn't have been any luckier. The exit door was straight in front of them. But as they approached, they noticed an emergency exit alarm bar on the door.

"You've got to be kidding me," John blurted out in frustration.

"Hold on a minute. These aren't always activated. The staff needs a way of taking out the trash, and I'm also sure a number of them are smokers." Matt walked up to the door. "I say we try it and then run like hell." He knew the authorities were closing in on them.

"What do we have to lose? Let's give it a go," John said. They still needed to get out of town.

Matt grabbed the emergency exit bar. "Here goes nothing." He carefully pushed the door and felt it give way as it slowly opened. Matt flinched, anticipating the sound of the alarm, but there was only silence. He smiled at John.

"That wasn't so bad," Matt said confidently.

"He pushed the door open further and stepped into the alley. He stood with his back against the door as John followed.

"That was a piece of cake. I can't believe I was worried," Matt gloated.

But Matt had spoken too soon; seconds later a blood-curdling alarm screamed.

"Holy . . . ," Matt blurted as he whirled around and slammed the door shut. "We've got to get out of here fast!" Matt yelled as they turned to run down the alley. They needed to get to the main street where they could hide in the crowds. As they neared the side street, an unmarked cop car drove past them up the hill with its lights on. They turned left and ran back toward the river.

They heard people yelling, but they didn't stop to see if it was directed at them. They sprinted past the movie theater and toward a boat dock at the end of K Street under the bridge. There were some abandoned buildings and warehouses where they could hide by the river. As Matt and John ran, they saw a hole in one of the chain-link fences ahead. They ducked through it and headed toward the water. They ran until they reached the waterfront boathouse. They looked around desperately. The door to the boathouse was locked, so they couldn't get inside. Matt hurried around to the side of the building, looking for another entrance.

"Matt, we've got to get away from here," John gasped, breathing heavily, a sense of urgency in his voice.

"I know. I say we take one of these boats across the river into Rosslyn. We can grab a cab from there. I doubt they'll expect us to cross the river by boat. And we're not getting across that bridge," he said, pointing at the Key Bridge. Traffic was backed up, and they could hear an orchestra of police sirens and car horns echoing in the night.

"It'll take us a while to make it across, provided we even find a boat," John said, skeptical.

"Do you have any better ideas?" Matt retorted. "We're running out of options. They know we're nearby. It'll only be a matter of time before they find us."

"I suppose you're right. We'd better grab one of these boats then. Do you see any with paddles?"

"I'll check the other side of the landing; you check this side."

They searched for anything that would get them across the river. Finally, John found a boat. He wanted to call out to Matt, but he knew that would draw attention—after all, they were trespassing. Instead, John sped around the building and almost ran into Matt who was trying to break the lock on a chain securing one of the boats.

"Hey, I found one that's not locked up," John said, panting. "It can fit the two of us. It's not a speed boat, but it should get us across the river. Follow me."

They snatched the metal boat and dragged it to the ramp, sliding it quietly into the water. They climbed in, grabbed the oars, and began rowing toward the opposite shore. Fortunately, it was a new moon, so they had the cover of darkness on their side. They rowed slowly to keep the wakes small.

They crossed the river and were nearing the other shore along the George Washington Parkway when Matt glanced over his shoulder. He glimpsed movements in the shadows; someone was sneaking around the boathouse. *Could it be the same guy who was following us?*

John looked at Matt as he rowed. "You okay? You're awfully quiet and acting a little squirrelly."

"I'm fine."

"You sure? You look like something's on your mind?"

"I think I saw the man who was following us near K Street." Matt pointed across the river toward the boat landing.

"It couldn't be. How could you tell from so far away? Besides, we lost him back at the restaurant." John shook his head.

"That's what I was thinking, but somehow he tracked us down, or maybe there are more of them."

"These guys don't waste any time. They're like cockroaches. They're everywhere."

"You're telling me."

The words had hardly slipped their lips when a police helicopter flew overhead. It buzzed the treetops and then headed along the river south toward the Memorial Bridge before turning around and heading back toward Georgetown.

Matt pointed at the helicopter. "Those guys are relentless."

They finally made it to the other shore and jumped out of the boat. Matt removed the drain plug from the back, and then they pushed the boat into the water and watched as it drifted from the shore and slowly sank.

They ducked under the trees and watched the helicopter circle overhead. Then it dipped to only a few feet above the water, the searchlight scanning the shore along the Georgetown waterfront park. The helicopter then hovered over the river and flashed its light toward the boat landing. Matt and John saw the man and then heard a loud voice from the helicopter speaker, but all they could make out was, "This is the FBI . . ." The helicopter's spotlight wavered and shone down on the mysterious man. Then gunshots rang out. The man in the black coat ran down the shore into the shadows toward the cover of the boathouse. They heard a second set of gunshots. Then there was the sound of rapid gunfire, like an automatic weapon. *Who was shooting at who?* The helicopter bobbed to dodge the gunfire. Moments later it flew away and headed down the river toward the Memorial Bridge.

"That was close," Matt said. "I wonder who that man is."

There was no response, so Matt turned and asked, "John, where are you?"

"I'm over here."

"Over where?"

"Behind here."

"I can't see you."

John popped his head up from behind a fallen tree. "Oh, I see you now. What are you doing way over there?" Matt could faintly see John's silhouette.

John dusted himself off and walked over to Matt.

"How'd you get over there so quickly?"

"When I heard the first round of gunshots I ducked for cover," John said. "It just so happened that I was able to find this log."

"I've never seen you move so fast," Matt chuckled.

"I didn't want to take any chances. I didn't know if they were shooting at us."

"It looked like they were shooting from the helicopter at that stranger, and he returned fire." Matt kicked some mud off his shoes.

"Do you have any idea who that man was?"

"Not a clue." Matt still wasn't sure if it was the man from the bookstore. He wondered if it was an NSA agent keeping tabs on him. He hoped it was.

"Where to now?" John asked.

"I say we head up the hill and make our way across the George Washington Parkway toward Fort Meyer Drive and then into Rosslyn. Route 66 is right there. That will be our best bet for catching a taxi out of town. I just hope traffic isn't backed up over there too."

"That works for me," John replied, a hint of relief in his voice that at least they were out of D.C.

34

In his conference room at FBI headquarters, Donovan was concluding the briefing when Agent Perez raced into the operations center in his professionally suave attire. Perez was of Latin-American descent, in his early thirties, average athletic build, light tan skin, brown eyes, and dark wavy hair that was faded on the sides and combed stylishly to the side on the top.

"Sir, we've got another update," he said breathlessly.

"More recent than the one we're finishing now?" Donovan asked mockingly.

"Yes. Agents spotted Matt O'Shea in Georgetown."

"I know. We sent out agents and a chopper. What's the word?"

"They were in pursuit by the K Street boathouse, and then we lost them."

"What do you mean you lost them? He was with someone?"

"Yes. Another guy, but we haven't identified him yet."

"Any clue who he might be?" Donovan stood with his hands on his hips, annoyed.

"Not sure at this point, but we'll find out."

"Do that. I want to know who's helping O'Shea. Is there anything else?"

There was a pause, and Agent Perez lowered his head. "Actually, there is. Someone opened fire on our helicopter. We don't know who it was or where it came from."

"What?" Donovan exclaimed, waving his arms about before slamming his fists down on the table. He leaned over fuming at Agent Perez who was standing to the side of the room by the doorway, keeping a safe distance. Director Donovan was known to throw things when he got upset.

"Who would be shooting at our helicopter other than O'Shea? And if it was him, how did he get a gun?"

"We don't know, sir. We need to find out. The pilots reported seeing a man in a long black coat and beanie down by the Georgetown waterfront. When they flashed their light on him, he opened fire."

Donovan stood, shaking his head in dismay. *What the hell is this turning into? That didn't meet the description of what O'Shea was last seen wearing.* "Listen up, everyone. I gave simple instructions to bring O'Shea in alive. Now there's been some shooting near Georgetown, of all places, which involved our team. We don't need any public attention on this situation: remember that. This is a code red national security issue. The last thing we want is to have the media all over this. Do I make myself clear?" He looked around the room for affirmation.

Heads nodded in agreement—all except one. Agent Burton stood along the back wall with his arms crossed and wearing a defiant expression.

Donovan noticed him. "Agent Burton, is there something you need to say?"

"No sir."

"Are you sure? You don't look too certain," Donovan said in an accusatory tone.

"I'm certain. There's nothing I need to say at this time, but I'll let you know," Burton sneered at the director, his tone dismissive.

Donovan gave him a stern look. "Burton, I want to see you in my office immediately after this."

The room fell silent, and all heads turned toward Agent Burton. He glared at Director Donovan defiantly.

"Yes, sir, with pleasure." He shrugged his narrow shoulders, pulled out his phone, and checked his messages.

Donovan turned to the rest of the room. "No one sleeps until we have O'Shea in custody. I want hourly reports. Do I make myself clear?" There were looks of acknowledgment across the room. "Let's get back to work." With that, Donovan stormed out and headed for his office.

Agent Burton waited until almost everyone had cleared out until he approached the door. He noticed smug looks from some of the remaining field agents, but he disregarded them. Burton didn't care what they thought. Most of them hadn't accomplished half of what he had.

Burton paraded out of the briefing room and down the hall toward Donovan's office, stopping for a drink of water at a nearby fountain. He figured if he was going to get a tongue lashing he should bide his time.

Guided by the rows of fluorescent lighting that lined the ceiling, Burton made his way down the long, drab, off-white hallway until he arrived at Donovan's office suite. He stopped but didn't go inside. Typically, Donovan's receptionist was at her desk talking up a storm, but she went home sick earlier, so it was only the director. Donovan was probably stressed because he had to check his own voicemail and email. *Heaven forbid that the world should ever come to that.* Burton stood a moment longer before walking around the reception desk and to the director's door. He knocked and cautiously popped his head inside.

Donovan didn't notice him in the doorway as he sat at his desk staring at his phone. Agent Burton waited a moment before speaking.

"Sir, you wanted to see me?" Agent Burton said politely.

The director continued to sit in a daze. Agent Burton spoke up again, this time a little louder. "Sir, you wanted to see me?"

Donovan gradually looked up with a blank stare.

"Sir, is everything all right?" Donovan looked down at his desk in deep thought. He didn't like the voice message he'd just heard.

Finally, Donovan nodded and motioned for Burton to enter. "Close the door."

35

Michael saw that he had a new text, one he assumed was from Godfrey. He opened the encrypted message on his phone and sat in disbelief as he read the words:

EMINENT ECLIPSE RISING

They were only three words, but he knew precisely what they meant. They had discussed the possibility of a cyberattack by Russia, North Korea, or China that could lead to a massive blackout across the United States, but they weren't certain if or when it would happen. "Eminent Eclipse" was the code name they used for the cyber defense project to combat the potential nationwide blackout. "Rising" indicated that the threat level was increasing to the point where an attack was likely or had already begun. For years there had been rumors of a cyber Armageddon or a cyber Pearl Harbor. Michael didn't believe that day had come yet. Given what the malware was targeting, he and his team assumed it was being used for cyber warfare and corporate espionage, but it was all speculation.

They'd received recent intelligence regarding blackouts that had occurred in the United States and other countries. The classified records all reported the presence of rare codes or malware in the systems. Recent reports indicated that the Chinese and the Russians were conducting cyber assaults on U.S. utilities, infrastructure systems, business, government, and financial systems. Michael and his team knew it was only a matter of time before something of epic proportions happened. Michael and his team assumed these smaller blackouts were a test of their enemy's capabilities. They couldn't identify the exact source of the code and stop the attacks, so they couldn't say with absolute certainty if it was Russia, China, or North Korea that was behind them. It could even be any number of lone wolves or small groups of rogue hackers behind the attacks. There was also the potential insider threat. They had been trying to figure out the "who" for months, but with no success.

Michael had no idea that a major attack was occurring. He hadn't heard about the security breach at Lucigen yet, or about the local power outage in D.C. that had begun Friday night. That was part of the reason Godfrey was trying so desperately to reach him.

Is this what he's been trying to tell me? But why would he risk texting the message, even if it was encrypted? Michael had served in the intelligence community long enough to know that nothing was ever truly secret, even internally encrypted messages. Godfrey had taken a huge risk in texting him. He must have found something of major significance.

Kate saw the look of horror on Michael's face. She reached across the table and put her hand on his. "What is it? You seem panicked."

"I can't tell you," Michael snapped at her. Kate pulled away and sat back in her chair.

"Why not?" she asked, crossing her arms.

"I need to get back to D.C. tonight."

"You what? But it's after eight. Even if you left for the airport right now, you don't know that you'd be able to catch a flight."

"Then I'll take the train or rent a car."

"What's so important that it can't wait until tomorrow?"

"I have to get back tonight."

"Does this have anything to do with your project?"

"You know I can't say." He wanted to tell her, but he couldn't. It was for her own safety.

Kate saw the look in his eyes. She recognized it from so many times before. She had learned over the years not to ask questions, so she turned away.

"I need to make a quick call. I'll be back." Michael got up from the table and headed for the back, looking for a more private location. He poked his head into the kitchen and saw Big Tony preparing dinner. Big Tony turned and saw him standing in the doorway. "Would you like to help?" he asked with a giant smile.

"Looks like fun, but not tonight. I don't want to get dirty," Michael said, motioning to his suit. "Besides, I need to make an important work-related call."

"Do you need a private place to talk?"

"Yes."

"I have just the place. My office is right up those stairs, first door on your left." Big Tony motioned up the staircase. "The door is unlocked. Make yourself at home." Tony smiled. "I'll have your dinner ready by the time you're back."

"Thanks. I shouldn't be long."

"Not a problem. Go handle your business."

Michael hurried upstairs to Big Tony's office and closed the door. It was dark and cluttered with files and papers. He shook the disastrous thoughts from his head and pulled out his phone. He stared at the text message in disbelief. *This can't be happening. It must be a drill.* They sometimes did that to keep everyone on their toes.

Michael pulled up Godfrey's cell number. He paused, not recalling a caller I.D. number or Godfrey's name on the text message. Usually, it contained a unique I.D. Michael had one as well. Surely he must have overlooked something. He went back and double checked the text. Sure enough, the message was from an unknown sender. Perhaps it was from a secure line.

Michael knew the only way to find out if it was a drill was to call Godfrey. He punched the number and listened as the phone rang a handful of times before going to a recorded message.

"I'm sorry, the number you are trying to reach has been temporarily disconnected or is no longer in service. Please try your call again later."

"What the . . ." Michael glared at the phone. *Maybe I dialed the wrong number.* He tried Godfrey's office number, but there was no response. *What's going on?* He hung up and tried one last time. *It has to work this time.* He listened as the phone rang, but again it went to the recorded message.

What's going on with his phones? Why would his personal cell number not be working? Michael tried the director's home number. There was no answer. He hung up and tried again. This time he left a message. "Director Godfrey, this is Michael Stevens. It's Saturday evening. I'm responding to an urgent message I received from you. Please call me as soon as you get this." He hung up and tried the director's work cell. After it rang a few times he was ready to leave a message when he heard someone pick up. Michael could hear breathing, but no one spoke.

"Director, is that you?" Still there was no response. The breathing got heavier. Michael asked again, this time a little louder. "Director, is that you?"

There was a faint muttering on the other end. Then Michael heard a sound he could not distinguish.

Michael asked again, "Director, are you there? Director Godfrey, this is Michael."

Then Michael heard some commotion as if furniture was being thrown around. The sound of a man's grunt echoed as if the wind had been knocked out of him or he had fallen.

"Sir, are you okay?"

Then Michael heard a strange voice with a Russian accent. "Who is this? Identify yourself."

Michael sat in dead silence, trying not to breathe, his heart racing. *Who is on the other end? What is going on?*

The Russian voice spoke again. "Identify yourself," Dimitri demanded.

Michael didn't know whether to respond. Perhaps he should make something up. Their phones were encrypted to conceal their numbers and block anyone from intercepting their calls. The stranger couldn't see his number on the director's caller I.D. unless the encryption program had been disabled.

"Who is this?" The ominous Russian voice sent shivers through Michael's spine.

Michael took a deep breath. "I'm trying to reach a friend. I must have dialed a wrong number. I apologize for the inconvenience. Good night." Michael started to pull the phone away from his ear when the voice on the other end spoke again.

"The friend you were trying to reach, what's his name?"

"Why do you ask?" Michael was getting suspicious.

"I'm curious."

"It's not important. I have the wrong number. I apologize."

"Michael, I know you're trying to reach Director Godfrey."

As his words lingered, Dimitri waited for Michael's response.

36

An elderly D.C. woman in her late eighties sat in a hospital chair in the darkness beside her husband of sixty-eight years. He had just passed away. His life support machines had stopped working. The hospital personnel had been unable to get the backup generators online in time. The computers that operated his machines had shut down when the power went out. She watched as the doctors and nurses tried desperately to save him, but without power, there was nothing they could do.

Distraught and heartbroken, the elderly lady had gently kissed her husband's hand as he had taken his last breath. Overcome with grief, she staggered as she attempted to stand. A nurse raced to grab her arm and steady her. The wife grabbed the bed rail and leaned over to kiss her husband on the forehead as she said goodbye. They had known each other since elementary school and married right out of college after he had joined the navy. He had served in World War II and suffered through the Great Depression. He was her one true love. Her world was empty now, her heart broken. She burst into tears, crying hysterically.

Trying to console her, a female nurse helped the woman sit in the chair beside the bed. Then the nurse had to leave to assist other patients, so she left the woman by herself. The widow leaned over and buried her face in her hands, tears pouring from her eyes as she sobbed alone in the darkness of the hospital room. Overcome by grief, she finally collapsed onto the floor, no one there to help her.

37

Matt and John approached Rosslyn as they made their way to Fort Myer Drive. They were scratched and exhausted and covered in dirt and leaves from trekking up the steep hillside through the dense underbrush, having climbed up the ridge from the river and the George Washington Parkway. They walked in silence along the road, each in his own world. The fall night air was brisk and damp as a light mist had begun to fall.

When they neared the main street, they looked for a cab. The traffic lights seemed to be working in Virginia. They turned and looked back over the Key Bridge. Traffic heading into Georgetown was backed up across the bridge. Cars were trying to turn around on the bridge, which only made the situation worse. They hurried anxiously along the sidewalk, checking regularly over their shoulders to see if they were being followed.

John pointed to a sign ahead that read, "Welcome to Virginia."

Matt turned to John and said, "I'm glad we're finally out of D.C."

"Me, too. Hey, do you think there are any cabs in that hotel parking lot?" John asked, pointing to his right.

They were approaching the hotel parking lot entrance when an unmarked black sedan screeched around the bend behind them. It sped toward them before making a sharp right into the parking lot in front of them, blocking the sidewalk.

Before they could run, the driver jumped out and stood with his door open as he banged on the roof. He wore a casual black athletic jacket and a solid black baseball cap. The shadow from the brim of his cap covered his face.

"Matt, get in now! I don't have time to explain," he said, half out of breath. Matt and John looked at each other not knowing what to do.

The man forcefully exclaimed as he pounded on the car roof with his hand, "Get in!"

Matt and John stood there perplexed. The man persisted, "Come on, Matt. We don't have much time. You there," he said, pointing at John, "you're coming too."

Matt wasn't sure what was going on, but the man knew his name. Matt turned to John and slapped him on the arm. "Let's go."

John looked at Matt as if he'd lost his mind.

"Yes, I'm crazy, but we're running out of options. Just get in."

Matt opened the back door and jumped inside. He slid to the other side of the back seat. He leaned over and peered out the open door at John. "Are you coming?"

John took a quick look around and then climbed inside. The driver got back into the car, slammed the door shut, and floored it. He made a screeching U-turn in the parking lot before speeding onto the road toward Route 66.

"Who are you? Where are you taking us? And how do you know my name?" Matt barraged the driver with questions.

Matt didn't get a response. The man didn't even acknowledge him. He focused on the road, occasionally glimpsing in the rearview mirror to see if anyone was following them.

Matt asked his questions again. The man responded, "What was that?"

"Who are you, and how do you know my name?"

The man eyed Matt through the rearview mirror. "You'll have your questions answered when we get to where we're going."

John chimed in. "That's great, but we want answers now."

The driver glanced over his right shoulder. "As I said, you'll have your questions answered when we get where we're going. Until then, just sit tight and be quiet."

A cell phone rang. The driver touched his earpiece. "Yes? Uh-huh. Right. Okay. Got it. Yes, they're with me now. Yes, both of them. We're on our way. Anything else? Yes, sir. Understood. I'll make sure that happens."

The driver touched his earpiece again and resumed the conversation. "Oh, yes, where were we?"

"We wanted answers," John responded, annoyed.

"That's right. Let's begin with introductions, shall we? I'm Riley. I'm on your side." He peeked over his right shoulder and winked at Matt. Matt gave him a quizzical expression as thoughts popped into his mind. *Is he with the NSA?*

"What do you mean you're on our side?" Matt asked.

"Precisely that. I'm part of an organization that protects the country from our enemies. You fell into a hot mess, and my team and I are here to help you out."

"How do you intend to do that?" John asked skeptically.

"You have nothing to worry about." There was optimism in Riley's voice.

"Not worry? It seems like the CIA, FBI, Secret Service, and just about everybody else are chasing us," John pointed out.

Riley grinned deviously into the rearview mirror. "The reason it seems like those organizations are chasing you is because they are." Riley paused to let the words resonate. Matt could tell from Riley's tone that he was serious. Matt could only guess what he'd stumbled across at work given the fact that someone was remoting into their systems and turning off power to the city. Even though Matt had been working undercover with the NSA for months on top secret cyber projects, he hadn't encountered anything like this before.

"You mean to tell me that the CIA and FBI are really after us?" John remarked in disbelief.

"Yes, as well as the U.S. Secret Service, Russian intelligence, the Chinese Ministry of State Security, and we imagine others." He said it so nonchalantly that they thought he might be joking. But they could tell from his somber demeanor that he was serious.

Matt wasn't sure how much Riley knew, but he hoped that he might provide more information. "What's going on downtown with the electricity?" Matt inquired, attempting to understand the severity of the situation. He was well aware of the cyber battles taking place across the world. Matt had been indirectly involved with some high-profile instances in recent years like Stuxnet, Heartbleed, and the Flame virus. He could tell from the day's events that something more significant was happening. He didn't want to blow his cover, so he had to be cautious. Matt still wasn't sure how Riley knew his name or who he was working for. Matt had been instructed during his onboarding before his undercover assignment began that in the event of a major incident or a compromise to his identity, the NSA would send a team for him. He wondered if this was it, though one man wasn't quite a team.

Riley glanced in the rearview mirror at Matt and said, "That wasn't just any security breach of your computer network at

Lucigen. It was much more. Washington, D.C., isn't the only city affected."

"What do you mean?" John asked, surprised.

"Oh yes, much more. This 'security breach' is part of something massive."

Matt inquired further: "How much can you tell us?"

"You will know everything there is to know, just not right now."

"Why not?" John wanted answers and was tiring of the generalities.

"All I can say is that what you've experienced in the past few hours dwarfs in comparison to anything you can imagine. These cyberattacks have been going on for decades. It just so happens that things are coming to a head. You both have the misfortune of getting caught in the middle of it."

The United States imports a significant amount of its electronics from China and other countries in Asia. Many people haven't been following the progress of investments in the United States, but a tremendous number of U.S. companies and businesses are now foreign-owned. A large number of U.S. ports and transportation firms are owned, at least in part, by foreign corporations and even foreign governments. That might sound absurd given all of the hype about homeland security to protect our nation, and it is. But this trend has been increasing as the dollar and U.S economy have weakened. The United States is losing its status as the world economic power as China, Russia, Brazil, India, and others become more competitive. The irony is that many of the politicians in Washington and business people in the United States don't want to admit this fact, or they know what's going on, but they're using it to line their own pockets.

"What we've been dealing with is one huge international game of chess. It's been in a long-term stalemate—until now."

"What do you mean, 'until now'? What's going on?"

"The scales have tilted."

"How so?" John asked, not quite following.

Riley was tiring of the questions and sensed their trepidation, so he pulled to the side of the highway and parked the car. He looked at both of them in the rearview mirror. They could only make out his mouth and chin because his ball cap and glasses covered the rest of his face.

"Listen, I know you want to know what's happening, but I'm asking you to trust me. I promise we will fill you in completely when we get where we're going." Riley was curt and direct. He cocked the gun that was sitting next to him in the seat. Both John and Matt heard the noise.

"Is that a gun?" Matt asked, nervously.

"Yes, but I only intend to use it if you don't cooperate." Riley wasn't joking.

"Fair enough." John, who had been leaning forward, slid slowly back into his seat.

"So now what?" Matt asked.

"After 9/11 and all of the terrorist events and threats, the government built out the Department of Homeland Security," Riley said. "Part of its mission was to coordinate security and intelligence efforts across the federal government. Frankly, I think it's done a pretty poor job. Not only that, you've got groups like the NSA, FBI, and CIA that are like little kids on the same playground who don't play well together. It's indicative of a much larger national security coordination problem, which is part of the reason my group exists. We are an elite joint U.S. government security unit that knows everything that's going on in the intelligence community. We make linkages across all agencies. That is the extent that I can tell you right now. You see, aside from the NSA, most of these organizations didn't have a real clue as to what's been going on in the cyber world until hours ago. Today, they realized what they didn't know. Frankly, it has them very worried, and rightly so. Now they're after what they think will be a major insight into what is happening."

"And what is that?" John asked.

"For one thing, they're after you." He pointed his finger at Matt.

Matt shook his head in disbelief. "After me?"

"Yes, which is why we need to get out of town and to a safe place."

"I never thought my weekend would go like this," Matt said.

"Me, either," John concurred.

"But what about the incident on the Georgetown waterfront? What about the helicopter and the gunshots? Who were they shooting at and why?" Matt wondered aloud.

"The helicopter was the FBI," Riley said. "They were after the two of you, or at least Matt. They may not know that John is involved yet. My guess is they will find out soon enough. The gunshots were for cover."

"For cover? Who fired first?" Matt asked.

"I'm assuming they did. We just returned fire." Riley responded innocently, knowing full well that his team had shot first.

Matt was perplexed. "There was a man near the marina. Is he one of yours?"

"Yes."

"Was it you?" Matt probed further.

Riley remained silent.

Matt raised an eyebrow. "Why would your guy open fire on an FBI helicopter?"

"The gunshots were a distraction. The man you saw was a decoy."

"A decoy?" John replied, surprised. "Why?"

"You needed a decoy to draw the helicopter's attention away from the river. The man purposefully made himself known. In the meantime, it gave you time to get across the river where I could locate you and get you out of town."

"Yeah, but now they think I'm armed and dangerous."

"Yes. That was a risk we had to take."

John slapped his seat and asked, "What do you mean 'you had to take'? I don't buy that for one minute. Now they think Matt is armed, and I'm convinced they won't hesitate to shoot if they see him—or me."

"I doubt that. Matt is too valuable. My orders are to bring him in alive. I'm sure the orders are the same for everyone else who's after him."

"Riley—if that's really your name—you haven't given us any reason to trust you." John's tone was arrogant and cynical. He wasn't much for listening to authority.

"You're right. I haven't given you any reason, yet right now you don't have many options, do you? You've got lots of people chasing you. I'm one of the only people you have right now on your side. You've got two options," Riley said as held up his pistol. "You can shut-up and listen to what I'm telling you, or I can put you both in the trunk until we get where we're going. It's your choice. What's it going to be?"

There was a long pause. Matt and John shrugged their shoulders at each other.

Riley lowered his gun and laid it back on the seat. Matt and John watched anxiously. Riley turned around and stared at them, his face still mostly covered by the baseball cap. They still hadn't gotten a good look at him. Riley reached up and took off his hat and glasses. He glared intently at Matt and John. Matt took one look and gasped in utter disbelief, recognizing him immediately.

"Now will you trust me?"

"You're the guy from . . ." But before Matt could finish, Riley had started the car again and was speeding off.

38

Trapped underground on a D.C. metro train, passengers were getting restless and beginning to panic. A concerned young mother dialed the emergency number.

"911 operator, what is your emergency?"

"We're trapped on a metro train!" the mother yelled frantically.

"Ma'am calm down. You're going to need to be more specific. Where are you?"

"On the metro," the woman panted. "You've got to help us. I can't breathe. It's dark and hot. We can't see anything. We're in a tunnel." The 911 operator could hear panicked voices screaming in the background.

"I need you to remain calm. Is anyone in need of immediate medical attention?"

"No, I don't think so. I can't see anything. It's suffocating in here. There are a lot of people on this train. You've got to get my baby and me out of here. I don't want to die!" The operator could hear the desperation in the woman's voice.

"Ma'am, you're not going to die. Help is on its way. What train are you on? What was your last stop?" The 911 dispatcher heard people tussling on the other end of the phone.

"Hey! Quit pushing me!" the mother shouted as she struggled against other passengers surging toward the exit.

"Ma'am, are you okay?"

"Get off of me . . . Quit pushing!"

The 911 operator could hear people squealing, and the woman on the phone was arguing with someone. A baby was crying in the background.

"Ma'am, what is going on? Talk to me."

"Let go, dammit! Quit pushing! Let go of my phone!"

"Ma'am, what's going on?" The operator felt helpless, unable to get the woman's attention.

"Stop it! Get off me! Where's my baby?" the woman exclaimed as she heard her baby wailing just a few feet away.

The operator overheard a wave of scuffling. "Ma'am, talk to me."

The passengers struggled to open the doors to get out, and they wrestled to get by the mother on the phone and her baby in the stroller.

A man hollered, "Hey! We've almost got the doors open!"

"Move! Get out of the way!" another man demanded as he pushed forcefully through the passengers, knocking the mother to the floor as other panicked passengers stampeded by her toward the opened doors. The baby's screaming eventually stopped.

"Where's my child?" The frantic mother groped blindly through the darkness trying to find her infant. She bumped into the side of the stroller that had been knocked over by the fleeing passengers. She hurriedly searched the stroller as other riders kicked her and trampled her as they fled the train and jumped onto the tracks. Her baby wasn't in the stroller.

"Help . . . help!" the mother cried. She dropped her phone as she frantically searched for her child until she felt a tiny, limp, lifeless arm.

"No! No! No!" the mother wailed as she attempted to pull her baby toward her. But it was too late. Her nine-week-old infant daughter had been crushed by the fleeing mass of passengers, her tiny neck broken, her nascent life snuffed out.

39

Back at FBI headquarters, Agent Burton closed the door to Director Donovan's office and stood at attention waiting to be lambasted for his misconduct during the meeting.

"Have a seat, Agent Burton." The director motioned to one of the chairs in front of his desk.

"There are some things we need to discuss, but I need to know that I can trust you."

"Of course, sir. You can trust me. What is it?"

"We're not the only ones after O'Shea, though I'm sure you're aware of that already." Donovan rocked in his chair with his hands clasped at his waist.

"What do you mean?" Burton uncrossed his legs and leaned toward Donovan's desk.

"I mean the CIA is after him, along with some other organizations."

"And what's the big deal about that? Aren't we all supposed to be working together?"

"Yes, of course."

"What seems to be the issue then?"

Burton leaned back in his chair and threw up his hands.

"It seems that in all of the commotion around here I missed a phone call from an NSA director." Donovan turned and motioned in the direction of his desk phone.

"An NSA director, sir?" Agent Burton's eyes opened wide in surprise.

"Yes."

"Which director?"

"The one for the Tailored Access Operations and National Cyber Security Division, Director Godfrey."

"Really? Why did he call?" Agent Burton asked in disbelief.

"That's not relevant. Godfrey said that O'Shea is one of theirs. Apparently he's been undercover working on their cyber projects. He seems to think this incident at Lucigen might be a breakthrough with one of their projects. They are trying to get to O'Shea first. Frankly, I think it's a load of nonsense. I think they're trying to cover up something, or they know he is somehow involved. The director advised us to stop our search and turn everything over to the NSA immediately. They will take it from there."

"They what?" Agent Burton squawked. "That's a load of crap. We've been tracking him since the beginning. I'll be damned if I'm going to let them take over." His tone rose as he spoke.

"I know, I know." Donovan signaled Burton to calm down.

"What are we going to do, director? It's this jurisdictional nonsense that pisses me off." Burton leaned over and crossed his arms on Donovan's desk.

"I can see that. But there's more."

Agent Burton, dismayed, slumped back into his chair. "But why is the NSA taking this on alone? Why are we left out?

Wouldn't they want our help?" Agent Burton fumed with frustration as Director Donovan filled in more details.

"The Secret Service is involved as well as Homeland Security. The team along with a handful of our agents has been onsite at O'Shea's office at Lucigen since earlier this afternoon."

"You never said anything about that in our update meeting earlier."

Donovan sat silent for a moment.

"Director?"

Director Donovan peered intently at Burton. "We were instructed not to be involved anymore because this is an extremely sensitive national security matter, and they believe there is a mole within the FBI."

"That's absurd," Agent Burton blurted, slapping his hand on the desk.

Donovan rocked back in his chair and threw up his hands. "That's what I've been told."

"How'd they come to that conclusion? Do they have an idea who it is?"

"They didn't say in the message."

"Did you call Director Godfrey back?"

"Yes, I just did. There was no answer."

"What did you want to see me about? Certainly, it wasn't this."

"I initially wanted to talk to you about your attitude in the meeting, yet in light of the message I've received from Director Godfrey, I'd like to postpone that conversation."

"Right now I'd like to discuss this O'Shea matter further. I want you to locate him and bring him to me."

"Is this going to be a one-man operation, or do I pull a team together?"

"Assemble a small team. Take Perez and Hawkins. You work well with them and can rely on them to keep this operation quiet. I can trust you all to get it done, no questions asked."

Donovan could trust Burton with the assignment, but he also would need a fall guy if things didn't work out as he had planned. Who better to take the fall than Agent Burton? He was known for his rogue behavior. If things went south, he could pin things on him.

"You will need something to assist you in your search."

"What's that?"

Donovan leaned over and reached into his side drawer. He pulled out a black metal case. Agent Burton examined it inquisitively.

"Come around here."

"What's in there?" he asked, pointing to the mysterious metal case.

"I'll show you."

"What are those?" Agent Burton asked, pointing at the open case.

"In simplistic terms, they're transponder homing devices, and this is how they're implanted." Donovan held up a jet injection gun. "They're used to track individuals. They're similar to the microchips implanted in animals."

"How does it all work?"

"Think of it as a GPS implanted under the skin."

"Why the homing device? Who's it for?"

"One is for you. The other is for O'Shea."

"For me? Why me?"

"This is a covert operation. We won't be able to communicate freely. The transponder will allow me to know where you are at all times as well as track your vital signs."

"Burton," the director said in a faint voice as he looked directly into his brown eyes, "I need you to trust me on this one. The assignment is critical to our nation's security and for the FBI. Will you do this?"

Agent Burton contemplated his task. It was a tall order. "What the hell, I'll do it."

"Excellent. I'll need to equip you with one of these tracking devices. The other, as I said, is for O'Shea when you find him."

"How will I contact you?"

"With this. It's a burner phone. The numbers are encrypted and untraceable should it fall into the wrong hands. You must keep it on your person at all times."

"So I find O'Shea, implant the device; notify you, and then what?"

"Bring him to me for questioning. I'll take it from there. You won't have to worry about a thing."

"I've got a question: how do I explain my absence and that of my team?"

"Say that I've put you on a special undercover assignment, in case anyone asks. I don't think anyone will. But just remember: lives and futures are at stake."

"What's this about an FBI mole?"

Donovan remained silent. The barrage of questions was making him uneasy. It wasn't the time or place to give Burton the full story. That was Donovan's business.

"Listen," he said, "there are times we do things that we don't agree with because it's our duty to our country."

Donovan liked living the high life and providing a lavish lifestyle for his family. He'd gotten into deep financial trouble years ago. A group of U.S. businessmen had bailed him out in exchange for favors, namely making some federal investigations stop and having vital evidence disappear, including witnesses. Donovan regretted his actions and hadn't realized at the time that the businessmen he'd helped had ties to Russia and the Middle East. By the time he found out, it was too late. He was trapped, and his associates knew it. He wasn't the mole Director Godfrey referenced, but his actions had caught the attention of other federal intelligence agencies that were tracking correspondence with questionable foreign individuals. Donovan sold out himself and his bureau, but this was a chance for redemption. By getting O'Shea and finding out who was behind the network security breach, he hoped he could restore his dignity, if only with himself, and absolve whatever wrongs he'd caused before things went any further. Finding O'Shea was the first step in that direction, and he needed Burton's help.

"Sir, with all due respect, you've lost me."

"I know. You're free to choose whether you want the assignment," Donovan said. "I only offer the opportunity because I think you are the most capable agent to lead it. So what's it going to be?"

Agent Burton pondered the offer. This unique assignment fascinated him. Meanwhile, Donovan watched him, waiting patiently.

"Okay, director, count me in."

"Great. I'll need to insert your tracking device. Please roll up your sleeve."

Agent Burton rolled up his sleeve and held out his right arm.

Donovan grabbed his wrist and turned over his arm. Then he pulled out an alcohol rub and wiped down Burton's lean, muscular forearm. Burton felt the cooling sensation as the alcohol evaporated.

Donovan picked up the injection gun and said, "I'd recommend sitting down. This procedure will only take a second.

You'll feel a sharp pain, and you may get nauseous and dizzy, but it will wear off shortly."

Burton hated the idea of an electronic tracking device being injected into his arm, and so he titled his head away. Donovan positioned the gun and pulled the trigger. Burton heard the sound of compressed air discharge. He winced as the pain shot through his arm and into his shoulder and neck. He started to feel light-headed, so he steadied himself against the desk.

"Are you okay?"

"Yes, I'll be fine. I just got dizzy there for a moment."

"You can take a look if you'd like."

Burton peeked at his right arm. There was a small red mark at the point of entry where he was bleeding slightly. He ran his fingers over it. It was tender. He also could feel a small cyst-like lump just under his skin.

Donovan noticed him flinch and said, "The pain will dissipate soon enough. Now step over here." Burton walked to where the briefcase was open on the desk. There was a control panel inside with a laptop-size computer screen. Donovan turned it on, and a satellite map of the United States appeared.

"Here, put your arm under this scanner. I need to calibrate the device. It will only take a minute." Donovan focused on the small computer case on his desk and entered some commands. Agent Burton put his forearm under a laser scanning sensor attached to the box. Donovan reached for Burton's arm.

"Hold it there for ten seconds longer."

Burton endured the procedure as Donovan adjusted the settings on the computer. "I think we're all set. Here, take a look." Donovan pointed at the small screen.

Agent Burton viewed the monitor that showed an aerial GPS image of a city. "I take it that red flashing dot is me?"

"That's correct," Donovan replied, nodding.

"Are you going to lug that computer case around all the time so you know where I am?"

"No."

Burton rolled his sleeve back down. "Then how will you be able to follow me?"

"Trust me. I'll locate you. Now when you find O'Shea, I want you to equip him with one of these tracking devices in his upper back. You may need to use one of these to make him unconscious so he won't resist," he said, handing Burton a small container of pills and a clear plastic case with a syringe and vial.

"What about that USB-like key you had earlier? What's that for?"

"For opening this." He handed Burton the black metal box on his desk. "You can use the computer in here to monitor the communication traffic across the intelligence community. It will let you access our systems as well as the NSA's and CIA's classified systems. It's a mobile SIPRNet system, and you will find the latest information you need about O'Shea in it."

"But sir, how is it that you're able to connect the NSA's and CIA's systems?" Burton paused as Donovan gave him a deadly stare. "Forget I asked."

"Don't worry. It's a joint intelligence system to which I have secret compartmentalized access. Unless things change, the next time we talk will be after you find O'Shea. Now go find Perez and Hawkins and bring them here so I can brief them. You can take these." Donovan handed Burton a black duffle bag to carry the items.

Burton glanced at his watch and saw that it was already late Saturday afternoon. It was going to be a long night. As he walked by the secretary's desk and into the hallway he could hear the

SIOC bustling with activity. He walked by the large glass windows and peered inside. It was just as busy as before the meeting. A dozen or so analysts were working diligently at their computer terminals while others talked on the phone. *Would the director tell the staff to stop their search or have them continue? What would the NSA do if they knew he hadn't halted the search? Who were they to call off the FBI's search?* Those and related thoughts ran through his mind as he continued down the hallway, through a series of secure doors, and eventually made his way to the parking garage elevators.

40

Michael stood frozen in Big Tony's office, not knowing what to say or do as the Russian's voice echoed in his ears.

The man repeated himself. "Michael, I know you're trying to reach Director Godfrey."

Michael paused. Who was this man?

"Yes . . ."

"That's what I thought."

"Who are you?" Michael demanded.

"You'll know when you need to." Dimitri wasn't getting what he needed from Godfrey, so he decided to go straight to what he believed was the next best source.

"What's that supposed to mean? What have you done with Director Godfrey?"

"The director is fine. You don't need to worry about him."

"Don't worry . . . I heard all that commotion as if someone where being beat up. I don't believe you."

"I don't expect you to believe anything. I'm telling you how things are," Dimitri barked.

The line went silent. Michael stood quietly in Tony's office. Finally, Michael let his temper get the best of him. "Who the hell are you?"

"You have no idea, but you will do what you're told. Do I make myself clear?"

"Or what?"

"Or we're going to have fun with the director and your lovely wife, Kate. I know you're enjoying your weekend in New York right now. How do you like the honeymoon suite? It's an elegant room. And you have great taste in Italian restaurants, from what I hear." Dimitri had no plan to hurt either the director or Kate, but Michael couldn't know that.

"I swear if you lay a hand on her I'll—."

"You'll what? You have no idea who you're dealing with."

Michael didn't know what to say. The man knew things. "I promise you, if you lay a hand on Kate I will hunt you down."

"Of course you will," Dimitri said dismissively. "Now, I'm not going to repeat this. You will do what I tell you when I tell you." His voice was direct and firm.

Michael paused. He didn't know what he was getting into. The man had threatened Kate. He swore that whoever was behind all of this would not get away with it.

"You're not saying anything," Dimitri said. "Do I make myself clear?"

"Yes," Michael responded reluctantly.

"Excellent. Now listen very carefully to my instructions."

Michael intently listened as he took notes.

41

Hours earlier, before tracking down O'Shea, Riley had been at FBI headquarters. He was surveilling the FBI's activity for the NSA to learn what they knew about Matt O'Shea and the security breach at Lucigen. Riley had been monitoring Director Donovan's calls and emails for weeks. The team Riley worked with had tapped Donovan's office and phones, so Riley had been listening to his conversations all day. He heard Donovan's conversation with Agent Burton and the message from Director Godfrey. Riley couldn't have Burton interfering with things. Riley had NSA associates who were embedded on Donovan's team months ago in an attempt to find the mole in the FBI. They were part of a joint cyberterrorism and cyber defense task force, but Donovan didn't truly know who they were working for. FBI headquarters was a short distance from O'Shea's company, so Riley and his NSA associates were able to keep tabs on them both.

As Agent Burton opened his car door, he heard the sound of footsteps approaching quickly behind him, and then he heard a gun being cocked. He spun around to meet an armed masked man about ten feet away.

"Who are you?"

"Let me see your hands. You and I are going to talk."

Burton did as he was instructed. "About what?"

"Your conversation with Director Donovan," Riley said, motioning with his gun for Burton to start walking toward the other end of the parking garage.

"And why is that? He was reprimanding me, if that's what you're talking about." Agent Burton didn't recognize the masked man's voice.

"Oh, really?" There was skepticism in Riley's voice. "You sure it didn't have to do with the search for Matt O'Shea?"

"I don't know what you're talking about." Burton moved forward.

Riley took a step back. "Easy there. Don't move."

"What do you know about Matt O'Shea?"

Agent Burton scoffed, "I don't know what you're talking about."

"I beg to differ."

"Why do you think I'm looking for Matt O'Shea?"

"I'm assuming nothing," Riley said with certainty.

"Then how are you so sure?" Burton stopped walking and turned, crossing his arms in defiance.

Agent Burton saw the masked man reach into his pocket and pull out a digital voice recorder. Riley pressed a button on the device. There was a brief silence before Agent Burton heard the director's voice. It was from the conversation they'd had earlier.

"Where'd you get that? Who are you, and why are you snooping around the director's office?" Burton uncrossed his arms and moved like he was going to engage Riley, but he stopped.

"It's precautionary for surveillance purposes. And who I am is of no importance to you right now."

"So you heard the entire conversation?"

"Every last word. I know exactly what you're up to." Riley reached under his jacket. "Put this on." He tossed a hood to Burton. "You're coming with me. Now turn around and put your hands behind your back."

Agent Burton did as instructed, and Riley handcuffed Burton's hands behind his back.

"Where are we going?" he asked as he angled his head to glance over his shoulder.

"Where we can talk in private." They moved through the garage to a black, unmarked, windowless government work van. Riley opened the rear doors. "Get in," Riley said as he grabbed Burton's arm and ushered him toward the back bumper. Agent Burton jerked his arm away.

"Suit yourself," Riley responded in an indignant tone.

Riley grabbed Agent Burton and shoved him forcefully into the back of the van. Burton hit his head on the metal floor as he fell. He cursed out loud and whipped around ready to fight, but it was futile given that his hands were cuffed behind his back, and he was wearing a hood. Riley climbed in behind Burton, dragging him further inside before closing the back doors with a loud thud.

Riley sat down on one of the metal benches along the side wall of the van. "Now where were we?"

"I don't know; you tell me," Agent Burton responded, indignant as he squirmed on the floor, working his way to a seated position.

"Listen. You have two options: either cooperate and this will be easy, or don't, and this will be difficult." Riley pushed the end of the gun barrel against Burton's forehead. "It's your choice."

There was a long pause. Agent Burton had no other options. Besides, he was curious to find out what this stranger had to say. He'd bugged the director's office, so who knew what other information he had that Donovan hadn't told him.

"Fine, I'll cooperate." He readjusted himself in his sitting position with his long legs outstretched and his arms behind his back to help prop himself up.

"Good. I figured you would. Although it doesn't seem like it right now, you and I are on the same side."

As Agent Burton sat, he replayed his conversation with the director in his head. Donovan said the FBI had been pulled off the case because there was a mole. Burton thought it might have been the director, but apparently that wasn't the case—or was it?

"You're the mole the director was referring to in our conversation, aren't you?"

There was a moment of silence before Agent Burton reasserted his accusation. "You're the mole, aren't you? That's why the FBI was told to stop its involvement in the O'Shea case."

"I wouldn't say I'm the mole."

"There are others?" Burton was bewildered by Riley's comment. *Could there be more informants the FBI didn't know about?*

"Yes." Riley nodded, even though Burton couldn't see him.

"Others within the FBI?" Agent Burton asked, raising his voice slightly.

"Yes."

"Is Director Donovan one?"

"I can't say for sure, but we have our concerns about him."

"You don't know if there are other moles within the FBI?"

"It's very possible. I can tell you there are moles within other intelligence agencies. I'm sure you're familiar with the National Security Administration and the Department of Defense. You heard of those employees recently in the news and all the files they released. I'd venture the Russians and/or the Chinese got to them, if not others."

"Really? How do you know?" Burton was always briefed on possible insider threats.

"We have our ways."

"I'm sure you do. Why were you snooping in the director's office, and why are you after O'Shea?"

"I tapped the director's office to find out certain information. I'm not after Matt O'Shea, at least not at the moment."

"You're not?" Agent Burton sounded surprised.

"No, but I do know where he is, or at least where he's going."

"How's that?" Burton asked, perplexed. He and his colleagues had been searching for O'Shea for hours and turned up nothing. Not only that, there were other intelligence authorities after him.

Riley sensed Agent Burton's puzzlement. "You're probably wondering how I know where he is already?"

Burton nodded.

"Well, it's similar to the way the director is tracking you with that device in your forearm, only O'Shea is carrying his."

"Carrying it?"

"Yes. It's in O'Shea's phone as well as the computer equipment he took from his office."

"What is O'Shea's role in all of this?"

"He's become inadvertently involved in a national security issue, as I'm sure you're aware, related to the blackout that's occurred in the city."

"Why all the hassle for just one man?"

"He's one very valuable man because of what he potentially knows and because of what he has in his possession."

"What do you mean?" Burton played dumb in an effort to glean more information.

"As you know, this all started with a network security breach at Lucigen that resulted in a power outage in parts of Washington, D.C. That wasn't a coincidence."

"Yes. I know that. But why did that turn into a major manhunt for one lowly computer software engineer?"

"We're after the source of the breach. We believe there is a massive cyberattack coming. We just don't know exactly how, when, or by whom."

"You think O'Shea knows something about it?"

"Absolutely. After the breach, O'Shea ran diagnostics tests on his computer to assess the extent of the damage. We believe he has those results and possibly even the code itself. Those may inform us about the next cyberattack."

"How do I fit into this?"

"I can't have you interfering." His tone was abrupt as he stomped his foot.

Just then Riley's phone rang. "Hello? Yes . . . Yes . . . Any news? Okay, I'm on my way." There was a sense of urgency in his voice. Matt was still in Georgetown, and Riley needed to get to him fast.

Burton had been sitting up, but Riley reached over and grabbed him under his armpits and dragged him to the other side of the van.

"Hey there, easy!" Agent Burton complained as he fought back against Riley.

Riley took a set of shackles and clasped them around Burton's ankles.

"What the . . . What are you doing?" Burton exclaimed as he kicked his legs and shook the chains.

"I can't have you running off talking to anyone, especially not Director Donovan."

Riley reached into his pocket and pulled out a syringe filled with a clear liquid. He took off the cap. "Be very still if you want to live."

Burton stopped squirming, breathing heavily through his nose. It gave Riley enough time to insert the syringe. Burton felt a brief, sharp pain in the side of his neck, and a burning sensation spread rapidly throughout his head and body. Burton started to resist, but before he could fight back his body relaxed, and he fell unconscious.

Riley grabbed his shoulders and lowered him to the floor of the van where he rested on his side. "There you go. That will keep you out of the way for a while."

Riley moved into the driver's seat. He checked to make sure no one else was nearby in the garage before he climbed out and locked the door behind him.

Riley walked a short distance to his car, unlocked it, and climbed inside. He reached into the armrest of his center console and pulled out a handheld computer device. "Now let's see where you are, O'Shea." Riley saw a satellite image of Washington, D.C., on his screen. Zooming in closer so he could see the building tops and streets, he spotted O'Shea's precise location. "There you are, not far at all." Riley started the car and sped off through the garage.

42

Michael stood in Big Tony's office as he listened to every task the Russian was asking him to do. He didn't know what to say. The Russian on the other end of the line meant business, and Michael didn't want to risk having anything happen to the director and, more importantly, to Kate.

"Now, did you get all of that?" Dimitri asked.

"Yes, I did."

"I want to make sure because you'll need to do exactly as I say."

"Yes, I understand."

"Good."

"What if I need to contact you?" Michael asked.

"Don't worry. I'll find you."

There was something about how he said it in his Russian accent that sent chills down Michael's spine. The man had Director Godfrey's cell phone, but how?

"How will you know when I've gotten to where I need to go?"

"I'll know," he said in a cold voice. "My associate will notify me. Now go." Dimitri ended the call.

Michael's mind wandered back to Kate. *What will I tell her? How can I explain all of this?* He stared at the desk and shook his head.

Then came a series of knocks at the door. Michael cautiously peered up to see who it was, but he remembered he had locked the door to the office. He leaned against the desk in silence. The soft knocks came again.

"Who is it?" he asked.

"Michael, it's me." He heard Kate's sweet voice. "Is everything okay?"

He didn't know how to answer that question anymore.

"Michael, are you all right?" There was deep concern in her voice.

"Yes," he replied reluctantly, even though he wasn't. The director had been kidnapped, and now Kate was at risk.

"May I come in?"

"Not right now. I'll be out in a minute." Michael reflected on the conversation he'd just had. It was going to be a long night.

43

"You're one of the maintenance guys at our company, aren't you?" Matt asked, surprised.

There was silence from the front seat. Riley was focused on the road. It was getting late, and there was much work to be done.

Matt asked again, this time leaning over the back seat: "You're one of the maintenance guys at our company, aren't you?"

Riley turned his head slightly and looked in the rearview mirror. Matt couldn't quite see the look on Riley's face, but then Riley responded: "Yes, I am. How else do you think I can get access to all parts of your building without being questioned?"

"But how did you locate us?" Matt asked, unsure as to how he could have caught up to them so quickly.

"It's my job. Besides, there are a lot of things I know about you." He paused momentarily. "And there's a lot I know about John, too." He glanced at John via the rearview mirror.

John leaned toward Matt, a skeptical look on his face. Matt returned the look.

Riley saw their reactions and said, "You both seem confused."

John spoke up first. "Yes, we are."

"Matt, who do you think called you last night while you were waiting outside the Laughing Jack?"

"That was you?" Matt was dumbfounded.

"Yes, but you didn't answer. I was one of a couple of people attempting to reach you last night. One of your bosses called you too." He was referring to Godfrey. "We called to warn you about the breach. That's why you were told to go back to your office. You obviously ignored the directions."

"I thought it was a prank call."

"No, it was all too real," Riley stated matter-of-factly.

"How is it you knew where we were? How are you tracking us?" Matt asked.

"There are a couple of ways, but one is in your pocket."

When Matt went undercover he was given a watch and a phone equipped with a tracking device. He was instructed to keep both on or near his person at all times. He had forgotten about them in the heat of the moment.

Riley saw Matt's eyebrows raise as a light bulb went off in Matt's head. "So do you know now?"

Matt wiggled in his seat and pulled his cell phone from his hip pocket.

"That's it."

John looked at the phone in Matt's hand. "With that?"

"Yes, with that. Nearly every phone now is equipped with a GPS transponder. I believe you also have some items from work in your bag." Riley gave Matt an implicating look. "You can go ahead and pull them out. We'll need those later."

Matt gave him a baffled look. *How the hell does he know all of this?* Matt reached into his backpack and pulled out the computer parts he'd taken.

Riley looked in the mirror and said, "That seems about right."

Matt reached back into his bag and pulled out the rest of the items, setting them on his lap. There were a couple of thumb drives, a motherboard, the cellular network card, wrinkled computer paper, and some knotted wires and cables.

John glanced at Matt. "What are you doing with all those? Did you steal them?" John was mystified as to why Matt had so many computer parts in his bag. "Are those all related to the security breach?"

Matt gave John a nod, but he didn't want to say it. Riley took the liberty of speaking up for Matt.

"Yes. Matt needed to take the evidence because it contains vital information about the breach of your network systems."

"What type of information?" John asked.

"Crucial information. Those computer components may contain malware. The nasty, vicious kind that destroys entire control systems and computer networks and takes out power to anything that's connected to it that it can infect."

"Are there other computer devices with malicious code?"

Riley gave John a stare. "Lots more; more than you can imagine."

"Define 'lots' for me."

Riley gave John a stern glare in the rearview mirror. "Hundreds of billions."

"Holy . . . You mean to tell me there are billions of potentially compromised computers and electronic devices in the world?"

"That's precisely what I mean," he said, his tone cold and grim.

"How did they get there?" John probed further.

"That's what you will find out once we get where we're going. For now, I'd suggest that you both rest. It's going to be a long night. I'll wake you up when you need to pay attention. For now, we'll be on Route 66."

Matt and John leaned back in their seats as they zoomed down the highway, heading west toward the Shenandoah Mountains.

44

Director Godfrey awoke to find his hands and legs unbound and felt the softness of a bed under him. The bed was small, more like a cot, with just a plain white sheet, pillow, and blanket on top of a thin mattress. He rubbed his eyes and stretched his arms. It felt good to be free. As the blurriness fled from his eyes, he examined his hands and wrists. There were faint red marks from where the ropes had been fastened. He sat up and squinted around what appeared to be a prison cell. He was in a holding room of some sort, but it was unusually bright because the walls were painted white.

He banged on the wall nearest the bed. It appeared to be made of solid concrete. The ceiling was unusually high, almost fifteen feet. Radiant lights beamed down. There was a metal door with a small rectangular glass window and a narrow opening under it about chest high. A tiny metal sink and toilet were squeezed into the back corner. The chilly, dry air was a stark contrast from the hot, musty room filled with cigar smoke where he'd been before. He sluggishly crawled out of bed and moved to the door in an attempt to peer through the window, but he couldn't see anything.

"Good evening, director." The voice of Dimitri echoed against the walls. Director Godfrey searched to see where the voice was coming from. Dimitri was speaking through a microphone built into the metal door. "I see that you're awake. I trust that you got some rest."

"Is that you, Dimitri? Where am I?"

"Yes, it's me. You're in a holding cell."

"But where?"

"We need to keep you in a secure place for your own safety." He intentionally avoided responding to the question about where. Godfrey didn't know that he was being held at a U.S. government facility in New York City.

"What do you want with me?"

"You have knowledge that we believe will help us."

"How so?"

"We need to know more about Michael Stevens and Matt O'Shea."

"I told you everything already."

"Yes, but we believe you're holding back information, specifically about the code you're working with. That said, we will continue to ask you until you provide us with what we need. Godfrey, right now I need you to step away from the door, turn toward the back of the cell, and put your hands behind your head."

Godfrey stepped back and did as instructed. Then he heard the metal bolts of the door unlock and the hinges creak as it slowly swung open.

Dimitri entered the room with two armed guards. Godfrey glared at him. "You're not Dimitri. You look nothing like the man I knew."

"You are partially correct." After he went into hiding, Dimitri had undergone reconstructive surgery on his face so no one would recognize him. He did so because the KGB had killed his family and was looking for him. But his idiomatic expressions and voice still gave him away.

Dimitri motioned to the two guards. They covered Godfrey's head with a black hood and handcuffed him before escorting him out of the cell. Then they all walked a short distance down the hall to an interrogation room. It was empty except for a single chair in the middle with a metal table against one of the side walls. There were solid gray concrete walls on three sides, and a wall length, two-way mirror on the fourth side, facing the chair.

The guards sat Godfrey down in the hard steel chair, situated his arms behind the chair, and secured them to a steel ring that was anchored by a metal floor plate at the base of the seat. They strapped his ankles to shackles in front of the chair.

Godfrey heard the sound of several light switches being flipped on. Although he was blindfolded, he could see glimmers of the bright lights through the cloth. Once he was properly secured, one of the guards removed Godfrey's hood. The intense beams shining into Godfrey's face blinded him. He could feel the heat from the lamps radiating in his direction.

As Godfrey tried to divert his eyes from the light, he heard Dimitri's voice again.

"Come now, Godfrey. There's no reason to withhold information from an old friend."

"Withholding?" he blurted out. "That's nonsense. I've told you everything I know. You still haven't told me why my team is under surveillance, let alone why you've kidnapped me."

"First, we need to locate Michael Stevens and Matt O'Shea, and we need to do it tonight."

"I already told you that Michael and his wife are in New York City for the weekend. I don't know where Matt is. What else can I say?"

"Where are the Stevens' staying?"

"I don't know. Why would Michael tell me that?"

"We checked your call logs. It appears you've been trying to reach Michael a handful of times since yesterday. What's that all about?"

"Nothing," the director replied nonchalantly.

"That's crap, and you know it. Nobody calls half a dozen times in a twenty-four-hour period unless it's important, especially late on a Friday night. There's something you're not telling us. What is it, Godfrey?" Dimitri sounded desperate for answers.

"My sense is that you already know why I was calling him."

"Then why don't you just tell me what I want to hear? Why were you trying so desperately to reach Michael?" Godfrey wasn't going to inform him that he knew about the breach at Lucigen even before it occurred. That's why he was calling O'Shea, to get him to go back to the office to try to stop it before things got out of hand. Godfrey also knew about all of the scans and diagnostics tests O'Shea had conducted after he'd discovered the breach, but he didn't know what Matt had found, if anything.

Director Godfrey paused and sat in silence before changing topics. "What is this place?"

"Like I said before, it's a holding facility," Dimitri replied curtly, annoyed with Godfrey's attempts to avert the questions.

"Are there other people here?" Godfrey asked.

"Yes."

"Who do you work for? Who funds all of this?" the director asked, moving his head in a circle.

"We have our sources."

"Are you with a government organization?"

"Partially."

"What do you mean by 'partially'?"

"Exactly that."

"How can you work 'partially' with a government organization? That's the most ridiculous thing I've ever heard."

"Let me put it this way, then. We're associated with many governments. And we have employees who work for the government, U.S. and foreign. You might commonly refer to them as moles, similar to O'Shea's role at Lucigen."

"Who funds you?"

"Various sources, but primarily the private sector. We own the rights to many patents, and we retain financial holdings in various companies, mainly in the energy, medicine, defense, and technology industries. We maintain our independence, yet at the same time we have almost an infinite source of funding as well as access to the information we need to do our work. The U.S. government doesn't want to be directly associated with us for obvious reasons, but we are closely linked. Someone has been meddling in our business affairs, and we're trying to find out who. The code you and your team found is almost identical to one we discovered in the control systems of our companies and our organization. We want to know how it got there and what its purpose is."

"That sounds most unfortunate," Godfrey responded sarcastically. "What other governments are you working for? The Russians? The Chinese? The North Koreans?"

Dimitri paused before responding. "Every country and organization has dirty work it needs done and special intelligence gathering that's required to protect its citizens, and then there are the particular personal business interests."

Dimitri knew that organizations and governments that preferred not be involved, at least not directly, were willing to pay top dollar for his services. No business executive or company

wanted to be linked to corporate espionage, stealing trade secrets, or intellectual property from other global organizations
and competitors. That could destroy consumer and shareholder
confidence and negatively impact financial markets and stock
prices. And there were government officials, both U.S. and foreign, who didn't want to be associated with or linked to various
types of clandestine activities. That way they could claim igno-
rance if anything were exposed.

"Are you working for the Russians?" Godfrey pressed again.

"No. Definitely not the Russians."

"No?" Godfrey asked, surprised. He was certain that Dimitri
had defected to Russia. It didn't make sense how Dimitri could
have gotten back into the United States undetected, let alone
kidnap a senior NSA official like himself. It wouldn't be long
before a search party was dispatched to find him. *Dimitri must be
working with someone inside the NSA, but who?*

"Years ago when I worked with you at the CIA, the Russians
tried to turn me against the U.S. As I told you before, they
threatened to kill my family and relatives. I did what I needed
to do."

"That whole media story about you and your friends being
caught in a storm off the coast of Portugal and your boat sinking
was a lie."

"The story was true."

Dimitri and his friends had, in fact, been caught in a horrible storm. Their boat was torn apart and eventually sank, leaving him as the sole survivor. His naval training had served him
well, and he was able to survive for a few days by floating on the
remains of the broken boat with life preservers tied together.
He was rescued by a fishing vessel one night when they saw the
homing beacon light on his life vest.

The captain and the crew nursed him back to health while at sea. They returned to the mainland to a small fishing town a week or so later. The captain gave him some money because Dimitri had lost everything at sea, including all forms of identification. He found a tiny motel and stayed there for a couple of days until he figured out his next move. While at a café one morning, he heard the news on TV about the sailboat and his friends, and how the Portuguese Navy found no survivors.

Two weeks passed, and the authorities were still conducting searches for survivors, but they found none. Dimitri used the situation as a chance to go underground. He had no plans to defect or to support the Russians. But the Russian FSB apparently didn't believe that he'd died. Dimitri later found out, as he said earlier, that the FSB had killed his family. They were tortured and then gunned down in their home. It was reported in the news as a brutal robbery, but Dimitri knew better, and he vowed to get even. Dimitri located one of the CIA's safe houses in Lisbon. He broke in and was able to get cash, equipment, and a create fake I.D.—including a passport—so he could get out of the country. He reconnected with some retired intelligence expat colleagues in Europe and North Africa who helped hide him in exchange for his assistance with some Russian and Chinese matters. It was a chance for revenge, so he eagerly accepted.

Godfrey shook his head. How could he not have known, even after all these years, that Dimitri was still alive? Not only that, how could Dimitri have reconnected with the NSA without him knowing? More importantly, who at the NSA and CIA was helping Dimitri?

"You seem baffled, Godfrey."

"I am. How were you able to stay hidden all these years? It's been over a decade. Why didn't you contact me? I would have helped you. What are you working on now? Who are you work-ing with?"

Dimitri wanted to answer his friend's questions, but there were national security matters at hand. "Godfrey, I need your co-operation. I need to know about Michael's project and O'Shea's role in all of this."

Godfrey was about to respond when the phone in Dimitri's pocket started ringing.

Dimitri pulled it out and looked at the caller I.D. "If you will excuse me for a minute." Dimitri stepped out to take the call.

45

Michael exited Big Tony's upstairs office with a solemn, exhausted expression. Kate stood in front of him, confused and concerned. He motioned for them to head down the hall toward the steps.

"You need to take dinner back to the hotel and wait for me in our room. Don't open the door until you know it's me. I'll knock hard once, pause, knock hard three times, pause, and then knock three more times. Seven total knocks, you hear me, seven. If anyone knocks in any other way, don't answer."

Kate gasped and put her hand over her mouth. "Oh, my gosh, Michael, are we in danger?"

"For the moment we're both safe. We need to make sure it stays that way, so there are a few things I need to do tonight." Michael tried to sound confident, but he was concerned that something terrible might occur tonight or was already happening with Eminent Eclipse.

"For the moment?" Kate's voice trailed off.

"Everything will be okay, but for now I need you to please do what I say and go back to the hotel. Lock the door behind you and wait until I come for you."

"When will that be?"

"Honestly, I don't know. It may be morning before I return."

"Morning?"

"Yes."

"Are you going back to D.C.?"

"I can't tell you anything. Please . . . just do as I say."

"What if I need to call you?"

"Don't. I'll contact you when I have a better handle on things. Whatever you do, don't involve the authorities."

"Michael, I'm scared. I've never seen you like this. Please be careful."

"I will." Michael stood solemnly at the top of the steps.

"What will we tell Big Tony and the others? Should we leave together? I don't want them to see you rush out without an explanation. They may ask questions that I can't answer." Kate was nervous.

"I'll leave first. I'll tell Tony that I have a surprise for you and that I have to get back to the hotel before you do. I think that's believable." He smiled lovingly at her, and she smiled back. He stepped closer and put his arms around her and gazed deeply into her eyes. "I love you. Everything will be all right. Trust me."

She gazed back at him. "I do trust you. I'm just scared."

"I know, but we'll get through this together."

"Yes, we will."

He leaned over and gently kissed her on the lips, reluctantly pulling away as he looked deeply into her eyes. She must have sensed it as well. When Kate saw the loving look on Michael's face, she perked up.

"I know. You don't have to say anything."

He smiled back at her and then said, "I need to go now." He tried to pull away, but he didn't want the moment to end. He didn't know if or when he would hold her again.

"You'd better get going." She pushed his arms gently away. Then she reached up and pulled him closer to kiss him again. "I love you."

"I'll see you soon." He pulled his arms away and hurried down the stairs. Big Tony was still in the kitchen. He heard the footsteps coming, and he checked to see Michael rushing by the door.

"Hey, where are you off to in such a hurry?" he hollered as he poked his head out of the kitchen.

"I have a surprise for Kate, and I need to head back to the hotel."

"What kind of surprise?"

Michael gave Big Tony a subtle nod and a wink that a guy would understand.

"Ah, okay then." And then Big Tony chuckled before he added, "But you haven't eaten yet." Tony held up his hands in disappointment.

"I know. Can we get everything to go? Kate will take it with her."

"You sure you don't want to stick around to eat?"

"Tony, I appreciate all your effort to make this a special dinner. I wouldn't run like this if it weren't important." Michael was sincere.

"When will you be back?" "Very soon, perhaps even tomorrow. How does that sound?" There was a cheerfulness in Michael's voice.

"That sounds great."

Michael reached out and firmly shook Big Tony's hand. "I'll see you again soon, my friend."

"I look forward to it."

As Michael headed for the door Big Tony hollered, "Mama will be upset that she missed you! I'll tell her you said goodbye!"

"Thanks. I appreciate that."

Michael then hurried outside, flagged down a cab, and climbed inside.

"Where to?"

"The West Side docks. I'll give you the address when we get closer."

"You got it," the driver responded in a thick New York accent.

As they sped off, Michael glanced back toward Il Romano. He could fend for himself, but he worried about Kate. Michael would do everything he could to make sure she stayed safe.

46

In the back seat of the car, Matt and John struggled to sleep. The seat was uncomfortable, and they had too much on their minds. Both stared aimlessly out the side windows into the darkness of the surrounding forest.

Finally, John reached down and snatched the motherboard out of Matt's backpack. "I can't sleep. My mind is too damn busy trying to figure out what the hell is going on. You mean to tell me this motherboard has malware and a backdoor built into it? Does anyone know about this?"

"Yes and yes." Riley gave John a smug look.

"Are you going to tell us why this is on Matt's computer?" John continued.

"Not now, but we will tell you when we get to our destination."

"Why not now? No one else is around. It's not like anyone is listening."

"You'd be surprised. I'm leery of discussing what we already have."

"How so? Are there bugs in the car's computer system?" John asked, sarcastically slapping the back of the driver's seat.

But as he looked into the mirror and saw Riley's face, he realized this was no joke. "So there could be malware in the car too?"

"Yes. Anything with a computer or electronic component could contain malicious software, whether it was put there intentionally or downloaded inadvertently."

"And why would someone put malware in a car?"

"Because many conversations take place in a car. It's a great location to gather information. Most new cars rely on computers, even if they aren't fully run by them. There's the movement toward driverless cars. Consider all of the disruptions and accidents it would cause if cars were to suddenly stop working or malfunction because of computer system errors."

Matt interrupted the conversation. "Where are we going?"

"A secure, remote location where we can talk more openly. We'll also be able to more precisely examine the computer parts you took and what you were able to save on your thumb drive."

John shook his head. "How far is it?"

"A decent distance. You see, the level of this national security situation has elevated to a code black status, so we're going where my colleagues can help."

"I thought the security levels only went to red. Are we being attacked? Do we have a cyber Pearl Harbor happening?" John asked sarcastically.

Riley looked sternly at them in the mirror. His expression was clear.

"Really? You're serious?" Matt asked. He struggled to get the words out.

"Level black means an attack is happening. You've clearly heard talk about a possible cyber Pearl Harbor," Riley said.

"Yes. Those conversations have been going on for years in the cyber communities." Matt had held such discussions with his hacker friends many times, but he never considered such a thing would actually happen. But then that's why the original Pearl Harbor had happened: nobody thought it would to the United States.

"We don't anticipate this being a cyber Pearl Harbor."

"That's a relief," John said as he sat up in his seat.

"From what we know, it could be much worse than that." Riley had their attention now.

"What? Are we talking cyber Armageddon?" John asked.

"Maybe not, but it could be close. That's why we need Matt's help."

"What makes Matt so special?"

"Perhaps Matt will tell you." Riley glanced at Matt through the rearview mirror.

Matt looked at Riley. *Does Riley know I'm working undercover for the NSA? Does Riley know about my background at MIT and side activities as a hacktivist?* Matt wasn't prepared to say anything—not yet. He wouldn't risk blowing his cover until he absolutely had to. Riley was alluding to something, but for all John knew, Matt was just a regular computer network engineer like himself.

"I don't know what he's talking about, John," Matt said, trying to deflect the conversation. "How long before we get to this secret place? Surely you can divulge that much information," Matt pleaded in a continuing effort to move the attention away from himself.

Riley glimpsed at them again through the mirror.

John was on the edge of the back seat with his elbows on his knees. He was eager to hear more.

"I know you both want more information, but I've revealed all I can for now. We have a distance to go. I'd recommend that you two try to get some rest. I'll wake you when we're close."

Matt and John were exhausted and anxious as they leaned against the seat and closed their eyes to try to get some sleep, but the specter of a major cyberattack against the United States weighed too heavily on them, especially on Matt. He had seen firsthand what was going on at Lucigen. The thought of worse events happening nationwide was almost too much to bear.

47

In a secure government bunker in the Shenandoah Mountains miles outside of D.C., Osmund, the Director of the North American Cyber Command, anxiously paced back and forth in the command center. "How long before they arrive?"

"Within the next couple hours. They're on their way right now, sir," an analyst responded before refocusing his attention on his computer.

"Do we know who all is coming?"

"Riley is on his way."

"Does he have the asset?"

"Yes, but he's been potentially compromised."

"Compromised? In what way?"

"There are two of them." "Two?" Osmund asked, surprised. "Do we know who the other one is?"

"Yes. In addition to Matt O'Shea, Riley has O'Shea's work colleague, John Knox. John has been helping Matt. We don't know how much Matt has told him, though. Riley picked both of them up near Rosslyn. What will we do now?"

"We'll handle it. Once Matt arrives, we'll find out more and decide how to proceed."

"Yes, sir."

"In the meantime, continue the work with your team. We need to know when and where the next cyberattack will occur. Have the technicians restored power around the National Mall yet?"

"No, sir."

"And what about the traffic lights and metro train situations downtown?"

"It's only gotten worse the past few hours, sir."

Traffic lights were either out or working intermittently. They received reports of car accidents and backups across the city. Driving through downtown had become nearly impossible. Traffic blocked the bridges leading out of the city to Virginia and Maryland. Emergency responders and police couldn't do anything. The metro trains were stopped, and passengers were trapped in tunnels across the city.

"What other systems have been affected?"

"None thus far in the D.C. area, but we're closely monitoring all of the industrial control systems and infrastructure networks in the metro area. I'm going to check the status across the country. Reagan National still seems to be online."

"What about the White House?"

"The backup power systems have kicked in, but the Secret Service has locked down the East and West Wings and secured a perimeter as a precaution."

"Good. Let me know of anything else."

48

The bright lights from the interrogation room beamed down at Director Godfrey. Dimitri had left the room to take a call and still hadn't returned. The director sat in the chair, his arms and legs secured. Godfrey wished that he was still back in the holding cell where he had been free. He squinted as he looked into the lights. Godfrey heard a metal door open, and Dimitri finally returned.

"Sorry, but I needed to take that call."

"What do you want with me, Dimitri?" Godfrey asked for what seemed like the hundredth time.

"I'll tell you. The project you have Michael working on has progressed past what it was supposed to. He may have learned things beyond his clearance level. And Matt O'Shea has a key role in this as well. You have no idea of the magnitude of what we're dealing with and what you've created with this project of yours."

"Where are you getting your information? Michael never told me much other than his regular updates each week, and I didn't get updates from O'Shea."

"And what were those?"

"We identified and were tracking an unfamiliar malicious code. It was infiltrating government and private computer networks and the Internet. We couldn't break it, let alone trace it or find the source. It continually changed locations, and the code itself mutated."

"Changed locations and mutated?"

"Yes, the physical location could not be traced. Before we could hone in on it would change again."

"So the code was changing locations and mutating almost instantaneously."

"Exactly."

"How could that be? What type of code does that?" Dimitri asked rhetorically.

"I don't know, to be honest. Your guess is as good as mine. It was not unlike the Heartbleed bug regarding its ability to bypass SSL and secure firewalls, or Stuxnet that targeted programmable logic controllers in factories and power plants, but yet very different in the sense of it being untraceable and unable to combat. It has semblances and traces of the Fawkes virus written by the Red Fox hacker, but it's not entirely his code. Someone modified it. We think something was built into the computer hardware or firmware of our industrial control systems from the beginning. That's how it's able to bypass the firewalls and security systems."

"What locations did you identify?"

"As I said, it changed all the time."

"I heard that, but there were recurring patterns. Could you identify a region or country?"

"Yes."

"Which ones?"

"There were a number of them in Asia, the Middle East, and Eastern Europe."

"I need specifics."

"China, North Korea, Russia, and Iran were most prominent."

"Now we're getting somewhere. What about the others?"

"There were others, but they didn't show up regularly."

"And what were those?"

"Nigeria, Egypt, Syria, Columbia, Venezuela, and Cuba. Those are the ones I recall from the briefings."

There was a silence, and then Dimitri spoke. "That means the network is more extensive than we initially thought. Were there any patterns in the codes among those countries?"

"That's what we were trying to decipher, but we didn't have any luck. We ran algorithms and simulations but couldn't discover any anomalies in the code vectors we were able to decode."

"Did you discover anything else?"

"Not really . . . Wait. There were a couple of things. They all seemed to cycle through a U.S. location at some point along the code path sequencing. Also, we were able to plot latitude and longitude, but they didn't make sense. A number of them were over the ocean or other bodies of water or in remote geographic locations where human populations are scarce. We wondered if the code might be getting routed through airplanes, cell phones, or even satellites so a particular ground location couldn't be pinpointed. That was one theory. We'd never seen anything like it and haven't had a chance to test our hypothesis."

"Do you know how the code was being transmitted?"

"We're not sure. We believe it could be by satellite or cell towers, but most likely it's over the Internet." Godfrey tried to feed Dimitri some morsels, but he wasn't going to reveal all that he knew.

"Hmmm . . ."

"You seem perplexed. Is this not similar to what you already know?" Director Godfrey asked.

"Something doesn't add up."

"How so?"

There was no response. Godfrey experienced an eerie feeling. A metal door opened, and Godfrey heard the footsteps of someone else enter the room. Then he heard whispering.

"Hello? Where'd you go?"

"I must apologize, Godfrey, but there are urgent matters that we must address. We'll continue this conversation later."

"But where are you going, Dimitri? What are you going to do with me?" Godfrey squinted into the bright spotlights. He could vaguely make out Dimitri's silhouette in the background.

49

The New York City Yellow Cab pulled up to a large metal and brick warehouse on the west side docks of Manhattan. Michael looked up at the expansive structure and then to the surrounding buildings. The area was deserted. It was late Saturday night, and he doubted anyone would be working. It felt sketchy.

"Here we are," the cabbie said as he draped his arm across the top of the front seat.

Michael rechecked the address he'd written down, uncertain if he was in the right place. "Are you sure this is it? This place looks abandoned."

"This is the address you gave me."

Michael pulled out his wallet and paid the driver before climbing out of the cab. He then surveyed the premises of the massive, ominous warehouse, but there was no one in sight. Except for one single light near a loading dock ramp, the place was dark. Off to one side of the loading dock there was an access door that was propped slightly open with a brick. Michael walked apprehensively to it and peered inside before opening the door cautiously.

The light from the street and the skylights above cast shadows on the interior walls. Michael eased inside and gently closed the door as he stood in the shadows while his eyes adjusted to the darkness. The warehouse was void of human life. There were wooden pallets and crates stacked nearly to the ceiling to form temporary walls throughout the vast facility. Michael stepped away from the door and crept along the exterior wall. He listened carefully for any movement or noises. He used a small flashlight on his keychain to read the labeling. From what he saw, the containers held electronics or computers, mostly from China. As Michael explored the interior perimeter of the warehouse, he came to another loading dock on the opposite side from where he had entered. There was a forklift parked by one of the doors. He placed his hand on the motor. It was still warm. Someone must have used it recently. He quickly searched again for any sign of life but saw none. *Why would someone bring me to a warehouse full of electronics and computers from China?*

Then he heard footsteps swiftly coming up behind him. Before he could turn or run, he heard a voice.

"Good evening Mr. Stevens. I'm glad to see you arrived. I take it you didn't have any trouble finding the place?" The voice in the shadows wasn't the one from his earlier phone call. The other man had a Russian accent. This man spoke perfect English.

"No, not at all. But I wasn't sure I had the right place."

"It can be deceptive. It's that way for a reason."

"What is this place?" Michael asked, looking into the rafters and motioning to the columns of crates surrounding them while flocks of pigeons nestled on the beams. The flapping of their wings echoed as they resettled themselves on their perches.

"This is a Customs warehouse."

"I figured that."

"Why did your Russian associate send me here?"

"Are you sure you want to know?"

"Yes, but before you tell me, what are you doing with Director Godfrey? And why did your associate threaten to harm my wife?"

"I have nothing to do with Director Godfrey or your wife. They are my colleague's concern. He will not harm them as long as you cooperate."

Michael ruffled his brow. He wasn't sure whether to believe the man. "Okay, we're alone now, so let's talk."

"Follow me."

Michael trailed the silhouette of the man to the center of the warehouse, an open space about the size of a basketball court. The moonlight beamed through the skylights and illuminated a small, flat, rectangular box in the middle of the floor.

"Is that a laptop?" Michael asked.

"Yes, it is."

"What's it doing in the middle of the floor?"

"It's there to demonstrate something."

"And what might that be?"

"Patience."

The stranger hid in the shadows. Although Michael still couldn't see his face, he could see that he had a tall, slender, athletic build. He wore a ball cap and a black sweatshirt with a hood to cover his head. Michael saw him pull something out of his pocket. He didn't know if it was a gun.

"What is that you have in your hand?" Michael asked, hoping the response would alleviate his anxiety.

"It's a remote."

"A remote? For what?" It didn't matter as long as it wasn't a gun.

"It's a detonator."

"A detonator!" Michael exclaimed. That was worse than a gun. "Wait just one second: is that laptop a bomb?"

"Step back a little further. You may want to hide behind one of those crates."

"My God, that's a bomb!"

"Not quite. It has a different purpose that I'll demonstrate. I'll explain so you'll understand why we brought you here. What I'm about to show you is the result of one of the applications of what you and your team have discovered. Now step back." The stranger was going to activate the malware in the computer, which would cause it to overheat and catch fire.

Michael did as instructed, stepping back and ducking partially behind a crate. In the silence of the warehouse they heard a faint buzz. Michael reached for his phone. He had put it on vibrate, but it wasn't vibrating.

"Is that your phone?" Michael whispered. Then he stepped toward the stranger. Michael saw him checking his phone. Brody, the stranger, had just received a warning text from Dimitri. Brody was only a short distance away, but he began jogging in Michael's direction. Michael didn't know what was happening. Brody approached him quickly and waved his arms, signaling for him to get down.

Suddenly, Brody broke into a sprint and yelled, "Get down!"

Before Michael could react, Brody smashed into him like a linebacker, and they fell to the ground behind some crates just as an explosion erupted. The warehouse illuminated with flashes of light followed by a plume of smoke. The sound of a metal door being smashed echoed off the rafters.

"Run for it!" Brody's yell seemed distant as his voice reverberated in Michael's ears.

Michael sat up, his vision blurred from hitting his head when he fell. Everything seemed to be occurring in slow motion, and his world was spinning. He heard shouts and loud voices approaching him as the warehouse filled with smoke. *Had the man blown up the laptop? Was the building on fire?* His eyes and skin burned. His military training led him to conclude it was tear gas.

"Run for it, Michael!" Someone grabbed his arm and pulled. Michael tried to gather himself, but he was dazed and couldn't focus. *The strangers, the laptop, the explosion.* He tried to gather himself. *Was this a raid?* Michael was kneeling and grabbing the back of his head.

"Michael, we've got to go now."

Michael felt himself being lifted off his feet and his arm thrown over a man's shoulder. The man wrapped his other arm around Michael's back. Michael heard more strange voices clamoring around him. They hurried out a back entrance to a parked car. The man helped Michael into the back seat and slammed the door. Michael fell over in the seat, his head pounding. Then he blacked out.

50

Flight 784 from Chicago to Washington, D.C., was coming in for a landing at Reagan National Airport.

"Control tower, this is TransAir Flight Alpha seven eighty-four. We're on our approach heading two seven zero toward runway bravo echo five."

"Alpha seven eighty-four, you are cleared for landing. Please continue on your current heading."

"Roger that, control. We'll be touching down shortly."

"Copy that."

The captain and co-pilot were conducting their final approach instrument checks in preparation for landing when the runway lights in the near distance went out.

"Captain! Did you see that?" The co-pilot blurted as he pointed out the cockpit window.

"I did." The captain then grabbed the radio. "Tower, this is flight Alpha seven eighty-four. Are you aware that the runway lights are out?" There was no response. He radioed again, but there was still no response.

The co-pilot turned toward the captain. "What do we do? Can we divert?"

"We don't have time. We'll be touching down in minutes. We've got to make an emergency landing."

"But we don't know where the runway is."

"Just maintain current heading and descent. We'll make an instrument and visual reference landing. Let's hope we don't overshoot the runway. Otherwise, we'll end up in the Potomac," the pilot said as he continued his landing sequence protocols.

The captain peered up from the flight controls. "That's odd." He pointed toward the National Mall and the Capitol Building on their left. "All the lights are out."

The co-pilot leaned over to get a better look.

The captain refocused his attention on the landing and turned on the intercom. "Attention, crew and passengers, this is your captain speaking. We're approaching Reagan National Airport. We'll be touching down in a few minutes. Please prepare for an emergency landing. I repeat, please prepare for an emergency landing. This is not a drill."

The startled passengers glanced frantically at each other, not knowing what to do. They plastered their faces to the windows, anxiously trying to see what was going on outside. Most of the city and the surrounding metro area were dark.

The chief flight attendant's voice then crackled over the intercom. "Please stay seated and make sure your seat belts are securely fastened and that your seats and tray tables are in their upright and locked position. Please assume the emergency landing position by placing your head between your legs and wrap your arms around your legs to brace for impact."

One middle-aged woman started screaming. "I don't want to die! I don't want to die!"

Another young family held hands and prayed out loud. A young professional woman hastily tried to call her fiancé, but she was shaking so much that she dropped her phone on the floor. Other passengers began to scream hysterically. Through the cockpit door, the captain could hear the passengers in the main cabin.

The captain turned to his co-pilot. "Whatever happens, it has been a pleasure flying with you."

"You too, sir."

The captain turned on the intercom one more time. "This is your captain speaking. Please brace yourself and prepare for an emergency landing. We'll be touching down shortly."

The flight crew strapped themselves into their seats. As the aircraft descended, it clipped the runway approach lights, throwing the plane off balance. The pilot attempted to level the wings before touching down. The impact jolted the flight crew and passengers, ripping off the landing gear as the plane crashed onto its undercarriage and skidded along the runway, ripping the right wing. The high-pitched screeching of metal and flying sparks stopped as the aircraft eventually skidded to a halt at the end of the runway.

The two pilots looked at each other. "Are you okay?" the pilot asked.

"I think so. How about you?" The co-pilot, a little shaken, managed a thumbs up.

"Good. Let's check on the crew and passengers."

They unbuckled themselves and tried to unlock the cockpit door, but it was stuck. The pilot and co-pilot could hear the passengers' cries for help. They fought to open the door, but to no avail.

The captain grabbed the ax from its compartment and told the co-pilot to step back. He then wielded it feverishly. After several powerful blows, the door finally gave way, and the two men squeezed through. The cabin was filling with smoke, and they could barely see past the first class seating area. The flight attendants had responded quickly to their emergency protocols and were assisting the passengers to the emergency exit doors and activating the inflatable slides. They could hear the flight attendants yelling instructions.

The frightened passengers moved to the exit doors nearest them, climbing over seats and each other as they fled. The exit door behind the cockpit was open, and passengers leapt onto the slide to escape the smoke.

The captain turned to his co-pilot and said, "Hurry, we've got to get these people off the plane."

The co-pilot started helping passengers out of the main exit door when he called back to the captain. "Sir, we've got a problem. The number two engine is on fire. We've got to get these passengers off before it . . ."

He had just helped a little girl onto the slide when the explosion from the engine knocked him off his feet and into the galley near the cockpit. The captain bent down to help him up.

"Peters! Peters! Get up!" There was no response. He'd been knocked unconscious.

The captain dragged him to the exit and pushed him down what remained of the ramp. The shrapnel from the explosion had punctured the inflatable slide. The captain raced back to the business class section. No more passengers were coming his way, but he needed to make sure everyone was off the plane. He knelt and crawled along the floor toward the back of the aircraft. The floor was hot from the fire. He stopped when he entered the economy seating area. The explosion from the engine had ripped through the main cabin near the back of the plane. He could feel the heat from the flames ahead of him, and the smoke was burning his lungs and eyes.

The captain called out, "Anyone in here?" There was no response. He yelled again, the smoke filling his lungs. "Is anyone else on the plane?" Still there was no answer. He didn't know that the passengers in the rear of the plane hadn't made it off in time and had been consumed by the inferno.

The captain crawled back toward the cockpit as fast as he could. He smelled burning flesh and jet fuel as he made it to the front exit. The flashing lights on the runway from the emergency responders gave him hope as the firefighters raced to battle the flames and get the passengers to safety. He paused, entranced by the chaos and inferno around him. The slide was damaged so he had to lower himself down as far as he could. He hung there dangling about ten feet above the ground, unable to see what was beneath him. He released his grip and dropped from the main entrance of the plane. As he landed, he felt the bones in his right lower leg and ankle fracture as he tumbled to the ground with a thud, crying out in agony. He tried to stand, but he couldn't bear any weight. He dragged himself along the tarmac away from the plane, arm over arm, reeling in pain. Luckily, the firefighters noticed him and pulled him to safety. The captain beheld the surreal spectacle before him, the entire plane engulfed in flames as black smoke billowed into the sky. Bloodied and burned passengers littered the runway as emergency personnel raced to attend to their injuries. Shrill wails from some passengers filled the air.

Dear Lord, what happened? the captain wondered, and then he passed out on the tarmac.

51

Dimitri left the interrogation room for a short while to take care of an urgent matter before returning. Director Godfrey sat waiting anxiously in the silence, the lights shining down on him. Angst flowed through his body as he heard the door open and the sound of footsteps walking towards him. Godfrey squinted at the silhouette of a man standing over him. Squirming in his chair, he tried to free himself, but his hands and arms were tightly secured. Godfrey closed his eyes, lowering his head as his body tensed, not knowing what was going to happen. Then he felt the chains and cuffs loosen around his ankles and wrists. Opening his eyes, Godfrey noticed that the bright lights had been turned off. Everything was blurry until his eyes adjusted. As he sat there dumbfounded, he rubbed his eyes and blinked to get things back in focus. He pulled his arms around in front of him and rubbed his wrists. Then, he bent down to rub his ankles. It felt good to be free. The man was still behind him, but he heard a familiar voice.

"Plans have changed, my friend. You are free to go." Dimitri walked around the chair to face Godfrey.

"What?" Godfrey exclaimed. "Dimitri, what's going on?"

"We have all that we need. We no longer require your assistance."

"Now what?"

"We will return you to Washington. You are to speak of this to no one. We will know if you do. My colleagues will escort you to the airport. We have a plane waiting." Dimitri motioned toward the door.

As Godfrey stood, he glared at Dimitri. "I'm not going anywhere . . . not until I get answers." Godfrey moved toe-to-toe with Dimitri.

"Well, my friend, a colleague of yours may convince you otherwise."

"What are you talking about?"

Dimitri motioned to the wall with the long two-way mirror and signaled. The metal door opened and a man entered. Standing there in disbelief, Godfrey recognized him immediately.

Dimitri turned to the man who had just entered. "I've got something that requires my immediate attention. I'll be back later. In the meantime, I'll leave you two alone to talk."

52

When Michael regained consciousness, his head ached and his eyes burned. He painfully sat up to view the room around him. He was lying on a dark leather sofa in what appeared to be a business office. It was dimly lit by a single desk lamp across the room. There was dark mahogany furniture, and a set of brown bookshelves spanned the length of one wall. He guessed it to be a law office. There were wide, tall windows with thick wooden blinds looking over the city. The floor was made of aged wood and peppered with fine area rugs. The room was hot and muggy, and the smell of cigar smoke filled his nostrils. He had no clue that Director Godfrey had been in the same room only hours before.

He rubbed the back of his head from where he had hit the ground earlier. He tried to recall what had happened, but his memory was fuzzy. He attempted to shake off the haze that clouded his throbbing head as he sat up and steadied himself against the arm of the sofa. He heard a chair roll across the wooden floor by the desk. With the faint lighting, he squinted to see who was making the noise.

"I see you're awake and alive."

"You could say that," Michael replied, stroking the back of his aching head.

"You took quite a fall when I tackled you," Brody's voice bellowed, echoing in Michael's ears.

Michael bent forward to try and see past the desk light. The stranger leaned into the light. He was a rugged man, probably in his late thirties or early forties. He had a well-trimmed, short beard. He was still wearing a black pullover sweatshirt with a hood that concealed the rest of his head. A shadow covered part of his face. His look was sharp and keen like an eagle. Michael couldn't detect any other distinguishing features.

"Who are you?" Michael forced out the words. They resonated in his head like a ringing bell, making the pounding worse.

"You can call me Brody."

"Brody, eh?"

Michael didn't recognize the voice from the earlier phone call. "Are you the one who ordered me to the warehouse?"

"No, that was my colleague." Brody was referring to Dimitri.

"And who is he, and who does he work for? He sounded Russian."

"Right now that's not relevant."

"What happened back at the warehouse? Was that a raid?"

"Yes, it was."

"What were they after?"

"They were after you and the contents of the warehouse."

"Me?" Michael asked, perplexed.

"Yes. It appears you are a wanted person."

"But why me?" he asked, even more confused.

"It seems people think you know something important regarding a national security matter."

"But I don't."

"Are you so sure?" Brody asked. "Think for a moment, and then answer that question again."

Michael sat facing Brody, hunched over, his elbows on his knees and his hands under his chin. He still couldn't think of why anyone would be chasing him.

"I'll give you a clue. It has something to do with your NSA job."

Michael thought about his work projects. He had suffered a concussion from the fall earlier, so he was having difficulty remembering. Then it came to him. *Could this have anything to do with Eminent Eclipse, their cyber defense project for the U.S. utilities and infrastructure systems?*

Brody noticed the shift in his demeanor. "It looks like something clicked. What do you say now?"

"I'm still not sure, but I have some ideas."

"Such as?" Brody probed.

"There's this covert cyber project that only a small group knows about."

"Why don't you tell me about it?"

"I can't. It's classified at the highest levels." Michael scowled at Brody.

"I'm aware of that. I know you all have identified a malicious code that's infiltrated many computer and industrial control systems across the country. It's affecting utility companies, banks, businesses, and much more. You've got a man working undercover at Lucigen, a Matt O'Shea. I didn't know the NSA hired college rejects. Does that about sum it up?"

"But how do you know all of that? Only my boss and a handful of other people in the NSA and White House know about this." Michael didn't know it, but Aiden had told Brody.

"Shall I keep going, or do you want to tell me what you know?" Brody leaned across the desk, his hands clasped in front of him.

"Where do I begin?"

"Anywhere you like."

Michael was about to say something when they heard a knock at the door.

Brody pushed himself away from the desk, reached into a lower drawer, and pulled out a pistol. Brody placed his left index finger over his mouth, signaling for Michael to keep quiet. As he slowly stood, his chair creaked. Michael cringed at the sound. Neither of them knew who was in the hallway. Brody stepped cautiously to the door and stood to one side. Then he waited. There was another series of knocks. Brody remained calm and quiet. Michael was getting anxious. He didn't know why Brody was hesitating so long to answer the door, but because he was armed, he figured he wasn't expecting company. Then there was a third series of knocks, but that one was different. It sounded as if someone was tapping a tune or Morse code. Brody braced himself. He reached down and put his hand on the door knob. He steadily raised his pistol when the same knocks came again. Then there was a voice in the hallway.

"Brody, it's me. I know you're in there; open up." The tone of the man sounded distressed or coerced. Michael recalled the instructions he had given to Kate about the number of knocks on the door and in what rhythm. He developed an uneasy feeling in his stomach. *Kate. Had she made it back to the hotel all right?* He had to get ahold of her and find out. He reached for his phone, but it wasn't in his pocket. He noticed it on the mahogany desk next to the lamp.

Brody eased back from the door as he steadied his gun, ready for anything. He motioned for Michael to move to the back of the office near the large wall of bookshelves. Michael gingerly stood and stepped backward until he reached the wall, his eyes fixated on the door. Seconds later, Brody moved stealthily toward Michael. Brody stopped by the desk to grab the phone and a few other things from the drawers, putting them in his pockets. Michael stood with his back against the bookshelves. When he was only steps away from Michael, Brody reached around his back and pulled out another pistol. He whispered to Michael, "Do you know how to use one of these?"

Michael gave him a snide look as he nodded. Michael had been a navy officer, so of course he knew how to use a gun.

Brody handed the gun to Michael who cradled it in his right palm. It had been months since he'd held a gun. The heavy metal was warm and hard against his flesh.

Brody whispered to Michael, "Watch the door."

"What are you going to do?"

"I'm getting us out of here," Brody said.

The knocks at the door came again. This time someone pounded louder. "Brody, let me in. I know you're in there."

Brody entered something into his phone and then put his hand on the wall. The sound of a latch opening was heard, and the bookshelf began to move, revealing a secret room behind it. Michael focused on the office entrance, anticipating that someone might break through the door at any moment.

Brody tapped Michael's arm. "Come on."

Michael had zoned out briefly. The pain was still radiating from the back of his head into his back and shoulders, making it difficult to concentrate.

"Come on; we've got to go," Brody whispered with a sense of urgency, motioning for Michael to hurry.

Michael snapped out of it and slipped quietly behind the threshold. No sooner had they stepped behind the closing bookcase wall did they hear the sound of the office door being smashed. They heard a flurry of shouting voices for a few seconds, and then all was silent.

The safe room they had just entered was dark. Brody switched on a red light that provided some illumination. Michael saw computer equipment and a workstation. It was a safe room only large enough for a handful of people. Brody switched on the computer terminal and monitors and footage of the office appeared on the screens. They could see a half dozen armed men in masks rummaging around, but they couldn't hear anything.

Michael turned to Brody and asked, "Is there any way we can listen to what they're saying?"

"Sure," he whispered.

Brody sat down, put on a headset, and adjusted the knobs on a control panel that looked like it had come from a music recording studio with all of its buttons and switches.

Brody put his hand up to the headset. "They're saying something, but it's faint."

Michael focused on the monitors. There were two men in the bottom center of the screen with their backs to him. Unlike the other armed men dressed in all black and wearing masks, one wore a dark business suit, and another wore a light gray athletic jacket and jeans.

"What are they saying?"

"Shhh . . . I'm trying to listen," Brody said as he waved Michael off.

Michael stepped back and quietly watched the screens with his arms folded.

"They're looking for you," Brody said.

"For me? Why?"

"They haven't said yet. I'm guessing the same reason we were just discussing—your NSA project."

"Who are they?"

"I'm not sure."

"What about those two men there?" Michael pointed at the bottom of the screen.

"I don't know."

"Can you zoom in on them? What are they saying?"

"Give me a second."

"Is it someone you know? They called your name."

"I know they did, but I didn't recognize the voice. I won't know until I get a good look at them."

"Can you switch camera angles? Do you have other cameras around the room?"

"Of course. Can't you see all the different monitors?"

The man in the business suit turned slightly to the right in the direction of the bookshelf, pausing momentarily.

"Oh, no . . . do you think he heard us?"

"That's impossible. The room is sound proof."

The room they were in was encased in concrete and reinforced with steel. Someone could shoot a gun, and there was only one chance in a thousand that a muffled sound might be heard.

Brody zoomed in on the two men and adjusted the speaker settings to hear what they were saying. He switched camera angles to the front to get a better view of them, but the camera across the way only captured one of them. He brought the camera into focus.

"I knew it."

"Knew what?"

"They're colleagues of mine, at least the one in the suit is," Brody said. "I assumed he might come looking for me when I

didn't respond to him, but I didn't expect an armed entourage."
Brody could see Dimitri directing the men to search everything.
Michael looked closer at the man in the jacket and jeans.
"Hey, that's David."

"David who?"

"He works in my unit at the NSA in Washington. What he's
doing here in New York, I have no idea."

"I have a similar question."

"Brody, why are they looking for us?"

"I don't know. Let me listen further."

"What are they saying?" "Be patient." Brody held up his
hand to silence Michael again. "They are in a rush, and they
need to find you soon. My colleague isn't happy with David."

"Why?"

"Something about needing information that you have on a
national security matter."

"I don't know what they could want," Michael lied.

"It has to do with the cyber project you're leading. It's something about a code. The Russians. The North Koreans. The
Chinese. A cyberattack against the U.S. Does any of that ring
a bell?"

"Are you sure they're not after you, Brody?" Michael asked,
diverting the conversation, especially because one of the men
was Brody's associate.

"Yes, they're after me too."

"But why would your colleague be after you, and why would
he have one of my task force members with him? David wouldn't
come willingly to New York. He lives in Maryland. Someone coerced him." Michael was troubled.

"Your guess is as good as mine, yet they appear to be working together to find you."

"Yes, that much is clear. Do you think these men were the ones at the warehouse?"

"It's likely, but I couldn't say for sure. These events are all related, and we need to get to the bottom of it." Brody changed the camera angles again.

The men on the screen moved feverishly as they searched the office, turning over tables and chairs and ransacking the desk and file cabinets. One of the men approached the bookcase and started grabbing books and pulling them down. Michael jumped back.

"Do you think they know we're in here?" Michael was edgy as he watched the books fall from the shelves.

"I don't think so."

"Do we have any other way out?"

"Yes."

"How?"

"I'm sitting on it. There is a trap door under this seat."

Brody reached under the chair, feeling around with his hands. "There it is." Brody inserted his key into the underside of the seat. He turned it, and the sound of hissing air being released from a passage underneath was heard. Brody stood as the floor lifted and the chair moved out of the way to reveal a tunnel. Michael peered inside and saw a ladder leading down.

"Where does it go?"

"Down," Brody said without a hint of humor.

"Apparently, but does it take us to another room?"

"Yes. It's several floors below us. We should be able to exit through there, or at least stay there until things are safe."

"Won't they have people waiting for us downstairs or outside?"

"They might, but we'll deal with that later. Right now, we need to get out of here."

Brody extracted a CD of some sort that wasn't much larger than a silver dollar. He slipped it into a tiny plastic case and put it into his pocket.

"What's that?"

"It's a recording of everything that's gone on in the room the past twenty-four hours. We'll review it later. Right now we need to leave."

"Won't they be able to access these computers too? What about your colleague? Won't he be able to access the room?"

"No. It's secured with biometric access." Brody never let Dimitri know about the safe room. But Brody didn't know that Dimitri had searched his office and copied his biometric profile, including his voice recognition and fingerprint access. Brody questioned whether Dimitri might be playing both sides, the United States and the Russians. He wasn't to be trusted. Dimitri had his own doubts about Brody joining their project and had been vocal with Aiden about it since the beginning. Bringing Brody on had been Aiden's idea.

Dimitri was supposed to be elsewhere questioning Director Godfrey. Why had Dimitri come back so soon? The situation raised more doubt for Brody, but he wasn't going to say anything to Michael about it. Brody had made a deal with the Russians to give them the classified information once they'd gotten it from Godfrey or Michael. O'Shea was another matter. Brody knew that the NSA was using O'Shea as a pawn. Brody also agreed to turn over Dimitri to the FSB in return for a large payment and asylum in Russia. Dimitri must not have collected the information he needed from Godfrey. Otherwise, he wouldn't be here. Brody couldn't take any chances. He would need to deal with Dimitri accordingly.

Michael stared into the dark hole. A wave of cool but stale air rushed upward.

"You first." Michael gave a nod in the direction of the opening.

Brody began to crawl down the ladder into the hole and then stopped. "Come on. We don't have much time." There was urgency in Brody's voice.

The door of the safe room was being unlocked. But how? Brody said they couldn't gain access.

Brody reached for Michael's leg. "Move it. Our time is up." Brody heard the latches unlock and the door start to open. He wasn't going to stick around to find out how Dimitri had gotten access.

"Grab the key from under the chair," Brody hollered up from below Michael.

Michael grabbed the key and pulled it out of the chair. The floor panel lurched forward. Michael's heart raced as he watched the floor close above them, knowing that at any minute the armed men might be upon them.

"Come on, come on!" Michael mumbled to himself as the trap door closed just in time. A sense of relief rolled over him, yet only momentarily. He found himself engulfed in a damp, cool darkness. It took a minute for his eyes to adjust as they picked up the narrow, hazy track lighting running vertically along the ladder and tunnel walls. He saw Brody's silhouette twenty feet below him. Michael followed and descended into the void, the metal bars of the ladder cold and clammy as he grasped each rung.

53

Back at FBI headquarters in Washington, Director Donovan paced back and forth in his office. It had been too long since he'd received any status report on Matt O'Shea. More troubling was that he hadn't heard anything from Agent Burton who was supposed to find Agents Perez and Hawkins and return to his office. Donovan looked at his watch. It had been almost an hour. He had hoped they would have something by now. He left his office and stepped into the corridor. Oddly, there was no one in sight. The hallway was silent except for the sound of voices in the distance. He walked to the SIOC control room and passed the glass windows. The center was still a flurry of action despite the late hour. He knew his team would work around the clock until they located O'Shea. Donovan quietly stepped into the center and leaned against the door frame. He didn't see Burton anywhere.

Hawkins was sitting at a desk and noticed Donovan standing there. He stood quickly from his computer terminal and approached him. "Sir."

"Hawkins, any word on O'Shea or his accomplice?"

"No, sir, not since agents spotted them in Georgetown. We haven't received any updates in hours."

"How could they just disappear? We have agents all over."

"We do. They're combing Georgetown, and we've broadened the search radius into Rosslyn, just in case they managed to escape across the river. We also set up checkpoints on the Key Bridge and Rock Creek Parkway. If they make any moves, we'll know it."

"What are you doing to secure the city?"

"We're coordinating closely with the D.C. Police Department and other local authorities." They activated the D.C. National Guard and were working with the navy and marines based in the city. Large portions of the city had lost power, and the roads, for the most part, were gridlocked. No one was moving unless it was by foot or helicopter.

Donovan shook his head. He couldn't believe what was going on, let alone not being able to do much about it. They needed to find O'Shea. He was behind all of this. Donovan was certain.

"If we need to work with the mayor and president to institute martial law across the city to maintain order and safety, then we'll do it."

"Understood," Hawkins replied, nodding.

"Have you seen Agent Burton? I instructed him to get you and Agent Perez about an hour ago. He was supposed to have you all come to my office. I have a special assignment for all of you."

"No, sir. I've been here the entire time. I think Perez stepped out to grab some coffee. He should be back any minute."

"Do you want us to look for Agent Burton when Perez returns?"

"No, that won't be necessary. I'll call Burton when I'm back at my desk. Carry on. I'll be in my office if you hear anything from Burton or about O'Shea. And make sure the city is secure."

"Will do." Hawkins motioned with a partial salute before returning to his computer terminal.

Director Donovan stepped out of the doorway and walked down the long hallway back to his office suite. He didn't know where Burton had disappeared to or why it was taking so long to find O'Shea.

54

After driving for over two hours into the Shenandoah Mountains, Riley exited the highway and drove down a two-lane service road. He reached over and slapped the backside of the passenger seat head rest. "Wake up, you two. You'll need to see where we're going."

Matt and John jumped, startled. The pair had finally dozed off. Matt rubbed his eyes and stretched his arms. John ran his fingers through his hair as he yawned.

They were in the country. There weren't many lights, and for the most part, it was pitch black. They didn't know how long they'd been riding, but they could make out the silhouette of the Shenandoah Mountains across the horizon under the sliver of a new moon.

John watched the outlines of the trees pass by. There weren't many cars on the road at that hour. Just then a wave of exhaustion washed over him, and he slouched in the back seat.

"Are you okay?" Matt asked.

"Yeah, I'll be fine. I just got tired all of a sudden. I didn't realize how late it was."

"It's been a long day for sure, and it seems like it will be a long night as well. I could use some more sleep myself." Matt released another huge yawn.

Riley hit the brakes and turned quickly off the road without warning. If Matt hadn't been wearing his seatbelt, he would have flown across the back seat. Matt threw out his hands to catch himself.

"Hey! We could use some advance notice here!" Matt blurted out, but Riley didn't respond.

"Did you hear me?" Matt was annoyed.

There was still no response. Riley focused intently on the road. The beams from the headlights illuminated the narrow farm road. They wound their way through a cow pasture toward the base of the mountains. They drove for several miles before they entered a forested area. Riley slowed down and turned on his high beams just before the paved road dropped from under them. They felt a jolt as the car rumbled onto a gravel road lined with trees and dense brush on both sides. Crushed rocks were ground under their tires as the car kicked up a plume of dust. Low-hanging branches scraped the sides of the car as they navigated a canopy of trees and brush.

John had an eerie feeling as he stared out the window. *Where are we going? And what is so important that they would bring us all the way out here to the middle of nowhere?*

Riley suddenly slammed on the brakes, and the car skidded to a halt. Matt and John threw up their hands to catch themselves against the back of the front seats. Dirt and dust enveloped the car, and Matt and John couldn't see anything outside. Riley waited for the cloud to settle and then slowly backed up.

"Why are you reversing?" John asked.

"I think I missed my turn."

"Great," John muttered. "Where did we pass it?"

"Not too far back." Riley turned on his spotlight near the driver's side front window. As he reversed, he scanned from side to side. "There it is." Riley pointed to the left down another gravel road that was almost hidden by overgrown bushes.

"I don't see anything," said John, frustrated.

"It's on that tree in the distance."

Matt and John took a closer look. There was a "No Trespassing" sign posted on one of the trees about twenty yards away.

"That sign?" John exclaimed, pointing.

"What's so special about that?" Matt wondered aloud.

"That's what I'm looking for." Riley backed up a short distance and then turned down the narrow road. He drove another quarter mile or so until he reached a chain link gate with a large "GOVERNMENT PROPERTY – NO TRESPASSING" sign on it.

"What is this place?" Matt asked.

"I'll show you." Riley grabbed his flashlight from the passenger seat and got out of the car. He leaned inside the driver's side window and smirked at Matt and John. "Wait here."

"What do you think he's doing?" John asked.

"I don't know, but I'm going to find out." Matt opened the door and walked along the road toward Riley. John climbed out of the other door and scurried behind him.

"What are we doing here?" Matt asked.

"There is an underground bunker back there." Riley pointed into the darkness on the other side of the fence.

"You mean one of them there secret government bunkers?" John asked sarcastically.

"Precisely."

"Why did you bring us out here?" Matt asked.

"Because, with all that's going on right now, it's one of the safest places we could be. Trust me."

"Are we going inside?" John asked with trepidation. He didn't like the idea of going underground. He was claustrophobic because his stepfather used to lock him in a dog kennel in their basement with the lights off when he misbehaved as kid.

"Yes."

"How big is this bunker?" Matt asked.

"It's massive enough to run the key parts of the U.S. government if things came to that, which from the reports I'm getting, could happen very soon."

"You're kidding, right? So it's like the size of the Pentagon?" John asked, astonished. "And all underground? But how?" John was in deep disbelief.

"It's not nearly that expansive, but it's big enough."

"But how could the government build something so massive without anyone knowing about it?"

"I'll explain later."

Although Matt had only worked undercover for the NSA a short while, he was aware of the underground operations centers outside of D.C. He'd never seen one, but he knew of their existence. In the event of a major cyberattack or missile attack on Washington, he was instructed to make his way out to the remote command center. Matt hadn't been told the specific location, only a local address near D.C. that would serve as a rendezvous point. He was instructed that a transport vehicle would meet him and take him the rest of the way. Perhaps Riley was one of the transporters.

"Where's the main entrance?" Matt was interested in seeing the command center he'd heard about during his onboarding.

"Through there." Riley motioned to the area on the other side of the fence. He stepped closer to the chain link gate. It was secured by a large metal chain and a bolt lock. Riley pulled something out of his pocket and started fidgeting with the lock. The latch opened, and he removed the chain. He pushed the gate open wide enough for the car to drive through before hustling back to the vehicle. Matt and John instinctively followed him.

Riley looked at both of them and pointed at the back door. "Get in."

Matt and John followed his instruction and climbed into the back seat.

Riley drove through the gate before stopping and getting out of the car. He pushed the gate shut, wrapped the chain around it, and replaced the bolt.

They drove another quarter mile or so down the winding gravel road until they came to a large opening in the trees at the base of a mountainside. As Riley shone his spotlight, they could see the old mining equipment and metal shipping containers that lined the perimeter of the clearing. There were a dozen or so tall mounds of overgrown dirt and gravel that were spread about, the remnants of mining excavation. The shipping containers were worn and rusted, and the earth-moving equipment, conveyor belts, and cranes showed the rust and age from having been abandoned decades earlier.

"You were serious. This facility is an old mine," John said.

"Yes. It was closed by the federal government many years ago for safety reasons. At least that's what the authorities told the public. We, of course, know better. Once the government took it over during World War II, we began further excavations to expand an underground command center in the event of a major nuclear attack on Washington. The cold war and the nuclear arms race with Russia expedited the completion of the project. Now we're in a different type of arms race with Russia, not to mention China, Iran, and North Korea, who are building their nuclear capabilities. We are now in a cyber defense arms race. We have to be ready for any form of attack be it cyber, nuclear, chemical, or biological."

They drove ahead to what appeared to be the mine entrance. "No Trespassing" and "Danger" signage covered the facade. Riley stepped out of the car and walked to the entrance where he opened a small metal door that was part of a larger door about the size of a loading dock bay. He unlocked the door and slipped inside, partially closing the door behind him. John and Matt got out of the car and went over to where he'd disappeared.

"Riley?" Matt hollered into the darkness. The only response was the echo of his voice off the cavern walls. "Riley, where'd you go?" Still there was no reply.

Seconds later they saw a white flashlight beam, and Riley appeared from the shadows.

"I had to unlock the entrance door. I'll need both of you to help open it. The electronic mechanism appears to be disabled, so we'll have to open it manually."

Riley walked over to the side of the large metal door and grabbed one of the latches. He pulled down on the lever, and they heard the bolts of the door retract with a loud clunk. "Now, help me push this open."

The three men pushed as hard as they could. The massive door swung open as the rusted hinges creaked. They pushed it open wide enough to drive the car through.

"I'm going to need one of you to get out and spot me as I drive inside," Riley said.

"I'll do it." Matt volunteered and slid out of the car. "I'm ready when you are."

"All right."

Matt waved Riley toward the opening, guiding him inside. Once Riley cleared the threshold he stopped the car and leaned his head out of the window. "You'll want to spot me from here to make sure I'm on the lift properly."

"The lift?" Matt asked.

"Yes. There's an elevator that will take the car down to the lower levels."

As the headlights illuminated the tunnel, Matt could see the lift a short distance ahead. Matt guided the car forward until he was standing next to the lift. Riley drove a little further until he entered the platform. It gave way slightly under the weight of the vehicle. Matt waved his hands, signaling Riley to stop. Riley put the car in park and set the parking brake.

"How do we activate the elevator?" Matt asked.

"You see that metal box back by the door that looks like a circuit box?" Riley shined his flashlight on the wall to the left behind them.

"Yes."

"Open it. On the right side, about chest high, you'll notice a round button that's sticking out that's about the diameter of a ping-pong ball. Push it, and a green light will come on."

"Then what?"

"You'll have to hurry. There's a ten-second delay before this platform lowers. That should give you enough time to close the gate behind us and get into the car."

"Fair enough." Matt found the button that Riley had described and pushed it. The green light came on, and they heard the sound of motors and gears engaging. Matt then ran to the car, closed the security gate, and climbed into the back seat just as the platform began to descend.

After descending slowly for nearly ten stories, the platform halted. Riley waited momentarily to make sure it had stopped completely. Two metal doors then opened sideways in front of them. Riley drove into a vast open area. It looked like an enormous underground parking garage with all of the support columns, but there were no cars. Matt and John watched as the elevator platform doors shut behind them with a thud. Matt noticed there was no armed security presence. It seemed strange.

"How did they build this place? It must have taken years and hundreds if not thousands of workers, not to mention tens of millions of dollars. Where did they put all of the dirt and rock? Didn't people see all of the work trucks? Surely people must have known." Matt was aghast.

"The project began almost a hundred years ago. It's been upgraded multiple times since then. I don't have time to go into the full history, but the U.S. military and federal government constructed it."

"The military? Really?" John scoffed.

"Yes. Thousands of years ago the Greeks, Romans, and other great civilizations constructed their cities and castles with secret underground tunnels. What makes you think we couldn't do the same? The Romans had their tunnels and passageways through and out of the city in the event of a siege. If you look into the history of D.C., there is an extensive tunnel network throughout the entire city that links Capitol Hill to the House and Senate buildings, to the White House, and to other buildings like the Treasury. The location of many of the tunnels is secret, but others are not. Even today you're able to take a small train from Capitol Hill under Independence Avenue to the House and

Senate buildings. That design was intentional. For many reasons over the years government officials and other persons of stature had to be able to make their way throughout the city undetected for their protection. In the event the city was ever attacked, they needed a way to escape to a safe place outside of the city."

"I suppose you have a point," Matt said, shrugging. "But how did they decide on this part of Virginia—or West Virginia—or wherever we are? Where are we exactly?" Matt inquired.

"I can't tell you the particular town. All I can say is that we're somewhere in the Shenandoah Mountains."

"How come you can't tell us exactly where we are?" John asked, finally speaking up. He hadn't seen any signs for a town when they left the main road.

"Listen, we don't have time to discuss any more of this right now."

"Where's the armed escort?" Matt asked facetiously. "I figured there would be a security detail of some sort."

"Yeah, what's with that? I would have figured the same. There's not a single person anywhere," John said.

"Some parts of this facility have been decommissioned. Federal government budget cuts over the years have significantly impacted our operations. Fortunately for us, the government isn't our only source of funds."

"That's nice. Where do we go now?" Matt asked.

"To the main operations center. It's nearby, but we will need to drive there." As Riley shifted gears and drove to the opposite side of the garage, the entire area suddenly went pitch black.

"What's happening?" Matt and John asked, almost in unison.

"No need to panic. These blackouts happen from time to time. It's part of the outdated electrical system. The backup lights should initiate any minute."

The three men sat in silence. Riley drove cautiously with his high beams on. When he arrived at the far side of the garage, there was an opening to a tunnel. It was wide enough to fit two or three cars side-by-side. Riley put the car in park. The bunker was quiet except for the muffled hum of the engine.

"Where does that lead?" John asked as he pointed over Riley's shoulder.

"To the command center. The tunnel links this entrance to the central installation."

Matt's eyes were still adjusting to the darkness. "How come the backup lights haven't come on yet?"

"They will. Like I said, it usually takes a few minutes." Riley paused. *Why haven't the backup lights come on? They should have by now.* Just then the lights clicked on. "There they go," Riley said, relieved.

They continued driving through the long tunnel for an eighth of a mile. They exited the tunnel and drove into another expansive opening half the size of a football field with a sixty-foot-high domed concrete ceiling. The space was brightly lit from above with a series of spotlights running the length of the dome and down the walls. On the far wall about twenty feet off the ground was a reflective window that spanned the length of a semi-trailer. It overlooked the cavern they had just entered. Under it was a metal door.

"You weren't kidding when you said they could run D.C. from here. It looks like they have enough parking," John joked in astonishment.

There were several dozen black government cars and SUVs parked on the far side. Riley's black sedan would fit right in.

"We're in part of the Shenandoah State Park. Franklin D. Roosevelt established the park in December of 1935 during his presidency. But this project began well before his election. Remember how I said the military constructed it? This project started twenty to thirty years before FDR took office. They managed to build this without anyone noticing for a couple of reasons. In 1933 they established the Civilian Conservation Corps, which was under the control of the U.S. Army at the time. When they created the park, they relocated hundreds of families from the area. The army also restricted access. Therefore, they were able to do construction and excavation without anyone knowing. Given the minerals in the region, it was also a profitable mining operation that helped fund our military operations and manufacturing during both world wars. There are also caverns along the Shenandoah Mountain range that made the excavation in some sections easier. The caverns simply needed to be reinforced."

"This is impressive," John said.

"Our forefathers were visionaries. They knew what they were doing."

John hadn't given his question much thought before he asked, "What happened to the people who stumbled across the project and the workers who built it?"

Riley responded, "I don't know. Your guess is as good as mine."

"This is the perfect cover. Just tell people you're mining in the park and they wouldn't assume otherwise, certainly not back then. The focus was on the war and foreign enemies, not on what the U.S. government was doing in its own backyard. There is a lot more distrust of the U.S. government now."

"Exactly."

"Where else do they have these covert facilities?" Matt asked. Given his undercover role with the NSA, he was aware of the facilities outside D.C., but he wanted to know if there were more.

"I'm not sure exactly, but they're all over. If I had to guess, installations exist in Boston, New York City, Colorado, Montana, Wyoming, the Dakotas, and New Mexico. I bet you never imagined you'd be involved in all this when you got out of bed this morning . . . And we're here." Riley brought the car to a stop alongside a black Suburban and got out.

Matt and John looked around at the other parked vehicles while Riley walked over to the metal hydraulic entrance door where there was a keypad and scanner screen on the wall. Riley put his hand on the glass scanner. With his other hand, he punched a series of numbers into the keypad, and a tiny red light by the door turned green. There was a loud clank as the bolts released. Riley grabbed the handle and opened the heavy door. Stopping momentarily, he turned and motioned for Matt and John to join him.

As they stood there, John spotted a security camera by the door. "They're watching us."

"We're always being watched." Riley's voice trailed off. "One of you hold the door."

While they waited, Riley stepped to the trunk of the car. Matt and John could hear metal clinking as Riley set a couple of black duffle bags on the ground.

John walked to the rear of the car where Riley was looking through a black bag.

"What's in there?" John asked.

Riley ignored him as he continued with his business.

John gently nudged the bag with his right foot. It was bulky, and there were heavy metal objects inside.

"Are you going to tell us what you're doing, or do I have to take a look for myself?" John asked.

There was still no response from Riley. Finally, John decided he'd squat to take a peek. He'd barely bent down when he heard the sound of a pistol cocking. He soon found himself staring at a gun barrel.

"I wouldn't do that if I were you."

Panic raced through John's body as he stared down the barrel. "Don't shoot!" John pleaded as he stepped back, his trembling hands in the air.

Matt lunged away from the door, and Riley pointed the gun at him.

"What's this all about?" John asked.

Then Riley calmly locked the pistol and handed it to John. "You might need this at some point." His tone was firm and direct. He looked at Matt and smirked. "You didn't think I was actually going to shoot him, did you?"

Matt wasn't sure what to say, so he said nothing. Riley smiled, pulled out another pistol, and handed it to Matt. "Do you guys know how to use those?"

"I do," Matt said, finally feeling safe and confident.

"I think I do," John said. John's experience with guns was limited to paintball, the arcades, and Duck Hunt on Nintendo. He'd never shot a real gun.

"Let me give you a quick lesson. Here's how you load and cock it. Then you hold it like this, point, and pull the trigger. And don't forget to take the safety off. Here, you try." Riley handed the gun to John. He removed the clip, reloaded it, cocked the gun, and pretended to pull the trigger.

"You got it now?" Riley asked.

"I get the idea."

"Good."

"But why do we need guns? I thought you said your colleagues knew you were coming?"

"They do. I like to be prepared for anything." Riley put one of the bags back in the trunk and threw the other backpack over his shoulder. "This is where you two find out what this is all about. Are you ready?"

"I suppose so," Matt reluctantly replied as he stood holding his backpack.

"Great. Let's go." Riley reentered his passcode before slipping inside. "All clear. Come on," he said as he motioned for them to follow.

The two followed closely behind Riley despite their misgivings. The heavy metal door closed behind them with a loud thud, and the sound reverberated throughout the dark corridor. The electric metal door bolts locked behind them. The overhead lights in the hallway activated. There was no going back. Riley hustled down the long illuminated corridor. He stopped and realized Matt and John hadn't moved. "Come on, you two. It's this way."

55

After Michael left the restaurant, Kate grabbed the packaged dinner that Big Tony had prepared for them and caught a cab back to the hotel. Kate sat quietly on the couch in the honeymoon suite. The excellent Italian dinner that Big Tony had prepared sat untouched in a brown paper bag on the kitchenette table. Kate wasn't hungry. Her stomach was in knots. She didn't know what was going to happen with Michael. In all the years they'd been together, this type of situation had never happened.

She trudged across the living room into the bedroom and opened the suitcase. She moved the clothes aside and reached to the bottom. There was a small compartment with a zipper. She opened it as Michael had instructed her. There was a piece of paper with a combination number on it. She stood up and strode over to the bedroom closet to find the safe. Michael told her that in a case of an emergency, he had hidden some things in it. She considered this an emergency.

She knelt down in front of the safe and entered the code, and opening it, she peeked inside. There was a hard black metal case about the size of a small shoebox. She reached in and pulled the case out. There was a lock on it, but Michael had given her the key before he left the restaurant. She carried the box to the dresser, set it down, and opened it. There was a gray foam cushion inside that she removed. Under it was a pistol, a cell phone, a set of car keys, a fresh stack of bound $100 bills, and a box that looked like a metal cigarette holder. She opened the smaller case to reveal some items that looked like computer chips and components. She'd never seen anything like them before. She wondered why Michael would leave them for her. She put one of them in the palm of her right hand. As she examined it, something caught her eye at the bottom of the box. There were a handful of small, shiny things about the size of sesame seeds in small glass cases. She picked them up. *What are these?* She lifted them to the light to examine them closer. Interestingly, they were some type of electronic device, but she didn't know what. She did know they were important if Michael had left them for her. She put the items back into the case. As Kate was closing it, she noticed a folded piece of paper and opened it.

> *Dear Kate,*
>
> *If you're reading this, you've found the box that I left for you in the safe. These items are all for you to protect in case anything happens to me. I need you to hold onto and hide what is in the box. I'm sure you're wondering what all of this is. The gun is precautionary. The keys are to a car parked at the hotel. I want you to go to our special place outside of town. If anything happens to me, or if you don't hear from me for twenty-four hours, go there. Wait until either I or someone from the agency contacts you on the phone. It's a secure phone, and it's untraceable. Only a few people from the NSA have the number. They will*

be able to protect you. Give them the items in this box, especially the disk and thumb drive. They will know what to do with them. I can't tell you what everything else is, but guard it with your life; it's vital to our national security. I'm sorry to have gotten you involved in all of this.

I love you.
— Michael

They had taken a cab from the airport, so she didn't know how Michael had gotten keys to a rental car. But there was a hotel valet tag on the key chain, so that would make finding it easy. She needed to get to their secret place. When they got married, Kate wanted to do something nice for Michael, so she had taken him to a cottage in upstate New York. It was on a quiet little lake near a large private home built like a Swiss chateau. It was a peaceful getaway where they had a quaint stone cottage all to themselves. They enjoyed their week on their own private lake. Michael spent the days fishing, and Kate read and took long walks through the woods. She reminisced for a moment by the dresser . . .

Then she returned to the present and picked up the gun. It was heavy. It had been years since she had held one. She never wanted Michael to have guns in the house, but given the nature of his work, there was no way around it. He taught her early when they were dating how to shoot. She had never used a gun before she met Michael. He wanted her to learn just in case she would ever need to use one. She hoped that day wouldn't come.

She opened the chamber to see if the gun was loaded; it wasn't. She reached into the case, grabbed a clip, and loaded it. She cocked the gun and made sure the safety was on. She was going to set it down on the dresser when she heard a knock at the door. *Michael?*

56

Michael and Brody descended several stories down the ladder through the dark tunnel until they entered a similar safe room. Michael surveyed the area before stepping off the ladder.

Brody moved to the desk and hit a button. The ladder retracted into the tunnel. Then Brody hit another button, and the ceiling door closed with a muffled thud.

"Where are we now?" Michael asked. "This looks like the room we were in before."

"It's another safe room. We are several floors below the other office."

"We should be able to leave then, right?"

"It's not that simple. You know that colleague of mine upstairs?"

"What about him?"

"This safe room opens into his office. Well, it's not his real office; it's just his cover."

"How do you expect us to get out then? We can't go back to the other room, and if we walk out of here chances are someone will see us. We're trapped."

"Not entirely."

"There's another room below this one?"

"Unfortunately, no," Brody said.

"How do we get out of here then?" Michael asked. "We can't just wait around."

Brody sat down at the workstation. "I'm going to get these computers online. We can activate the cameras and see if there's anyone outside. We don't want to exit this room blindly." Brody knew that when Dimitri didn't find them upstairs, it wouldn't be long before he came looking for them downstairs. They had to work quickly.

"That's great and all, but what about anyone who might be in the hallway? What are we supposed to do about them?"

"I can activate the hallway cameras too. I have access to all of the cameras in this building. We should be able to see if there is anyone on the floor. If we can make it down the hallway to the staircase, we'll be okay. We only have a flight of stairs to go down to get to the back alley. There should be a car waiting for us there. Now help me with these computers."

"Is this the same system you have in your office?"

"Yes, but it's been modified."

"What's my colleague David doing mixed up in all of this?"

"I honestly don't know." Brody assumed that when Dimitri couldn't locate Michael fast enough, and he wasn't getting answers from Godfrey, that he'd find another way to get the information about the NSA's cyber surveillance projects. That's why Dimitri had kidnapped David and had sent men to track down Michael's wife at the hotel. Dimitri needed leverage in case Michael or Godfrey refused to talk. Brody wanted the information to sell to the Russians and the Chinese. He knew that Aiden or Dimitri would never provide it, at least not willingly. He assumed that Dimitri had found out that something wasn't going as planned, which is why he came looking for them. Dimitri had tipped Brody off about the raid at the warehouse, but Brody didn't know who was behind it.

Brody knew they didn't have much time; Dimitri could come downstairs at any minute. If Dimitri was able to access the safe room upstairs, Brody wondered what else had been compromised. He wasn't certain how much Dimitri knew, but he was not to be trusted. He had never trusted him.

By now the computers were online, and the cameras were activated. Michael checked the monitors. He didn't see anyone in the office or down the hall.

"Looks like we're in the clear. We should leave now." He breathed a sigh of relief.

Then something caught Brody's attention. He turned so swiftly he almost knocked Michael off balance.

"Hey, I said we were in the clear. There's nobody out there," Michael said.

"Not so fast."

Michael hadn't noticed the men on one of the screens. They were wearing black, and the lights in the hallway were out, so they almost disappeared in the blackness.

"It's just as I thought." Brody pointed at the screens.
"What?" Michael asked.

"Look, they're coming down the hallway."

Michael moved to take a closer look. He saw the silhouettes of armed men sneaking down the hall along the walls. "Holy . . ."

It was hard to distinguish the men, but they were sure it was the same ones from upstairs. The men were heavily armed. They surrounded the exterior office door.

"What are we going to do? They'll come in any second."

"Hold on."

"We don't have time. We have to act now." Suddenly Michael felt dizzy and began to stagger.

"Are you okay?"

"I'm feeling light-headed all of a sudden."

Brody leapt over to Michael. "Here, you need to sit down." He grabbed Michael's arm and helped him to a chair before racing back to the computer. Brody didn't like what he saw. The men congregated outside the office door. Michael was hunched over with his elbows on his knees and his hands on his forehead as if he was about to get sick.

Brody watched as Dimitri entered the office with a gun pointed at David's back. The other armed men followed inside before fanning out around the office. "They're here," Brody said ominously.

57

In the confined location of an undisclosed interrogation room in New York City, Godfrey stared in disbelief at his chief of staff, Aiden. It made no sense why Aiden and Dimitri would be working together, let alone behind his back.

"Aiden, what the hell are you doing here?" Godfrey asked, astounded.

"Well, sir, I came to check on you."

"How did you know I was even in New York? I didn't tell anyone. How did you know anything had happened to me? And why are you working with Dimitri?"

"Michael called me last night and again today."

"He did?"

"You sound surprised."

"Why would Michael be calling you?"

"Because I'm your chief of staff, and I keep a close eye on you and everyone else on the team. Michael sounded troubled. He said you tried reaching him and that he had called you back, but there was no answer for hours. Because he knows you live with your phone attached to you twenty-four/seven, he figured something was up. That's why he called me," Aiden said.

"But where are we, and how did you find me?"

Aiden smiled. "You forget I have my ways of monitoring people. Remember, that was one of the reasons you hired me. You wanted me to keep tabs on you and the others." Aiden had put a tracking device in Godfrey's phone as well as in the phones of the other members of the task force.

"But why am I here? And where are we?"

"We're inside one of our buildings."

"We're what!" Godfrey exclaimed. "No, it can't be." Godfrey knew there was no way they could be in the basement of an NSA building. They had moved him to another location. He was certain of that. He remembered the warm, musty room and the smell of cigar smoke. He had no idea what time it was or if it was day or night. But Aiden was telling the truth; they were in one of *their* buildings, just not an NSA building. They were in one of Homeland Security's holding facilities in New York City.

"But . . ."

"But what? What's so hard to believe?"

"How come I didn't know we had these facilities? I'm the director, damn it. I should be aware of these things. Did you know all of this was here? How long have you known about this? How and when did you get to New York?" Godfrey fired off his questions.

Aiden didn't answer. He simply stared at Godfrey.

"You've known about this, haven't you?" Godfrey pointed accusingly at Aiden.

"I didn't know that you had been detained here until some hours ago, but I have known about these facilities for some time, yes. We have many holding facilities here in New York." Aiden was lying through his teeth. He was working with Dimitri to arrange everything—the kidnapping, the interrogation, the deceptions. No one else had the level of access to Godfrey, his whereabouts, or his office. Aiden needed to know more about Godfrey's cyber surveillance project.

"Why didn't you tell me?"

"It was on a need-to-know basis, and you didn't need to know. Besides, if questioned, you could honestly deny the facilities' existence or your involvement."

Godfrey was quiet. For the most part, it made sense. He was one of the most senior directors at the NSA. With all the scandals and conspiracies that plagued the security agencies as of late, it was probably best that he didn't know about everything.

"I suppose you're right. Why all the commotion though, and why was I being held, let alone interrogated like a criminal? Who's behind all of this? Did you have a hand in any of this, Aiden? I'll have their head and yours if I find out that's the case. I can assure you of that." Godfrey shook his finger at Aiden.

"No, sir. As soon as I found out you were detained, I did everything I could to get you out of here. You won't believe the strings I had to pull. Dimitri contacted me to let me know you were here."

"Oh, really? Dimitri, of all people?"

"Yes."

"Why would Dimitri want to help me? . . . Who is in charge of this operation? It sure as hell isn't me."

"I honestly don't know." Aiden lied again. He was orchestrating all of the charades, but he couldn't tell Godfrey that.

"Bullshit, Aiden. Cut the crap. Who did you talk to in order to have me released?"

"I didn't get his name."

"Why not?"

"He didn't give it to me." Aiden continued his lies.

"Isn't that convenient."

Aiden was tiring of all the questions. He couldn't afford to tell Godfrey that he was behind the interrogation and that he had been working with Dimitri and Brody all along. Aiden had been keeping tabs on Godfrey and his team's activities since he'd brought on O'Shea to work undercover at Lucigen. It wasn't meant to endanger him in any way. Aiden was there to protect Godfrey and the interests of the agency—and the country. Besides, Godfrey had never really told him why he'd hired O'Shea, so Aiden took it upon himself to find out. Aiden didn't have all of the information, but he knew that Godfrey had taken and rewritten O'Shea's code. It made sense once he found out why. Godfrey was leading his own covert cyber surveillance program, but Aiden had never known why until recent months. He hoped through the interrogation that Godfrey might provide more information and a clear rationale for his actions, but he didn't. When Aiden realized what Godfrey was doing, he saw an opportunity for himself.

"Sir, with all due respect, I still think it's better that you not know all the details. It's best if you leave things up to me and the others." There was a tinge of arrogance and insubordination in Aiden's voice.

"What others?" Godfrey demanded.

Aiden paused. "You know . . . the others—Brody, Michael, the team."

"Michael's involved with you in this too? And Brody? You're saying that I should just let you all handle whatever it is that's going on while you leave me in the dark? I'm your boss, dammit." *Who does Aiden think he is? Michael's involved in this? I don't believe it. Michael would never go behind my back with something like this, but Aiden and Brody might.*

Aiden recognized the look of disgust on Godfrey's face. "Listen, sir. I can assure you that we are protecting you and the interests of the agency and the country."

"Protect me!" he blurted out. "I don't need your damn protection, Aiden. Have you lost your mind? Have you forgotten who you work for?"

"No, I haven't. It's difficult to explain, sir, because of what you know and don't know. That is why you were being questioned. They believe you have information that may help them."

"It was more like an interrogation. Who are 'they,' and what the hell do they want?" There was disdain in his tone. "Why was I being detained?"

"It has to do with the cyber defense and surveillance project Michael is working on with the team."

"Where is Michael, by the way?"

"I'm not sure exactly," Aiden said, "but he'll be joining us soon enough."

"I thought you would know because apparently you know everything." Godfrey was losing his patience.

"Not everything, sir. I don't know his specific whereabouts." Aiden knew Michael was in New York City, but it was true that he didn't know exactly where, at least not at the moment. Aiden didn't know if Brody had found Michael yet. Brody left earlier to meet with Michael after they moved Godfrey from Brody's office to the underground holding facility downtown. Neither of them had heard from Brody, so Dimitri had gone to look for them.

"Have you talked with Michael at all the past day or so?"

"How could I? Someone kidnapped me on Saturday, or at least I think it was Saturday. What's today? Have you talked to him at all?"

"No," Aiden said. "He just left me an urgent message that he hadn't been able to reach you. That's when I searched my sources and found that you were here. I also checked with the NSA's Travel Department, and they said you'd booked a last-minute trip to New York earlier this afternoon."

"When do we get out of here?" Godfrey wanted to return to headquarters and get answers.

"We'll leave soon enough."

"What do you mean? Dimitri just told me I was going to the airport."

"We'll go when we're done here. There's been a massive cyberattack against major network and industrial control systems across the country that involves at least one member of your unit, Matt O'Shea. This has compromised the safety of you and your staff. There was a distinct incident yesterday at Lucigen in D.C. where Matt works. I'm escorting you out of here, and then we're going to meet with Michael. A national disaster is happening that threatens our security, and we need to know who is behind it and why. More importantly, we need to know how we can prevent further damage across the country. Right now the malware that was discovered is like a bull in a China shop inside of our computer systems. Hopefully, it'll explain more as to why you were brought here and why Dimitri is involved. You'll get all your questions answered eventually. You must be patient."

Aiden then walked toward the door and motioned for Godfrey to follow.

58

Meanwhile, back in his office at FBI headquarters, Director Donovan sat at his desk staring keenly at his computer screen. *Where are you, Agent Burton?* Donovan typed his login information. He navigated through the command prompts until he located Agent Burton's profile. Donovan saw that his radio transponder was still active and navigated to where he could identify Burton's location. He typed in a series of commands until a satellite image of earth from space appeared. He zoomed in until he could see the outline of the Washington, D.C., metro area.

"Now, where are you?" Donovan continued to zoom in. "So you're still in D.C . . ." As the image grew larger and closer, Donovan saw that Burton was still near FBI headquarters. In fact, it looked like he was still in the building. Donovan pulled up the building schematics. *Is he in the garage? How can that be?* He pulled up Burton's vital signs indicator and saw they were abnormal. His heart rate and blood pressure were unusually low. *This reading can't be right.* Donovan pulled out his handheld device and opened his tracker application. It showed the same information that was on his computer screen. *There must be a mistake, some issue with the transponder calibration settings. There's no way he can still be in the building, let alone have these readings. There's only one way to find out.*

Donovan logged off his computer, grabbed his handheld tracker, and headed to the elevator bay nearest the underground garage. While waiting for the elevator, he checked the indicator display on his device. It showed that Burton was nearby. He stepped onto the elevator and hit the button for the second level. Once there he marched into the garage as he checked his device. The locator showed that Burton was less than thirty yards away. *Why is he still in the garage? If he's sleeping on the job, I'll have his head.*

Donovan followed the homing signal on his handheld device through the garage until he approached a black van parked at the far end opposite the elevators. His tracking device beeped rapidly, indicating that Agent Burton was nearby.

There were no windows in the van, so Donovan circled around to the driver's door to check if it was unlocked. It wasn't, and there was no one inside that he could see. From his angle, he couldn't see if someone was in the far back, so he unclipped his pistol and, with the butt, smashed the driver's side window. He reached in and unlocked the doors before going around to the rear doors. *Burton, you'd better not be sleeping in here.*

Not knowing what to expect, Donovan held his pistol in one hand while he grabbed the door handle with the other. He swung the rear doors open and lunged back.

"What the . . . *Burton?*"

59

Riley, Matt, and John made their way down a long, faintly lit corridor of the underground bunker.

"Where's security, or at least someone keeping an eye on things?" John asked.

"Don't worry. Like I said, there's always someone watching. I have no doubt of that." Riley motioned toward the ceiling where there were tiny, discreet security cameras. Each had a flashing red light.

"They're watching us?" John asked, knowing the answer but feeling the need to ask the question anyway.

"Very much so. My colleagues have been monitoring Matt for quite some time." Riley turned to Matt and John who were walking behind him. "Come on. We need to hurry."

The three men continued down the long, dark hallway. The air was dense, forcing them to breathe heavily, and the squeaking and clopping of their shoes echoed loudly. The buzzing of the ventilation system overhead could barely be heard.

The men came to a four-way intersection and stopped.

"Which way do we go?" Matt asked.

"This way." Riley motioned to the left.

As they rounded the corner the lights went out.

"Now what?" Matt said.

"Easy fellas, no need to worry."

As they waited in the darkness, Matt's heart raced feverishly as he felt it pounding. John was breathing faster as his anxiety level rose.

Riley patiently kept his wits about him. Moments later, just like before, the lights came back on. Then a loud, deep voice echoed from an intercom above. "Welcome, gentlemen.

We've been waiting."

60

Michael and Brody watched as Dimitri and his armed entourage of masked men in black uniforms entered the office with Michael's colleague David. Michael gathered himself while Brody worked quickly to devise a plan for their escape. Dimitri and his men didn't appear to be searching for anything. Dimitri stood near the door with his gun fixed on David as they exchanged words. Brody knew that at any point Dimitri could enter the hidden surveillance room.

Brody kept a close eye on the men. One of the armed men looked directly into the wireless cameras hidden inside a sculpture on the mantle. Michael and Brody watched as Dimitri and David engaged in a heated conversation. Dimitri didn't like what David was telling him.

"What are they saying?" Michael asked impatiently.

Brody held up his hand. "I can't quite hear. Let me try something else." He tweaked a few more knobs on the control board. "That's more like it. The man in the suit is arguing with David." Brody still hadn't told Michael his colleague's name. He knew working for Godfrey, Michael might know of Dimitri's story and disappearance. He didn't want Michael to know that Dimitri was alive.

"Arguing about what?"

"Not sure. I just picked up the conversation."

Michael watched and waited, tapping his foot, as was his custom when he was nervous.

"My colleague wants to know more about your cyber project. He believes David knows where you are, but he's not saying anything," Brody said as he pointed his finger at Michael.

"How could David possibly know where I am? He has no way of tracking me."

"Clearly others know we're in the building because someone followed us from the warehouse. They just don't know exactly where in the building we are."

"What else are they discussing?"

"My colleague isn't happy." On the screen, Brody and Michael saw Dimitri pound on the desk and wave wildly with a gun in his hand. He marched to David in the middle of the office and pointed the gun at David's head.

"This doesn't look good." Michael and Brody watched as Dimitri cocked his gun.

Michael gasped and reached for the computer screen as if he could somehow help his colleague.

Dimitri and David exchanged more heated words before Dimitri moved toward the fireplace. One of the armed masked men kept a gun fixed on David. They continued watching as Dimitri stood in front of the fireplace, silent. Brody changed camera angles to get a better view.

David flailed his arms as they bickered. Finally, he waved off Dimitri and turned in the direction of the door.

"You're not going anywhere." Dimitri raised his gun and unloaded a series of rounds into David's back. He staggered head-first, reeling in pain as he reached for his back. He grabbed the nearest chair, knocking it over. Dropping to his knees, he fell on his side.

Michael jumped back, startled by the gunshots. "He shot David!"

"It looks like it," Brody responded coldly. Dimitri was not to be trifled with; he would do whatever it took to get what he wanted.

Dimitri stomped about the room pointing the gun at his men as he yelled orders.

"What's he saying?" Michael asked.

"I don't know. I don't understand Russian."

"Russian!" Michael blurted. "Those men are Russian?"

Brody thought Dimitri might be playing both sides. In his mind, this only confirmed his suspicions. Brody just didn't know at what level Dimitri was involved with the Russians. Had Dimitri been selling government secrets?

Michael and Brody continued to watch the scene unfold on the monitors.

"Leave him here," Dimitri said in English. "We'll come back for him later. Right now we need to find Brody. We know he's around here somewhere."

Michael gave Brody a suspicious glare.

Brody knew he was a marked man. He couldn't risk getting caught. Perhaps Dimitri learned that he was colluding with the Russians and Chinese.

Dimitri motioned for the men to leave, and they filed out of the office. Dimitri didn't bother to check if David was still alive. Once all the men had exited, Dimitri closed and locked the office door.

Brody changed camera views to show the hallways. He and Michael watched as the group moved down the corridor toward the elevators. For the time being, they were in the clear.

61

Kate stood in the honeymoon suite with the gun in her hand. The knocks at the door sounded again. She stepped out of the bedroom and tiptoed near the door, not sure what to do. Kate recalled what Michael told her about how he would knock when he returned. *Seven taps,* she remembered. And she was not to open the door for anyone else.

"Room service," a man's voice sounded from the other side of the door.

Room service? She hadn't ordered room service, and Michael certainly would not have ordered it given their last interaction at the restaurant.

"Room service." The man knocked again.

Didn't I put the "Do Not Disturb" sign out? Indeed, in her rush and angst to get back to the hotel, she had forgotten to put the sign on the door. *Drat. What am I going to do?* Michael told her to put the sign up so no one would bother her unless they had a really good reason to come knocking.

She would call the front desk. They would know if room service had been ordered. She peeked through the peep hole. There was a man dressed in a white hotel uniform who looked like a member of the kitchen staff. Next to him was a food cart with plates covered with metal domes. A bottle of champagne was on ice in a bucket. Kate swooped over by the couch, grabbed the phone, and dialed the front desk.

"This is the front desk. How may I assist you?"

"Good evening," Kate whispered. "With whom am I speaking?"

"This is Connie. How may I assist you, Mrs. Stevens?"

"Can you tell me if my husband ordered room service, or if someone did on our behalf?"

"Sure. Why do you ask?"

"Because there's a man outside our room saying he has room service for us. I didn't order room service, so I wanted to check."

"Of course, Mrs. Stevens, let me check that for you. Give me just one minute, please. Is it okay if I put you on hold?"

"Yes, but please hurry."

"Thanks. I'll be right back."

There was a pause that seemed like an eternity to Kate.

"It appears our hotel manager provided the room service. It was a courtesy for your special weekend. Congratulations, by the way."

"Fine, thank you." *Would Michael have told the manager about our occasion? Why would the manager be sending room service at this time of night? Wouldn't they have asked first before sending it up? Michael said not to open the door for anyone, not even him unless he gave the special knock.*

"Connie, would you mind putting me through to the manager?"

"Certainly. Is everything all right?"

"Yes, of course. I'd just like to thank him."

"Oh, yes. Let me put you through. Give me one second, please."

Kate waited anxiously while Connie dialed the manager.

"Mrs. Stevens, it doesn't look like he's at his desk. He's not answering the phone. Would you like me to page him? It would only take a moment." Kate didn't want to seem paranoid, but she had learned from Michael years ago that you could never be too cautious.

"If you could page him that would be great."

"Just one minute while I put you on hold."

"Okay."

There was a brief silence before the background music started. As Kate waited, the man outside the door knocked again. She checked her watch. He must have been out there for at least five minutes. *Why hadn't he left? Even if I didn't put up the "Do Not Disturb" sign, he should have gotten the hint that no one was answering the door.*

"Mrs. Stevens?" Connie's voice broke Kate's whirlwind of thoughts.

"Yes, Connie."

"I paged him, but he didn't answer. Would you like me to leave a message?"

Unknown to Connie and Kate, the manager wasn't answering because he had been bound and gagged by two men and left unconscious in a storage closet in the hotel basement.

"No, that won't be necessary. I'll try him again later." She had to think hastily. She didn't want to sound alarmed, but she was concerned by the unidentified man outside her door.

The knocks came again, followed by a man's voice. "Mrs. Stevens, this is the manager on duty. Are you in there?"

"Hold on, Connie, it sounds like someone else is at the door."

That was quick—a little too quick. Kate put down the phone and snuck over to the door. She peered through the peephole again to see two men: the waiter in the white kitchen outfit and a second man, well-dressed, in his early forties. He wore a tailored navy blue or black suit and silver tie with a shiny name tag on his jacket that she couldn't quite read. He was heavy set with a strong chest and shoulders, but handsome. He had short, dark brown hair. His dark, well-trimmed beard was a tad longer than a five o'clock shadow. Neither of the men showed much of an expression.

"Mrs. Stevens? It's the hotel manager. The front desk paged me. I'm coming by to see if everything is okay."

Kate carefully placed her hand on the doorknob. She stared back at the phone she'd set on the end table. She wasn't sure what to do. Once again she recalled Michael's advice: Do not open the door under any circumstance, not even for him unless he knocked as he had explained. But everything seemed all right. She had spoken with Connie about the room service. She had checked with the manager. Now the manager was apparently outside her door. Certainly it would be fine to let them enter. But first Kate went back to the phone.

"Connie."

"Yes, Mrs. Stevens. How may I help you?"

"Honestly, I don't know."

"You seem alarmed. Are you sure everything is all right?" There was sincere concern in Connie's voice.

"I'll know in a few minutes."

"Is there anything I can do?"

"There is, actually. I'm going to leave my phone off the hook. I don't want you to hang up. If you hear anything unusual, I want you to call security and get them up here right away; do you understand?"

"But Mrs. Stevens—" Connie was troubled by Kate's last comment.

"Connie, I need you to do this for me."

"But I don't understand. What's going on?"

"I'm not sure right now, but I need you to go with me on this. Will you do that?"

"Yes."

"Thank you. Put your phone on mute so it won't pick up any background noise from the lobby."

"Yes, ma'am."

"Hopefully, I'll be back on the line in less than five minutes."

"Sure," Connie replied. Her heart was pounding. She was disconcerted and didn't know what was happening. It was late, and she was the only one at the front desk. There weren't many guests checking in or loitering in the lobby. She checked her watch. *It'll only be five minutes.*

On the other end, Kate put down the phone raced around the bedroom to hide the black metal box under their bed, the two men knocked again.

"Mrs. Stevens?" one of the men hollered.

She composed herself before returning to the door. She kept the safety latch on as she cautiously opened the door.

"Good evening, gentlemen," her voice was pleasant as she tried to appear calm.

"Hello, Mrs. Stevens. How are you tonight?" the man who said he was the manager asked.

"I'm just fine, thank you. To what do we owe the pleasure of this visit?"

"Your husband called earlier and said you two were here for a special weekend. On behalf of the hotel, I wanted to provide you with a nice evening meal and dessert."

"That's awfully kind of you, but we already ate dinner. We just got back."

"That's alright. We'll just drop this off and be on our way. Perhaps you both may get hungry later."

"I'd prefer that you not. My husband isn't feeling and he's sleeping on the couch. I don't want him to be disturbed. Good night." She didn't want them to know she was alone.

She began to close the door when the manager wedged his shoe in the door.

"We'll only be a minute," he said abruptly with a dubious smirk.

"That won't be necessary. Please remove your foot," she said forcefully. She gave him an angry stare. Kate sensed the tension and knew opening the door had been a mistake.

"I apologize, how rude of me," he said as he gave her a smug look and leisurely pulled his foot away.

"Good night." Kate hurriedly closed the door and leaned up against it and sighed.

A series of loud knocks shook the door.

What now dammit. I told them to leave. She spun around and started opening the door to tell them off when they kicked it open, knocking her back as she fell to the floor. Before she could react the two men were on top of her. The manager straddled her chest and restrained her arms while the other took a syringe from his pocket and injected a drug into her arm.

"Connie!" Kate tried yelling as loud as she could while she fought to keep the man's hand away from her mouth.

Connie had been listening intently. "Mrs. Stevens? Mrs. Stevens? Is everything okay?"

"Connie . . . help . . . " Kate pleaded, but her voice was barely audible, the man on top of her had forced a napkin into her mouth.

Connie wasn't sure what was going on. She couldn't hear what Kate was saying.

Kate flailed her arms and legs attempting to fight back but she was no match for the two men. As the drug took affect her body relaxed and went limp.

"Mrs. Stevens?" Connie cried out. Something was wrong.

Connie put down the phone. *What about the manager? I'll page him again, but first I need to call security.* She picked up another phone at the front desk. "Security, it's Connie at the front desk. I need you to go up to the honeymoon suite right away."

"What's the problem?" the guard asked.

"I'm not sure, but I think something's wrong. I was just on the phone with a guest, and it sounded like she was in trouble."

"All right, we'll check it out."

"Thank you."

The security guard hung up the phone. *It's probably just some drunken guest that accidentally dialed the front desk. I'll check on it later.* He whirled around in his chair to continue watching the Knicks' game on television.

Upstairs in the honeymoon suite, Kate's world had gone dark as she lay unconscious on the floor. The young man dressed as a waiter checked her pulse. "She's still alive."

"Good, we need to keep her that way," the man dressed as the manager replied.

"How do we get her out of here?"

"Will she fit under the food cart?"

"I don't know. I saw a laundry cart down the hall. The cleaning staff must have left it there."

"Go get it."

The waiter quickly returned with the cart. The two men lifted her into it and covered her with linens.

"Let's go. Take her downstairs to the laundry room near the loading dock. I'll meet you there as soon as I can."

The two men exited the room and headed down the hallway toward the elevator.

"You take this one," the man dressed as the manager said. "I'll wait for the next one. It's best not to be seen together."

The waiter then pushed the cart onto the elevator as the door closed behind him.

62

Members of the Dallas Fire Department were responding to what began as a one-alarm fire just after dinnertime in an uptown high-rise apartment complex. The fire started on the sixth floor where a couple was cooking dinner, and a grease fire ensued. They didn't have a fire extinguisher in their apartment, so they weren't able to contain the flames that spread rapidly through the kitchen and the rest of their apartment. Flames and smoke consumed their residence in minutes. For some reason, the building's sprinkler and alarm systems hadn't activated. Dispatch received the initial 911 call from the couple, and a handful of engine companies arrived on the scene. The firefighters quickly made their way into the building to assess the situation.

"Chief, I just heard from our men inside. The fire is spreading rapidly," a lieutenant called out. "The sprinkler systems never activated."

The chief gave him a confused look. "How can that be? We just checked the alarm and sprinkler systems across the city recently."

"I don't know, sir, but we've got to do something quick. Our ladders only reach to the eighth floor, and we've got residents on the twentieth."

Just then another firefighter ran up, panting for breath. "Chief! Chief!"

"What is it?" The chief held up his hand indicating the man should take a second to catch his breath.

"Chief, I just checked the alarm control panel on the first floor . . . None of the alarms have gone off in the building. Not a single one. Many of the residents don't even know there's a fire in the building."

"What!" The chief looked up as flames burst from the windows of the apartments on another floor. "Not a single alarm has gone off?"

"I'm afraid not, chief."

"What about other 911 calls?"

"The only one that's come in to dispatch was the first one."

"My God, what's going on? All of those people in there . . ."

Another firefighter yelled, "Chief, our communications are down."

"What do you mean?" the chief snarled.

"All of our radio and phone communications are down. I can't reach anyone at dispatch, and I don't know where our people are in the building."

"Dear Lord, help us," the chief muttered. Then he saw something smash through one of the apartment windows about nine stories up.

"Watch out!" one of the other firefighters yelled.

Luckily, the men heard the warning and jumped out of the way as a table crashed onto the sidewalk. A man and a woman leaned out of the broken window, screaming for help. The firefighters on the ground couldn't make out the words, but they knew the people were terrified. Smoke engulfed the couple as they leaned further out of the window. The firefighters looked up, knowing there was nothing they could do. To their horror, holding hands, the couple leapt from their ninth- story apartment, their arms and legs flailing as they plunged to the pavement. Even the veteran firefighters who had seen plenty of tragedy in their careers were stunned. Many couldn't hold back the tears. But the chief, whose heart was breaking, knew he had to remain firmly in charge despite the tragic circumstances.

"Get dispatch on the line now, dammit!" the chief yelled. "We need more engines!"

"But chief, like I said, our communications are down. We've got nothing."

Another firefighter ran up to the chief and said, "Sir, I've got more bad news."

"What?" he snapped as he whirled around.

"We don't have any water pressure. Our hoses are useless."

"You've got to be kidding me. Those hydrant pipes aren't supposed to lose pressure. What in God's name is going on here? Nothing we need is working."

The firefighters stood around the chief with blank, hopeless stares, some still trying to hold by their tears. All they knew was that there was nothing they could do to contain the fire. There was an explosion, and the firefighters looked up as more flames burst from the building. They heard the eerie cries of trapped resident s being burned alive. They watched in horror as more residents leapt from their windows to their deaths. What started as a small apartment fire would consume the entire apartment complex, taking hundreds of lives—men and women, children and the elderly, and the firefighters who had bravely entered the building in a doomed effort to save them.

The chief stared at the fiery carnage and shook his head in disbelief. Never before had the veteran firefighter cried at the scene, but this had become more than even he could take. "God help us all," he sobbed.

63

In the interrogation room, Godfrey paused before joining Aiden at the door.

"Come on, we've got go." Aiden motioned for Godfrey to follow him. Reluctantly, Godfrey did so, heading through a series of narrow, winding tunnels until they eventually exited into an underground parking garage. There was a black SUV with a driver waiting for them. Godfrey breathed in the stale air.

Aiden opened the back passenger door and ordered Godfrey to get in. Godfrey gave him a hesitant look. Aiden prodded, "Come on. We need to go. There's not much time."

Aiden knew there was only a brief window to get to Michael. Dimitri was looking for him at the safe house, and Dimitri had sent his men to capture Kate at the hotel before the Russians could take her. Brody was supposed to meet with Michael at the warehouse and then take him back to the safe house after he showed him the stockpile of computer equipment. Aiden knew he could trust Dimitri, but he wasn't so sure about Brody.

Aiden and Dimitri had worked together for years, even after Dimitri's disappearance and supposed death. He, Godfrey, and Dimitri had been long-time colleagues in the intelligence community, even though Aiden was some years younger than the other two. When Dimitri disappeared after the boating accident near Portugal, Aiden suspected foul play. He searched for Dimitri through his intelligence channels and finally found him. Aiden had been helping him avoid detection ever since. Given Godfrey's role in the NSA, Aiden couldn't tell him about Dimitri. Aiden intentionally sought out the chief of staff position with Godfrey to keep a pulse on things at the agency and elsewhere in the intelligence community. The stature and access that role provided suited his purposes well.

The SUV wound around the final incline as it exited the garage. They entered a courtyard with a roundabout that featured sculptures in the middle. The forty-story glass building towered over them as they circled the courtyard. Godfrey saw the row of international flag poles outside the black fence, and finally he knew exactly where he was. He'd been there many times before, though on his own accord.

"The United Nations in New York City . . ." Godfrey's voice trailed off in disbelief. *How?* He couldn't make any sense of it as he grabbed Aiden's shoulder in utter amazement. "You have a lot of explaining to do."

64

At the safe house in the hidden surveillance room of Dimitri's office, Michael and Brody waited to ensure that Dimitri and his entourage had left the floor. Brody accessed a series of security cameras to ascertain where Dimitri had gone. He didn't see him anywhere, so he assumed he and his men had left the building. They were at least out of the office and off their floor, which would give him and Michael time to exit. Brody pointed to the screens.

"I think we're in the clear." Brody said. "We should get going." He checked the hallway cameras one last time before he engaged the hidden door activation mechanism. There were several loud clunks as the bolts unlocked. The door to the safe room squealed as it opened. When there was enough room for them to exit, Brody paused the door. He didn't want to open it fully in case they had to reenter quickly.

Brody motioned to Michael. "Come on, let's go." Brody slipped into the office. Michael followed Brody's lead, cautiously poking his head around the side of the door. Brody looked at David's motionless body lying face down on the floor.

"We've got to get out of here, Michael."

"Wait. What about David?"

"I'm sorry, Michael, but he's dead. There's nothing we can do."

Brody stepped around David's body and moved to the door. He put his ear up to it to determine if he could hear anything. It was silent outside. But as Brody turned to step away from the door, he heard something. It was barely audible, but it sounded like someone groaning.

"Do you hear that?" Brody waved for Michael to come over.

"Hear what?" Michael crept over to Brody and leaned against the door to listen.

"That groaning noise. Listen again." Brody cupped his hands against the door.

"Where's it coming from?"

"I can't tell. It's getting louder though."

Michael stood quietly. "Wait. Yeah, I do hear it, but barely. But I can't tell where it's coming from, either."

"Heeerrrree . . ." David grunted with all his effort.

Michael and Brody spun around and ran over to him. "David—we thought you were dead." Michael knelt beside him.

David squinted up, surprised to see Michael. "What are you doing here? Where am I?"

"You're in an office building in New York City, but don't worry about that now. We'll get you out of here."

65

In the parking garage of FBI headquarters Director Donovan stood with the rear van doors open as he looked at a man lying shackled in a fetal position.

"Burton!" Donovan climbed into the back of the van. He shook the man, but there was no response. He removed the black hood from Agent Burton's head. He was unconscious, but he still had a pulse.

"What's going on?" He lightly tapped Burton's pockmarked face to see if he could get a response. "Burton, wake up." There was no response.

Burton was alive, but Donovan had no idea how Burton had ended up like this or who had done this to him. Donovan climbed over the passenger seat and looked in the glove compartment to find a set of handcuff keys. He grabbed them and unlocked the shackles around Burton's ankles and wrists. After removing the tape from Burton's mouth, he sat him upright against the side of the van.

"Burton, can you hear me?" Donovan grabbed both of his shoulders and shook him lightly. Burton's head tilted, limp.

Donovan noticed a quarter-sized bruise on the side of his neck, so he examined it further. He saw a tiny red dot in the center where something had been injected. Whatever the substance, it had knocked Burton out. Donovan needed to get Burton back to his office and wake him up. He needed to know what happened and who did this.

There was a medical clinic on site at the FBI, but Donovan didn't know if the physician would still be working this late on a Saturday. At the very least he'd be able to access the clinic and get some smelling salts or epinephrine to revive Burton. Donovan would have to move him on his own; he couldn't risk getting help.

Donovan checked Burton one last time. He was faintly breathing but still unconscious. Donovan crawled out of the van and closed the back doors. He needed to hurry to the clinic but would stop by his office first. Perhaps there would be something on the garage surveillance cameras that might show him who did this to Burton and when they did it.

66

The hotel waiter and man dressed like the manager met in the hotel's basement laundry room. "What do you want me to do with Mrs. Stevens? We can't keep her here in the laundry room." The waiter pointed to the laundry cart where Kate was hidden under a pile of linens.

"No, we can't." The other man checked his watch.

"Where should I take her? I can't just grab a cab."

"Take the utility van. It's parked in the alley outside of the rear loading dock. Drive her to the safe house. Dimitri will meet you there. I'll meet you there later."

"What if Dimitri isn't there?"

"Dimitri should be there by then if he's not already. I'll send him a message to let him know you're on the way. I'll call you later. I need to take care of something first."

"You got it." The waiter pushed the cart to the loading dock door and opened it. The utility van was backed up to the door. He opened the back door of the van and wheeled the cart inside. He closed the door and looked back. His associate had already left. The man in the suit changed into a security guard uniform before he set out for the lobby.

The waiter activated the loading dock door and crawled under it. The waiter jumped down from the loading dock, climbed into the driver's seat, and headed to rendezvous with Dimitri.

67

Connie paced anxiously behind the front desk. She didn't know what to do. She kept looking at her watch. *Why haven't I heard anything from security yet?* She reached for the phone to call security again when she saw an unfamiliar guard enter the lobby.

"Security! Security!" she called out desperately as she ran toward him.

"Yes, what is it? What can I do for you?" he asked calmly.

"It's Mrs. Stevens."

"Who? What about her?"

"She called to ask for help several minutes ago. She's in the honeymoon suite."

He listened calmly as he nodded. "Yes. Uh-huh. What else did she say?"

"All I heard her was, 'Connie, help.' That's when I called you guys," she explained as she pointed to the security patch on his shirt. "But I don't recognize you."

"I'm new. I just started this week. We got your message. I was making my rounds, so I checked on Mrs. Stevens."

"And what did you find out?"

"She seemed perfectly fine when I was there. She thanked me, and then I continued making my rounds."

Connie didn't believe a word of it. She knew everyone at the hotel, even the new hires, and she didn't know this guy who claimed to be a guard. But she didn't want to let on.

"If it would make you feel better, I'll call right now just to make sure."

"Yes, it would." Connie began to calm down.

They walked over to the front desk.

"Okay, let me see the phone." The guard reached across the counter to pick up the phone, but Connie grabbed it and dialed the Stevens' room number. The impostor heard ringing on the other end. He knew no one would pick up.

Connie said, "There's no answer."

"At this hour she and Mr. Stevens must have retired for the evening," the impostor suggested. "She said her husband wasn't feeling well when I spoke to her earlier."

"But I heard her call for help. It couldn't have been more than twenty minutes ago," Connie pleaded.

"Look," the guard said forcefully, "I was just up there, and she was fine. You're over-reacting. I'll check on them again when I make my next round. Besides, it looks like you've got things to deal with." He motioned to the guests who were waiting at the front desk. "If you don't hear anything from me, you can be sure everything is fine."

The impostor didn't give her a chance to respond as he made a line toward the elevators. She stared him down as he left. He must have sensed her watching because he turned, waved, and smiled half-heartedly. Once he rounded the corner, he made his way swiftly to the stairs. He had somewhere else to be. Dimitri would be waiting.

68

David was crumpled on the floor of Dimitri's office as Michael knelt next to him. "David, can you walk?" Michael asked as he attempted to help him up.

"I don't know," he said, gasping as if the wind had been knocked out of him. "It feels like I got hit by a truck," he said as he finally regained full consciousness. If they didn't get him to a hospital soon, he would die. David struggled to keep his eyes open, and he was losing blood fast.

"Who were those men with you?" Michael tried sitting David up, but it didn't work.

David stared up at Michael. "I don't know. One minute I'm in my house in Maryland, the next minute I'm being escorted off a private jet at LaGuardia." David coughed, and blood sprayed from his mouth.

"Did they say what they wanted, why they kidnapped you? What were they looking for?"

"They wanted information about our cyberterrorism and surveillance projects against the Russians and Chinese. They were looking for you and the guy you're with." David glanced at Brody.

"You must be the one. I didn't tell them anything, I swear." Bloody drool seeped from David's mouth and down his chin.

Michael bent closer. "Who were you arguing with?"

Before David could answer, Brody interrupted. "We'll have time for questions later, but right now we need to get out of here." Brody wanted to get David alone to question him, but he would need to keep him alive first. He needed to know what Dimitri was after and why.

"Dimitri. I think I heard him say Dimitri." David tried to stay awake but faded in and out of consciousness.

"Enough . . . we've got to go!" Brody did what he could to hurry them up.

"Do you know why they left in such a hurry?" Michael asked. He still wasn't ready to leave.

David struggled to stay conscious as he began to go into shock. "I can't recall exactly, but his phone rang. Something about a woman . . . somebody's wife . . . at a nearby hotel . . . and leverage," he gasped, coughing up more blood as he began to tremble.

Michael deliberated. *A woman at a hotel . . . leverage . . . certainly they couldn't be after Kate.* But there was no way for him to know. "Why did they leave you here?" Michael asked. He assumed they would have finished the job.

"I don't know." David did his best to keep his eyes open.

"David, stay with me. We're going to get you out of here." Michael squatted down behind David and wrapped his arms under his armpits and lifted him.

David looked up with a blank stare, his body limp. Brody could see David's lifeless eyes and that he had stopped breathing.

"Michael, it's too late. He's dead." Brody placed his hand gently on Michael's shoulder. "I'm sorry, but there's nothing more you can do. We've already been here too long."

"He can't be gone," Michael said as he knelt over his young colleague, shook him, and called out, "David! David!"

Michael began to start CPR, but Brody pulled him back. "We've got to go while we still can."

"We can't just leave him here." Michael was on both knees next to David's lifeless body.

"We have to."

Brody reached for Michael, but he batted his hand away as he stared at his dead colleague.

"We're not leaving him behind."

"We'll come back for him," Brody said softly. Michael reached over and closed David's eyes before sluggishly standing.

Brody then moved to the door and tried to open it, but it wouldn't budge. "It's locked."

Brody paused, then he motioned for Michael to step back. Brody pulled something out of his bag and knelt down by the door as if he was going to pick the lock. Instead, Brody set something by the door and then hurried toward them shouting, "Get down behind the desk! Do it now!"

Just then a muffled explosion blew debris across the room as a small plume of smoke and dust filled the space. Michael and Brody poked their heads over the desk. Brody stood up and dusted himself off as he watched the door swinging from the hinges. "Just as planned. Come on, let's go."

Michael and Brody made their way to the freight elevator. Moments later the elevator opened in the basement maintenance area. Brody turned to Michael and said, "I'll grab the car. Meet me in the back alley. It's that way." Brody pointed toward the end of the hallway. "Go straight until the corridor ends, then make a left. You can't miss it. You'll see a red metal door with an 'exit' sign on it."

Brody then hurried off in the opposite direction as Michael made his way toward the alley exit.

69

Riley, Matt, and John remained silent in the hallway when the voice over the intercom bellowed out again: "We've been waiting for you."

John waved at the camera on the ceiling. "You have? That's nice. Where's the welcome mat?"

"Who are you?" Matt asked.

"You will find out soon enough." It was Osmund, the Director of the North American Cyber Command Center known as NA-C3.

Riley pointed to the end of the corridor. "There."

The men made their way to the end of the hall to an enormous steel door. There was a key pad to the right with a biometric security scanner. Matt had seen similar ones during his trips to the NSA.

John asked, "Are they going to let us in?"

"No need. I can do it." Riley put his hand on the screen and entered his passcode. A moment later, they heard the bolts of the large door unlock, and it opened with a rumble.

Riley signaled to Matt and John. "Come on. They're waiting."

They were astonished by what they saw. It was a large control room with massive screens that took up an entire wall nearly twenty feet high and forty feet wide. There were rows of computer terminals in a half-moon shape arranged in theater style. They all faced the wall of screens, and each seat had its own computer workstation. It looked like a shuttle launch control center. There were at least three dozen staff operating the computers while additional staff scurried about to conduct other urgent tasks.

The trio noticed a man standing on a small balcony overlooking the action. He was an older Caucasian man, probably in his late fifties or early sixties, average build, handsome, with short gray hair brushed neatly to the side. Osmund was clean-cut and well-dressed. He sported a dark gray suit with a white dress shirt but no tie. He was tall with narrow shoulders. Despite a generally unimpressive physical frame, his presence still commanded authority. His booming voice fit his towering figure. As Matt examined him more closely, he experienced the strange feeling that he knew him from somewhere, but he had no idea where.

Four marine guards armed with assault rifles greeted them. One of the marines approached with his gun fixed on them. "Face the wall and put your hands on your head."

The three of them did as they were instructed. The other marines searched them. They took Matt's backpack that contained the computer components and confiscated the guns that Riley had given them.

A loud, deep voice sounded from behind them. "Make sure you search them thoroughly. We need everything."

Riley resisted as he was searched. "What the hell is going on, Osmund?"

"We can't be too cautious. The situation is dire, and we believe it may be the result of an inside job at the NSA."

"What's with all of this?" Matt complained. It looks like you're at war."

"We are at war, Mr. O'Shea," the older man said as he stepped down from his perch.

"You're serious, aren't you?" John said.

"Dead serious." Osmund strode over to them.

"Why are we here?" Matt asked. *None of this was part of my NSA job description.*

"Because we need your help."

"You need our help? How? We don't even know why we're here or what's going on." Matt had difficulty talking as his face was still pressed against the wall.

"More specifically, we need Matt's help," Osmund said as he moved closer.

"Matt? You're kidding, right?" John sneered.

"No, I'm not." Osmund stood directly behind them.

"How is it you need my help? It looks like you've got plenty of personnel here."

"True, but the specialized knowledge and expertise we need, well, you're one of a very few who have it. That's why we need you in particular."

"What could I possibly do?"

"Come now, Matthew. Don't you remember the Fawkes virus?"

Matt remained silent. No one had called him Matthew in years, not since he was in middle school. And not only that, no one knew he'd written the Fawkes virus. He'd never told anyone about it, and he'd done it under the hacker alias of "Red Fox."

"I heard about it years ago," John said, but he had no idea how it related to Matt.

"It's a code," Matt spoke up.

"Matt is correct," Osmund replied.

"I get that, but a code for what?" John asked.

"Matt, why don't you tell John about it?"

"I'd rather not. It's better that John not know, for his own safety. Can we put our arms down and turn around now? This is tiring." Osmund knew about Matt's code, but Matt didn't know how he could have found out about it.

"Yes, of course." Osmund gave the armed guards a nod, and they backed away and lowered their guns. "Please come over here." Osmund motioned for them to stand by a railing that overlooked the facility.

"What is all of this?" John asked as he waved his hand widely.

"This is the North American Cyber Command Center, and right now we're incredibly busy."

"Who are you?" Matt asked.

"I'm the Director, Director Osmund."

Matt was confused. He thought he was working for the NSA's Tailored Access Operations. Matt hadn't heard of this cyber division at all. He wondered if who he was working for at the NSA was involved in this program.

Osmund spoke up. "We've been working on some special projects, one of which may be of particular interest to you, Mr. O'Shea. We believe it's the reason behind the whole fiasco at Lucigen and around the country."

"And what would that be?"

"I'll show you." Osmund directed their attention to the screens on the wall where there were satellite views of major cities around the United States, but a number of the screens remained dark.

"Those look like cities," John said.

"You are correct," Osmund responded.

"And why are we looking at satellite images of cities?" Matt asked.

"Because we're hoping to see something. Let me rephrase. We anticipate seeing something."

"And what is that?" Matt asked.

"Just wait."

"You brought us all the way out here to the middle of nowhere to show us a bunch of satellite views? I could have just used Google Earth on my own damn computer," John uttered, annoyed as he pointed to the monitors.

"Yes and no. There are things we can tell you, and there are things we can show you. In this case, you'll understand better if we show you."

"Fair enough. So what are we waiting for?" Matt asked.

"Do you have the computer components you took from your office?" Osmund asked, looking at Matt.

"How do you know I took anything?"

"We have our ways. I need those components."

"Why?"

"Those components are necessary to show you why you're here."

"They're in my backpack." Matt motioned to the bag, and one of the guards set it on top of a nearby desk and rummaged through it. He pulled out the memory cards, thumb drive, and motherboard along with the other components. The guard then carried them to Osmund. Matt watched as Osmund examined everything closely.

"Plug these components into our system and test them," Osmund ordered, signaling a nearby technician. The tech inserted the motherboard into an open slot and plugged the thumb drive into the USB port. Some command prompts popped up, and the tech began keying in information.

"What are you doing?" Matt asked.

"We're running a malware diagnostic scan and a trace."

"Why?"

"We're looking for patterns and any abnormal connections."

"And what might those be?"

"A distinct pattern. You noticed the code profile when you ran the diagnostic in your building, didn't you?"

"Yes. I noticed the code and a strange pattern in Lucigen's control systems. I'd never seen abnormalities like those before, but I didn't have much time to examine them. Someone hacked into my computer overnight, and when I arrived at the office Saturday morning, I noticed the security breach. Not only that, someone was remotely controlling my computer even while I was sitting at my desk. I found a cellular network card attached to my motherboard."

"Of course you did. Do you have a printout of your diagnostic test or a copy of the code on the thumb drive?"

"Yes."

"Where is it?"

"It's also in my backpack."

Osmund motioned for the guard holding the bag to check it. He pulled out the wrinkled stacks of paper.

"Bring that to me." Osmund examined the papers. "Hmm . . ." He wasn't sure what to make of them.

Matt gave Osmund a cockeyed look and asked, "Who hacked my system at Lucigen?"

"We have some idea. That's part of the reason you're here—to help us figure out who is doing this and to stop it from happening again."

"Where do you think the attacks are coming from?"

"We've traced them to China, Russia, and North Korea, though we haven't been able to trace the exact source of the code. It continually mutates."

"That's strange," John said.

"I agree," Matt added. He was familiar with mutation strings, but he'd never seen them used against an energy company.

"It's most interesting what we've discovered."

"How so?" Matt asked.

"Just the overall code itself. It's a form of communication between computer systems, but we didn't know for what purpose until last night."

"And what purpose is that?" Matt asked.

"To take out all of our nation's industrial control systems and infrastructure."

Matt had known long ago exactly what could happen, and the NSA had briefed him on scenarios as part of his undercover assignment.

"All of our country's infrastructure could be impacted: telecom, power, gas, water, Internet, you name it," Osmund said. "Anything controlled by a computer and connected to the web could be taken offline just like that." Osmund snapped his fingers. "Worst of all, it's already begun."

John ran his hand over his head as he grasped the severity of the situation.

"How do we stop it?" Matt inquired.

"We can't right now, unfortunately. And therein lies the problem."

"What do you mean?"

Osmund directed their attention to the large screens. "You've already experienced a brief taste of what it'd be like if our control systems go down and the chaos it would create."

John wore a quizzical look, but Matt knew exactly what Osmund meant. "You mean the traffic lights. They were out in D.C. as we escaped the city. There was complete gridlock."

"Exactly. The power disruption last night and today in parts of D.C. was not due to the thunderstorm. It was because of a cyberattack. I'm afraid that other control systems across the city and country have already begun to go down too. The traffic lights across D.C. have been knocked completely offline. It's good you got out when you did. Power in most parts of D.C. also has been taken out, at least those parts controlled by Lucigen. That's what our adversaries were doing when they hacked your systems. We've been able to thwart them for the time being and restore power to parts of the city, but we won't be able to hold off their continued attacks for long."

"How come?"

"Unfortunately for us, this looks like an inside job, which means that as soon as we close off one access point to our infrastructure systems, another one is created. Someone is actively operating and directing this code. Somebody is intentionally attacking the U.S. infrastructure. The events thus far have been sporadic. It hasn't been full-scale nationwide yet, but most major U.S. cities have been impacted in one way or another. Power and communications are the two systems most affected. The situation is dire. People are dying."

"What do you mean? Dying how?" John asked.

"There," Osmund said as he turned to face the giant monitors on the wall. "See that screen on the far left."

"It's almost totally blacked out," John said.

"Well, my friends, that's St. Louis. Most of the power to the city has been taken out—even auxiliary power for generators and backup systems. The hospitals and other medical facilities have no power, which means anyone on life support will die. Some already have. Emergency personnel can't respond to 911 calls because their phones are down. And because the traffic lights are out and the city is in gridlock, help couldn't get through anyway."

Osmund entered some commands into the computer nearest him and then said, "Look at this." On another large monitor he zoomed in from a satellite. They could see the Gulf of Mexico. He zoomed in further to the southern part of Texas. He continued narrowing the view until they saw Houston, but it didn't look like a typical satellite view of city lights at night.

"What's up with the lights on the screen southeast of the city?" John asked as he pointed at the image.

"Those aren't city lights. Houston is ablaze. The strange shapes of light you see are massive fires. Those are oil refineries outside the city that are burning. Someone hacked their computer systems and overrode their safety controls, causing the systems to overheat. There were explosions in many of the plants that created a domino effect. The fires have been burning for hours. There is no way to contain the fires because the city water systems and fire hydrants have been disabled. The explosions at the plants wiped out the surrounding infrastructure. The smoke being released into the air is extremely toxic. If the local residents aren't able to evacuate or are downwind from the fires, they will be consumed by the flames or asphyxiated from the poisonous smoke and gases."

John couldn't believe what he was witnessing. "You can stop of all this, can't you? The country will be in ruins if this continues."

Osmund solemnly lowered his head. "You are correct. Unfortunately, disasters like this are occurring all across the country as we speak, and there is little we can do right now to stop them."

"There must be something!" Matt exclaimed passionately.

"There is something you can do." Osmund turned to Matt with an air of hope.

"What is that?"

"You can find a way to reprogram or stop the code that's causing all of this damage to our systems. We don't know who put it there or how, but we can at least attempt to override it."

Matt gave him a baffled look. "You want me to do what? How could I possibly do anything?"

Osmund moved closer and put his hand on Matt's shoulder. "Because you wrote the foundational code, that's how."

Matt pulled away. "What? What are you talking about? I didn't cause this. You can't blame me for what's going on."

"I'm not saying that you did, and I'm not blaming you at all. The code we're dealing with has foundational elements that you wrote, the same one you wrote when you were at MIT that you put on open source for the whole world to see. Someone modified it, and we don't know who, although we're all seeing why. How it went from something that could have transformed our nation's cyber security efforts into this destructive malicious code in our control systems nationwide, we have no idea."

Matt knew exactly what Osmund was talking about. The program he had written was part of his thesis that nearly got him kicked out of MIT. The intent of his code was to revolutionize cyber security and cyber defense monitoring for the United States. But someone had acquired and modified it for their devious purposes. They used it to penetrate banks and companies to skim money to fund their nefarious activities. They got caught when they attempted to manipulate the stocks and commodities on the New York Stock Exchange. The attack on the NYSE was in no way subtle, and it immediately alerted the authorities.

After Matt left MIT and anonymously joined various hacktivist communities, he learned one of the names given to the many projects using modified versions of his code was the Robin Hood Project. The aim of the project was to take money from wealthy companies and individuals and redistribute it to those in need. It was a noble cause but difficult to execute. Matt learned more about the Robin Hood Project after he'd been hired to work on covert projects for the NSA. No one bothered to tell him more specifics about how his code was being used. He remembered the day in college when the FBI raided his apartment and took all of his computer equipment and other electronics. The FBI said everything would be destroyed but, apparently, that was not the case, and the NSA had gotten hold of it.

"Sir, this mother board and cellular network card are hot." An analyst at one of the computers whirled around in his chair.

"Hot?" John asked. "Yes, hot. It's transmitting a signal."

Matt hurried to the analyst's workstation. "Can you trace it?"

"We'll try."

"See if you can map it for us," Osmund instructed.

"What are you mapping?" Matt asked.

"If the cellular network card is transmitting back to its host, then that may help us locate its source."

"And how accurate is your trace capability?" Matt asked.

"Very accurate," Osmund said.

"What do we do while the system runs its trace?" Matt asked, wondering what was going to come next as he watched the devastating destruction occurring on the screens in front of him.

"We wait."

70

The cab pulled up outside a dark hotel near the Birmingham airport. Guests stood outside of the main lobby entrance. The businessman exited the cab, grabbed his bags from the trunk, and headed for the door where some people were smoking.

"What's with the lights?" he asked as he approached the lobby door.

"The power's out, can't you see?" said an elderly, crotchety white woman sitting on a bench. Her Alabama accent was nearly as thick as the smoke she and her friends were bellowing.

"How long has it been out?"

The old woman titled her head back, took another long drag of her cigarette, and blew another plume of smoke. "Too damn long, if you ask me."

The old man next to her—her husband, perhaps—spoke up. "About two hours, I'd say."

"That's not bad."

The husband looked up at him. "They say it could be out a whole lot longer."

The businessman cordially waved to the couple and walked into the dark hotel. Candles dimly lit the lobby while guests sat quietly in the chairs and sofas. It was stuffy, and the air was stale. Some of the guests fanned themselves with folded newspapers. They didn't look happy. The businessman strolled to the reception desk.

"Good evening."

The young man working the reception desk was reviewing something on the counter. "Good evening, sir."

"I'm here to check in."

"Our computers are down. I'll have to check you in manually."

"What's with the power?"

"Apparently a transformer or power station nearby blew up. It knocked out power to this whole area."

"You don't say. Any idea how long before it comes on again."

"No clue. The last time we talked to the utility company they said it'd be a few hours, but that was a few hours ago. We can't get through to the power company anymore."

"No one is answering your calls?"

"No. All we get is a busy signal. What's your last name?"

"Henley."

The young man looked through a printout of the guest registry. "Here you are. Just one night?"

"Yes. I fly out in the morning. Do any of the hotels in the area have power?"

"None that I'm aware of. Some of the guests called around, but everybody seems to be in the same situation."

"Is your restaurant open? I could you use a bite and a drink. It's been a long day. I'm starving."

"No, sir. I'm sorry, but it's closed for the night. No power, you see."

"Yes, of course. Is there anywhere else I can get something to eat? It looked like there was a gas station across the street."

"You can try."

The young man fumbled with something on the desk. "Sir, I apologize, but our room key scanner isn't working. I can't make a key for you."

"Don't you have a regular key that's not electronic that you can use to let me into the room?"

The young man stared at him in frustration. "I'm so sorry, sir, but all of our hotel rooms only have electronic key entry."

"So you're saying I won't be able to get into my room tonight."

"I'm sorry, sir, that's the case right now. You're welcome to wait here in the lobby with the other folks, though."

The businessman glanced at the other miserable-looking guests. The lobby resembled an emergency shelter with people sitting and lying everywhere.

The businessman gazed at his watch. It was late, and he had a flight to catch early in the morning. His patience was dwindling. "I don't have time for this nonsense. Where do you expect me to sleep tonight? I paid for my room in advance, and I have a flight to catch in the morning." He slammed his hand down on the counter.

"Sir, please calm down. If there was something we could do, we would."

The businessman snatched his bags and stormed out of the lobby. He approached the elderly couple he had passed on the way inside and asked, "Are y'all going to try another hotel?"

A slender, casually dressed, middle-aged black man sitting on the curb with his teenage daughter answered first and said, "Ain't no other place to go, my friend. Believe me. I've tried callin' at least ten hotels."

"What did you find out?"

"No one's answerin' or the line was busy."

"Have you tried calling a cab?"

"I can't get through to them neither. You heard me. Ain't nobody answerin' their phones. It looks like we're not the only ones in this situation. It's the damnedest thing. I ain't never seen anything like this around here before."

"Well, I'm not just going to stand around here."

"Suit yourself. It's late. Good luck tryin' to find a room."

"Thanks." Frustrated, the businessman hiked through the parking lot toward the gas station. He saw that the lights were out there too. As he neared the road, he saw headlights approaching from what looked like a taxi. He stepped out and waved it down. "Taxi! Taxi!"

The taxi slowed and came to a stop. The driver rolled down his window. "Can I help you?"

"Yes, I need a ride."

"Where to?"

"The nearest hotel."

"How near?"

"Someplace close to the airport. I have a flight in the morning."

"I hate to tell you, but I just came off the highway, and it looks like power is out for at least a few miles. I can drive you further and see what we find."

"Please do."

"Go ahead and hop in."

The driver popped the trunk. The businessman put his bags in and climbed into the back seat.

"Do you know why the power is out?"

"Not a clue. We sometimes lose electricity with tornadoes and storms and such, but I've never seen anything like this. We haven't had a storm in weeks."

"The hotel staff said a transformer or something blew at a local power station."

"Damn squirrel or something, I bet. That would knock out the power." The cabbie put the car in drive and pulled away as he sped in the direction of a major intersection. He was texting and didn't see the tractor trailer fast approaching from his right. The stoplights were out, and the cab driver didn't even slow down to yield. There were flashes of headlights, brief screams, and the sound of metal crashing and glass shattering. Then all was silent except for the wailing of a car horn coming from the mangled taxi.

71

They slowly approached the exit gate of the UN parking lot in New York City when Director Godfrey asked, "Aiden, how the hell did I end up here? You had me detained in the basement of the UN building?"

"Sir, I will explain everything, but right now we've got to go." There was a sense of urgency in his voice.

"Aiden . . ."

"It doesn't matter. We've got to get away from here. We don't have much time. Look," he said, pointing to the left. There was a small caravan of black cars and SUVs with tinted windows quickly approaching the gate.

"Who's that?"

"I don't know. It could be Dimitri." Aiden recognized the vehicles from the satellite antennas on the roofs.

The black SUVs pulled up to the gate, and the driver in the lead vehicle rolled down his window to talk to the guard. They exchanged words, and the driver held out his badge. The guard stepped inside his small building to open the gate. Aiden gestured to the driver to pull toward the gate. As they neared the exit, the lead vehicle that was approaching from the other direction had entered and driven toward them. Aiden's driver drove slowly as the two vehicles approached each other. The tinted back passenger window behind the driver rolled down. Dimitri poked his head into the opening. Aiden's driver lowered his window as well. Aiden leaned over as the two men faced each other.

Dimitri spoke first. "Where are you going?"

"I'm taking Godfrey to the airport. He's got a flight back to D.C." Aiden pointed to the back seat.

Dimitri angled his head so he could look into the window. He saw Godfrey behind Aiden.

"And what about you?"

"I couldn't find Michael, and his colleague David wouldn't talk, so I searched for the next best thing."

"And what is that?"

Dimitri flipped on the overhead light and reached to his right. Aiden could see that it was another person, a woman. Dimitri propped up the unconscious, attractive brunette. Aiden knew exactly who she was. Godfrey moved in his seat to get a better view and recognized her immediately as well. There was no mistake. It was Kate Stevens, Michael's wife.

Godfrey tapped Aiden's shoulder and whispered, "What the hell is Kate doing here?"

Aiden brushed Godfrey's hand away. "Not now, Godfrey." Aiden returned his attention to Dimitri. "What do you intend to do with her?"

"I wasn't able to locate Michael. He's still got to be with Brody somewhere. If Michael knows we've got his wife, he'll find a way to get to us," Dimitri said as stroked Kate's hair.

"No word from Brody?"

"None. The plan was for him to rendezvous with Michael at the warehouse on the west side. They were supposed to return to the safe house afterward, but that was hours ago. You know I've had my doubts about Brody. I think he's playing us."

"And what about David?" Aiden checked to see if he might be in the vehicle as well.

"We had to leave him back at the safe house. We'll recover his body later."

"Body? I said no casualties—certainly none of our own," Aiden fumed. He knew something like this might happen. Dimitri had become unpredictable.

"He wouldn't cooperate."

"Dammit, Dimitri, you know better," Aiden said as he pointed angrily at Dimitri. "We're going to find Michael and get David. You take Kate inside. We'll be back." Daggers leapt from his eyes as he glared at Dimitri.

"Fine, suit yourself." Dimitri smugly waved off Aiden and closed his window. There was a pause before his SUV lurched ahead and sped off toward the underground garage, the other vehicles following closely behind.

Aiden spun in his seat. "Godfrey, the airport will have to wait. We're going to get Michael and David from the safe house."

Aiden reached down by his leg to grab a black bag. He set it on his lap, unzipped it, and pulled out a small laptop. He opened it and turned it on.

Godfrey recognized the bag. "That's mine, isn't it? You took that from my office."

"Yes, it's yours. How else do you think I'd be able to find Michael and you when I'm on the move?"

"Aiden, when this is all over . . ."

Aiden defiantly held up his hand to silence Godfrey. "Please, Godfrey, not now. You'll thank me later, I guarantee it." Aiden typed away.

"What are you doing?" Godfrey leaned around the front seat to view the computer screen.

"Like I said, I'm locating Michael. I know you already knew he was here in New York with Kate. That's why you came up here in the first place, wasn't it? It'd be easier to deal with him here than to take him back to Washington."

It didn't take Aiden long to find Michael once he synced up to the satellite GPS program. "Just where I thought he'd be—in the safe house building. It's a short drive from here."

"But Dimitri said he couldn't find him there."

"That's Dimitri. I, of course, have the benefit of being able to sync with the transponder device that we implanted on him. It's the same way you were able to locate Michael in New York initially."

"What about David?"

"He appears to be there as well, at least that's what's showing up in the system map from his transponder." Aiden slapped the side of the driver's seat. "Let's go. We've got to hurry. If my hunch is right, they're going to need our help soon."

Meanwhile, as Dimitri and his caravan descended through the UN parking garage, his phone beeped as an alert came through. He glimpsed at the screen. "Damn it!" he roared as he pounded his fist on the seat. "Turn around now. We're going back to the safe house."

The driver didn't hesitate, whipping the SUV around the corner, the tires screeching as they made their way back to the garage exit. The vehicles trailing Dimitri followed suit and sped after him.

Dimitri received a notification alert that there had been a security breach at his office. Someone had tripped his office security alarm.

Brody. I knew he was there.

72

After making it across town, Aiden and Godfrey were blocks away and approaching the safe house when Aiden noticed a familiar man running across the street to a car. The man was wearing a dark hoody over his head and blue jeans.

"Slow down and pull over!" Aiden shouted at the driver. The driver did as instructed.

"What's going on?" Godfrey asked.

Up ahead, about a block away, Aiden pointed at the man who had just hobbled across the street and was climbing into a dark sedan. "That looks like Brody."

"How can you tell from here?"

"From that gimpy gait he's had since he was shot in the leg. He'll lead us right to Michael and David. We'll wait here and follow him."

They watched as the car pulled out and headed down the street a couple of blocks before turning into an alley. Aiden pulled up his laptop again to check the location of Michael and David. He opened a satellite image of New York City and zoomed in.

"Godfrey?"

"What is it, Aiden?"

"It looks like Michael is still nearby. From what I can tell on the satellite images, he's in the rear of the building in the alley."

"What about David?"

"There's no signal. I don't know what happened. David was visible earlier."

"Where was he during his last signal transmission?"

"I'll check." Aiden searched the system. "It indicates that he was last in the building, but I'm not getting any readings from his transponder."

"What about his vitals?"

"Nothing. The system shows there were irregularities in David's heart rate about twenty minutes ago and then, just like that, the signal stopped. What do we do?"

"We'll wait a little longer."

Just then Aiden's phone began to vibrate. He pulled it out of his pocket and looked at the incoming text message. It was from Brody.

Caution. David is dead. Killed by Dimitri. I've got Michael. He's been shot too. Russians . . .

Aiden stared at the screen, shaking his head. Something didn't make sense. Did Dimitri kill David and shoot Michael too? Or was it the Russians? It seemed unlikely it was Dimitri. He'd just seen him barely twenty minutes ago. He hadn't said anything about Michael other than he couldn't find him or Brody. Dimitri mentioned shooting David, and his transmitter showing his vital signs indicated he was dead. Aiden pulled up Michael's profile on the laptop to check the diagnostics on his transmitter. All of Michael's vitals were normal and active. He knew that wouldn't be the case if he'd been shot. *Brody isn't telling the truth.*

Godfrey saw that Aiden was working on something on the laptop. "What are you doing now?"

"Brody just sent me a text message. He said David is dead, killed by Dimitri. Michael has been shot, but that doesn't make sense. Michael's vital signs are reading normal. He started to mention something about the Russians, but the text ended."

"I think we need to go down that alley and check things out." Godfrey reached for the door.

"Wait a minute." Aiden grabbed Godfrey as he started to open the door. "Look." Aiden pointed to a small entourage of black vehicles that had just come from behind them down the street and pulled in front of the safe house.

A handful of men in suits got out of the vehicles and ran inside. Another man impatiently exited the back seat of the lead SUV as he scanned up and down the street before heading inside.

"That's Dimitri," Godfrey said. "What's he doing back here? I thought he'd still be at the UN building."

"I don't know, but apparently something brought him back, and quickly. I don't know why he didn't call to let me know he was coming." Aiden checked his phone to see if there were any missed calls or messages, but there were none. "I don't like what's going on."

"Do you think Kate is still in the back of that SUV?"

"She has to be. Dimitri got here too fast, and he doesn't trust his men enough to leave her behind."

"We've got to get her then," Godfrey said as he reached for the door.

"What?"

"Yes. We've got to grab Kate while they're inside." Godfrey started to open his door, but Aiden pulled him back.

"And then what?"

"You said Michael is still in the alley."

"Yes, I did. It doesn't look like he's moved from there."

"Don't you think it's strange that he and Brody aren't going anywhere? We're going down that alley to get them." Godfrey grabbed the door.

"In that case, you'll need this," Aiden said as he reached into a small bag and pulled out a pistol that he handed to Godfrey.

Godfrey checked the clip and chamber to make sure it was loaded. "Let's do this."

Aiden tapped the driver's shoulder. "Pull up closer to that alley and then wait until we signal you. Be ready to drive, and fast."

The man nodded.

"Ready when you are."

Aiden pulled the pistol out of his shoulder holster. Aiden and Godfrey flung open their doors and raced across the street and down the sidewalk until they neared the alley. They took cover behind some crates as the rain poured down.

Godfrey squatted closer to Aiden and pointed at the parked vehicles. "You get Kate out of the SUV. I'll cover you."

"You got it." Aiden readied himself and then took off, ducking in and out behind trash cans and dumpsters that lined the storefronts as he sneaked up behind Dimitri's SUV. He could see in the side mirror that the driver was still inside. Needing a distraction, he noticed a loose, broken brick on the sidewalk. Picking it up, he launched it at the SUV's rear window, but it bounced off. *Damn bulletproof glass.*

Startled, the driver leaped out of the SUV with his gun drawn, and then he hunkered down to take cover near the door. No one else got out. The driver cautiously made his way to the rear of the vehicle, giving Aiden a clear line of sight to take a shot. Aiden poised himself, and then fired several rounds into the man's chest before he fell to the ground. Aiden ran to the rear passenger door to check on Kate. She was lying on her side in the back seat. Aiden unclipped her seatbelt. He poked his head around the back of the SUV and signaled to Godfrey for help. Pelted by the rain, they carried her swiftly across the street where their driver was waiting with the back hatch of their vehicle open. They lifted her inside.

"Two more to go." Aiden helped the driver close the rear door. Aiden and Godfrey sped back across the street to the alley entrance.

"You go. I'll cover you." Aiden motioned for Godfrey to head down the alley.

Godfrey cautiously made his way along the wall, stepping in and out behind the dumpsters and boxes that lined the narrow street. He saw Brody's dark sedan parked down the alley.

73

At the safe house, Michael stood outside of a back maintenance door on the loading dock. It was raining, so he stood under the awning. Michael stepped to the edge of the platform so he could see down the alley. There was a dead end to his right, so there was only one way out. He watched as a dark blue four-door sedan turned into the alley and rapidly approached.

Brody had seen the black SUV that had trailed him from a couple of blocks away. When he turned down the alley, he noticed that it hadn't driven past him, so it must have pulled off. It looked suspicious, but Brody couldn't get a good look at the driver, and he didn't recognize the vehicle. Brody wasn't going to say anything about it to Michael, but he would need to stay alert. Dimitri or Aiden could be following him, but he couldn't know for sure. If he was going to have to make a break for it, he might have to sacrifice Michael even without the information he needed. Dimitri and Aiden were probably onto him by now. He hadn't answered any of their calls or texts. He would have to deal with Dimitri and Aiden separately.

Brody pulled up to the loading dock at the back of the building and lowered the window. "Come on, let's get going." He didn't want to wait, especially not on a dead end. It'd be a kill box if they got stuck.

Brody pulled out his phone and sent a brief text. Then he reached under his seat before he sprang out of the car, leaving it running. As he dodged the rain, he raced to the loading dock and leapt up the stairs. "What the hell is going on? What are you waiting for?"

"It's David. We can't leave him behind," Michael pleaded.

"We discussed this before. I said leave him." Brody got in Michael's face. "Listen, any minute now this place could be crawling with Russians and who knows who else. We've got to go."

Brody was facing the street at the end of the alley when he saw a couple of men run by. Brody stepped to the edge of the loading dock for a better look. An uneasy feeling crept into his stomach.

"Brody, what are you looking at?"

"Nothing."

Michael didn't believe him. He could tell that Brody was anxious about something. "What'd you see down there?"

"Nothing, I told you."

"I'm not sure I buy that." Michael began to feel unsettled. The cold November rain and the darkness of the alley weren't much comfort.

Brody was concerned. Things were going south, and quickly. He needed to get out of there, with or without Michael. If Dimitri or Aiden didn't get to him first, his Russian or Chinese clients certainly would.

Brody checked the alley. There was movement at the end of it. He saw a solitary figure moving in and out of the shadows.

In the darkness and rain, there was no way he could tell who it was. Then a man darted from one side of the alley to the other, ducking behind a dumpster.

"There's someone in the alley down there," Brody said, alarmed.

"Where?" Michael hurried over to the edge of the loading dock by the steps.

"Over there." Brody pointed down the alley to a large dumpster along the wall.

"I don't see anything."

"Take a closer look. I swear I saw a man hide behind that dumpster."

"I still don't see anything," Michael said as he peered through the raindrops.

"He's there. He's got to be."

"I don't . . . wait; I think I saw something move." Michael thought he saw a man stick his head around the dumpster, but he couldn't be certain.

"Well, there's an easy way to find out," Brody said. Then he smiled as he pulled out his gun equipped with a silencer.

"What are you doing, Brody? You don't intend to fire that, do you?"

"Of course I do. Look. David is dead, and someone is snooping around the alley. I think this is a trap. I'm not going to get caught here." Brody cocked his pistol.

"How can you be so certain?"

"I can't. It's only a hunch, but I've learned to trust my instincts." Brody glared down the alley to see if there were any other movements. Then they saw him. A man in a dark suit ran from behind a pile of trash closer toward them before crouching behind some crates.

"Did you see him?" Brody asked. "Now do you believe me?" Brody paused. "I'm sorry, Michael." Brody was only a few steps from Michael when he whirled around aimed the gun at Michael's midsection. Michael hardly saw it coming, but he was able to sidestep enough so that the shots only grazed his side and arm. Michael staggered backward, grabbing his side. Before he could catch his balance, Brody lunged at Michael, punching him in the face and knocking him into the crates. Michael fell hard and crashed through the boxes. Confused and disoriented, Michael didn't know what to say or do as he watched Brody standing over him.

Brody didn't want to kill him, so he wasted no time and leapt down the steps into the rain and sprinted toward his car. He took one last glance back at Michael who was lying in the pile of cardboard boxes. Brody climbed into the car and accelerated backward down the alley toward the street, flying passed Godfrey who was hidden behind the crates. He slammed on the brakes and turned sharply onto the street, his tires squealing as he skidded onto the rain-soaked asphalt, nearly hitting an oncoming car.

Aiden and Godfrey watched Brody race away, but they didn't open fire. They couldn't afford to draw attention to themselves. Michael stumbled to his feet, stunned. *What just happened? Why did Brody shoot me?* He staggered to the edge of the loading dock. The rain was still pouring down, but Brody was long gone. Michael grabbed his right side to try to stop the bleeding. He was losing blood rapidly and getting light-headed, so he propped himself against the wall.

At the end of the alley, several sedans pulled up along the street to his left. As he watched, a group of heavily armed men got out of their cars. The men ran toward the entrance. At least they weren't coming in his direction.

He made his way down the stairs, steadying himself against the wall. He needed to get to a hospital, and soon. He hobbled to the end of the alley, hiding in the shadows. He'd only gone a short distance when he heard yelling behind him. A man had just come out of the loading dock exit. Fortunately, his back was to Michael, so he didn't see him stumbling the other way.

Michael didn't know if it was Dimitri and his men or the entourage that had raided the warehouse earlier. He hurriedly searched for a place to hide. He ducked behind a dumpster and pile of trash near the dead end of the alley to watch the men from a distance. Two men were standing at the far end of the alley. Michael knew there was only one way out, and they were blocking it. He'd have to wait until they were gone.

Michael worked his way further behind the dumpster, the empty cardboard boxes, and the bags of trash. The smell of rotting garbage filled his nostrils and made him nauseous. He pulled the plastic bags and boxes around him to conceal himself as best he could, resting his head on a cardboard box. He held his nose and closed his eyes temporarily. Strange voices approached. He prayed they wouldn't find him. His body weakened as his side and arm burned from the gunshots. *What would they do if they caught me? Who were they, and what did they want?*

His thoughts whirled. Everything was cloudy. He couldn't think straight. As he lay there, he thought of Kate. *Kate! Where was she? Was she okay?* He wondered if he would ever see her again. He pictured her face and warm glow, and it made him smile. The rain slowed to a drizzle. The sound of people running and splashing through puddles was only a short distance away. He closed his eyes and saw Kate's face in front of him. Then he blacked out.

74

Back in the underground North American Cyber Command Center, Matt and John watched all of the activity on the large wall monitors. They watched as coding strings ran across some screens while analysts checked satellite images and looked for control system network updates on others.

"How are you two holding up?" Riley quietly asked Matt and John.

"I'm doing all right," Matt said softly, even though he was exhausted.

"I'm okay," John said as he sat at one of the temporarily empty workstations. Then he took a closer look at the monitors and noticed the names of the cities under the images: Los Angeles, San Diego, Portland, Seattle, Las Vegas, Chicago, Atlanta, St. Louis, Memphis, Dallas, and Philadelphia. "That explains all of this craziness."

"Exactly. You both are seeing what's happening in real time across the nation. The White House is extremely worried. Our country is under attack." Riley pointed somberly toward the screens.

75

When Michael finally regained consciousness, it was to the sound of familiar voices. As he gradually opened his eyes, he found that he was resting against the back seat of an automobile. His head hurt, and his side burned. He tried to rotate his body to get more comfortable.

"Easy there," Godfrey said as he put out his hands to steady Michael.

"Director Godfrey? Where am I? What are you doing here in New York? You're supposed to be in D.C."

"It's a long story. You should rest. You've been shot."

Michael groaned in pain as he sat up taller in the seat. "What happened? Where's Brody? Where's David?

Godfrey repeated himself. "You've been shot. We're taking you to get medical help. Brody drove away."

Michael drifted in and out of consciousness. "Kate!" Michael shouted suddenly as he straightened up and hastily began searching for her.

"Easy Michael. We've got her too. She's safe." Godfrey put his hand on Michael's shoulder. "You need to rest. We're headed to the hospital."

Michael fought to stay conscious, but he finally passed out.

76

Dimitri and his men scoured the building searching for Brody and Michael. They'd gone to Dimitri's office where they discovered that the door had been blown open. Dimitri was the first to enter the room. David was lying face up, dead. Dimitri searched his desk and office to see if anything was missing, but nothing had been taken.

One of the armed masked men called out to Dimitri. "It looks like the door was blown from the inside."

"You're right, but how? And more importantly, who?" Dimitri waved his hands in a circular motion and said, "Search for any evidence of the explosive device." Dimitri then stormed to the entrance of his surveillance room and opened a hidden access panel. He entered his passcode before putting his hand on the fingerprint reader. The large steel door began to creak open, and he stepped inside. A light on one of the monitors was blinking, so he grabbed the computer mouse and moved it back and forth to wake up the screen. He typed in his login information and searched through the system access logs. Someone had accessed his system within the last two hours and downloaded files. Dimitri shook his head. *Brody must have taken the top-secret files. I knew they were right under my nose. I knew it.* Dimitri stormed out of the surveillance room and hit the button to close the door behind him.

"Let's go," Dimitri ordered his men. "They can't be far away."

The armed men hurried out of the office and down the hall. Dimitri stayed behind momentarily. He sauntered over near his desk and gazed out the window. Soon his phone rang.

Dimitri picked up the phone. "Hello."

"Dimitri." The man's voice had a thick Russian accent.

"Yes."

"Your time has come, comrade." The man on the other end spoke in Russian.

"Who is . . ." But before Dimitri could finish his question, his phone exploded, knocking him against his desk before he fell to the floor, dead. Brody had tipped off the Russians and sold Dimitri out to save his own hide.

77

With Dimitri and his men out of the way, Brody knew his best chance to escape Manhattan was to get to LaGuardia. There was a private jet waiting, and he expected that Aiden and the others would be headed there as well. The UN headquarters wasn't far from where he was. The Queens Midtown Tunnel would be his fastest route out of town. Brody sped through the city streets, swerving in and out of cars and racing through stoplights. Brody had blown his chance of getting the information he needed from Michael. Although he stole the top-secret intelligence files from Dimitri's computer, he couldn't deliver everything on his end of the deal. With only one-half of the records, the information he had was useless. Driving along East 40th Street toward the tunnel, Brody knew he was a marked man. He passed 3rd Avenue, turned onto Tunnel Entrance Street, and drove a couple of blocks until he saw the tunnel entrance.

"Dammit," Brody shouted as he slammed his hand against the top of the steering wheel. He was staring at bumper-to-bumper traffic. The route was under construction. Brody opened his door and stepped into the rain. There were blinking yellow and

orange lights ahead. He looked back as cars began to line up behind him, blocking his ability to go anywhere. He climbed into
the car and was tapping impatiently on the steering wheel and
shaking his head in frustration when a man dressed in a white
construction helmet and a long orange trench coat with reflec-
tors waved to get Brody's attention.

Brody held up his hands and mouthed, "What do you want?"

The man motioned for Brody to open his window. Without
thinking, Brody lowered it, regretting his decision immediately
as he saw the gun barrel. He was unable to react fast enough to
grab his pistol from the center console. The man in the construction jacket fired several rounds into Brody's head and chest.
The muffled gunshots from the silencer were easily drowned out
by the jack hammering. Brody slouched in his seat as the rain
poured into his open window.

The gunman tucked his gun into his jacket and casually
walked away. As he did, he pulled out his phone to send a quick
text in Chinese: "It's done."

78

FBI Director Donovan got what he needed from the onsite medical clinic and swung by his office to check some things on his computer. He avoided stopping by the SIOC for the time being as he needed to figure out what had happened to Agent Burton. He opened his computer system and accessed the internal security cameras located in the garage.

Now let's see who did this. Donovan initiated a quick scan from every angle of the last hour or so of footage, but he saw nothing unusual. He found a view that showed the van, but it was at the far end of the garage. Donovan couldn't make anything of it. As he fast forwarded through the material, it turned into scrambled static. He continued, and the image of the van showed up again. He checked the time stamp before replaying the video. There was almost thirty minutes of blank tape when all of the garage cameras had been disabled. Someone had tampered with them. *This doesn't do me any good.* He slammed his fist down on his desk. He got up to check on Agent Burton again when his phone rang.

"Hello?" he answered in an annoyed tone.

"Director Donovan," Aiden said matter-of-factly.

"Yes, who is this?"

"You were instructed to cease your search for Matt O'Shea."

"I don't know what you're talking about."

"Don't play dumb, director. You have an unconscious agent in a van in your garage, an Agent Burton, I believe. You sent him after O'Shea. Meanwhile, your entire team has continued to search."

"How do you know that? Who are you?"

"I know because one of my men put your agent in the van. He'll be okay. He was drugged. We couldn't have him getting in the way, but he should be waking up soon."

There was a long pause before Donovan spoke again. "What do you want?"

"I want you to do what you were told. You were instructed by Director Godfrey to cease your search for Matt O'Shea."

"And if I don't?" Donovan's tone was defiant.

"You don't know who you're dealing with. We're watching your every move. How do you think I knew about Agent Burton—and you? We're aware of your business dealings, director. Just be glad we haven't come after you yet. You're in over your head and should be ashamed of the things you've done." Godfrey wasn't the only one Aiden had been watching. He'd had a number of key members of the intelligence community under surveillance. He couldn't have Donovan interfering with his plans.

Donovan sat quietly. *How did the man know all of this?*

"Call off your search now. We have Matt O'Shea in our custody."

"Who does? The NSA?"

Aiden paused. "Who is of no importance to you. Just know that we have him."

"But what about the security breach at Lucigen?"

"We've got it handled."

"Not from the reports I'm getting and what I've seen on the news, you don't. There's a national disaster going on in cities across the country."

"You let us worry about the technical side. You'll be briefed by the appropriate authorities when the time is right. Until then, stop your activities and speak to no one. We'll be watching and listening. In the meantime, I strongly suggest that you and your agents work with the D.C. Police Department to secure Washington. Things are getting out of hand already across the city." Aiden then ended the call.

Donovan sat back in his chair. "Son-of-a . . ." He slammed his phone down, aware of his predicament. The man on the phone knew about his underhanded dealings, but Donovan knew above all else that he needed to secure the city. That was his priority, and he couldn't avoid that responsibility. Donovan jumped up and hurried back to the operations center to look for Agents Perez and Hawkins. He would have to worry about his personal situation later.

79

One of the technicians brought Riley a stack of file folders and reports that Osmund had requested.

Riley reviewed the documents before handing them to Matt.

"Here, Osmund asked that I give these to you."

"What are they?"

"They're reports that I think you'll find enlightening. They should help explain some of what's going on."

In bold letters the cover page read:

TOP SECRET

Matt opened the packet and skimmed the introductory pages before flipping through the other parts of the report. The Index page listed cities and dates as far back as the sixties. There were numerous blackouts listed all the way back to 1965. There was a chronological index of events with the report containing more specifics related to each occurrence. Other material detailed the full range of cyberattacks around the world:

2016 - **Sri Lanka** Nationwide Blackout
2016 - **Kenya** Nationwide Blackout
2015 - **Pakistan** Blackout
2015 - **Turkey** Blackout
2012 - **India** Blackout
2009 - **Brazil** and **Paraguay** Blackout
2008 - **Venezuela** Blackout
2008 - **Zanzibar** Power Blackout
2007 & 2005 - **Brazil** Blackouts
2006 - **Queens, New York** Blackout
2005 - **Malaysia** Electricity Blackout Crisis
2005 - **Atlantic** Power Outage
2003 - **London** Blackout
2003 - **Italy** Blackout
2003 - **Northeast U.S.** Blackout
1999 - **Southern Brazil** Blackout
1978 - **Thailand** Nationwide Blackout
1977 - **New York City** Blackout
1965 - **Northeast U.S.** Blackout

The list went on. There were dozens of massive blackouts documented from around the world.

Matt looked up from the report. "You mean all of these are linked?"

"You got it," Riley said.

"So this malicious code that was in my computer and in the industrial control systems across the country is the cause of all of these outages?"

"Maybe not the only cause, but it's unquestionably related to the more recent events. You'll notice the incidents have increased significantly since 1999."

John snatched the report from Matt. "Why is that?"

"It started with the Y2K bug. It was the perfect opportunity to penetrate our computer systems. It was quite brilliant. Do you remember the panic everyone had in the U.S. and around the world about the Internet and computers crashing?"

"Yes, I remember. How did those devices and malware get in there though?" John asked.

"The manufacturers put them there. They used the rush to update all of the world's computer systems as a chance to embed the malware without drawing attention."

"I'm not following you. Why would the manufacturers put hardware bugs and malware in our computers?" John asked.

"Very simple: to spy on us and steal our intellectual property and sensitive information. Where do we import most of our products from, especially our electronics and software?" Riley motioned to the array of computers and electronics around the room.

"Mainly China," John said.

"Precisely. The Chinese aren't exactly our best friends, are they? We trade a lot with them, and they own about thirty percent of our national debt. They also have close ties with North Korea and Russia. Do you remember in 2006 when there were fears raised by Capitol Hill when the U.S. Department of State ordered thousands of computers from a Chinese company?"

Congress, for good reason, was concerned that the computers had been compromised. Not only that, the same company had acquired majority stakes in other U.S. computer companies. And that company is still a principal computer supplier today to many government and private sector organizations. What's worse is that even after U.S. authorities warned companies about the threat, they still bought their machines and network mainframes from overseas because they're less expensive. The recent incidents where hackers stole credit card and other sensitive information from U.S. companies and the U.S. government occurred because they're using foreign-manufactured computer equipment that's been infected with malware since day one. It had just been dormant and waiting to be activated."

"I vaguely recall those stories," Matt said. "Were all of those concerns valid—from Congress and the rest of the U.S. government?"

Riley paused. "I'm not at liberty to say." Riley's response was enough of an answer for Matt.

Osmund had been observing the conversation and slipped in behind them to listen. "Allow me to frame this differently so you might better understand. Keep in mind this is just one reason behind those devices and malicious code that you found on your computer. There are other purposes, which I will explain as well. Those devices and the malicious code aren't the only issues we have to contend with right now."

"Have at it." Matt signaled for Osmund to continue.

"Have you ever had the power go out at your house?"

"Yeah, a number of times when I was a kid," Matt replied.

"And what was that like?"

"We were scared and disoriented at first, but my parents reassured us that everything would be okay. Sometimes it happened while we were sleeping, so we didn't even know. The power was usually back by the morning; we rarely went more than a day or so without electricity." Matt wasn't sure where Osmund was going with the conversation.

"Now envision that same power outage on a national scale. Imagine that it's not only your electricity that's been cut off, but your water supply, gasoline stations, phone, Internet, and your financial institutions. Worse yet, you don't know when any of it will come back online. It could be days, weeks, or months. Not only that, the U.S. would have no control over anything, at least not immediately. The U.S. would be catastrophically disabled, and it would be utter turmoil and chaos across the country, including leaving our borders unsecured."

"What I don't understand is why now?" Matt asked. "Why would other countries like Russia and China want to disrupt our power grid and risk creating pandemonium in the global economic marketplace? Many countries, China in particular, rely heavily on the United States for business and trade."

"We have the same question," Osmund replied, "and we don't know the answer. What we do know is that our enemies are employing technological guerrilla warfare and cyberattacks using various types of malware. That cellular network card you found on your computer can be activated through the Internet or through a portable transmitter that is, essentially, a specially-equipped laptop or smart phone. That code you found is what makes all of this possible." Osmund then directed their attention to the screens on the wall. "They can take out our industrial control systems even if we completely isolate them from the public Internet. They're connected without us even knowing. They're always in contact with their command-and-control servers back home, wherever home may be."

"Since you can't crack the code, why don't you just find the command-and-control computers and take them out?" John asked.

"If only it were that simple, we would." There was despair in Osmund's voice.

"Do you know where those computers are?" John asked.

"We don't, at least not exactly. They can be operated remotely from almost anywhere in the world as long as they have a power source and a link up to either the Internet or satellite."

"This is unreal," John lamented.

"I can assure you it's all too real," Osmund said. "It's happening as we speak. We've been able to penetrate a number of the transmitters, which has helped us tremendously. We were able to reverse engineer them for our counterintelligence purposes, which is the only reason we know as much as we do. But there are still many unanswered questions."

"Wouldn't they help you find the others if they're all somehow interconnected?" Matt asked.

"You would think. The command-and-control computers don't refer to each other in any way, at least from what we can tell. Somehow, they're putting out a signal with instructions that the other computer systems are constantly listening for, so it isn't possible to find the addresses of the other systems by penetrating any one of them. Hell, we can't even figure out for certain how many might be involved."

There was no way to know. It was a similar dynamic during the Cold War days when the Russians would hide commands for their sleeper cells and spies in specially worded ads in sections of newspapers. It was sometimes possible to tell who sent the orders, but there was no way to know who was reading or acting on them. The recent events with lone wolf terrorists or hackers are similar. There were broadcast signals and instructions to diverse audiences globally, but the individuals receiving and acting on the information were nearly impossible to identify, track or predict.

"If you know the patterns of these signals, couldn't you just look for every computer that has ever sent or received one of them?" Matt knew there had to be a solution.

"We've been working on that, but the sources constantly change location, and the code itself morphs."

"How is it you've been able to narrow the location down to individual countries then?" John asked.

"We've created a plot map of everywhere we've counted the hits based on the signal transmissions. This diagram is what we've come up with thus far." He turned to the large screen and waved to the data analyst. "Lee, pull up the map."

A large satellite image of the world appeared. There were red dots for each one of the hits. It looked like the type of plot map that the Centers for Disease Control use to illustrate outbreaks. The computer virus was becoming a global pandemic.

Lee was in his late twenties, Asian, short and slightly built. His black hair was buzzed on the sides and styled in a hip fashion on top. He wore thick, dark-rimmed glasses.

Matt and John studied the map that spanned the full length of the wall.

"That's a lot of dots," John said, stating the obvious.

"Yes, it is." Osmund stared at the countless dots on the screen.

"How many are there?" Matt asked.

"We don't know. We've been tracking them for years."

"There have to be trillions of dots." Matt was making an ill-fated attempt to count them.

"Try over eighty trillion. We're able to locate the key regions and countries from the groupings."

"I see what you mean," Matt said as he stared at the plot diagram. The countries Osmund had mentioned were covered extensively in red dots.

"Do any of these show a distinct pattern in their beaconing frequency?" John asked.

"Surprisingly, no. The signals are like snowflakes in that regard. Each one is unique, and each message is encrypted."

"That's interesting," Matt said. "Can't you at least cluster them to identify centers of gravity? I would expect if a mobile transmitter is nearby, you would see a pattern of the message being replicated by the closest compromised devices, almost like ripples in a pond."

"We've tried, but we've come up short each time."

"You should at least be able to locate a city or neighborhood or something."

"We've been able to determine some of the cities, but even searching for a mobile laptop in a city like Beijing or Moscow is like searching for a needle in a haystack. The signals continually move. Plus, differences in the speeds of networks are throwing off our ability to find any explicit ripples, and sometimes there are interruptions in the transmissions that have lasted for days or weeks and, in some cases, months."

"Could it be that these transmitter devices and command-and-control computers are all sending the same command on a predefined schedule, like throwing dozens of stones in a pond?" John suggested. "If we know they're portable, then maybe they're always on the move." John's wheels spun as he worked to make sense of it all.

"I'm not sure I follow," Osmund said.

"Could the transmitters be in an automobile or airplane or something that is continually on the move? How is it that some of these show up over the ocean or other bodies of water? Could people be carrying them?" John paused and reflected on what he'd just said. "What about routing the signal through cell phones?" Think about it," John said. "Most people in the world—even in underdeveloped countries and regions—are walking around with little computers in their pockets, and they're always connected. How would anyone know what their phone was doing all day? And there are all sorts of data on there that would allow the software to be unique to the user but still appear random."

Everyone listened to what John was saying and tried to analyze it. Transmitting signals and code through cell phones was extremely likely.

"John, I think you might be on to something," Osmund said. They had considered cell phones before, but they hadn't taken into account all the human variables.

"Your theory is logical, and it could explain the movements and permutations we've identified. Perhaps the code is somehow being changed as it passes through each phone based on an individual's physical movement and location. That would explain the uniqueness in that each code pattern is like no other, even if it's routed through the same device more than once. It's an ingenious concept and impossible to trace. The challenge, then, is how to disable the cellular implants to be able to identify the command beacon and source of the code while not harming the devices. Or better yet, figuring out a way to rewrite the code while it's active, which is something Matt can help with."

"Excuse me, guys," Lee said. "I overheard your conversation and did a quick analysis."

"What do you have for us?" Osmund asked as he turned toward his top tech.

"Well, sir, there are instances where the tracer hits were in one place for several minutes or longer."

"What are you saying, Lee?"

"I'm saying it's possible to more narrowly pinpoint a location based on what you were just discussing about the cell phones."

"Keep going," Osmund said.

"I'll have to run more tests, but it looks like, in some cases, what we were tracking has been in a single location for minutes, if not hours, or even returned to the same place."

"How'd we miss that?" Osmund stood with his hands on his hips, annoyed that they'd overlooked something so obvious. They had explored the cell phone theory before but had failed to consider the GPS locator apps as a variable that would cause the code to morph.

"We weren't looking for it, so we didn't find it," Lee said. "It wasn't until I overheard your conversation that it hit me. It was so obvious that we glossed right over it. Using human movement to manipulate code permutations as they pass from one person to the next is brilliant. It's a mathematical wonder; the possibilities are infinite and would have been nearly impossible to track— until now."

They had been looking for variables based on common artificial adaptations from computers, code sequences, and the algorithms themselves. They were looking for technical variables. They hadn't considered the human variables related to movement that could be used to modify an algorithm. Things were becoming clearer. If the transmission and permutations of the code were based on human movement, they could remove those from the equation and see what they came up with or, better yet, figure out a way to disable those applications on the phones to more specifically isolate locations. But that'd be hundreds of millions of phones. It was a long shot, but they might be able to identify their target source locations or find a way to disrupt them.

"Great work," Osmund said as he towered over Lee, putting his hand on his shoulder in a complimentary manner. "See what else you can find. We've got to work quickly."

"Thanks. I will." Lee shrugged and headed back to work. He didn't care for public recognition.

Osmund was thrilled with the new hope this theory entailed. He redirected his attention to Matt and John.

"Here. Let me see that." Osmund took the report from Matt and flipped through it. "Read these paragraphs." Osmund handed it back to Matt who read silently:

> *The President announced on August 16, 2003, his concern for the blackout and the potential impacts they might have on the economy and against the country's fight against terrorism. The administration emphasized the need for changes to the U.S. national energy policy, critical infrastructure protection, and Homeland Security. During the blackout, most systems that would detect unauthorized border crossings, port landings, or detect unauthorized access to many vulnerable sites, failed. There was considerable fear that future blackouts would be exploited for terrorism. Also, the failure highlights the ease with which the U.S. power grid could be taken down. The President further mentioned the dramatic impact such events would have on the economy and the operability and security of the country.*

Matt somberly lowered the report and set it on his lap. "The latest plan is to knock out our power grid. That would impact everything. But this excerpt from the president is over twelve years old. The government knew about all of this even back then?" Matt asked rhetorically.

Osmund was keenly aware that anything could happen during a massive power outage, especially one that could last for an extended period. Everyone in the country could be without water, electricity, gas, Internet, and phone service. Not only that, any navigation system, financial or medical institution could be shut down. It would be catastrophic, a modern-day Hiroshima, except a technology virus would be the weapon.

"None of the incidents on this list over the last forty-plus years were accidents?" Matt glared at Osmund in amazement.

"We doubt it. The more recent occurrences were the result of the code we've been discussing—your code."

In the past, the U.S. government hadn't had the technology or experience to detect the malware, so they assumed the incidents with the power companies were accidents or glitches in the various control systems or a result of systems simply being outdated. Over time, they learned that wasn't the case. All of the events were intentional attacks not only on the United States but against other countries as well.

"Here, read this paragraph." Osmund flipped through the report to another section and gave it back to Matt, who quietly read:

> *The Task Force also found that the energy company in question did not take remedial actions or warn other control centers until it was too late because of a computer software bug in the energy management system that prevented alarms from showing on their control system. This alarm system stalled because of a trace condition bug. After the alarm system had failed silently without being noticed by the operators, unprocessed events started to queue, and the primary server failed within thirty minutes, resulting in a blackout.*

The excerpt was based on the U.S. Northeast blackout of 2003. All of those attacks had been going on right in front of their faces. Matt's company was one of the latest victims, but it was happening all across the country.

"What have you been doing about all of this?" Matt demanded as he shook the report in Osmund's face.

"Everything we could. Believe me. We've been trying. Just look at this entire operation dedicated to these issues for the last decade." Osmund made a sweeping motion over the command center around them.

This impending wide-scale cyberattack against the United States was just like other preventable situations, including the U.S. economic crisis of 2008. There were warning signs for years about the financial institutions and the economy, but no one paid attention, or they dismissed what they saw. No one, certainly not the government or financial institutions, thought it would ever happen. They'd been blinded by their arrogance and greed while the very threat stared them in the face.

"If we don't act, the U.S. will experience a nationwide blackout?" There was a deeply troubled look on Matt's face.

"It's already begun," Osmund said. "You've seen it firsthand." His team had been monitoring what was going on across the country, especially the last twenty-four hours. He knew that if they didn't stop further damage soon, the U.S. would be in utter disarray for months if not years.

There were more recent examples of plane crashes, train accidents, submarine and satellite collisions, and security breaches where hackers had taken information from government organizations and private sector companies. Enemies of the United States were becoming more emboldened. Years ago the Chinese had hacked into the Pentagon and acquired detailed information on U.S. military weapons systems and aircraft. It was also odd that with all the vastness of the oceans and outer space, there were instances of nuclear submarines and satellites colliding. Years ago such incidents were almost unheard of, but in recent years they were happening regularly. They weren't coincidences. In nearly every instance, the follow-up reports cited software or hardware failures in the computer and navigation systems.

"It's all in here." Osmund tapped the top of the report Matt was holding.

"These events didn't happen that long ago," Matt noted, glancing up from the document.

"No, they didn't. There is evidence everywhere around the world that cyberattacks are happening regularly to various degrees."

"Regarding the cyberattacks on the Pentagon," Matt asked, "how do you think they managed to bypass the firewalls and systems as secure as the Pentagon's?"

"As I mentioned before," Osmund said, "hidden access was most likely manufactured into the computers' hardware and software from the beginning." To Osmund's right was a small pile of documents on the desk. He picked them up. "There's more. Take a look at these." Osmund handed Matt another set of documents.

Matt scanned through the brief summaries of events:

* *August 14, 2008 – Surging demand tests power lines in New York City . . . Five years after record blackout, electricity infrastructure lags.*
* *November 19, 2008 – NYPD opens counterterror center . . . the center will eventually receive data from devices designed to detect any radiological and biological threats.*
* *February 11, 2009 – U.S. satellite destroyed in unprecedented space collision with Russian satellite . . . there have been only three relatively minor collisions between such objects in the last 20 years . . . Never before have two intact satellites crashed into one another allegedly by accident.*
* *February 16, 2009 – British and French nuclear submarines collide . . . Although both are fitted with state-of-the-art technology aimed at detecting other submarines; it appears neither saw the other until it was too late.*

- *June 1, 2009 – Jetliner lost at sea . . . Jet's disappearance a mystery.*
- *June 25, 2009 – Deadliest metro train wreck in Washington, D.C., history . . . Federal investigators found anomalies in the metro equipment that senses trains and transmits speed commands.*

Matt was deeply troubled. "These are all events in the past ten years." He could only imagine all of the other attacks that weren't listed.

"That's correct. And that's only a fraction of the ones that are captured in that report. None of our politicians will openly say it, but the United States has been at war for years—cyberwar."

Osmund knew there were even more recent reports, but those were the only records that he had on hand that were at a low enough sensitivity classification level he could share with Matt. The latest reports from recent weeks were even more disturbing. Countless cyberattacks were occurring daily around the world at an alarming rate with greater effectiveness and devastation. He knew it was critical that they locate the source of the code and stop it. "Believe me," Osmund said. "Those who know the real implications are doing everything they can to win this war. That's why our organization exists—to support and defend the United States from foreign and domestic enemies. Unfortunately, we don't know what the next target will be."

Matt glared at Osmund. "Nearly everything these days requires electronic components and microchips that could be infected by this virus."

"Exactly. Buildings, cars, phones, planes, satellites, transportation, security, banking, communication, energy, water . . . the list goes on."

This cyber threat was all the more reason for the United States to manufacture its products in America. By the United States continuing to acquire so much of its electronics overseas, especially in China, it was providing foreign governments and businesses direct access to its most valuable asset, its intellectual property. That is a competitive economic edge the U.S. is losing due to cyber espionage of trade secrets and information. Worse yet, many companies have no way of knowing what foreign manufacturers and intermediaries are installing in their electronic devices, the software that's produced by them, or the software that's downloaded onto computers from the Internet by their employees. If the U.S. government and major corporations could be hacked, the average citizen was even more vulnerable.

There were alarmists and conspiracy theorists who warned about impending cyberattacks, but they were usually disregarded. Besides Osmund and his team, there were only a limited number of others in the intelligence community who knew the full extent of the cyber threat, and many of them were moles working for the NSA.

"Are the CIA, FBI, and NSA computers vulnerable to hackers?" John asked.

"Possibly. They're probably being attacked as we speak. Every day there are hundreds if not thousands of attempts to hack into government and private sector computer systems. Take a look at these examples." Osmund handed Matt another report, and he read:

- *April 21, 2009 – Chinese hackers gained access to Pentagon's newest fighter jet . . . also gained temporary access to the Air Force's air traffic control systems.*
- *July 7, 2009 – Social Security code cracked; numbers may have been compromised.*
- *July 9, 2009 – Cyberattack traced to N. Korea . . . Hacking effort that began July 4 crippled many U.S. websites.*

John looked over Matt's shoulder as he read the report and said, "It doesn't make any sense that so few people know the extent of what's going on, let alone what to do about it. All of the signs are so obvious."

"Say what you will; it is what it is," Osmund said. "There are those who know about it, but they don't want to alarm the American public. It could create mass hysteria."

"How did this cyberwar start?" Matt asked.

"We used similar intelligence gathering strategies against the Russians, Japanese, and Germans after World War II. We bugged electronic equipment and products that we exported to them. Decades later, it appears our foreign counterparts have pulled a similar trick on us."

What Osmund and the others didn't fully understand was that nearly every U.S. computer system and network had been infiltrated, and the virus was spreading fast. It was only a matter of time before it was too late. It would be game over, checkmate.

"You all have been combatting this for years," Matt said, "and you expect me to crack this code and magically stop all of this now?" Matt motioned to the dozen or so images displayed on the wall monitors.

"You had the fortune, or misfortune, of stumbling upon it," Osmund said. "Your code has found its way back to you after all these years. As you saw in the reports, more of these occurrences are taking place. You noticed the exponential growth since 2003. Now, it seems, you may be our last hope."

80

Michael awoke in a New York City hospital bed to the beeping of machines and a burning pain in his right side. He wiggled his fingers and toes to make sure he still could, and then he noticed an IV in his forearm. He attempted to sit up, but he was simply too weak.

"Kate!" he cried. "Kate!"

Two nurses raced into the room to calm him.

"Where's Kate—my wife—where is she?" he asked, frantically looking around the room for her. Then he heard a familiar voice.

"Michael, she's okay." It was Godfrey. He'd been in the corner reading the newspaper.

"Director Godfrey? What are you doing here? What am I doing here?"

"It's a long story. You were shot. Kate is okay, though. She's right here." Godfrey pointed at the bed on the other side of the room.

The nurses helped Michael sit up so he was able to see Kate. He saw that she was alive but unconscious.

"Kate!" He reached for her hand, but the beds were too far apart.

"She'll be fine, Mr. Stevens," one of the nurses said as she checked his vitals. "She was drugged, but we're flushing her system. She should be awake soon and ready to go home by tomorrow."

"Brody?" Michael struggled to say the name.

Aiden had been outside the room to take a call, but he stepped in again in time to answer: "We've taken care of Brody."

"What?" Michael was groggy from the pain medicine and was slow to comprehend. "The Russian—what about the Russian?"

"Oh, yes, Dimitri," Aiden said. "He's been handled too." Aiden then approached the foot of the bed. "Michael, you don't need to worry about Brody or Dimitri. We will fill you in later. The important thing is that you and Kate are safe. We'll have you home soon enough."

"What about O'Shea? Where is he?"

"He's in a safe place in our underground cyber command center outside of D.C.," Aiden said. "He's in good hands and well away from all of this."

"Michael," Godfrey said as he placed his hand on the bed rail, "Aiden is right. We will discuss everything later. For now, you need to rest."

"Where am I?"

"You're in a New York City hospital." Godfrey then tapped the bed rail. "We'll get you taken care of and out of here before long." He smiled at the nurses. "Isn't that right?"

Michael titled his head to look at Godfrey. "I thought you were in trouble . . . You called me . . . It was urgent . . . You called for help . . . I heard banging . . . the Russians . . . Eminent Eclipse . . ." Michael rambled incoherently as he wrestled to stay awake.

"Aiden and I talked. We've got everything under control. You just rest."

Michael fought to keep his eyes open, but as the exhaustion and medication overcame him, he collapsed on the bed and fell asleep.

81

She was a single white mom of twenty-three, so her mother babysat on the nights she had to work. There were no businesses near the cramped two-bedroom, first-floor apartment that she shared with her mom. She lived in a rural area off a two-lane gravel road. Her high school sweetheart had gotten her pregnant their senior year, so she never started college, but she had been saving money to go back to school. The only job she could get was waiting tables.

One night her ex-boyfriend from high school was at a house party and got into a fight. He was drunk and high when he got into an argument over some drugs and stabbed another man. Luckily, the victim survived. But her boyfriend was arrested and sentenced to fifteen years in prison. She was stuck raising her son alone, except for the help from her mother.

Her hair was ratty and frizzy from waiting tables in a dingy, greasy roadside diner. She had finished her night shift and was headed home to her five-year-old son when the gas light on her dashboard came on. She still had a thirty-mile drive home down a dark, two-lane highway, so she figured she should fill up if she could find a station open so late. She never remembered it being so dark. Then she saw the faint lights of a truck stop in the distance. As she approached, she noticed all of the gas pumps were occupied. There were even a few cars waiting.

She drove in and pulled behind one of the cars waiting in line. She noticed a group of customers congregating near the cash register inside the convenience store. They were having a heated argument with the attendant on the other side of the safety glass. She couldn't tell what they were saying, so she got out and walked inside.

"Turn on the pumps, dammit!" a tall, heavyset, bearded truck driver yelled as he pounded on the glass window.

The brown-skinned clerk spoke into the intercom in his foreign accent. "Sir, the pumps aren't working."

"Bullshit! I need gas, dammit! I've got a delivery to make by morning."

"Sir, there is nothing I can do. I'm sorry. Our pumps have been off for the last hour or so. Perhaps you can try another station."

"You're the eighth location I've stopped at on this damn highway. I've been driving for miles. No one has any gas, or their pumps aren't working. What's wrong with you all? Don't you know people need gas?"

"Sir, I don't know what to tell you. I'm sorry."

"You're all a bunch of fucking crooks. Open up. I'll turn the pumps on my damn self."

The single mom slipped further away down one of the aisles where a casually dressed short, pudgy, older black gentleman was looking for snacks. "Excuse me, sir, do you know what's going on?"

"Apparently those folks can't get gas. The pumps don't seem to be working."

"What about you?"

"Oh, I don't need gas, my dear. I filled up yesterday. I just stopped off to pick up a few things. My wife had a craving for some chocolate, so I'm being a good husband." He smiled kindly at her.

"That's very loving of you. This situation looks pretty bad. That truck driver is pissed. I'm worried he might do something."

"He does look angry. If you'll excuse me, I'm going to go before this situation gets out of hand." He moved to the checkout counter where the clerk remained behind the glass barrier.

"I'll take these, please," he said, holding up a handful of snacks and candy bars.

The clerk spoke into the intercom, and his words crackled out of the speaker in the middle of the window. "The register stopped working a minute ago."

"That's fine. I'll pay cash."

"The register isn't working."

"I heard you the first time," the old gentleman replied kindly.

"I can't take your money, sir, because the register isn't working anymore. It won't even open." The poor clerk was at a loss. He could see that the customers were becoming more confrontational, and he was helpless.

The short, older black man looked confused. "I'm sorry, but how come I can't pay for these? I have cash." He pulled a ten-dollar bill from his wallet and held it up for the clerk to see.

"Hey, old man, keep your money," the gruff truck driver said as he pushed the man's hand down. "As a matter of fact, why don't you go ahead and take those? They're on me."

"That's very kind of you," the old black man said as he looked skeptically at the truck driver. Then, with a puzzled look, he glanced at the crowd of restless travelers.

"Well, go on. You got your stuff; now get out of here," the trucker commanded as he motioned to the door.

The old man hurried out, glancing over his shoulder, still confused.

The trucker turned to the rest of the customers standing around him. He towered over most of them by nearly a head. "As a matter of fact, why don't you all take whatever you want?"

The clerk didn't like the sound of things. "Sir, how do you intend to pay?"

"With this." He reached behind his back and pulled out a gun. He pointed it at the clerk, who put his hands up and backed away from the glass.

"Will that be a problem?"

"No, no, not at all," the poor clerk stammered.

The other startled customers hid behind whatever display or shelf they could, scrambling toward the back of the store.

"Don't worry; I don't plan on shooting any of you. Go ahead and take what you like. He's not going to stop us." He pointed his gun in the direction of the clerk who had ducked behind the counter. The clerk grabbed his cell phone from his pocket and called 911, but he could barely control his trembling fingers and kept dropping his phone. Finally, he managed to type the numbers and hit "Call."

The phone rang once before the operator picked up. "911—what is your emergency?"

"My store is being robbed. Please help. I'm at the truck stop on Exit 59."

"Sir, you're going to have to be more specific. What is your exact location? What road? What is your . . ." The operator hadn't finished her sentence when the line cut out.

"Hello . . . Hello? Are you there?" the clerk said, but there was no answer. The clerk slowly crawled to his knees and peeked over the counter. "Oh, dear Lord." People were taking items off the shelves, pushing over displays, and snatching drinks and food out of the fridges as fast as they could. A scrawny pimple-faced teenager raced out the door with a case of beer.

A short, fat biker with a leather jacket and tattoos covering his arms and neck grabbed a hammer out of one of the tool-kits on sale and started pounding on the glass where the clerk crouched behind the counter. "Let me in there!" the biker shouted. "Give me your money!"

The frightened clerk knelt behind the counter as the biker continued to pound away at the shatterproof glass. There was nothing the clerk could do. Thoughts of his life flashed through his mind. Would he ever see his family again?

82

Director Donovan sat at his office desk having just briefed Agents Perez and Hawkins on the situation. Donovan decided he needed their help with Agent Burton. When they returned to the van, Burton had slowly begun to regain consciousness. Perez and Hawkins helped Donovan walk Burton back to the director's office where they laid him on the couch.

While Burton regained his wits, Donovan directed Perez and Hawkins to follow up with the entire team and make sure the city was secured. After an hour or so had passed and Donovan was confident that D.C. was under control, he turned his attention back to finding Matt O'Shea. After Donovan received the call from Director Godfrey to end his search for O'Shea earlier in the day, Donovan sensed something wasn't right. The latest call he'd received only solidified his skepticism that the NSA was up to something. As a result, hours earlier he had dispatched a field team to track Godfrey and his staff.

Donovan had received word a short while earlier that Director Godfrey had made a last- minute trip to New York City. Aiden, his chief of staff and Michael Stevens, his deputy, also had been located in New York. Donovan didn't know why all three men were in New York City separately—and on a Saturday. When Godfrey failed to check into his hotel after he'd been spotted by FBI agents leaving LaGuardia in a dark SUV, Donovan knew something was wrong.

His New York field agents also reported a government raid on a warehouse on the West Side docks that contained recent shipments of computers and components from China and where Michael Stevens had last been spotted. Donovan needed to get to the bottom of it. Burton was sitting on the sofa rubbing his head when Agents Perez and Hawkins paraded into the office. Hawkins spoke up: "Sir, the National Guard is securing the city, and the mayor and president have declared a state of emergency. Most cell phone reception is down, so we have to patrol block by block and building by building to notify people of the situation. The D.C. Police Department is directing traffic to clear the roads. We're gradually locking down the city. It's just taking time as we mobilize everyone."

"Good work. I've got another task for you all. I need you three to go to New York, tonight, and I mean immediately."

The three men all gave Donovan confused looks. Burton's head pounded, and the last thing he needed was to be on an airplane. "Sir," Perez said, "with all due respect, you want us to do what?" Burton was hunched over with his head in his hands, looking up with a grimace.

"You heard me. I need you all in New York tonight."

Perez approached Donovan's desk. "Sir, if I may . . ."

"You may not. This matter is not up for discussion. The rest of our team is looking for O'Shea. I need you three in New York. Director Godfrey and Deputy Stevens from the NSA have disappeared, and I worry something is wrong, especially with what's going on out there." He pointed outside in reference to the mayhem across the city.

Hawkins walked up to Perez who was standing with his hands on the back of one of the chairs in front of Donovan's desk. "Sir, the city is in chaos and the roads are blocked. The D.C. police won't have the streets cleared for hours. How do you expect us to get out of here?"

"There is a helicopter waiting on the roof. It will have you in New York in less than two hours. I need you to go directly to Manhattan."

Burton finally gained the strength to stand. "Is New York experiencing what we are here? If so, it's going to be a bitch getting around there." He rubbed his neck as he wobbled, his headache barely subsiding.

"Fortunately, it doesn't seem that this cyberattack has hit Manhattan too horribly. Either it was better prepared, or it wasn't the primary target. Now you all need to go. There's no time to lose."

"Who are we looking for when we get there?" Hawkins asked.

"I need you to locate Director Godfrey, Aiden, his chief of staff, and Michael Stevens, Godfrey's deputy."

Burton had to sit again, so he plopped into one of the chairs in front of Donovan's desk. "How are we supposed to do that?"

"You let me work on that from here. I'll put out a call to the state and federal authorities to be on the lookout for them. As soon as I get word, I'll let you know. They've got to surface sometime. When you find them, let me know, and I'll give you further instructions. Now go." Donovan pointed at the door.

Agents Hawkins and Perez helped Burton as they all made their way to the elevators. Donovan watched as they left. After they were out of earshot, he sat at his desk and called the NYPD and their Manhattan FBI field offices. Though he was hesitant, he contacted the NSA's Manhattan office as well. Surely they would know where three of their own were.

83

Osmund's and Matt's conversation was interrupted by a panicked voice calling from a nearby computer terminal.

"Sir, I think we have a major problem." It was Lee.

Osmund whipped around in the direction of the voice.
"What is it?"

"You'd better see for yourself." Lee motioned frantically to
his screen.

Osmund rushed to the computer.

"Sir, it's worse than we'd anticipated." Lee displayed a computer control system schematic on one of the large wall monitors. Osmund stared blankly at the screen. "Talk to me, Lee;
what are we looking at here?"

"It's the control systems for the Calvert Cliffs nuclear plant
in Maryland. The cooling pumps have just been disabled."

"What! Dammit, man, can you get them back online?"
Osmund realized what it meant if they couldn't get the cooling
systems reactivated. It would result in a nuclear meltdown that
could take out Washington, D.C., and most of the East Coast.
The plant was on Chesapeake Bay, and millions of gallons of

toxic water and nuclear waste would be released into the ocean if the nuclear rods melted down and the plant blew up. The damage would be catastrophic.

"Sure, I could get them back online if I had access to the program that turned them off in the first place. But it looks like it's the same malware knocking out power to dams and power stations across the country. This instance is the first nuclear reactor that's been attacked. Whoever is behind this wants to make sure D.C. gets it good. Those bastards plan to wipe out the East Coast. The good news is that this latest instance provided me information about the malware's attack vector that I think Matt may be able to use as a way to access the code. It's worth a shot."

Osmund reached for Matt. "We need you on one of these computers, now. Get on that one right there." Osmund pushed him in the direction of the workstation on the other side of Lee.

Matt lunged forward, surprised by the force with which Osmund had pushed him. "Easy there." Matt caught himself on the back of the chair before sitting in front of the computer. "All you had to do was ask," he complained as he gave Osmund a dirty look. "What do you want me to do?"

"Break into that code—your code. You need to disable it and stop any more of this destruction." Osmund shook his finger at Matt like an enraged school teacher.

Matt flippantly waved him off with a sweeping gesture. "Quit calling it 'my code,' dammit. My code was never intended for this. The government took it, all of my computer equipment, and my research years ago. I almost didn't graduate because of you bastards." Matt angrily wielded his fist in Osmund's direction.

Matt didn't know if the NSA was behind his MIT debacle, but the FBI sure was. Agents had escorted him back to his apartment from campus like a criminal and raided his apartment. He lumped all government authorities into the same category: lousy, lying, scheming bastards.

"Who knows what you all did with my code? I bet it's one of your own, probably some disgruntled son-of-a-bitch that's behind this. You all pissed off the wrong person, and he's getting even. This shit show will teach you for ruining my life and stealing my code in the first place. Serves you pricks right."

"Enough already!" Osmund roared and stomped his foot, the echo reverberating off the walls. For a brief moment the room went deathly silent as all of the staff's eyes fixated on Osmund, his fury so palpable that everyone felt the temperature rise. No one dared move.

"I don't even know what I'm looking at or working with here," Matt said, breaking the silence. "You said yourself you're not able to isolate the transmission signal or the code. What do you expect me to do? It's not like I have a magic wand to fix this mess. I can't do anything until it's located, and I have access to a code I can reprogram. You've got to give me something to work with, anything. This garble does me no good."

"Lee, show Matt what you found from this latest attack." Osmund hollered across the room at the analyst who had been running diagnostic scans on the motherboard and cellular network card from Matt's computer. "Any update on that signal tracer yet from Matt's equipment?"

The analyst yelled back, "I'm working on it! It's still hot and transmitting a signal."

"Well, hurry the hell up, dammit. We're running out of time."

"Sir, I'm working as quickly as I can," the poor analyst responded in despair.

"I don't need excuses; I need solutions. If you don't locate where that source code is coming from, we can kiss our asses goodbye. Do I make myself clear?"

The analyst retreated sheepishly into his chair. "Yes, sir."

Osmund pivoted to Lee. "What's the update on those nuclear reactors?"

Lee had been typing frantically, doing anything he could to bring the cooling systems back online. "Sir, it's crappy. Nothing I'm attempting is working. Their security software is blocking me from accessing their systems. The coolant levels around those rods are beginning to drop."

"How much time before the plant starts overheating and does damage to the reactor cores?"

"Three, maybe four hours at most. After that, we're pretty much screwed."

"Shit," Osmund said as he shook his head. "Keep doing what you can. In the meantime, let's pray for a miracle."

84

At a downtown Baltimore hospital the power had gone out, all the computer and building control systems were offline, and the backup generators had shut down. The surgical team surrounded the unconscious teenage patient lying on the operating table. He had multiple gunshot wounds and had just been transferred to the intensive care unit from the emergency room. They had stabilized the victim and were preparing to operate when everything went dark.

"What the hell?" the surgeon gasped as he was about to make an incision.

"What happened?" asked a technician as he squinted in the darkness.

"I have no idea," a nurse remarked.

There was a palpable sense of concern within the surgical team. They stood in the dark for what seemed like an eternity, but the power didn't come back on. The lead surgeon finally spoke: "Perhaps a transformer blew. The backup generators should come on soon. They'd better. We can't operate in the dark, and this patient is going to die if we don't do something fast." The surgeon turned toward the young OR tech. "Mark, go see what's going on."

Mark grabbed an emergency flashlight. He shined it around the operating room, noticing the nervous looks on all of his colleagues' faces. Mark made his way out to the main corridor where medical staff and security guards with flashlights ran anxiously up and down the corridors yelling orders. Mark grabbed an ER technician by the arm as he sped by.

"Hey Todd, what's happening? We're in the OR, and everything blacked out. We've got a gunshot victim who's going to die if we don't get the power on soon." Mark was frazzled.

"All our systems are offline. Every last one of them." Todd shook his head in dismay.

"But what about the backup power? The generators should have kicked on by now."

"Nothing. They're fried, dead, kaput. Everything's down."

Mark got noticeably more worried. "What do we do? What about the patients?"

"It's bad. We've already lost two patients who were on life support, and I'm afraid we'll lose more if the power doesn't come back soon. The ICU just radioed for additional assistance. They've got patients coding and can't do anything about it."

"Is it just our hospital?" Mark asked.

"No, it looks like the entire downtown is blacked out. I don't know what happened. Some of the ambulance crews radioed in about twenty minutes ago to say that traffic was a mess. All of the traffic lights have gone out, and the roads are just one city-wide parking lot. They can't respond to their 911 calls. One of the paramedic crews en route to a car accident victim in critical condition is stuck on the road. They can't get the victim back here."

"Has anyone called the power company?"

"The landline phones are down, and the cells aren't getting a signal. Our two-way radios are working, but they have limited range. We also don't have any water pressure. Look, I've got to go. I'm needed back in the ER." Todd raced down the hall, the ray from his flashlight bouncing up and down.

Mark watched in disbelief as other hospital staff and security guards rushed intensely by him. *Lord, help us.* He ran back to give the surgical team the bad news. He knew in his gut that the patient was going to die, and there was nothing they could do but watch.

85

At the New York City hospital, Director Godfrey and Aiden left Michael's room and found an empty staff office to discuss the situation.

"Director, things have gotten way out of control." Aiden had been monitoring Godfrey's activities all along and knew he might be behind some of this, but he didn't know the full extent.

"I know. What do you propose we do?"

"I'm not sure. Michael has been shot, Kate has been kidnapped and drugged, we've got a dead NSA analyst, and we've got other dead bodies on the streets of New York City."

"Yes, I know. Blood is on my hands, and there's more to come," Godfrey said as he bowed his head.

"Director." Aiden put his hand on Godfrey's shoulder.

Godfrey slowly raised his head and looked up. "Aiden, I need you to do something for me."

"What is it?"

"Do you still have the entrance code to my office?"

"Yes, of course."

"I need you to go back to D.C. tonight. There is something in my desk drawer that I need you to get."

"What?"

"You'll know when you see it. It's my journal." Godfrey reached into his shirt to pull out a metal chain that held a small key. He removed the chain from around his neck. "You'll need this to open my desk and access my computer."

Aiden sensed a heaviness in the room. "Director, what's this all about? Is there something you need to tell me?"

Godfrey stared at the key in his hand. "No, Aiden, there's not. Everything you need to know is in my desk drawer."

Aiden knew Godfrey wasn't telling the truth. He'd known him long enough that he could read him, but he decided not to push it. "Anything else?"

"No. I just need you to go immediately back to NSA headquarters. I will make sure Michael and Kate are taken care of." Godfrey's voice trailed off.

"Okay, if you say so."

"Now go. Call me when you're at my office. I'll be here. Michael and Kate aren't going anywhere tonight."

Aiden left the office and sped down the long corridor toward the elevators.

Godfrey followed him into the hallway. He waited to make sure Aiden was on his way before going back into Michael's room.

It was late, and the overnight hospital staff was nowhere to be seen as Godfrey turned the corner toward Michael's room. He strolled by the nurses' station where a middle-aged nurse sat in front of a computer.

"Good evening," he waved sheepishly.

"Sir, can I help you?" she asked.

He stopped momentarily at the counter. "No, thank you. I'm just here visiting Michael Stevens in room four sixteen." He gestured down the hall in the direction of Michael's room.

"Visiting hours are over."

"Yes, I know. Michael and his wife were admitted together. I'm Michael's boss. I brought them here. They don't have any family in town, so I'm making sure they're both okay for tonight."

"I'm sorry, sir, but only immediate family is allowed to stay past visiting hours or overnight." The heavyset, crotchety old nurse with her frayed blondish-gray hair stood but was still a head shorter than Godfrey.

"I understand. I won't be long. I just want to check on them one last time before I leave." He smiled warmly in an attempt to show he was well-intentioned.

"Okay. If they need anything just hit the call button." The nurse cautiously sat as she hawkishly eyed him.

"I will. Thank you." He graciously waved over his shoulder as he strolled down the hallway.

Godfrey knew Aiden had been up to something. He just didn't know what. Godfrey had lost all trust in Aiden, especially because he was most likely responsible for his kidnapping and interrogation. He was also the only one with access to Godfrey's office or computer, so Aiden had to have been the one the night before who was in his computer system. Godfrey pieced it all together and didn't like what he saw. At least Aiden would be on his way to Washington shortly, so he'd have him out of his way for a while.

Godfrey called to let Osmund and his team know about Aiden's potential involvement and that Aiden was headed back to NSA headquarters. Osmund and his men could take care of Aiden if matters came to that. Godfrey needed to be far from it, if and when it happened. They needed to catch Aiden in the act. There was nothing else Godfrey could do. Everything he had planned was falling apart. He never intended for any of this to happen. Americans were dying because of him, and Michael had almost been one of them. *I don't know if I can live with myself.* Someone had to take the fall. He started this, and he would end it.

Matt O'Shea had disappeared off the radar for hours, but luckily he had been picked up and taken to their North American Cyber Command Center. Godfrey hoped that O'Shea would be his scapegoat for the malicious code and the attacks. After all, he was the one who had written the source code years ago at MIT. He hoped that by hiring Matt under the auspices of making him an undercover cyber specialist that he'd be able to use him if needed. Matt's computer program for surveillance and cyber defense had been brilliantly written. It was almost foolproof, except for a few minor errors that Godfrey had corrected, or so he thought. Godfrey had his own plans for the code. His special covert cyber surveillance project had been working out superbly over the past couple of years until Aiden's apparent interference.

Godfrey slipped into one of the medicine storage rooms. After he grabbed what he needed, he peered into the hallway to see if anyone was coming before he returned to Michael's room, quietly closing the door behind him.

Meanwhile, Aiden exited the hospital and headed to the parked vehicle where a driver waited for him outside the main entrance. As he approached the SUV, he stopped. The driver rolled down the passenger window and asked, "Sir, are you ready to go?"

Aiden didn't know what it was, but he got a strange feeling in his chest. There was something about Godfrey's last words: "I'll make sure Michael and Kate are taken care of..." Aiden knew that could have a couple of meanings. Given the current circumstances, he wondered if Michael and Kate might be too much of a liability. There was something Godfrey wasn't admitting.

"Sir, is everything okay?" the driver asked.

"Wait right here. I'll be back." Without hesitation, Aiden spun around and raced back into the hospital.

Godfrey bent quietly over Michael who was soundly sleeping. The last dose of morphine had kicked in and knocked him out. Kate was fast asleep in her bed on the other side of the room.

"I'm sorry about all of this Michael," he whispered. "None of this was supposed to happen. I was only doing it for the sake of our country, for our national security. You, of all people, would understand. We have to make sacrifices, and sometimes that involves innocent people's lives. You and Kate were never supposed to get mixed up in this, not this way."

Godfrey never meant for any of this to happen. He was merely trying to send the country a message, to make a point. He couldn't get national leaders to listen to his warnings about the threats from Russia and China, let alone North Korea. No one would take him seriously. They didn't want to believe that the United States was on the brink of a major cyber war. Godfrey never expected the country's enemies to gain access to his program and use it against the United States. But Godfrey had lost control of the code, and this nightmare was the result. It had to end, and it had to end tonight.

Michael stirred in his sleep but didn't awaken. Godfrey moved to the other side of the bed to sit in the chair nearest the door and watch the news on TV. The sound was muted, but he could see the riots and destruction taking place in cities across the country that had lost power and other infrastructure. He knew there was nothing he could do to stop it. It was too late. O'Shea was his only hope, but he didn't even know if he could help at this point. He prayed that the fail-safe self-destruct feature of the code that he'd written would eventually trigger, thus limiting further damage. Godfrey had wanted to win more support and funding for his cyber security and surveillance programs and secure his place in U.S. intelligence history. He never planned this disaster; it was beyond his imagination.

Godfrey reached into his pocket and pulled out a syringe and a small vile containing a drug. He rolled up his sleeve before extracting the drug from the vile into the needle. The drug would paralyze him and then cause him to go into cardiac arrest. It should be a quick death. No one would know except him. He would have time to dispose of the syringe and vial before the drug took effect. It was his only way out. He couldn't envision going through a high-profile trial, let alone spending time in prison. He was too old and proud. He wanted to spare his family the embarrassment and shame of all he'd done. The thought of his lovely wife and family being harassed unsympathetically by the media troubled him. At least this way he could die quietly on his own terms as a patriot. The fate of the country would be left in others' hands. He had confidence in Osmund and his team. Godfrey had done enough.

Godfrey inserted the syringe into his forearm. The warm tingling sensation radiated up his arm as the drug entered his vein. Just then Aiden barged into the room.

Startled, Godfrey fumbled and dropped the syringe on the floor.

Aiden glared at Godfrey. "What are you doing?"

Godfrey tried to play it off, though he was beginning to sway as the drug took effect. "Nothing, nothing at all. What are you doing back here? I was just making sure they were okay before I left for the night."

"I bet you were." Aiden strode over to Godfrey.

"Aiden, stay right where you are," he said, holding up his hand as he staggered in an effort to stand.

"What did you have in your hand?"

"I don't know what you're talking about," Godfrey said as he swayed, unable to keep his balance.

"Bullshit. What are you up to, Godfrey?" Aiden looked down at the floor and saw the open syringe by the chair.

"Nothing. I was just leaving. I thought you'd be on your way to the airport by now."

"I'm sure you were hoping that," Aiden said with an air of sarcasm in his voice.

Godfrey began to get dizzy, so he held out his hand to steady himself.

Aiden stepped closer. He noticed Godfrey's sleeve was rolled up. "What have you done?"

Godfrey rolled his eyes before plopping into the chair, bracing himself as he fell back. He sighed deeply and whispered, "It's over, Aiden." Godfrey's head sank against his chest.

Aiden knelt in front of Godfrey. Picking up the syringe Aiden exclaimed, "What are you doing, you crazy old man?" Aiden shook his head, knowing Godfrey was taking the easy way out. Godfrey began to drift in and out of consciousness.

"It's all my fault, Aiden, all of this." Godfrey motioned wildly with one arm as he propped himself up with the other. "How did I ever come to this place? I have nothing left."

"What are you talking about, Godfrey? I'll get help."

"No, don't." Godfrey raised his hand to reach for Aiden.

"But Godfrey, you'll die."

"I know. It's my time. It's what I deserve," Godfrey gasped. "Aiden, there's something I must tell you. The code . . ." Godfrey coughed and wheezed.

"What about it?"

Godfrey struggled to breathe as he sat hunkered over. "It's all my fault."

"What do you mean?" Aiden asked as he leaned closer.

"I let it go too far," Godfrey confessed in a voice so weak it was barely audible.

"I don't get it."

"I don't expect you to, but you will. The code," he coughed again, struggling to breathe, "I took the code from O'Shea."

Aiden slid closer to Godfrey, propping him up with a hand against Godfrey's shoulder. "I know that. You had me and Michael recruit him and then asked us to keep an eye on him. I know all about it."

"But I modified his code, Aiden, and they got access to it."

"Who Godfrey, who got access to the code?"

"The Russians," he said, panting, "and the Chinese," he gasped, forcing the air into his lungs. "And the others. I don't know how. It was auctioned off. Someone sold us out. They sold me out." Godfrey struggled with every breath.

Aiden put his hands on Godfrey's shoulders and shook him. "What have you done?"

"I released the code into our systems."

"What systems? NSA's?"

"Yes, and others across the United States."

"Which ones, Godfrey? I need to know," Aiden demanded.

Godfrey stared at the television and watched the breaking news of the national catastrophe that was unfolding.

"It's too late." Godfrey nodded at the TV. "That one," he said as he feebly pointed at the room light. "And that one." He motioned to the electronic medical devices alongside Michael's bed. "And those . . . all of them . . . utilities, infrastructure, control systems, banks . . . The code is everywhere. I did it to protect our country."

Godfrey figured that with him being able to centrally monitor and control all of the computer networks and infrastructure systems nationwide that he would be able to keep the country safe, but he was wrong. He had released the code into all of the systems as part of his surveillance program, but now all those systems had been compromised. The code was being used against America by its enemies.

"How do we stop it?"

Godfrey could only shake his head. "What have I done, Aiden? I've lost my wife, my family, my country."

"Dammit, Godfrey, tell me how to fix it?" Aiden vigorously shook Godfrey's shoulders. Unbeknownst to Godfrey, Aiden had been going behind his back and using the code for his own purposes. Aiden didn't know the extent of Godfrey's activities and worried that he might be implicated if he was somehow linked to what Godfrey was doing.

"Eminent Eclipse, Stuxnet, the Flame virus, the presidential election . . ." Godfrey slouched further, his chin resting on his chest. "I've been involved with it all."

"Who else knows what you've done?" Aiden asked, and then he slapped Godfrey, but he only glared at Aiden with an empty stare.

"No one knows . . . not even Michael or the team."

Godfrey hadn't even told Osmund or the White House. Godfrey couldn't afford to have anyone else know his plans. Godfrey slowly looked up and spoke as drool ran down his chin. "You've got to get to O'Shea. You've got to get back to my office. O'Shea is the key. He's the one who can stop all of this. You'll find everything you need in my desk. You have the key. You must go." Godfrey tried to push Aiden away, but Aiden pushed Godfrey back so he could raise his head.

All the while, Michael and Kate lay there oblivious in their beds. The drug should have killed Godfrey several minutes ago, but he was defying its effects to share his story with Aiden.

"You're not dying on us yet, you son-of-a-bitch. You started this whole mess. Now you're going to make sure it's finished." Aiden got to his feet and whispered into Godfrey's ear. "Besides, I need you to take the blame for all of this fiasco. I'm sorry it all had to happen this way."

Godfrey's eyes suddenly opened wide as he gulped for air.

"Godfrey, before you die, I want you to know that I was behind it all. Your intentions were good, but you were sloppy, old man. As you take your final breaths, know that I sold you out. I re-programmed the code for my purposes, my benefit, not yours. And as you die now, know that I'll be enjoying life far away from here soon while, even with your death, you'll take all of the blame. I'll make sure of that. You and your family will be shamed. Meanwhile, I'll be the national hero who discovered your plot and stopped it."

Godfrey steadied himself against the back of the chair. There were daggers in his eyes as he glared angrily at Aiden and his devious smile. "I should have known I couldn't trust you, you traitor."

"Come now. I was only taking after you, my mentor," Aiden mocked.

Godfrey used all of his strength to push himself upright in the chair so he could look directly at Aiden. "Your day will come too, you son-of-a-bitch," Godfrey gasped.

"Perhaps, but yours has already come, old man." Aiden lunged forward and put one hand over Godfrey's mouth and the other behind Godfrey's head, suffocating him.

Godfrey flailed about and grabbed aimlessly at Aiden's arms, but he was too weak to pull them away. Godfrey reached into his suit coat to draw the gun from his chest holster, but Aiden pinned down his arm. Aiden slammed Godfrey's head against the wall before finishing him off. Godfrey's body went limp, and he slumped over in the chair, lifeless.

Aiden hastily looked around at the scene. Taking a handkerchief from his pocket, Aiden wiped the gun in Godfrey's holster. Using his handkerchief again, Aiden picked up the used syringe and vile that had been kicked near Michael's bed during the struggle. Aiden opened the hazardous materials box, dropped the syringe inside, and tossed the vile in the trash can.

Aiden noticed that Michael and Kate were still sound asleep. He looked at his watch and realized that he needed to get back to Washington.

The nurses were making their rounds and were headed toward the room. One of the nurses called out as she trotted toward Aiden. "What's going on in there?"

"He's had a heart attack. You've got to help him." Aiden pointed back toward the room, waving for her to follow him. Once she entered the room, and with her attention focused on Godfrey, Aiden slipped out and made his way to the SUV that was still waiting for him. As Aiden pulled away and turned down the street toward the airport, an FBI helicopter carrying three FBI agents was landing on the hospital's rooftop helipad.

86

The engines of the private Leer jet were fired up by the time Aiden's vehicle arrived on the tarmac at LaGuardia. Aiden climbed out of the SUV and ran toward the aircraft. The pilot who was standing at the bottom of the airplane's staircase motioned to Aiden and yelled, "Sir, it's time to go!"

Aiden scurried up the staircase into the plane. He watched as the SUV pulled away. Once inside, a flight attendant closed and sealed the door behind Aiden as he made his way to his seat in the back. He buckled himself in and zoned out momentarily, but he did hear the final words of the pilot's welcoming announcement: "We'll be touching down in Washington, D.C., within the hour. Please sit back and enjoy the short flight."

Aiden felt the plane lurch forward as it made its way down the tarmac to the main runway. He pulled out his phone and searched through his contacts. He found the number he was looking for and pushed "Call." The phone rang a couple of times before a man on the other end picked up.

"Hello, this is Director Donovan."

"Director, this is Aiden from the NSA, Director Godfrey's chief of staff."

"Oh, yes. I figured you might be calling soon. Word has it that the NSA has been busy in New York City the past forty-eight hours."

"How'd you know we were in New York City?"

"Well, you guys at the NSA have your ways of gathering intelligence, and we here at the FBI have ours."

Donovan had received the latest word from his field agents that the Russians and Chinese were after several U.S. government intelligence officials and a possible former CIA defector in New York City. When Michael Stevens ended up in the hospital with multiple gunshot wounds, another NSA agent was gunned down in his car, and Director Godfrey died of an apparent heart attack in the same hospital as Michael, he knew there was a problem.

"You and your agents were supposed to get to O'Shea first. I can't believe you let him get away," Aiden rebuked Donovan.

"I know. Things weren't supposed to happen this way."

"No matter. My people at the NSA have him now, so I'll be able to deal with him once I'm back in Washington."

"Have you been watching television?" Donovan asked.

"No, but I've heard the news."

Donovan sat at his desk with his head propped up on his hand as he rubbed his forehead. "Then you've heard the Hoover Dam has been taken offline, and most of the West Coast has lost power as well as many other areas across the country. They're blacked out, and millions of others are without phone service or water. Our infrastructure systems are going down piece-by-piece throughout the United States, Washington, D.C., included."

"No, I didn't know it was that bad," Aiden responded, not entirely surprised but half-heartedly concerned nonetheless.

"There have been widespread power outages. We have reports that there's more to it, though. I'm sure you'll hear about it soon enough from your people in D.C. I wonder how the White House is going to spin this. You've got your work cut out for you, Aiden. We're locking down D.C. and have instituted martial law and curfews. D.C. has been impacted, but not as bad as other cities."

Aiden had heard all he needed. "Look, I've got to go. I'll be in touch after I land. We'll discuss this more then."

"Okay. Good luck."

Aiden ended the call and reclined in his seat, shaking his head. What a mess. Things were never supposed to get this bad. *How are we going to explain this?*

Aiden needed to reach Riley and find out what was going on with O'Shea. He scrolled quickly through his contacts to find Riley's number. The phone rang repeatedly before going to voice mail. *Dammit, Riley, where are you?* Aiden dialed again and listened as the phone rang; this time Riley picked up.

"Hello?"

"Riley, is that you?" There was a clear sense of urgency in Aiden's voice.

"Aiden, thank goodness. Where are you?"

"I'm on a jet back to D.C. from New York City. I've got to get back to NSA headquarters. Where are you? Where's O'Shea?"

"We're in the Cyber Command Center. O'Shea and John are here."

"John? John who?"

"Matt's friend. He's been helping Matt. It's hard to explain."

"I need Matt at NSA headquarters in the next hour," Aiden snapped.

Riley was taken back by Aiden's abrupt request. Matt needed to stay right where he was, helping them at Cyber Command to crack the code. They'd just begun to make progress.

"You heard me," Aiden said forcefully.

"Have you seen what's going on across the country?" Riley asked.

"Yes. That's why we have to work fast. That's why I need O'Shea at NSA headquarters with me. Godfrey is behind all of this," Aiden barked.

"Godfrey?" Riley exclaimed. "But why? How? He's supposed to be protecting our country, not destroying it."

"He was trying to protect it. He didn't do this intentionally—at least I don't think he did. Godfrey only told me a fraction of the details, but he said everything we need to know is in his office. He said O'Shea is the only one who can help me stop it. Godfrey modified O'Shea's original code for his own purposes. He thought he would be protecting the country from cyber threats and terrorism through his own covert cyber surveillance program, but his plan backfired. The Russians and Chinese, among others, got access to the code and turned it against the United States."

"But how?"

"I don't know. That's what I've got to find out, and that's why I need O'Shea's help. How soon can you get him to NSA headquarters?" Aiden asked.

"We'll fire up a helicopter now and have him there in no time. Where are you, Aiden?"

"I'll be at the NSA in about an hour. I'm on a jet right now back to Washington."

"Aiden, we may not have that long." There was despair in Riley's voice as he looked up at the destruction on the screens before him. "The cooling pump systems at the Calvert Cliffs nuclear plant in Maryland have been taken offline. The coolant levels around the rods are dropping."

"When did that happen?"

"About an hour ago. We've got two to three hours at most before the plant reaches meltdown levels."

"Shit. We'll have to do whatever we can with the time we have and hope for the best." Aiden knew when he sold access to the code that there would be attacks on power plants and other industrial systems, but he never thought a nuclear plant would be targeted. That was never the agreement. It raised the severity of the situation to a whole new level, and he was unprepared to handle it.

Riley paced back and forth in the North American Cyber Command control room. "How do we get onsite at NSA? We don't have authorization to enter their airspace, and they sure as hell aren't going to let us land a helicopter there with what's going on across the country."

"You let me worry about that. When you're en route, I want you to call the following number." Aiden rattled it off. "I'll take care of the rest. You got that?"

"Yes, sir."

"Let them know you're working with Director Godfrey and me, and this is about Red Panda Eminent Eclipse. Give them your flight plan coordinates and other information. You don't have to say anything further. They will give you clearance to enter NSA airspace. If you have any issues, call me immediately. Got that?"

"Yes."

"Good. I'll see you in the next hour—and hurry."

Riley lowered the phone and put it back in his pocket.

"Who was that?" Matt asked.

"Your employer."

Perplexed, John glanced at Matt. "Why is Lucigen calling Riley?"

Riley interjected before Matt could respond. "It's Matt's other employer."

John was even more confused. "I don't get it. What's going on?"

Riley turned to John. "Matt works undercover for the NSA. He has for quite some time. He's one of our covert cyber security agents."

John turned back and forth between Riley and Matt.

"Don't worry about it. Come on. We're leaving." Riley motioned for them to follow him.

"Where are you going?" Matt asked.

"We're going for a ride to NSA headquarters."

Osmund had stepped away momentarily and was talking with one of the analysts reviewing the latest events when he overheard the conversation.

"Sounds like you guys need to get to NSA, and fast. We've got a chopper ready. I'll have our men take you there immediately." Osmund waved to a marine standing by the door who trotted over. "I need you to escort them to the helipad."

"Yes, sir, right away, sir." The marine turned to the three men. "Come with me, please."

As Matt walked by Osmund he grabbed Matt's arm. "Here, you may need this. It's encrypted and untraceable." Osmund handed Matt a burner phone. "Make sure it's on at all times and that you're able to hear it ring. I'll give you updates from here. If nothing else, you've got to get that cooling system at Calvert

Cliffs back online. If you don't, nothing else matters. Now get going, you don't have any time to waste."

"You got it." Matt feigned a salute to Osmund.

"And Matt, one more thing: watch out for Aiden."

Matt gave Osmund a puzzled look. Osmund had received an earlier call from Godfrey forewarning him about Aiden. Godfrey didn't provide many details other than he was concerned that Aiden might be attempting to undermine their agency and could be involved with providing intelligence secrets to foreign governments.

The three men exited the main control room where a small motorized vehicle was waiting to escort them to the helipad.

87

When Aiden's jet landed at Baltimore-Washington International he deplaned and boarded a government helicopter to NSA headquarters. A vast stretch of darkness spanned the horizon toward D.C. The pilot radioed the air traffic controllers with the necessary information to let them know Aiden was en route.

"Sir, you have permission to enter NSA airspace," a controller replied.

"Thank you. We'll be landing shortly."

Aiden's helicopter was approaching the NSA grounds when he saw the blinking white, red, and green lights of another aircraft closing swiftly in the distance. *That must be O'Shea.* Aiden checked his watch. *Right on time.*

Aiden jogged away from his helicopter and shielded his face as he waited in the distance for O'Shea's copter to land, his hair blowing as the rotors spun and kicked up dust around him. When the other helicopter touched down, three men leapt out and trotted toward Aiden. He recognized Riley and O'Shea but not the third man.

"Welcome to NSA headquarters, gentlemen!" he yelled above the spinning helicopter rotors.

The four men hurried toward the entrance and entered through the main glass doors into the lobby. Aiden turned to Riley and John and said, "I think it's best if you two stay here while Matt and I go upstairs. We can handle this. But stand by in case we need anything."

Riley gave Aiden a skeptical look. It was unusual that he wouldn't want him and John to go with them, but he wasn't going to push it. Someone needed to stay with John because he didn't have top-secret clearance. And besides, Aiden outranked him. Riley nodded. "Okay, we'll wait here. Call if you need anything."

"We will." Aiden grabbed Matt's arm and said, "Come on. We don't have much time."

88

Back at the New York City hospital, the FBI agents were finishing their interviews with Michael and Kate about what had transpired earlier, but neither was much help because both had been asleep or unconscious through most it. Besides, Michael was hesitant to share what all he knew until he had a chance to talk with Godfrey and his superiors at NSA. As the last agent was about to exit the room, Michael sat up slightly and called to him. "Wait. Before you go, I forgot to ask. No one has said anything about Director Godfrey. Where is he? Is he okay?"

Agent Hawkins turned to Michael and said, "I'm sorry; he's dead. He had a heart attack last night."

A wave of melancholy washed over Michael as the sense of loss hit him in his gut. The director had been a friend and mentor. He had the utmost respect for Godfrey. He was a stalwart, the backbone of many of the major national cyber security initiatives designed to keep the country safe. He had done so much, many things he could not receive public recognition for because the projects were so secretive. Michael knew about them though. He recognized the patriot and selfless servant the director was to his country. Michael couldn't believe he was dead. He flopped back in his bed and stared blankly at the ceiling.

89

Once inside the NSA building, Aiden and Matt made their way through the labyrinth of corridors and secure doors until they arrived at Godfrey's office. Aiden entered a key code on the touch pad on the wall. They heard a beep, and then the sound of the door unlocking. Aiden grabbed the handle and opened the door, peering cautiously inside. The office was dark, but as he stepped inside the motion sensor lights activated. He turned to O'Shea. "Come on. We've got to hurry."

Aiden walked briskly to the director's desk and sat. He knew which drawer to open. He'd been snooping on Godfrey for some time. He pulled out the key that Godfrey had given to him at the hospital and opened the bottom drawer. There he grabbed a silver metal box that he placed on top of the desk. Aiden then took a small electronic chip key from the chain around his neck and inserted it into a keyhole on the side of the box. Placing both thumbs against the two thumb-size indentations on the front of the box, he waited for the system to read his fingerprints. There was a click, and the locks opened. He raised the lid and peered inside. There was a journal, some random papers, the director's passport, several stacks of money, and an odd-shaped

USB drive. He knew the USB was a key. He had his own version, but he needed the director's to be able to access certain network drives and files within Godfrey's computer. Aiden reached down and inserted the key into the front side of the computer. He put the director's badge into the common access card I.D. reader and turned on the computer, waiting for it to boot up. As the login screen appeared, he grabbed Godfrey's journal. Thumbing through the pages, he found what he was looking for. He entered the director's username and password into the prompt on the screen. A few seconds later, the computer authenticated the credentials, and the screen refreshed as the main desktop appeared.

Godfrey hadn't given Aiden much information when they were at the hospital, but he said everything would be in the journal. Aiden feverishly searched through the pages while Matt stood over his shoulder, not knowing what to do. Aiden quickly found what he needed, the location of the source code in his computer files. Aiden navigated through Godfrey's computer folders until he located the right file. He double clicked and opened it. Scrolling up and down, he scanned the code before turning to Matt. "This is all you from here on out. This is the source code that's causing all of the nationwide destruction. Godfrey took your code and reprogrammed it, but I don't know how he modified it. I need you to stop it or override it."

"What? Godfrey is behind all of this?" Matt asked, shocked.

"It would seem so. There's no time to explain; I need you to do as I say. Here, sit." Aiden stood so Matt could sit in front of the computer. Matt placed his fingers over the keyboard and awaited Aiden's instructions.

"Ready when you are. What do you need me to do?"

"Go down to the bottom of the code. I'm going to give you some instructions to enter into the command prompts." Godfrey told Aiden that the passcode was in his journal, but Aiden didn't know where. Then Aiden found what he believed it to be. *This can't be it. It's too simple.*

90

Aiden stood over Matt's shoulder as he sat in front of Godfrey's computer. "This might be easier than I thought," Aiden sneered.

"What do you mean?" Matt spun around and stared at Aiden.

"Here, I'll take care of this." Aiden wanted to be the one who stopped the attack. He wanted the credit even though he was behind it.

"But I thought you needed me to modify the code."

"I thought so too, but I believe the passcode is right here," Aiden said as he thumbed to a page of the open journal.

"Really?" Matt said surprised.

"Here, stand up."

Matt got up and Aiden sat. He opened the journal, placed it on his lap, and read the last entry on the page. It was dated nearly a month ago. Aiden shook his head as he browsed the text before turning the page.

"What is it? What's in that book?"

"Nothing, just some of the director's work notes." Aiden lied. Godfrey had laid out his plans in a manifesto: what he had done, why he had done it, and how. It was as if he were confessing in his notes in the hope that doing so would provide some personal justification. Perhaps he felt guilty. For a moment, Aiden felt sorry for the director. Godfrey had sacrificed everything for his country—even his life. Aiden regretted that, but Godfrey would have to take the fall.

"Are you going to stop this or not?" Matt pointed forcefully at the screen.

"Yes. Give me a minute."

"We're running out of time."

Just then the cell phone in Aiden's pocket beeped. He pulled it out and checked the caller I.D. Getting up, he stepped briskly away from the computer, setting the journal down on the desk.

"Where the hell are you going?" Matt reached for Aiden's arm, but he pulled away. Matt didn't know what could be more urgent than the task at hand. There was a nuclear plant approaching a critical meltdown, and Aiden was taking a damn phone call.

"I'll be right back. This is an emergency." Aiden walked out of the director's office.

Meanwhile, Matt sat at the computer terminal and scrolled through the code, recognizing it immediately. They weren't lying. *These sons-of-bitches took my code and rewrote it for their own purposes. I'll be damned.*

Aiden scouted the hall to make sure no one was coming. He scrolled through the text messages, smiling as he read them. In disappointment, he shook his head knowing what he had to do.

#0908194 – $145M
#09112001 – $155M
#1271941 – $250M
#06141946 – $255M
#10261947 – $265M
#11072016 – $300M

Aiden touched the text entry box and typed a group message: "Bidding on hold. Item possibly compromised. Stand by for further instruction." Aiden then pushed "Send" before putting his phone back in his pocket.

91

Aiden finished sending the text in the hallway outside of Godfrey's office and was reaching for the door when it flew open.

"What are you doing out here?" Matt was panting heavily.

"I was just finishing up."

"Finishing up what? Do you see what's going on?" Matt pointed in the direction of the TV screen on Godfrey's wall. He had turned it on to check the news.

The image on the screen showed a strip mall. The camera zoomed in to show hundreds of people rioting in the parking lot. Businesses and cars were burning, and smoke was filling the air. People were looting the stores and fighting over groceries and water. Police lights were flashing on the screen, and the occasional police officer ran by chasing a looter. Gunshots rang out in the background.

"What's going on? Where is that?"

"I don't know yet, but it's chaos."

Aiden watched the TV. "What a disaster. I can't believe Godfrey let this happen."

"Aiden, where's the passcode? Right now this program is read-only. I can't make any edits. We've got to get the nuclear plant back online, get the power back on, and stop any further damage."

"Get Godfrey's journal. We don't have a minute to lose."

O'Shea cocked his head. *Apparently we do since you've been outside for the last five minutes.*

Aiden hurried to the computer and sat down. "Now where was I?" He grabbed the journal and thumbed through the pages to the passcode. "Here it is."

"What are you waiting for? Go ahead and enter it." Matt hastily tapped on the computer screen. "You're wasting time."

Aiden shot Matt a nasty look. "We can't rush this. It could make matters worse if I enter the wrong passcode." Having a hydroelectric power plant like Hoover Dam go offline was one thing, having a nuclear facility lose electricity and meltdown near Washington, D.C., was something completely different. Aiden knew he would have a lot to clean up, but that's what he'd wanted. All of these events should help secure his position as Godfrey's successor, and guarantee the necessary support for Aiden's new plan for national cyber security programs.

Aiden pulled up the code and opened the command prompts as he skimmed the text on the page. It was handwritten but legible. Aiden knew the director loved his wife more than anything. It would only make sense that the passcode was their wedding anniversary. *How ironic: the very work that killed his marriage eventually killed him. What a shame.* Aiden typed the eight numbers into the computer and hit "Enter." *There, that should do it.*

Almost immediately he got a response. Aiden didn't like the pop-up that appeared on the screen.

Access Attempt Failed
1 of 3

"Dammit." Aiden slammed his fist on the desk. "The passcode didn't work."

Perhaps Aiden had entered it too quickly and made a mistake. Aiden tried entering the date again, this time slower to make sure he correctly typed each number. He hit "Enter" again.

Access Attempt Failed
2 of 3

"Shit." Aiden's heart raced. If the next entry was wrong, he'd be locked out of the file, and there would be nothing he or Matt could do. Aiden didn't know why the passcode wasn't working. He had used it before to access the program files. Godfrey must have changed it in the last day or so and didn't write it down. With Godfrey dead, Aiden had no way of accessing the program file to disable the code.

"Do you think Godfrey would have made the passcode so simple?" Matt asked. "It goes against all the principles of creating a password. He, above all others, knew that. He'd never use any personal dates for something so crucial."

"True." Aiden went along with it, but he knew that was the passcode. He'd used it the day before. Aiden reflected on the conversation that he'd had earlier with the director. *O'Shea is the key. Only O'Shea could stop it. What did he mean? Obviously, Godfrey's wedding date wasn't the passcode anymore.*

"What do we do now?" Matt asked as he tapped on the back of the chair while Aiden appeared lost in thought.

It had to be something else meaningful, but what? Aiden turned to Matt. "Before Godfrey died, he said that you were the only one who could stop this, that identifying you was the key. Does that make any sense to you?"

Matt racked his brain. *How am I the key?*

"Matt." Aiden grabbed O'Shea's arm.

Matt pulled away. "I'm thinking; give me a minute." Nothing came to him. He was staring intently at the desk when something caught his eye. "What's that?" He reached for the journal on Aiden's lap.

"What? This?" Aiden held up the small, hardbound book.

"Yes. There. It looks like a page is loose or a bookmark is sticking out. See, right there."

Aiden flipped the journal upside down and shook it. An MIT photo I.D. fell onto the floor. "Who's this?" he asked, holding the card up to get a better look. The student's name had been intentionally scratched off to make it illegible.

Matt moved closer.

"What's this doing in here?" Aiden flipped over the card to look at the back. "What do you make of this?" Aiden handed Matt the photo I.D.

Matt grabbed the photo and recognized it immediately. "I know what Godfrey meant now."

Aiden gave Matt a baffled look. "I don't get it."

"I wouldn't expect you to. Now get up," Matt demanded.

"Why?" Aiden glared at Matt with a perplexed look.

"You heard me. Move your ass. I know what the passcode is." Matt waved the photo in Aiden's face.

"That thing? It's just an old student I.D.," Aiden scoffed.

Matt put his hand on the back of the chair where Aiden was sitting. "You will know in a minute. Now let me sit down."

Aiden got out of Matt's way.

Matt opened the command prompts on the screen. He placed the photo I.D. in front of him. *Godfrey was no idiot, and he needed something simple. This made perfect sense.* The front of the student I.D. card contained a barcode with eight numbers under it. Matt carefully typed them into the computer.

90566123

He checked the numbers three times to make sure they were correct before hitting "Enter." Then the computer beeped, and the message he expected appeared on the screen:

PASSCODE CONFIRMED
ACCESS GRANTED

Aiden leaned on the desk. "What did you do?"

"I figured out the passcode. It was this." Matt waved the I.D. in front of Aiden. "Take a close look. What do you see?"

"I see an I.D. for an MIT student." The words had barely left Aiden's lips when it finally hit him. He couldn't believe he didn't notice it in the first place. "The student I.D. number is the passcode, isn't it?"

"You got it."

"Have you ever seen the student in this picture?" Matt asked as he held the photo next to his own face.

Aiden gasped. "It's you. But you look so different." In an instant everything made sense. Godfrey had taken Matt's code, so it was only fitting that the passcode would be Matt's old student I.D. number.

"I do look a lot different. I changed my whole image after the incident at MIT. I thought you would have known that. I didn't want anyone to recognize me, but we still have plenty to worry about. What's our next move?"

"I need you to check the code and make sure it's intact," Aiden said. "Figure out how Godfrey modified it and if there's a way to reverse what he did or, at least, to stop what's happening. If it's true that the Russians and Chinese compromised the code, then we need to rewrite it so they can't continue using it."

"I can do that," Matt said, "but it's going to take time."

"How long?"

"It could take hours. From what I can tell, Godfrey did a lot of half-ass patchwork in here. It looks like the work of an amateur. Are you sure Godfrey made these modifications?"

Aiden gave O'Shea a smug look. "He must have."

"I would have thought, given the director's position and experience, that his code writing skills would have been better than this crap. Let me see what I can do."

"We still don't have a lot of time, so you need to hurry." Aiden motioned for Matt to get to it.

As Aiden was stepping away from the desk, his phone rang. "What is it, Riley?"

"You're not going to believe who just walked into the lobby: the secretary of defense."

"What? The secretary? He's here now?" Aiden was beside himself.

"You heard correctly. He's here in the lobby talking with staff."

What's he doing here? Aiden began to panic. He wasn't expecting the secretary to get involved, certainly not right here and not right now.

"Apparently," Riley said, "the secretary decided to come here personally to address this disaster."

After Osmund had received the disturbing call from Godfrey at the hospital, he had called the secretary of defense to give him an inside report on what was happening, including with the Calvert Cliffs nuclear installation. Osmund informed the secretary about Godfrey and that Aiden and O'Shea were headed back to NSA headquarters. As soon as he could, the president evacuated the White House, and all key personnel headed for the continuity of operations facility outside the city. Meanwhile, the secretary of defense had left the Pentagon for NSA headquarters.

"The secretary just left the lobby, so you've got less than ten minutes until he joins you," Riley said. "And Aiden, he's beyond pissed."

"Thanks for the heads up." Aiden ended the call and turned to Matt who was rapidly typing.

While Aiden was on the phone, Matt had located the back door he'd written into the original source code. He breathed a sigh of relief. Even though Godfrey had modified his code, the back door was still intact. Matt had learned early in his programming days at MIT to always create a back door for his codes because you never knew when one might be needed. Given the nature of his program, he'd included several back doors in case one or more were discovered or compromised. He reviewed the code and saw that the fixes were going to be much simpler than he had feared. Whoever reworked the code had done it in such a way that it could be reprogrammed easily. Not only that, it was so the programmer almost wanted someone to hack it from the outside. But what made less sense was that the programmer had built quick fixes and fail-safes that would prevent serious damage that couldn't be stopped or reversed. Someone wanted damage to be done, but only if it could be limited and controlled.

"How are things coming along?" Aiden asked.

"I'm almost done." Matt was updating the code and adding some new features, including updating his back door entry sequences along with other hidden security features. If the NSA or anyone else tried to use any part of the code again, Matt would know, and he'd be able to gain remote access from anywhere in the world. Not only that, he'd be able to control and even disable it with only a handful of keystrokes. He saw what his code could do in the wrong hands, and he wasn't going to let that happen again.

Aiden sat on the desk next to Matt and said, "I thought you said it would take hours."

"That's what I thought, but I found a way inside and was able to make the necessary changes much quicker than expected."

Just then the phone in Matt's pocket rang. It was the burner that Osmund had given him before he left the command center. There was no phone number I.D. on the screen, but Matt answered anyway.

"Hello? Osmund?"

"Matt, are you at Godfrey's office yet? Have you gained access to the code?"

"Yes, and I'm here with Aiden."

"You need to get those cooling systems at Calvert Cliffs back online ASAP."

"Oh, shit." Matt had been so caught up in reprogramming his code to make sure he'd be able to access it in the future that he'd forgotten about the nuclear plant.

Matt heard someone in the background. It sounded like Lee. He was barking orders and checking for updates on the nuclear plant status. Since Matt, Riley, and John had left for the NSA, Lee had been actively monitoring the situation at Calvert Cliffs. He was in continual communication with the plant managers and engineers on site. After the primary cooling system had been taken offline, the control rods were moved into place to stop the nuclear fission reactors. The rods were still too hot though, so the engineers on site manually activated the backup cooling system, a self-contained diesel generator designed to spray coolant on the rods to keep them at a manageable temperature. Unexpectedly, the generator had gone out minutes before Osmund called Matt.

"Matt, give me your status. Are you able to link into the code and disable it?"

Matt rapidly entered some commands. "Hold on . . . almost there . . . Got it. I'm where I need to be."

Matt heard Lee yelling to Osmund who put the phone on speaker. "Matt, are you still there?"

Matt heard more voices and commotion in the background. Then a distinct voice spoke; it was Lee. "Matt, you need to hurry the hell up. Those reactors are overheating."

"I'm working as fast as I can, dammit." Matt rattled away at the keyboard, entering commands and trying to find the one to disable the code sequence targeted at the nuclear plant control systems.

"Matt, hold on." Lee then carried the phone back to his work station where he had the plant manager at Calvert Cliffs on another line.

"Harry, are you there?" Lee asked, trying to get the attention of the plant manager.

"Yes, go ahead." Harry was huffing and puffing as he paced in the plant's engineering control room.

"How are things looking on your end?" Lee asked.

"Bad, very bad," Harry responded. "None of our backup safety cooling measures are working."

The emergency core cooling system had been designed to rapidly cool the core and make it safe in the event of an accident. Most nuclear plants were equipped with multiple systems to ensure a meltdown wouldn't occur. But all three at Calvert Cliffs had been disabled or failed.

"Harry, I need more specifics; talk to me."

"Our peak core temperature is rising. It's over the minimum safe threshold now. Something needs to happen fast. I've got less than ten minutes before the nuclear reactor cores begin to suffer damage!" Harry's heart was racing, and he was sweating. He hit the emergency evacuation alarm. Seconds later the sirens wailed a deafeningly shrill warning throughout the plant.

The coolant in the Unit 1 reactor had dropped below sustainable levels, and the temperature was increasing rapidly to critical levels at over 500 degrees Celsius, nearly double the standard operating temperature. The Unit 2 reactor wasn't in much better shape. When the temperature reached over 800 degrees Celsius, the plant would suffer damage to its nuclear cores. And at over 1,200 degrees, a meltdown would begin.

"Matt, are you there? This is Osmund."

"Yes, I'm here." Matt was frantically typing. "Hell, yeah!" he cheered. He'd found the code sequence that was attacking the programmable logic controllers at the plant. "All right, time to work my magic."

"Matt."

"Not now, Osmund!" Matt barked, needing to concentrate. The wrong modifications to the code or a mistyped command entry would only make the situation worse.

Lee was still on the line with Harry. "Harry, what's going on?"

"Holy shit!" Harry exclaimed. "You can't be serious. We're screwed." Harry ran his hands through his sweaty hair as he watched the red lights and alerts pop up all across their system diagnostics screens. The plant was in the early stages of meltdown; damage to the reactor cores had begun.

An engineer burst into the control room with an update. Their last resort to cool the reactors was to flood the cores with water from the bay, but they couldn't open the intake valves to allow water to flood the containment vessels—not even manually. There was no other way to lower the temperature of the cores unless the cooling system came back online.

"Harry?" Lee said, trying to get his attention.

Harry was eyeing the engineer when he spoke into the phone. "We need to evacuate." The peak core temperature had risen to over seven hundred degrees. A meltdown was imminent.

"Give us five more minutes. I've got a guy working on it," Lee pleaded.

"We don't have five minutes!" Harry shouted.

"Osmund, what's going on with O'Shea?" Lee asked. "We need an update now. That reactor is going to blow if he doesn't get those cooling systems back online."

Matt was already stressed, but to complicate things, he heard banging on the office door. He looked up to see the secretary of defense barge into the office with an entourage of secret service agents and armed NSA guards behind him.

"What the hell is going on here?" the secretary demanded.

Aiden rushed to intercept him, but the secretary shoved him out of the way and headed straight for O'Shea. The secretary stormed to Godfrey's desk and aggressively shook his finger at Matt. "Who the hell are you, and what are you doing in here?"

Matt held up his hand, glancing briefly at the secretary. "Not now," he scolded before he continued typing.

"I'm the secretary of defense!" he shouted as he shook his fist at O'Shea and walked around the desk.

"I don't give a damn who you are. You won't be secretary of anything if you don't shut up and let me do this." Matt needed to reboot the plant's computer system before he could bring the cooling system back online. He needed someone at the plant to manually restart their computer systems for his software program updates to load and take effect.

The secretary paused, shocked. He'd never had anyone in his professional career talk to him in such a manner. Aiden felt compelled to interject. "Sir, this is Matt O'Shea. He's the only person in America right now who can stop of all this. Please let him do his work."

Matt glared at them. "Would you both please shut the hell up; I need to focus."

Aiden and the secretary quieted down like schoolboys in the principal's office. They slowly walked around the desk and stood silently over Matt's shoulder to watch him work.

On the other end of the phone, Matt could hear Lee hollering. "Matt! Talk to me man! What's your status?"

"I've modified the software with an updated run sequence, but I need the plant to manually restart its computer systems."

"You want the plant to do what?" Lee couldn't believe what Matt was telling him. Matt was asking a nuclear plant to shut down its computers while it was in the early phases of a meltdown.

"You heard me. Turn off the plant's damn computers and restart them."

"They may not be able to get them back online. Are you sure that's going to work?"

"No, but it's our only shot."

Lee turned to Osmund, "Sir, you're not going to believe this. Matt just instructed me to have the team at Calvert Cliffs restart their cooling system computers, manually."

"Give me that damn phone." Osmund thundered over and grabbed the phone. "O'Shea, are you out of your mind? That plant is going into meltdown, and you want them to turn off their computers? They may not be able to get them back online. Do you understand the consequences?" Osmund barked.

Matt took a deep breath. "I know it sounds crazy, but they've got to do it. We've got to try. The computers need to reboot with the software program updates I made to their systems. It's the only way to know if the changes I made worked."

Osmund yelled at Lee, "Tell them to shut down their computers now!"

Lee shook his head in dismay. He couldn't believe what was happening as he lifted the phone to his ear. "Harry, are you there?"

"Yes, but not for much longer." Harry was panicked. He was staring at the distraught faces of the other engineers in the control room. A meltdown would be catastrophic for the East Coast, and it was already starting.

"We need you to turn off and restart your cooling system computers."

"Are you out of your freaking mind?" Harry flailed his arms in protest as he stomped his foot.

"Just do it. I don't have time to explain," Lee said, trying to remain calm but with urgency in his voice.

Harry turned to an engineer who was monitoring the core temperatures and cooling systems. "Gene, I need you to turn off and restart your computers. Just do it. There's no time to explain."

Gene looked like a deer in headlights. Following orders could mean suicide and the death of millions of others. He froze. Harry leapt over to Gene's computer and shoved him out of the way. Harry opened the control panel to restart the systems. He pulled up the command prompt and hit "Restart." Then he waited. The monitor screen turned black. Several long minutes passed before the computer flickered back to life.

"Harry, tell me what you see," Lee asked. He was monitoring the plant's systems from his computer terminal and saw them go offline.

"The systems are coming back online, but slowly."

One of the engineers whose system was still online bellowed, "Sir! Our peak core temperatures are over 1,000 degrees. Damage to the reactors has started."

Harry anxiously thumped his foot on the floor and tapped his fingers on the desk. "Come on, dammit, restart." Moments later the main control screen appeared. "Yes!" he shouted as he shook his fist.

"Lee," Harry said, "the computers have restarted and are back online. I'm going to check the cooling systems." Harry navigated through a handful of screens until he reached the diagnostics program for the cooling system controls.

Lee couldn't tell from his computer whether the power plant's systems had come back online. Seconds later, Lee heard impassioned screaming on the other end of the phone. He didn't understand what the voices were saying, but they sounded horrible. Lee lowered his head and buried his face in his hands. *Oh, no; it didn't work!*

A moment later Lee heard Harry's elated voice, and he was shouting with joy as he jumped around and hugged the others in the control room. "It worked! It worked! Son-of-a-bitch, you all did it!"

The cooling systems were back online, and the core temperatures were dropping. Harry turned off the evacuation alarm, and the screeching sirens fell silent.

Lee sat at his workstation, still holding the phone, his palms sweating. Osmund towered over him. On the other end of the line in Godfrey's office Matt, Aiden, and the secretary all stared at the computer screen in anticipation. The last five minutes had seemed like an eternity.

Osmund grabbed the phone from Lee. "Matt, are you there?"

"Yes," he responded sheepishly, not knowing what had happened.

"It worked! Great job!" Osmund was happy and hopeful.

"It did?" Matt glanced back and forth at Aiden and the secretary. "It worked? Really?"

"Yes, I'm sure you can see for yourself," Osmund said.

Matt pulled up the plant's cooling system schematics on his screen. He could see that the temperatures in the reactor cores were dropping into the safe range. *Well, I'll be . . . It worked.* Matt sat there, part in relief and part in disbelief.

The secretary put his hand on Matt's shoulder and leaned forward to speak into the phone. "This is the U.S. Secretary of Defense. Who am I speaking with?"

"Sir, this is Mr. Osmund, the director of the North American Cyber Command Center."

"Good job, Osmund. Thank you to you and your team. I expect a full briefing tomorrow on what the hell happened. In the meantime, there's still work to be done. We're not out of the woods yet."

"Thank you. Yes, sir. I understand."

The secretary patted Matt on the shoulder. "Thank you. Sorry for my harsh abruptness earlier. I didn't know you were the only one who could help us." Then he glared angrily at Aiden. "And if it hadn't been for you and Godfrey, we never would have needed his assistance in the first place."

Matt refocused his attention on the computer screen. His work wasn't over yet. He continued to rattle away at the keyboard. After a few minutes he stopped. "There." He pushed the chair away from the computer and held his hands up in celebration.

"What did you do just now?" Aiden asked.

"The way Godfrey rewrote his code allowed for easy reprogramming. I'm finishing the changes right now and locking out whoever has had access up until this point. Whatever damage this code has been causing will be disabled for now, but this is only a temporary patch. I'll need additional time over the next twenty-four hours to make more extensive fixes to the code to prevent further damage."

"You've stopped the cyberattack?" Aiden asked, skeptical.

"I believe so, from what I can tell—at least for now."

Come take a look." Matt motioned to the screen where four words were flashing:

PROGRAM RUN SEQUENCE ABORTED

"What all did you change? I wasn't able to . . ." Aiden paused before letting anything more slip. He had been able to access and direct the code, but he hadn't been able to make any major changes. Doing so required super-user administrator rights that Matt apparently had acquired, just like Godfrey.

"Do you think I'd be dumb enough to write the type of program that I did and not include a backdoor? I was young, but I wasn't stupid. This situation is the exact reason I did it. How I did it is for me to keep to myself as my insurance card, just in case anyone tries to mess with me again. I'm not giving that up to anyone." Matt glared fiercely at Aiden and then at the secretary.

The secretary pushed Aiden out of the way and got face-to-face with Matt. "Is that a threat, young man?" The secretary was seething. There was a national crisis going on, and he hadn't slept the last two days. He had little patience or tolerance for attitude, even if Matt had just saved their asses.

"Not at all, Mr. Secretary. I'm merely protecting my own interests to make sure you sneaky government bastards don't screw me again and create another mess like the one you all created the past two days."

The secretary sat on the edge of the desk. "I see. I've heard a lot about you, O'Shea," he said as he crossed his arms.

"You have?" Matt couldn't believe the secretary knew his name let alone anything about him.

"Yes. You created a huge predicament years ago when you put the code you wrote at MIT on open source. It's amazing our economy didn't end up in worse shape than it did. You could have wrecked our entire financial system."

"With all due respect, sir, that's an exaggeration. Someone took my code and used it for their own nefarious purposes. It was likely one of your people," Matt remarked as he shot a smug look at Aiden. "Besides, I didn't cause any of those economic issues. The U.S. economy was already suffering before you and the president took office. You talk about my fiasco. Look at what your own National Security Agency has been doing. They've been spying on American citizens and companies for years, not to mention the countless trade secrets that have been stolen and sold to fund covert government programs. I'm sure there's more but, unfortunately, I didn't have the chance to read everything. You can see for yourself." He tossed Godfrey's journal across the desk, and it slid into the secretary's thigh. When Aiden had stepped out of the office earlier, Matt skimmed through it and had taken many key photos with his phone. He was shocked by what he learned and was even more stunned that Godfrey had written it all down. It seemed odd. Why would he write down facts so damning? It was as if he, or someone, wanted it to be discovered.

The secretary stood and moved closer as he eyed O'Shea. He towered nearly a head taller than Matt. Matt pushed his chair back.

"You've got a lot of nerve, O'Shea. How much do you know?"

"Enough to make sure you all don't harass me in the future and to ensure I get a new life far from here. You wouldn't want me going to the media with what I know, would you?"

"Is that a threat?"

"No, it's a promise." Matt sat with his legs and arms crossed as he confidently rocked in his chair.

"You can't have your old life back. But what I can give you is a new life."

"And how do you propose to do that?" With his hands on his knees, Matt rocked forward in the chair toward the secretary.

"You leave that to me. I'll make the arrangements."

Aiden stood silently to the side but felt compelled to speak. "Sir."

The secretary turned, annoyed by the interruption. "What is it, Aiden?"

"How are we going to explain all of this to the American people and the president?"

The secretary paused. "Very carefully." He marched to the office door and opened it before turning back toward O'Shea. "If you'll excuse us for a moment, there are some matters I need to discuss with Aiden."

"Certainly." Matt hurried to the door, sensing a storm brewing.

The secretary held the door open. "Please wait outside. This will only take a few minutes." Matt saw the bolts of lightning in the secretary's eyes and knew that Aiden would be on the receiving end soon.

Matt sheepishly left the office as the secretary closed the door behind him. Matt waited in the hallway with the Secret Service detail.

The secretary signaled to Aiden and commanded, "Sit down!"

Aiden defiantly moseyed over and sat. He watched as the secretary paced in front of him like a tiger about to pounce.

"What the hell has been going on around here? I've got a national security crisis on my hands and a dead NSA director. Have you been watching the news?"

"Well, sir, with everything going on with Godfrey and O'Shea, not really." Although Aiden hadn't been watching the news, he knew full well what was happening.

Hundreds if not thousands of U.S. citizens had been killed, injured, or missing across the country because of the cyberattack. Cities and towns had lost water because the pumps at the water plants had been taken offline. Many were without electricity. Mobile phone networks had been shut down in parts of the country. The only way for many to communicate was through satellites and two-way radios. Even the satellite communications were spotty because the government was having to route the signals through its NATO partners. Transmissions through the country's undersea cable network had been disrupted on both coasts. Nearly the entire air traffic control system was knocked out, and there were downed airplanes scattered across the country, not to mention all of the stranded passengers at airports nationwide. There was rioting in the streets and looting across the country. People were killing each other over food, water, and other necessities.

"This is a national disaster of historic proportions, and you let it happen under my watch. Your ass is on the line." The secretary was fuming.

"Mr. Secretary, with all due respect, this was all Godfrey." Aiden threw up his hands as if he had nothing to do with it.

"Really? I've known Godfrey a long time, and it doesn't strike me that he'd pull a stunt like this and put our country at such grave risk."

"Sir, it's true. It's all in his journal. And he told me just before he died."

"He told you? Really? What did he say?"

"He confessed that he was behind everything. He took O'Shea's code and modified it for his own ends. He embedded the code in our industrial control systems and networks across the country as part of a covert surveillance program he was overseeing."

"How'd he manage to do that without me or the president knowing?"

"I don't know. Godfrey died before I could ask him."

"And how did our enemies manage to steal Godfrey's code?"

"Like I said, I'm not sure," Aiden said. "That's what we need to find out."

Foreign entities had gained access to the code. Of course, that access was gained, at least partially, because Aiden was selling it to them.

"At least we've been able to stop this attack temporarily so things don't get worse, but our country has taken a significant blow. I never would have let this circus get this far," the secretary said. "Your program is over. We can't afford to have something like this—or worse—happen again. You and Godfrey have failed our country. I'm turning your operations over to Osmund."

"But sir . . ."

"Aiden, don't waste your breath." The secretary's tone was stern.

Aiden stood and said, "But sir, Godfrey's intentions were noble. And our programs have protected us from countless attacks. You know that as well as I do. Please don't make any rash decisions."

Aiden thought carefully before continuing. "We can take advantage of this. You and the president can leverage it. You can't just shut down our programs. Not now. Not after all of this. This only highlights the importance of what we're doing. We should expand our programs, not eliminate them."

"Aiden, once I have a full grasp of what happened here I will shut your programs down if I choose. In the meantime, I've got to figure out what to tell the president and the American people."

The secretary was still pacing like a caged tiger when one of the members of his security detail entered the office.

"Sir, good news."

"What is it?"

"Our control and infrastructure systems are coming back online. The White House executive offices have power again. We're getting reports that power is being restored across the country, and we've begun to reestablish communications. It looks like the worst of this is over."

The secretary snarled at Aiden. "I beg to differ. This is far from over. Aiden, I think we're done here."

The agent took one look at the secretary's expression and quickly ducked out of the office, recognizing his presence was no longer welcome.

"But sir, if not us, who will protect our country against another major cyberattack like this?" Aiden pleaded.

"This is the last time we will have this conversation. You and Godfrey have jeopardized the safety of this country and gambled with the lives of its people. I will not give you the chance to do it again."

"But sir, it wasn't my fault."

Just then another Secret Service agent entered the office. "Sir."

"What!" The secretary roared and whirled around, annoyed by the continual interruptions.

The agent jumped, startled by the secretary's harsh tone.

"Sir, you've got to get back to the White House soon. The president is on his way there now."

The president was returning on Marine One from the Continuity of Operations facility. He wanted to conduct a press conference first thing in the morning, but he needed to meet with the Joint Chiefs, NSA director, FBI director, and D.C. police chief first.

"Thank you. I'll be right there," and he motioned for the agent to leave as he turned toward Aiden one last time. "Now, if you'll excuse me, I have to explain this to the president so he has the facts to tell the American people."

Aiden wanted to defend himself again, but he held his tongue. His work wasn't done, and this fight wasn't over, but it was time for him to cut his losses and lick his wounds until he could gather himself. But there was another issue that he had to present to the secretary.

"Sir, one last thing before you go."

"What is it?" the secretary snapped.

"What about O'Shea and his friend John? What do we do with them? They know too much. They're liabilities."

"They are hardly liabilities. They are vital assets, and we need to protect them. Place them in the Witness Protection Program until we figure out a more permanent solution. Do you think you can handle that?"

"Yes, sir."

"Good. Then we're done here." The secretary stormed out of Godfrey's office and made his way back down the corridor with his entourage.

Aiden snatched a small glass candy bowl on the coffee table and hurled it against the wall in anger, smashing it to pieces. "Damn you!" Aiden screamed aloud. "You have no idea. The president would never have been elected, and you wouldn't have gotten your appointment if it weren't for us, you ungrateful bastard!"

Aiden had wanted to tell the secretary that Godfrey had been manipulating the U.S elections for some time. Godfrey had been involved with hacking the voting systems in a number of key states. He had essentially been electing officials he believed would fund his national security programs. What Godfrey didn't realize was that foreign governments had caught onto his scheme and we're using Godfrey's computer programs for their own benefit, including intervening in U.S. politics and hacking U.S. businesses and federal agencies. The American people believe their votes matter, but they don't. Godfrey had made certain of that. Godfrey had influenced the election of the president along with other key positions. Regardless, Aiden couldn't be tied to it, at least not directly. Many Americans believed the Russians, Chinese and other foreign governments were meddling in U.S. politics. Aiden would use that to his benefit.

Aiden sat at Godfrey's desk and picked up the director's journal. The secretary had forgotten to take it amid the heat of the conversation. Aiden would need it. Just then there were knocks at the door and O'Shea entered.

"Aiden."

"Yes."

"The secretary looked pissed when he left."

"He was." Aiden propped his feet up on the edge of the desk and reclined in the chair.

"What's next?" Matt asked as he moved closer to Aiden.

"You need to disappear for a while, both you and John. I'm putting you both in the Witness Protection Program until this whole mess blows over. I'll make sure you both have what you need, but you cannot speak of any of this to anyone. Otherwise, we'll kill you." The words came out of Aiden's mouth nonchalantly.

"What!"

"Yes. This can never get out, ever. Do I make myself clear?" Aiden's words lingered like an ominous fog.

Matt nodded. "So now what?"

"You'll be escorted to the BWI airport where a plane is waiting for you."

"And what about all my stuff at my apartment?" Matt asked.

"We'll take care of it; don't worry. Until we say otherwise, you don't exist. The good thing is that you have no immediate family or close friends, so no one will report you missing," Aiden said as he smirked deviously. He had orchestrated Charlie's car accident and death. He knew from the beginning that Matt could have no next of kin if he were to be closely involved with their projects. Aiden made certain of that. It was too much of a risk.

"What about work?"

"We'll take care of it all; now get going. The men outside will escort you and John to the airport. You must go now."

"And what about you?"

"I'll be in touch. In the meantime, I've got to clean up this disaster. We may call for your assistance again; now go."

92

Back at the North American Cyber Command Center, Osmund and his security team had been monitoring the radio waves during the blackout. They averted the near disaster at the Calvert Cliffs nuclear power plant, but they weren't able to stop the countless tragedies that had occurred nationwide. There were limited or nonexistent communications in many parts of the country. Secure government communications had been protected, but even some of those had failed. For the most part, major mobile towers and cellular channels had been disabled, and the public and private sectors were cooperating to restore them and other critical infrastructure systems as soon as possible.

Cyber Command had intercepted some encrypted text messages and phone calls that they hadn't been able to crack. Osmund turned to one of the technicians who was working on the messages.

"Any luck?"

"Not yet, sir," the technician replied as he tapped away on his keyboard.

"Keep trying. What's the status on our infrastructure systems?"

"They're coming back online little by little—the power, water, gas, telephone, and aviation. O'Shea did it. He stopped the brunt of the attack, at least for now." The technician flashed the latest update on the wall screens. "See for yourself."

The screens showed rotating satellite images of U.S. cities across the country. The monitors that had been black were now showing signs of life. From their computer reports and diagnostic tests, they saw that other control systems were coming back online too.

Osmund clenched his fist in a congratulatory manner. *Way to go guys, way to go.* But that didn't change the fact that a tremendous amount of devastation had been done across the United States. Many lives had been lost, and the rebuilding efforts would take weeks, if not months.

93

Meanwhile, back at the White House, the president had already met with his Security Council, the FBI, and the D.C. police. He was preparing for his morning press conference. Sitting quietly in the Oval Office, he reviewed his notes one last time before making his way to the press room. Dozens of reporters had packed the room, sitting and standing wherever there was space. The lights shone brightly from the back of the room. The president knew recent events would not be easy to explain as he looked down at the binder that contained his talking points. Although he'd conducted countless press briefings during his political career, this one would be like no other. He closed his eyes and gathered his thoughts before stepping out to take his place at the podium, the presidential seal mounted on the front, and a dark blue curtain with American flags on both sides of the stage serving as his backdrop. Before taking questions, he delivered an opening statement:

"Ladies and gentlemen, my fellow Americans: I come before you today troubled and saddened by the events of the last forty-eight hours. As you know, we suffered a temporary blackout in many of our cities across the country. Much of our nation's infrastructure including electricity, gas, water, telecommunications, and transportation went offline. We are still in a national state of emergency. Many network systems and power have yet to be restored. Many Americans are still without electricity, and other utilities may be out for days, if not weeks.

"I have directed the governors of all fifty states to immediately dispatch their National Guard units to maintain peace and order. Washington, D.C., will remain under martial law, including curfews, until further notice. I am deploying additional U.S. military troops across the country to restore order and to secure our borders from a potential influx of illegal immigrants that could include terrorists. The events that have transpired highlight the points my administration has raised consistently. Our infrastructure, including our power grid, is vulnerable. The events the last two days are the result of technology that is out of date with the needs and demands of our country. Due to the increased strain on our power grid and other industrial control systems, they finally gave way under the burden. As I've said in the past and continue to reiterate, the United States needs to work to become more energy independent, to focus more on renewable power sources, and to advance our national energy security policies to ensure this never happens again.

"The status of our power infrastructure and other industrial control systems has been and will continue to be a national security concern. We have learned from the past couple of days the type of chaos and destruction that is caused by a large-scale blackout and how vulnerable we truly are as a nation. Members of my Cabinet and Security Council are actively working to identify what caused these failures, and we will work tirelessly over the coming weeks and months to address their findings. For the safety of our nation, this can never happen again.

"In the coming days I will issue an executive order that will revolutionize and modernize our energy independence and dramatically improve our infrastructure, now and for the future. I will also introduce infrastructure and national security legislation that I will urge Congress to pass immediately. These initiatives are not a matter of politics. They are about doing what is right to secure our country's future and to protect our people. I have faith that we will rebound from this catastrophic event. We have the greatest nation in the world, and this tragedy will not change that fact. Our people are resilient and steadfast. We will unite to become better and stronger. We will move forward together. I'm honored to be your president and to lead you through this adversity and into a brighter future. Thank you. I'll now take a few questions."

"Mr. President," one of the reporters called out, "how do you explain this massive blackout that impacted so much of our infrastructure?"

"As I just stated, much of our infrastructure is outdated and collapsed under the heavy demand. Next question." He pointed at another reporter.

"How's it possible that something of this magnitude could have happened so widespread across the country? This wasn't an isolated event. Nearly the entire country was impacted in one way or another. How do you explain this?"

"As I said moments ago, members of my Cabinet are looking into this further and will do a full assessment of the damage, what happened, and why."

Another reporter spoke up. "Mr. President, we've heard rumors that this was a cyberattack launched by the Russians or

Chinese. We've heard Iran or North Korea may be involved too. What can you say about that?"

"I'm not going to speculate, and I'm not going to play into any media conspiracies. We're still gathering information. We have the most advanced security systems and the best cyber security professionals in the world looking into this."

The reporter probed further. "So you're not ruling out that this was a massive cyberattack by foreign governments or entities?"

"Like I said, our national security and cyber security teams are looking into all possible causes."

"Could this have been a homegrown attacker or insider threat, a lone wolf?"

"We are looking into all potential causes."

Another reporter spoke up. "Mr. President, what do you have to say to all those families who have lost loved ones the last couple of days, especially the elderly and hospital-bound, and those who were victims of the plane crashes or violence, the oil refinery and factory fires, and the countless other tragic events? We've heard reports that the death toll is in the hundreds if not thousands nationwide."

"My heart goes out to all the families of those who lost their lives. This is a terrible tragedy in our nation's history. The victims and their families have my condolences, and we will do all in our power to make sure that nothing like this happens again and that we repair the damage that's been done. The safety and security of our country are my top priorities."

Another reporter asked, "Sir, is it true that the U.S. lost its capability to launch nuclear weapons during this attack?"

"For national security reasons, I cannot address that point."

The president was becoming more annoyed with the barrage of questions, and he glanced at his press secretary who was moving to the edge of the stage. The president gave him a subtle nod, and he hustled to the podium.

"Thank you, but the president will take no further questions at this time. We'll have updates for you all once we know more. Thank you again." The president then headed for the Oval Office as reporters continued to shout questions they knew would not be answered.

94

Aiden was still in Godfrey's office at NSA headquarters completing some unfinished business on the computer. The long night had stretched into the morning. He had been watching the president's press conference on TV.

Well done, Mr. President. We'll see how long the American people believe that nonsense. You're just using this situation as a political platform to push your energy and infrastructure policies. You're making a mistake if you cancel our cyber surveillance programs. Clearly, the events this weekend didn't send a strong enough message about our network and infrastructure vulnerabilities to attacks by our enemies.

Aiden finished downloading the files that he needed before wiping Godfrey's desktop and computer network drives clean. Aside from a few crumbs that would implicate Godfrey in all of this, he didn't want to leave any traces, certainly nothing that would link him to the disaster. After he had removed the thumb drive, he shut down the computer. On the desk he noticed the framed photo of Godfrey and his family. Aiden briefly bowed his head. *I'm sorry, Director, but I had to do it. You, of all people, would understand.*

Aiden got to his feet and headed for the door. He checked the office one last time to make sure he had grabbed everything because he wouldn't be returning. He exited Godfrey's office, and the door locked automatically behind him. A private plane awaited him at the airport. He had a flight to catch out of the country. As he hurried through the labyrinth of corridors, he pulled out Godfrey's cell phone that he'd taken and sent another text. His work wasn't over yet—far from it.

95

In the Cyber Command Center the brief celebratory atmosphere had ended, and the crew was back at work. One of the analysts who had been trying to crack the encrypted messages sent during the blackout was making progress. "Sir, I think I've got something you might want to take a look at."

"What is it?" Osmund asked.

"I'm not sure what to make of it. It's a bunch of numbers and text."

"Put it on the screen so we can all take a look."

The analyst did as instructed. Here is what appeared:

#09081941 $145M #09112001 $155M #1271941
$250M #06141946
$255M #10261947 $265M #WH11082016
$300M

Osmund had an idea of what it was, but he wasn't going to say anything yet. He needed more information to confirm his assumptions. "I need to know where that message originated, and where it was received." Osmund snapped a photo of the computer screen.

"You got it," the analyst replied.

96

Escorted by their security detail, Matt and John were whisked away from NSA headquarters and to the BWI airport. They didn't know their final destination, but Matt hoped there would be plenty of white sandy beaches and umbrella drinks there. The two were exhausted and hadn't slept all night. It had been a long and crazy weekend. He needed to get away from all of it. There was nothing for him here anymore. After everything that had happened over the weekend, he wanted to be as far away from the United States and Washington, D.C., as possible.

John and Matt both slouched in the back seat of the SUV. Matt checked to see if there were other vehicles following them, but there weren't.

John looked in Matt's direction and said, "Some weekend, wouldn't you say?"

"That it was. I hope never to have one like it again," Matt sighed.

"You and me both. Is it true you were working undercover for the NSA?"

"Do we have to talk about that right now?"

"Sorry, I was just curious. I had no idea."

"The short answer is yes, but that's all I will say about it for now."

"Fair enough. I'd hate for you to have to kill me if you told more."

Matt gave John a serious look and punched his shoulder. "Not funny."

"Sorry, I shouldn't joke about those things."

Matt sat back and closed his eyes. He was glad this was all over. As he was dozing off his leg began to vibrate. He reached into his pocket and pulled out the burner phone that Osmund had given him. There was an unknown number on the screen.

"Hello?"

"It's Osmund. Where are you?" Matt detected the concern in his voice.

"We're in a vehicle on our way to BWI."

"Who are you with?"

"Two guys. I'm guessing they're Secret Service or NSA agents. It's some security detail. Aiden told us they'd have an airplane waiting to take us to a secure location far from D.C. I just don't know exactly where. No one has said anything. Aiden is supposed to meet us at the airport."

"I'm going to text you an image. I want you to let me know what you think."

"Okay," Matt responded, perplexed.

Osmund pulled up the picture he'd taken of the computer screen with the numbers on it and texted it to Matt. "Let me know when it goes through."

"Got it. I'm pulling it up now." Matt opened the image on his phone. "I'll do my best to make sense of it."

On the other end, the analyst sitting at the computer near Osmund spoke up. "Sir, we've just intercepted another text transmission. It was sent a short while ago. It's coming from a government-issued phone. I think I can hack into it."

Osmund responded to the analyst. "Do it and trace it. I want to know who it belongs to and where it's being sent from." He turned his attention back to Matt. "See if you can make sense of the image. I'll call you back shortly."

97

Still laid up at the hospital in New York City, Michael and Kate awoke to the sound of a nurse bringing in a breakfast cart. A middle-aged, blonde nurse set the tray down on the table next to his bed.

"Good morning, Mr. Stevens. You should be able to go home in a few days. Your wife will be released today."

"Good morning, I suppose." Michael shook his head, still groggy from the medicine. He squinted as his eyes adjusted to the morning sun slipping through the window from the other side of the room. He gazed lovingly at Kate who was sitting up on her bed and smiling at him with her beautiful eyes.

"Hello, love."

"Hello," he replied, beaming back at her.

Michael turned to the nurse who was arranging his tray. "What happened yesterday?" He scratched his head and rubbed the back of his neck, the pain in his side still noticeable.

"You were shot, sir, and someone drugged your wife."

"I remember getting shot, but I don't know how I got here. How did my wife end up here?" Michael fumbled about in his bed as he tried to sit up.

"Your work colleagues brought you both here. I'm just starting my shift, so I wasn't here last night. I don't know the full story; sorry. It sounds like it was a busy evening. The FBI and police are still here."

"Where's Aiden?"

"Who?" The nurse looked at him, confused.

"My other colleague. He's the director's chief of staff. Where is he?"

"I'm sorry, sir. I haven't seen him." The nurse continued setting out the breakfast trays for Michael and Kate.

Michael didn't notice the FBI agent who had been sitting in the corner. He was there on protective duty.

"Mr. Stevens."

Michael sat up to face the voice. There was a young, black FBI agent, probably in his late thirties, sitting with his legs crossed and his hands resting on the arms of the chair. He was athletically built and clean cut, probably former military judging from his build and haircut. He was dressed in a gray suit with a badge clipped to his belt. Michael could see he was wearing a shoulder holster.

"Yes. Who are you?" Michael asked.

"I'm Agent Burton. I'm here to make sure nothing else happens to you or your wife." He opened his suit jacket so Michael and Kate could clearly see his holster and badge.

"Who drugged Kate?" Michael asked.

"I can't give you the full details, but you will be briefed soon."

Michael rolled toward Kate who was starting to nibble on a piece of toast. "Who did this to you? Did you recognize them?"

"I don't know. I'd never seen them before. I don't remember anything after dinner. I remember going back to the hotel and someone bringing room service. That's it."

"Someone came to the room last night?" Michael's tone rose as he struggled to sit up in his bed.

"Yes."

"And you let them into the room?" Michael winced in pain as he faced Kate.

Kate cowered in her bed. "Not exactly." She didn't like to see Michael angry.

"What did I tell you? I said not to let anyone in under any circumstances."

"I know. I'm sorry. It's just that the men looked like they were with the hotel. They forced themselves into our room. I tried to fight them but they overpowered me."

Michael lay there shaking his head, dismayed. "That's exactly why I told you not to answer the door. Thank God you're safe. Do you know what could have happened? You could have been killed."

Kate's eyes opened wide as she turned pale. The fact that she could have been killed hadn't registered with her until that moment.

Michael looked at the nurse. "What was she drugged with?"

"I don't know. I don't have her toxicology report."

"Kate, how are you feeling?" the nurse asked.

"I've got a terrible headache, like I'm hung over."

Michael sat up to face Agent Burton. "What's next?"

"Kate will be discharged today, but you have a few more days before they send you home. We'll make sure you're briefed and up to speed on everything and that you get back to Washington safely."

"I appreciate that. What all has been going on?" Michael pointed at the TV where the president was about to conduct a press conference.

"How do I turn on the volume? I want to hear what he's saying."

"Here, allow me." Agent Burton reached up and turned on the volume.

"Thank you."

They all watched in silence. Agent Burton was already aware of everything that had happened, but this was the first that Michael and Kate had heard the full extent of the situation. They were stunned.

Kate was the first to speak. "This is horrible. All of those people without power, and worse, those who died," she said, putting her hand over her mouth, aghast.

"Was New York affected?" Michael asked.

"Yes," Burton said, "but not as bad as other cities. It seems like New York City was better prepared given its history of blackouts and terrorist attacks. The hospital lost power temporarily in the middle of the night but, fortunately, the backup generators kicked in. Other hospitals in the city and out in the boroughs weren't as fortunate. There are still people across town without power, but the authorities are working to restore it. Other cities across the country are in horrendous shape. It will take weeks if not months for them to recover from the damage. Parts of cities are burning. Dozens of oil, gas, and ethanol plants exploded, destroying everything around them. Other cities or towns flooded when dams or spillways opened. Many drowned or have been left homeless. Search and rescue missions are underway across the country."

Michael's head sunk. "I should have done more. We knew something like this might happen. I should have called Godfrey back sooner," he mumbled.

"Michael, you did all that you could. This had nothing to do with you," Agent Burton reassured him.

"But we could have prevented this." Michael slapped his hand against the mattress in frustration as he flopped back in his bed.

"I don't think that's true, sir."

"Why not?"

"Because it might have been an insider attack."

"But who?"

"I don't know, but your senior NSA officials will brief you on everything once they have more details. All I can say is that the situation is stable for now. We're working to get national and local security under control. If you'll excuse me, there are some things I need to check on." Agent Burton handed the remote to Michael before leaving the room.

Kate sat up in her bed. "Michael, is this related to the project you were working on?"

"Partly, yes. But we didn't expect this to happen, at least not like this, and certainly not now." He was in disbelief. "I'm sorry about our weekend," he said.

"It's okay; at least we're alive." She blew him a kiss.

He returned her gesture. "I love you."

"What's next? There's a national crisis, and it's far from over."

"But maybe the worst is over; at least I hope so."

"I guess this means you'll be working more hours, and I'll never see you."

"I hope not," Michael replied, cautiously optimistic. "I promise I'll make it up to you."

"Then I guess we'd better take advantage of the time we have together right now."

"What were you thinking? I'm expected to be in here a few more days, but you get discharged today."

"And what's your point?"

"I don't know how much fun I'll be. I'm not very mobile right now, and I'm in some pain. All I can do is lie here."

"And what's so bad about spending time with my loving husband?"

"Nothing, I guess."

"It's been forever since I've had your captive attention in one place for more than a night."

"Captive?"

"You know what I mean. This will be the longest we've been alone together in the past two years."

"I know, and it stinks that I'm laid up in a hospital bed."

"But I won't be." She gave him a deviously seductive and suggestive expression. "We'll make the best of this; you don't worry about that one bit."

Michael smiled warmly into Kate's eyes. "I married an amazing woman."

"Yes, you did, and don't you forget it," she said as she grinned ear to ear.

"I'm so happy to be alive and to be here with you."

"Me, too." She was glowing as she gazed lovingly at him.

98

The NSA team at the Cyber Command Center diligently scrambled to assess the full extent of the damage. The signal tracers they'd sent out hours earlier were finally returning with updates. An analyst was finishing the latest scan and compiling the results of his recent diagnostic where he had been able to break through more of the encrypted phone messages. "Sir, you're not going to believe this. The messages we intercepted . . . " He was unable to complete his sentence before Osmund interrupted.

"Yes, what about them?" Osmund moved to the analyst's workstation.

"They came from Godfrey, or at least his mobile device."

"What? Director Godfrey is dead. How can he be sending messages? Check the time stamps. It's possible the blackout caused a delay, and they're just now coming through. Let me know what you find out." Osmund grabbed his phone and called Matt.

"Matt, it's Osmund."

"What's up?"

"Have you made any sense of that image I sent?"

Matt could only guess what the numbers were. "They look like bids. It seems like someone is auctioning something off. And the others, I'm guessing, are bidder I.D. numbers."

"My hunch was the same."

"Where is the message coming from?" "You're not going to believe me when I tell you: Godfrey's phone."

"But Godfrey is dead. Who could be using his device?"

"Sir," the analyst cautiously interrupted.

"What?" Osmund spun around to face him.

"There's more. The last two transmissions came from near Fort Meade."

"Fort Meade? NSA headquarters? That makes no sense. Godfrey was in New York, so how's that possible?" Osmund was about to continue when he stopped himself. But his thoughts continued: *Aiden. It can't be. He was the last one with Godfrey, and he was at the NSA with Matt only hours earlier. Damn him if that son-of-a-bitch is auctioning off what I think he is.* Having worked together for years, Osmund had never trusted Aiden. Osmund sensed something was different recently, but he'd never imagined that Aiden could sell out his own country—until now. The call he'd received earlier from Godfrey only confirmed his suspicions.

"Matt, whatever you do, don't get on that plane." If Aiden was behind this attack, there's no telling what he'd do to Matt and John.

"Why not? What's going on?" Matt stared with a troubled look at John who was seated next to him in the back.

"Matt, whatever happens, do your best to stop that vehicle and get away. We're sending a team after you right now. Hang tight." Osmund ended the call and then yelled to the team of analysts and agents around him. "I need an exact location on O'Shea, now!"

Matt glared at the phone in his hand, shaking his head in dismay. He then turned and whispered reluctantly to John, "This isn't over yet."

Matt leaned over and muttered something in John's ear. John nodded. The driver glanced at them in the rearview mirror but quickly returned his attention to the road. Matt and John knew what they had to do. Matt quietly unbuckled his seat belt. John did the same. Matt waited only seconds before he made his move, springing over the driver's seat and frantically grabbing the steering wheel. The driver fought back as the SUV swerved, knocking the car beside it into the center median guardrail. Matt wrapped his arms around the driver's neck and strangled him. Restrained by his seatbelt, the front passenger attempted to fight off Matt, but John was all over him. John climbed over the seat and clawed at the passenger's face before starting to choke him. With arms and bodies flailing about in the front seat, the driver jerked the wheel sharply to the right, and it jumped the curb. Seconds later the vehicle flipped and was briefly airborne before tumbling violently off the side of the road and through the grass. Broken metal and shattered glass flew in all directions. The vehicle rolled several times before coming to a stop on its side. The SUV's horn blared, the driver's body crammed against the steering wheel, while all four men lay motionless and mangled, trapped in the smashed wreckage along the Baltimore-Washington Parkway.

99

Despite the widespread U.S. blackout, through his connections Aiden had managed to make it safely out of the United States. He left casualties behind: Godfrey, Brody, David and Dimitri, among others. His offshore bank account was full, and he looked forward to spending it. It was a week after the attack, and massive nationwide efforts were underway to restore order, power, and other utilities across the United States. Meanwhile, Aiden was enjoying the tropical sunshine on the island of Cuba. He planned only a temporary stay until he could make it further south on a cargo ship. His plan was to island hop and avoid major cities and countries, staying under the radar until he could disappear more permanently. His ship was leaving that night for Colombia. He had made arrangements with the Cuban and Russian governments for safe passage.

Aiden had learned from his sources that Matt and John had survived the car crash on the way to the airport and escaped, which troubled him. After the accident, Matt and John had been rushed to the emergency room where they had been triaged for their injuries. They were placed under protective custody by the

FBI, which was overseen by Director Donovan. If Aiden had to guess, Osmund would make sure that Matt and John were well guarded and kept away from the public and the media. Aiden knew that after Matt and John were discharged from the hospital, they would be sent far from Washington, D.C., to an unknown location. Aiden didn't worry too much about that though. If he had located Dimitri after all of those years in hiding, finding O'Shea shouldn't be too difficult. But for now, he had more urgent matters to handle.

It was a pleasant evening with a rosy red and orange tropical sky dotted by a handful of feathery clouds. The sun was setting over the Caribbean as Aiden donned his sunglasses. The warm, salty breeze gently blew through his hair and left the taste of the sea on his lips. The grit of the sand rubbed against his feet under his flip-flops. Alongside the beach, Aiden sat at one of a dozen or so small white plastic patio tables at the tiny roadside cabana on the edge of Havana. There were a handful of scantily dressed locals sitting around the other tables drinking beer and enjoying the picturesque evening. The restaurant's exterior wooden walls were adorned with old fishing poles and nets, and local Cuban beer signage hung from the awning above him. The short railing that encased the small, open-air terrace where he sat along the sidewalk was carved from driftwood. The sound of the waves in the background crashed against the sandy shore a short distance away. He turned toward the setting sun as its reflection danced across the water's surface. The smell of the island air and freshly-cooked seafood from the grill filled his nostrils as he breathed a sigh of relief. He sipped his ice-cold beer from his comfortable mesh-backed chair as he enjoyed the shade of the thatched umbrella that protruded through the center of his table.

The casually dressed waitress brought him another beer and took his dinner order before prancing back to the kitchen. Aiden threw his head back and polished off his beer before setting the empty glass down on the table. He snatched up the fresh beer the waitress brought and took a long gulp. It was glorious to be alive and to have made it out of the United States without incident. He casually held up his glass and quietly toasted his fallen comrades before taking another swig. He watched as the rush-hour traffic passed by on the avenue next to him, the sea of motorcycles and mopeds weaving in and out of the cars as they slowed for occasional speed bumps. The fresh smell of the sea gave way to car exhaust.

And so it was that Aiden didn't notice the mud-covered dirt bike approaching discreetly. The adult driver wore a backward red baseball cap and large, dark sunglasses. A shark-tooth necklace dangled over his tan hairy chest, and his tattered tropical shirt was half buttoned and flapped in the wind. His tattered blue jeans offered little protection from the engine heat as it coughed gray smoke from the exhaust pipe. His younger passenger wore a plain black T-shirt and cargo shorts with a beaten-up black, open-face helmet and shiny silver sunglasses. He carried a brown leather satchel strapped around his shoulder and had one hand around the driver's waist, the other inside the bag.

The dirt bike slowed as it approached the speed bump in front of the restaurant. As it did, the passenger cautiously removed a pistol from his pouch and took aim. Just steps away from the road, Aiden sat at his table finishing his beer when the first bullet entered his back and exited his chest. He lurched forward, spitting out his beer as he dropped his glass to the ground, shattering it. The other patrons and waitresses immediately took cover. Aiden clumsily stood up and spun to face his assailant when the second bullet entered his chest, piercing his lung. Stunned, he coughed a spray of blood over the table in front of him. He then stumbled and fell into it, knocking it over. He tried to stand but staggered and collapsed to the ground. Rolling over on his back, he began to drown in his own blood. Moments later, he saw a dark shadow standing over him, and the long silencer barrel aimed at his head. Aiden only heard the first muffled shot as the bullet entered his forehead, jolting his head back. The final two rounds entered his chest. Aiden's body convulsed with the force of the bullets' impact. The young man swiftly strode over beside where Aiden had been sitting and snatched up his duffle bag; it contained his personal effects along with Godfrey's journal and computer files. The young man made sure Aiden was dead before trotting over and climbing back onto the motorcycle. The men sped away, vanishing into the waves of traffic as dusk settled over Havana.

■ ■ ■

Osmund was sitting in his office in the underground North American Cyber Command Center when his secure desk phone rang. "Hello," he answered.

There was heavy breathing on the other end and the sound of car horns honking and loud island music blaring in the background. Then a man in a Spanish accent spoke: "The sun has set over the island and the cargo will set sail tonight."

Osmund didn't have a chance to respond before the caller hung up. He rocked back in his chair, rubbing his hands together, pleased by the news.

ABOUT THE AUTHOR

J.B. Chadwicks is a freelance writer, novelist, coach, dreamer, visionary, teacher, and entrepreneur who seeks to inspire and empower others. He encourages others to dream big and to persevere in pursuing their dreams and aspirations. He resides in Virginia with his wife where he enjoys travelling, hiking, fishing, sports, spending time with friends and family, and writing.

Made in the USA
Middletown, DE
10 August 2019